SERIAL DATER

BY

K.T. JAYNE

Published independently.

Cover design by Hiromi

e: k.t.jayne.author@gmail.com
ig: ktjayneauthor
w: kt-jayne.com

For Andy, thank you for your belief

THEN

CHAPTER 1: STAYING POWER

NOVEMBER 2013

Friday 1st: 17:54

He fumbled in the dark trying to hook his keys out of his hip pocket. 'Argh, balls.'

'Ah balls' chirped the three-year old at his elbow.

One hand hooked around a large predator, a polythene bladder of prey in the other; he cursed his luck on the coconut shy. 'Jae... hold this for me Monkey will you.' He grappled with the giant funfair shark. It rolled over his arm, swallowing his son whole. 'Got it?'

'Yuff.'

Shifting the bag of goldfish into his free hand, he lifted the keys and stabbed at the lock. 'Can't see a goddamned thing.'

The key snapped into place.

'A godaaa—'

'Yes, right Jae, OK now.' He shouldered the winter-swollen door ajar. Spider-leg fingers crawled in search of the light switch.

Contact. Click. Flash. Ting. Darkness.

'Oh great, the bloody trip.'

'The blud—'

'Jae, enough with the copying' he said, then turned his attention to the shadows in the hallway.

'Sal?'

Nothing.

'Saaaaal?'

'Mummmeeee. Mummm—'

'Jae shush, I'm trying to listen.'

Listen to Nothing.

He breathed in slowly, then blew out a long sigh of resignation. 'OK, she's gone for a lie down... again' he said, talking more to himself than to his son.

'Is it bedtime Daddy?'

'No, not bedtime just yet.' His eyes started to adjust. He cupped his hand around the dining room door frame and tried the light.

Nothing.

'Saaaal? You there?'

He patted along the wall of the entrance hall, making his way down until he felt the lacquered wood of the telephone table under his palm. He planted the fishbag. It wobbled and sloshed as he teased open the draw and took out the pencil-thin Maglite Solitaire. Wringing its neck to coerce it into life, he aimed the feeble stream of light towards the stairs. It trickled over the first step. He twisted the head of the torch again, hoping to flood the hallway. Jammed. Damn it.

The dining room door was open a slither. He crept down the hall, not sure why he was creeping, and nudged it wider. He swept the room. Sally's coat sat upright on the Chesterfield, like it was draped around the shoulders of the invisible woman. The light flitted over the cast iron fireplace, flaring off the surface of the studio portrait above it; himself and Sally lying on the floor laughing as a chubby-limbed Jae crawled towards the camera. It was a study in false sincerity brought into relief by the stark backdrop of super-white paper. He'd never liked the picture, flattering though it was. He saw it as an Elastoplast; an overstatement of connubial bliss. He was reminded of what lay beneath every time he looked at it.

His beam continued combing the scene by way of his wife's yawning, sloppy tote bag and came to rest on some papers scattered next to it on the lace tablecloth. A faint, sickly-sweet aroma of violets peppered the air. The smell gave him palpitations but he couldn't place why. He tilted the spot light up to catch the fuse box on the wall tucked between a tall, mahogany bookcase and the crescent of the bay window. The torch blinked on and off as if sending for help. Cursing, he slapped it against his palm, at first knocking it out, then at the third blow, bringing it back round. He eased himself past the dining table and popped open the breaker casing, running his finger along the row of fuses. Each trip switch had a sticker underneath it. The one labelled LIGHTS had flicked off. The switch offered some resistance as he levered it into the on position. The ceiling light momentarily flashed but he barely had time to squint before darkness thwarted the reflex. The trip had bounced back up.

'Odd... must be a fault' he said to no one. He made his way back to the foot of the stairs. Jae was treading water in the porch, swimming up and down with the shark.

'Where's my Mummy?'

'Dunno Monkey – probably upstairs. Hang on here.' He turned towards a noise of splish-sploshing beside him. Two silver-green pinholes of light froze in his beam. The tabby was at full stretch teasing the circling shadows in the fishbag with its paw.

'Psst. Norman. Ged-out-avit.' Norman bolted, leaping past Jae's grappling hands.

He stalked around the sweeping banister in a low squat like a vampire slayer. The grotesquery of the fair and the darkness had him spooked; he shook himself sensible. Squeezing the trigger on the baby gate at the foot of the stairs, he gingerly started to mount each creaking board.

'Mummmmeeee'

'Jae just stay there for a moment' he said, half turning back towards his son who was just boarding the first step behind him. 'Don't copy Daddy. Stay there.'

He held his breath; a vague queasiness swashing in his belly. His quickening heartbeat pulsed in his ears as, feet hesitating on every tread, he made his ascent. His search beam skimmed the no-man's-land at the summit.

No movement. No sound. Nothing.

Shrunken floorboards yelped in distress behind him. He spun around to come face-to-face with the shark's laughing black eyes and saw-toothed grimace. 'Jesus. Jae, I told you to stay put' he said, steadying himself against the balustrade. 'Fuck *me*' he breathed.

As he swooped the light round to his left it began to strobe again, rendering the scene in a series of flickering freeze-frames. The bedroom door half open. The foot of the bed. The lower rungs of the loft ladder. He slapped the torch across its face but it defied him. Was she in the bed? He couldn't tell at this distance.

'Sal?'

He edged closer.

'Sal? You in? You in bed?'

Thrub. Thrub. Thrub.

Closer still, he jabbed the bedroom door. It stuttered open as if spinning through a magic lantern.

Nothing.

Thrub. Thrub.

He turned towards the en-suite, forgetting that there would be no tell-tale slit of light under the door. 'Sal... Sal... you in the bathroom? What's happened to the lights?' His palms felt sweaty.

Nothing.

The resinous, bitter-sweet odour of frazzled plastic teased his nostrils. He twitched. Feeling for the edge of the bed, he lowered himself onto it and patted the flock-textured quilt as if he didn't trust what the staccato flashes of light were allowing him to see. It felt gritty to the touch.

Thrub. Thrub.

He swallowed and spoke softly. 'Sal... sweetheart... where are you?' Was it the trembling of his own hand that was causing a loose wire to open and close in the bulb? He smacked the spotlight, stunning it into obedience.

Something gently swept the top of his head, dragging his long fringe over his eyes.

'What the f—' He brushed his hair aside and tilted the torch upwards. It slipped from his clammy hand as his head was grazed again by the return journey.

'What the fucking fuck?' Dust hitched in this throat, forcing a cough. He frantically combed the bed for the flashlight and grabbed it. Swaying shadows rose and receded against the metallic-effect wallpaper, aping the cheap lighting effects of a ghost ride. The reflected torch beam flared in the mirror above the bed, blinding him.

He lowered the flashlight, squinted hard and waited for his eyes to adjust, striving to make out the source of the overhead pendulum.

'Mummmeeeeeeee'

***

Friday 1st: 09:42

Sally Capote's car pulled into the sweep through driveway of Top Tots nursery as if it were driving itself. Braking just shy of another car, Sally sat at the wheel wearing an expression of glazed porcelain. Her onyx eyes, varnished by antidepressants, were framed with uneven kohl lines and mascara-clumped lashes that looked like chocolate-coated spiders. She rubbed her Regency-rouged cheeks and sighed so deeply that inhaling again felt like an asthmatic effort. She switched off the ignition and swung her legs out of the car. Pausing for a moment, she eventually dragged herself over to the rear door.

Her three year-old son giggled at her through the window. 'Mummy? Why have you got that on your face?' His chubby finger reproached her vain attempt to mask her numbness. She didn't respond, but bent in to give him a lingering kiss on the forehead. Her head flopped down as if her neck had snapped. She shook her mop of brunette locks and stole a sharp intake of breath.

'Come on Sally' she said into her chest.

'Come on Mummy.'

She unclipped the car seat harness and scooped her boy out of the car, sliding him onto his feet. He bounced off like Tigger.

'Alfie, Alfieeee' he squealed at the sight of his lifelong best friend.

Sally fished his lunch bag out of the rear seat and followed him in.

'You OK Mum?' the stout, homely nursery nurse said, adopting a maternal frown.

'Yes, thanks.'

'Picking Jae up at five as usual?'

'No, his Dad will collect him today.'

'His Dad? On a Friday? OK. Does Jae know?'

'Yes, he knows.'

10:21

Once inside the front door she fell against it, heaving it shut. She closed her eyes. Tears teemed over her the brim of her lids, weaving rivulets of ink through the powder dusting her cheeks. She drew in a long, deep breath to stem the rising sobs.

Then another.

And another.

She was ready.

She tossed the toddler reigns onto the hall table and made her way into the dining room. Collapsing into the weathered leather of the sofa, she sat for a few pensive moments plotting her moves; choosing her words. She slipped her arms out of her coat sleeves and stood up, shedding her skin. Hooking up her bag she moved over to the dresser and pulled open a drawer. She lifted out a twee writing set of floral notelets and dropped it onto the dinner table. An almost-empty book of postage stamps followed close behind.

She let her handbag slide from her shoulder. It landed next to the scented stationary stirring the smell of violets. It conjured up memories of their holidays in the Lake District and the fragranced oil burner that infused every corner of their favourite mineral emporium with that same sweet aroma. It was there that he'd bought her the Tiger's Eye ring.

The one intended as a placeholder on her wedding finger. The one that, years later, still held its place.

She paddled around inside the bag looking for the Offensive Weapon. Her husband's Blackberry. The phone he used for work. She pressed and held the power switch until the handset glowed with tactless glee. Blinking hard to clear the water from her eyes, she opened the messages app and scrolled through the list. She tapped *Her* name.

Through misted vision, Sally laboured to read the accursed text:

Scotty babe. Your staying power is legendary ;-) Must do it again sometime soon.
Em xx

'Babe... she's calling him *babe*.' Not again. Emma? Really? Not again.

Holding her breath wouldn't quell the sobs this time. Her head fell into the cradle of her arm, her shoulders jerking with heartbreak. She sheltered there for a few moments, indulging her pain.

Then she pushed herself upright, dragged her sleeve across her face and ushered the notelets closer. Thrashing around in her bag for a pen, she rattled a prescription pill container. She snatched it, pushed and turned the child lock, tipped a small pile of benzos into her hand and necked them. Swallowing almost choked her. Not yet.

Finding the pen, she began to write before the inevitable fog of sensual deprivation descended. In a few short minutes she was done. She signed off with:

I thought you were my beginning, but all I can see is the end.

I have to go now, while I still can.

I love you. I love too much.

Your Sally xxx

She neatly folded the note, slid it into its sleeve, tongued the glue and smoothed down the seal. Flipping it she addressed the front and applied her last stamp.

She shoved the chair away with the backs of her legs, collected the letter and the Blackberry and, leaving the rest of the scene untouched, made her way back out into the hall. On the phone table she gathered a small pile of envelopes. She put hers amongst their number then shuffled them like a poker deck. It was a killer hand.

Still clutching the Offensive Weapon she scooped up the toddler reigns and turned to mount the stairs. Muscle memory obliged her to clip the baby gate shut as she started to climb. On reaching the apex she strode to the corner of the landing, plucked the loft hatch rod from its clip and stretched up to hook the catch. The accordion of aluminium steps brayed in protest as the un-oiled hinges expanded to reveal the stairway to heaven.

Then she made her way towards the bedroom, pushing the door ajar. The sunken ceiling, heavy exposed beams and squat, criss-cross leaded windows made for a gloomy atmosphere. She triggered the light switch in a futile effort to lift it.

On the dressing table an arc of family photographs mocked her melancholy: Sally looking boffin-like in her doctorate graduation robes as a fiercely proud Scott plants a congratulatory kiss on her cheek. The beaming couple on their wedding day, flanked by grinning relatives wearing shiny suits, fussy frocks and fascinators. The day two became three – both wearing the unmistakable expression of exhaustion and ecstasy that only comes with a first-born. And Jae, caught in the act of taking his first stumbling steps; the majestic glacial Screes of Wast Water dwarfed in the background by the momentousness of the milestone. Sally lifted the last frame and pressed her lips to the glass. She made no attempt to stem the hot torrent of tears.

She returned the picture to its rightful place in the story of their lives. Slipping off her wedding band and the Tiger's Eye, she placed them with the Blackberry at the centre of the gallery; a sacrificial offering to the shrine. Then she pressed the Play button on the CD player. Swirling violins soothed her malaise and whilst Dusty Springfield's achingly sorrowful voice implored her to stay, each stroke of the horsehair on steel stirred the undercurrent she needed to set herself adrift.

She turned and floated towards to the landing, leaving the bedroom door half open, then slowly mounted the stairway to heaven. The toddler reigns swung from side to side, the plastic buckle tapping the aluminium frame with each step, ticking out the countdown to Nothing. At the top she paused, struggling to see anything in the pitch black of the small attic space.

As her pupils dilated she started to make out the wooden joists stretching away from her and the overhead rafters triangulating above her like arms bent in prayer. She hoisted herself up through the narrow aperture, dragging her leadened legs beneath her. Twisting at the waist she planted herself on the ledge of the opening. She raised her knees up to her chin and pirouetted being careful to place one foot in front of the other on the neck of a joist, like a gymnast preparing to take steps on the high beam. Easing herself up onto her feet, she outstretched her arms and tiptoed little by little across the timber, stopping at the centre. She was about to perform the most complex manoeuvre of her routine. Building to the dismount.

Sally braced herself, and glanced down at her feet. The loft wasn't boarded, Scott had kept meaning to… but that didn't matter now. She unfurled and raised her hand to grab the overhead beam. She tossed the reigns over the rafter, threading one of the shoulder braces through the other to create a makeshift noose.

She tugged them to check the hold. The knot tightened around the plank as the nylon straps snapped together, cracking sharply against the stillness. It was secure. Placing her head through the dangling loop of the shoulder strap, she slid the adjustable buckle until the band pinched her neck. She swallowed, choked and briefly panicked, fingers clawing at the garrotte to loosen it, momentarily threatening to change her mind.

The rush of blood to her head started to subside; the Diazepam was kicking in. She inhaled slowly and deeply, contriving with the drugs to dampen the sickening surge of oxygen. She closed her eyes, conjured up an image her beloved little boy and whispered 'Mummy loves you Jae, it'll be better for you this way.' Sobs started now, wracking her body; tempting her to topple. She reached for the beam, steadied herself and took a moment or two to let herself cry.

She lifted her foot, flexing and pointing her toe as she prepared to alight. Then, as if in slow motion, she was air-bound.

Sally Capote's legs burst through the bedroom ceiling. Plaster dust and clumps of render spewed onto the conjugal eiderdown as she forced the bulb from its tear-drop pendant. It mimicked Sally, hanging by a thin sinew of cable; its lamp fizzing and popping as if putting up a final wave of resistance before the light inside died, and they both succumbed to blackness.

One more twitch.

Then limp.

Then.

Nothing.

***

18:11

His blood drained. His guts hit his throat. He couldn't bear to look, but couldn't bring himself to look away. Feet frozen. Head reeling. Heart lurching.

'Oh Sal. Sally. *Sally.*'

The halo from Scott's torch followed his wife's body, lifelessly swaying to and fro; dangling legs scored with cuts and grazes.

'No. God. *Please.*' He wrestled the light away from her and swept the room looking for any grounds she might have for leaving him. For leaving *Jae*. The light caught something on the dressing table, it glinted as he darted the torch from side to side.

Desperate now he crossed the room locking the object in his sights.

His Blackberry.

Scenes of familial joy surrounded the device, taunting him with happier times. He tapped its surface. It radiated a cold, despondent glimmer, ambivalently divulging its secrets:

Scotty babe. Your staying power is legendary ;-) Must do it again sometime soon.
Em xx

Scott sank to his knees. 'Sally no... no no no...'

CHAPTER 2: CHORUS

'Calm down Scott. We're here to help.'

'Fuck you fuck you fuck you'

'Jesus it stinks in here. Place is a tip. Looks like the kid's been left to wreak havoc. Chucked paper and crap everywhere.'

'Shut your little fucking mouth, or I'll rip your little fucking tongue out.'

'Scott, it's Doctor Leftwick. Try to calm down Scott, we're here to help.'

'Shut your little fuckin mouth... or I'll rip you little fuckin tongue out.'

'Why does he keep saying that? Who's he talking to?'

'It's not just rubbish. Take a look, there's bloody loads of 'em. Scraps of paper everywhere, covered in scribble.'

'What are they?'

'Dunno – shopping lists. But then there's a whole bunch of random ones. "*We miss you.*" "*We can't cope alone.*" And this one "*Why did you leave us?*" Notes to his wife?'

'Scott, can you hear me? Scott?'

'His pupils are dilated.'

'Drugs?'

'Citalopram wouldn't normally do that. Hard to say. He's clearly very agitated, possibly amphetamine.'

'Scott, it's very important that you tell me, have you taken anything apart from the medication I've prescribed for you?'

'Fuck you fuck you fuck you'

'Scott sit down, calm down. We need to take you into hospital so we can find out how best to help you.'

'Mr McCabe, I believe in your current state of mind you may pose a danger to yourself or to your son.'

'Fuck you fuck you fuck you'

'I want Mummy.'

'Get the boy out of here.'

'Calm down sir please, your son's upset. I need to admit you to hospital under section two of the Mental Health Act. I want to give you the opportunity to admit yourself voluntarily, but I should advise you that I can detain you without your consent.'

'Shut your little fucking mouth, *or I'll rip your little fuckin tongue out.*'

'Is this his hand writing? Do you recognise it?'

'Erm... this one is, and this. Some of them, I'm not so sure, some don't look like his.'

'Daddy-daddy'

'He's still in nappies, is that normal at his age?'

'Pretty much. Believe me I've seen worse.'

'He's terribly sore, poor little mite.'

'It's OK sweetie. Daddy's not feeling very well. You're OK sweetheart. We're going to help Daddy.'

'Where's my Mummy?'

'Is there anyone Jae can go to until we can make arrangements?'

'Me. Aye, I can. I'll take him.'

'And you are?'

'Roy. I'm Scott's uncle.'

NOW

CHAPTER 3: WHY?

OCTOBER 2016

Friday

He squeezed the damp dish cloth between his fists. It mirrored his wringing gut. The mornings were always the hardest part of the day. Thank God it was pub day. Not that any other day was dry, but the pub always held promise.

'*Jae*, for fu—'

Jae's head shot round and seized his Dad in a 'you're-about-to-say-a-bad-word' glare.

'...for goodness sake mate, you're nearly seven, can't you get most of your breakfast in your mouth by now?'

Jae's blank expression betrayed his missing of the point. 'I'm *six*. And I *hate* porridge.'

'Porridge? I thought I gave you…' Scott flicked open the breakfast cereal cupboard above the drainer. Several bulging sacks of Scottish oats lay across the shelves like sandbags. A porridge bastion.

'You don't like porridge…' he drummed his fingers on the door.

'Peter likes porridge.' Jae stood his spoon upright in the stodge.

'Who's Peter? A mate from school?' There was hope in his tone.

'No, he's my friend. He comes out when we're here. Sometimes.'

'Oh, right.' He rubbed his eyes. '*That* kind of friend.'

Scott's head was pounding, as it so often was this early in the morning. He grabbed one of the semi-bled bottles of red wine from last night's guilt trip and, half disgusted with himself for overindulging and half pissed off that he'd neglected to cork it, started to pour its contents down the drain. It sloshed over the drainer and into washing up bowl.

'I'm thirsty Daddy; can I have some of that juice?'

'You don't want this stuff sweetheart – it's adult's juice.' Guilt compounded. Scott switched duties, tipping a puddle of purple syrup into the bottom of the bright green cup. As he twisted the tap head, cold water gurgled through the concentrate. Watching its foam bubble and pop made him glaze over, his vision blearing like a procrastinating auto-focus.

The chill of the dilute flowing over his hand snapped him back into the moment. 'Oh sh—' his hand sprung open. The cup hit the basin and relieved itself of its contents. The juice swam blindly into the waiting pool of red wine, swirling around the bowl.

'Bugger.' Scott shook the water from his hand and reached for the tea towel. 'Try again' he said, grinning at Jae. This time he stayed on task, replenished the drink and carefully placed it on the small vinyl-covered table top in front of his son.

'Thank you.' Jae astonished Scott. Was this *his* boy expressing spontaneous gratitude?

'*Good boy* Jae, very nice manners fella.' A broad smile swept across his face. It was contagious – Jae grinned back.

'Right, matey, what d'you want on yer butties?'

'Peanut butter.'

'No can do. School rules.'

'I had it yesterday.'

'Get away. You sure?' Scott salvaged two slices of bread from a past-its-sell-by bag and sniffed the crusts for signs mould.

'I *did*. Daddy you always forget stuff.' He watched as Scott slathered the slices with butter. 'If I had a new Mummy would she remember stuff?'

'New Mummies aren't that easy to come by Monkey. Believe me.'

The truth was that even if new Mummies were in plentiful supply, he didn't feel ready to find one. During the three years since they'd lost Sally, it felt to Scott like he was teetering precariously on life's tightrope, with Jae the only counterbalance that kept him from falling. The months following Sal's suicide saw him reaching the edge of reason and seeking solace in a measure of pharmaceutical research he hadn't indulged in since his University days. Following the sectioning and several trysts with Social Services, which almost resulted in Jae being permanently taken into care, Scott had gradually plateaued into a more stable state of mind. Albeit it one that was now foggy with the residue of cut-price Merlot.

'Daddy, who do you think would win, a polar bear or a tiger?' Norman strolled into the kitchen, took a perfunctory sniff of her bowl before dismissing its contents and weaving a figure of eight around Scott's ankles. The tabby, being too idle to make it as a farm cat, had adopted them during Scott's recovery. She was given her misnomer by a three-year-old Jae who'd mispronounced 'woman' when mastering the basics of boy animals and girl animals. The name had stuck, as three-year-old-coined names do.

'Ooh, that's a tough one. I mean a polar bear is bigger,

and they are very vicious. But then a tiger is a natural hunter and has those huge claws and big sharp teeth. I can honestly say I don't know son' he said, wedging quarters of a limp jam sandwich into a plastic take-away tray.

'I'll bet *Norman* would beat him. She's like a tiger.' Jae leant out of his chair and tried the grab the cat's tail. Norman's proprioception had the better of him, flicking it out of reach with split-second precision.

'Norman? She's stuff-all good for a mouser.' It was true. Since her nameday, she'd gained girth and lost pace.

'Who do you think would win out of a polar bear and a crocodile?'

'Oh I reckon the crocodile might have the edge there. He'd grab the polar bear in his big jaws and give him the death roll.' Scott started to spin on the spot. Oh Christ, he shouldn't have done that with a hangover. It was too much for Norman; she vaulted out of the cat flap.

'Mind you, ya don't tend to find crocodiles and polar bears in the same place, fella. They come from different countries.' He kneaded his temples, astounding himself with his insightful knowledge of the animal kingdom.

His pirouette had left him facing the back wall. It was only then that he noticed a small scrap of paper pinned to the corkboard, amongst the other notes-to-self memory joggers that Scott relied on too much.

Marg

Sandwich stuff

Crisps

Cat food

Christ, how was he supposed to remember the shopping when he couldn't even remember writing the list? He'd added something underneath that was harder to make out, written, as it was, in barely legible scribble. He leaned in closer to analyse the cypher:

Cuckoo

Fuckoo

Fuck you

Scott put his hand over his mouth. Cold beads of moisture pricked his brow.

'Who would win, a polar bear or a wolf?'

He rubbed his forehead as if it would help to massage memories to its surface. Had he really been that drunk? He could hope so. He trawled through his thoughts, trying to account for the lost time. '...*cuckoo*?'

'Cuckoo?' Jae said. 'I didn't say—'

'Sorry, matey, I was thinking out loud.' Is it happening again? That's what he was thinking. 'What did you ask?'

'Who would win, a polar bear or a wolf?'

'Ah, that's easy, the polar bear would win hands down. Unless the wolf was hunting in a pack of course...'

He tried to refocus himself on the present and Jae's obsession with hypothetical battles between animals from different continents. They were important to Jae, so they were important to Scott. Plus they opportuned rites of passage moments to discuss fight or flight, whether it is better to stand and face your fears, or to turn and run from them. Scott could deal with the hypotheticals.

'Would a polar bear beat a T-Rex?'

'Blimey Jae, the T-Rex would eat the polar bear for a light snack. But you know that dinosaurs don't exist anymore, don't you?'

'Yeah they're all dead. Are polar bears still alive?'

'Oh yeah, polar bears are still alive. They live in the Arctic. Or is it the Antarctic? Anyway, yes they still exist.' David Attenborough step aside.

Scott turned on the spot to clear away the much-maligned contents of Jae's bowl. He toed the pedal of the small bin, it begged him to feed it with the gluey remains of welded together oats. He obliged, prising it off Darth Vader's cape. It landed with a splat, slapping a jilted, half-finished box of Citalopram across its face. He looked at it wondering if he was doing the right thing, then let the bin lid fall. He'd forgotten to take them anyway, more often than not.

The annex dwelling they now occupied together was cramped compared to the farmhouse they had once called their family home. But that house harboured too many ghosts; some that he couldn't dispel, others that he sensed, shifting amongst the shadows of his memories, but couldn't summon. So two and a half years ago he'd moved them both into one of the modest two-bedroom tied cottages that, in the days when the estate was still his parents' dairy farm, were used for holiday lets when the B&B rooms in the main house were full. Scott was used to living amongst strangers, but he preferred not to share a body with them. And that's what haunted him just now as he looked at Jae and swallowed. It's not happening again. He was pissed is all.

He distracted himself by picking up yesterday's mail. Amongst the deck of unopened envelopes a single postcard depicted an ancient sandstone fortress set against an unblemished azure sky, framed by the sunburnt sprays of palms trees: *Alcazaba de Málaga* it proudly stated in a handwritten font. He flipped it over and re-read it.

Dear Scott,

Well, the best of the weather has passed but we still have an enviable 24 at the height of the day. Hope it's not too chilly back home. How's the farm? You getting along any better with Iain? I do hope so.

Your Dad and I were thinking of heading home for Christmas this time. Most of the expats here do, it gets very quiet. Would that work for you and Jae? Give him a kiss from Grandma. I miss him. I miss you both.

Love always, Mum xxx

'You can hope, Mater.' He tapped the card on his palm.

'I don't want to go to school Daddy.'

'Oh, *Jae*.' His sigh attested the all-too-familiar pre-school resistance. 'Why fella? What's up this time?'

'I might not finish my work. The teacher will make me stay in at break.'

'We've been through this before matey, just make sure you listen then you'll know what you're supposed to do.'

'Hmmm.'

'Is there anything else on your mind?'

'Hmmm.' He lowered his eyes, avoiding his Dad's scrutiny.

'*Is* there Jae?'

'This boy calls me idiot.'

'Which boy?'

'A bully called Josh.'

'How often has he said that?'

'He says it every time I say an answer in class.' He'd tried to brave it out but as the words formed his tear ducts joined his quivering bottom lip in mutiny, droplets swelling at their brim and tumbling down his cheeks.

'Oh for Chri— come here fella.' Scott gave him a manly embrace then, poised on one knee so that he could hold Jae's gaze with his own, rested his arm around his little lad's shoulder. 'Do you want me to talk to your teacher about it?'

Jae nodded and wiped his snotty nose on the sleeve of his school jumper. Scott resisted the detracting urge to sponge it.

'All right Monkey, I'll phone her today. OK?'

Jae nodded again, pushing the tears from his cheeks.

'Is there anything else worrying you sweetheart?'

He shook his head. Scott wasn't entirely convinced but time was getting tight.

'Come on fella, dry your eyes, it'll be fine. I'll talk to your teacher and we'll sort this Josh out.' With a fist to his little fuckin throat if I have anything to do with it, he kept to himself. 'Let's get a wriggle on now.'

'Dad – you're a nerd.' Jae prized his hand from Scott's grip as if being a nerd might be catching.

Scott stopped in his tracks, stalling their daily stroll to school. 'A nerd? How's that?'

'You're standing on a nerd drain.'

'A nerd dra—?' Scott shot a glance down to his feet.

'If it's just one drain, it's a nerd drain. If it's two drains it's good luck.' Jae elucidated the law according to year two.

He looked again. Both feet were planted firmly on a single, concrete utility access cover. It had him bang to rights. 'I'm a nerd, sure enough' he said, yielding to this obtuse new judicial system.

'If it's three drains it's bad luck...' Jae hadn't paused for breath, '... but you can cancel out the bad luck by saying toast.' He read Scott his rights.

'By saying toast?' *Of course.* Scott hesitated, 'Can I cancel out being a nerd by saying toast?' He pondered on whether being a nerd was somehow cool. To women, specifically.

'Yeah, you can cancel being a nerd by saying toast. And you can cancel out the good luck by saying toast too.' Scott couldn't imagine why, should you happen upon a double drain, you'd want to cancel out good luck. That's year two playground logic for you, logic in its truest form.

'Toast.' Had he hastily cancelled out nerd-cool?

Jae cupped his Dad's hand in approval. Clearly he'd redeemed his street-cred as far as his little lad was concerned. Scott slipped his other hand into his jacket pocket. His phone briefly buzzed against his palm. 'OK, what's this...?' He pulled it out and glanced at the glimmering calendar prompt across its midriff: **09:15 – 10:15: Trev**. 'Oh sh—' he paused and shot a glimpse at Jae, 'Oh sugar, I almost forgot.' His digital memory served his half-baked brain well; he couldn't afford to miss this appointment.

'Are those people?' Jae tugged him back to into the moment, pointing to a motley array of algae patches that dappled the tarmac.

'No Monkey they're just marks on the ground.'

'Mummy is buried in the ground but she's up in heaven.' It was almost a question.

'That's right; Mummy is up in heaven, looking down on us.'

'Where is she?' He skewed his head up towards Scott and

winked against the sun.

'She's up in the clouds.'

Jae searched the sky expectantly.

'Nice white clouds and blue sky today.' Scott's leaden sigh betrayed a heavier heart than his words implied.

'It's a lovely day. Is Mummy in one of those clouds?' By contrast Jae's ingenuous enquiry rang with inappropriate chirpiness.

'Yeah, she's up there looking down on us, making sure we're OK' he said, to reassure himself more than his son.

Losing Sally had torn him apart. He didn't claim to understand her depression, or her manic episodes, but there was something in her unpredictability that held him together. Perhaps her need for a mood stabiliser pulled him into focus, kept him present. Or maybe it was because Sally loved him; chose *him* over one of the others. Scott still gravitated towards his stabilisers; the ones that chose him. Or needed him, like Sally did once. Like Jae does now.

'Which cloud is she in? I can't see her.' Jae scoured the heavens.

'No we can't see her.'

'She's a ghost?'

'Yeah, she's a ghost.'

'She's a ghost so she's invisible?'

'Yes she's invisible, we can't see her.'

'We can't see her but she can see us.' Jae continued to comb the clouds in the sky, eyes darting left and right. Then, with a sudden squeal of delight, he said 'I just saw Mummy.'

'Did you?' For the briefest moment a tiny celestial light

flared in his heart. He wanted to believe. He gave Jae's hand a gentle squeeze. His little boy's smile looked like it would reach right around the back of his head and split it in two. Scott humoured him, 'Did you wave to Mummy?'

Jae raised his free hand and flapped it in an ebullient effort to reach the Other Side.

'Did Mummy wave back?'

'Yeah, she waved back.'

'Nice one.' Then he added under his breath 'She waved back.' Scott's abdominals were clenched so hard that he was stooping. He tried to relax - the 'Why did Mummy die?' question hadn't made an appearance.

Jae seemed to be stuck in the 'why' stage of development. Everything was still questioned to its 'why-est':

'Why does my chest bump up and down?'

'Because your heart is beating inside it.'

'But why?'

'Because it has to pump blood round your body.'

'Why?'

'Because that's how we stay alive – blood moving through our bodies.'

'Why?'

'Because blood carries oxygen around, and other stuff, it keeps us alive.'

'Wh—'

'Because... well, just because Jae, I don't know why. Google it.'

But then Scott was stuck in the 'why' phase too. Why *did*

Mummy die?

It was another question that Scott didn't have the answer for, at least not one that he felt he could share with the very person who needed to believe in him the most. He searched his soul for that answer every day. How long would 'because she was very poorly' serve as a justification for the little man losing his life source?

But for now at least he could lay that question to rest.

'Come on, let's go to *woik*...' Scott's tuneless, staccato attempt at *Little Green Bag* and his *Reservoir Dogs* swagger never ceased to delight Jae despite the daily nature of this school run ritual.

'Don't sing, don't sing!' Jae said this every day too.

Scott's potholed memory meant that he was perennially tardy, forever rushing from one nearly forgotten commitment to another. He'd developed several father-son customs to jog Jae along when he realised he'd shaved it too fine.

'Beat Daddy, beat Daddy.' He broke into a canter.

'Beat Jae, beat Jae.' Jae sprung into life like a gambolling lamb, little legs pumping hard, desperate to be first to the Whiston Primary school gate.

'OK, off you go Monkey. I gotta go see a man about a truck.'

'Bye Dad.' Scott noticed that Jae had taken to calling him Dad rather than Daddy when in or around the confines of the school.

'Bye fella. Give your Dad a kiss.' Scott crouched down and held his son in a too-meaningful embrace. He kissed his little velvet cheek. 'Love you Jae.'

Jae returned the kiss quickly, as if worried that this tender moment might get snapped by mocking peers. 'Love you

Dad.'

Then he was off, legs peddling across the brightly-painted tarmac of the playground, oblivious to the jump-step rules of the hop scotch blocks or the perils and rewards of the snakes and ladders. He mounted the three steps to the main entrance. Then he stopped, as he did every day, turned and searched the school gates for his Dad, locked on him and, with a hint of hesitation, waved.

For Jae this daily tradition was like clipping himself onto a line before stepping off the parental precipice into the daunting void of school.

For his Dad the moment was altogether more needy. Jae was the grounding path that connected Scott to Sally; his anchor to a lost life. Jae may have had Scott's eyes, but his fine cheekbones and warm smile were all Sally's. Life without him would be no life at all.

As he watched Jae turn away and melt into the bustling hive of small children filing through the double doors, a knot of dread twisted Scott's intestines. Having nearly lost Jae once, the sight of him being swallowed up would be seared onto his retina; a ghosted image that would remain with him until the stomach-settling second that he held his little lad's hand again.

Scott shivered the shiver of someone walking across his grave. He pulled up his collar and dipped his head down as if he were undercover, then turned away from the playground and cut across the front of the school gates in a bid to make a quick dash for home. Scott had, very consciously, stopped going into the playground and habitually stopped short of the school gates. Too many mornings of maternal cliques whispering behind cupped hands had deterred him anymore from entering into playground politics with the various huddles of 'there-but-for-the-grace-of-God-go-I' mums.

Three years on and the rumours still periodically swept round the playground, darting and swirling around Scott whenever he'd moved through the other school-run parents like a shark gliding through a shoal of fish. Hushed whispers shooting off at tangents as he passed by: 'That's the one, you know, the one whose wife...' He sometimes mused that he would have been subject to less damning speculation if he'd killed her himself.

In his haste to get away he jostled a young mum as she appeared at the gates. 'Oh, sorry' he said, eyes darting up to meet hers.

She flashed Scott a coy smile and held his gaze for slightly longer than necessary. 'No worries' she said, her smile broadening.

Nice teeth he noted... nice everything in fact, now that he'd allowed himself a moment to take her in. Did he know her, or her him? He dismissed the thought and brusquely excused himself, hunching up his shoulders to brace himself against the bitter breeze.

These brief encounters with attractive young mothers were commonplace. To those with the acquired taste, it wasn't difficult to work out why. If you gene-spliced a young George Best on a Chardonnay come down with Dave Grohl on a caffeine high you'd pretty much have Scott nailed. He had the erratic yet effortless sex appeal of someone who, despite the toll of hedonism, trauma and insomnia, was ruinously handsome.

His Anglo-Irish accent added to his enigma. It was a peculiar hybrid akin to that of a foreign footballer who'd played for a northern English club for many years. He didn't exactly 'lilt'; lilting was for southerners. Scott's dialect was more the-bastard-son-of. 'Ef Pater Schmaikel hed bane fro Derry, haida ended up soindin laike yiew' his cousin and fellow United fan, Bri, would say.

But it was his oceanic eyes that arrested most. Switching between clarity and vagueness; between euphotic sunlight and abyssal midnight. Fractured light reflecting his fractured soul.

Of course Scott was oblivious to all of this. He thought he looked like shit. He thought that women flashed their pearlies at him because they were Nice girls, being Nice. Scott was scared of Nice girls like a leper would be of touching the unafflicted. He feared that if he brushed up against them his melancholy would taint them. Become necrotic. Kill them.

He chanced a glance back to see if pretty-young-mum had lingered at the gates, hoping for him to have had second thoughts about making an exit. No such luck, she'd been supplanted by the simianesque school caretaker, bolting the black-clad, iron gates shut as if caging a dangerous beast.

Ah, probably just as well. He'd gotta see a man about a truck.

***

Scott jogged up the tractor-furrowed lane into the crescent-shaped, cobbled farmyard that posed as a modest preamble to his parents' sprawling farm estate. Directly opposite the front entrance gate stood a large, rustic-looking log cabin which housed the farm shop, cafe and dairy ice-cream annex. To its right was the customer car park, scabrous, puddled and in need of repair. To its left was the red brick Victorian farmhouse in which Scott was raised – the old B&B that he and Sally had taken over as their marital home after his parents had emigrated. Its latent, leaded windows he still struggled to look in the eye, for fear of the phantoms that his gaze might awaken.

Next to the farmhouse was *Store it with McCabe* – a squat reclaimed-brick building that acted as the office frontage for the self-storage units. Beside this there were a set of heavy duty, steel security gates that protected the lockups at the rear. Then on the other side of the gates were the three original tied cottages. One of the terraces was now home to Scott and Jae, another had been converted into an adjoining garage which Scott used as a home for his beloved Land Rover and for storing the trappings of his trapping.

The third tied cottage on the other side of the garage had been claimed for another office next to three barn-converted haulage sheds with dome-shaped, corrugated roofs, which collectively formed the relatively small logistics wing of the business that Scott now oversaw. He had once managed the estate in its entirety, but that was before his post-Sally meltdown; before most of the estate had been put in the hands of his cousin.

Trev Davies was waiting for him in the *Move it with McCabe* office. Trev was a pub acquaintance and a key account for Scott, one of the four big customers that kept his part of the farm business ticking over. He was a short, portly, ruddy-faced 53 year-old with thick, dark-rimmed glasses that magnified his almost-black eyes so that he bore a more than passing resemblance to a Slow Loris. Just like his mammalian twin, he may have looked like a harmless, cuddly Ewok but he had a toxic bite that could leave you for dead. If Scott kept his friends close, he kept Trev closer.

Like Scott's father, Trev used to be a farmer but had ditched livestock in favour of recycling. Resourcefully he bought and hauled all the waste malted wheat discarded by breakfast cereal manufacturers, treated it and then re-sold it to dairy farmers, animal sanctuaries and private customers as animal feed. He was a man in need of curtainsiders.

'Sorry mate.' Scott panted. 'Got caught up with one of the mums at the school gate' he said to cover his tardiness.

'Lucky bastard, rubbing shoulders with all that fanny every day. You're alright mate, I wouldn't fuckin climb over a juicy piece of beef curtain to get to you either. Ha-ha.' Trev's trademark blend of profanity and misogyny made Scott's use of vocabulary sound positively literary.

'What we got today then Trev?' Scott flicked open the top of his cigarette packet, teased out a tempting white stick and offered it to his valued customer.

'Ah, don't mind if I do.' He took the proffered gift then leant in to ignite it from the flame of Scott's outstretched Clipper.

'Coconut shells.' He exhaled a curl of tumbling smoke.

'Oh, yeah?' Scott mumbled between pursed lips as he raised the flame to his own tab.

'Yep. Grind the fuckers up; mix the granules in with the feed. Acts as friggin fantastic lubricant in feed dispenser; helps with scratching the cows' guts to get 'em regurgitating. Bloody gold dust' he said.

'Lubricant? Beggar me I never knew...' Despite already being familiar with the insight, Scott humoured him. Trev was a man of pride. He was also a man with a fat wallet.

'Ay mate, that reminds me.' Trev side-tracked the conversation excitedly. 'Talk about lube, have I got a fuckin story for you. Critch told us this in the Clover last night, 'kin funny it is.'

'Ah, if it's a Critch tale it'll be comedy – g'on.'

'This mate of his is havin this big fuckin extension done to his house. Oak-framed fuck off conservatory. Anyway that's besides the point. All you need to know is the bill for this fucker was 80 big ones. The guy's 'kin loaded, more money than fuckin sense if you ask me...'

'Aye.' Scott coughed out an accordant chuckle.

'So he comes home one afternoon to take his wife out

for lunch – she's not expectin him coz he's usually a total fuckin workaholic. Anyway, he gets in through the door, hears these scrapin and gruntin sounds. At first he thought it was the ruttin dog draggin his balls across the hessian floor tiles, 'til he gets closer to the dining room... the fuck off conservatory is being built onto the dining room... Anyway that's besides the point. He realises it's no fuckin dog, well not in a manner of speaking, bitch maybe...'

'G'on—'

'His wife is only straddled over a Black an' fuckin Decker workmate, arse in the air, gobblin one chippie with another of the fuckers knobbin her bollock deep. I'd have done my fuckin nut mate; I mean I wouldn't be accountable... But do you know what this guy did? He keeps schtum, gets his phone out; shoots a fuckin video. Emails it to these lads' gaffa sayin he wants to meet for a pint—'

'Well, I'll be bloody jiggered.'

'Straight up. One pint, pie and mash, and threat to become a publicist later and he's havin his fuckin 80 grand extension done for sweet FA. His wife still has no fuckin idea he seen it. Plus he's got all the evidence he needs if she ever gets fruity in the divorce courts. Bloody beautiful.' Trev cast his fag butt to the floor triumphantly.

'You're friggin joshin me mate.'

'No word of a lie my son – I've even seen the fuckin video. Boss it is, I'll mail it to ya.'

'You're all right mate...' Scott started to gesture a polite refusal.

Trev gave him an uneasy look as if to say *What? Not one of us?*

'...You're all right, you are mate.' Scott adjusted. 'Yeah send us it. Sounds class.'

Trev's jaw momentarily unclenched, but then his saucer eyes lit up like pools of fire. 'I tell you what for fuckin nothin mate, he's got more patience than me. If I found my wife like that I'd string all three of the fuckers up, cut the fuckin balls off those boys and make her wear them for earrings. I mean if I ever caught *anyone...*'

Trev pressed his finger into Scott's chest with painfully sharp pang. He surveyed Scott intently with his magnified shark-black eyes. Scott swallowed; his heart began to canter.

'Ha. I'm just fuckin you about, ya saft get' he said after an uncomfortable pause. 'Josie wouldn't go for scruffy gobshite like you if you were that last fuckin man alive.' Pot and kettle came to mind - whilst Trev's weight could seriously do with being kept in check, he was still punching way above it.

Scott's inner infidel was starting to twitch and squirm within its slippery membrane. Could Trev know? Would Josie have really let anything slip?

It was four years or more ago. Sally's spirit had been gradually bleeding into the atmosphere, she'd become a translucent ghost of herself, scarcely visible to the untrained eye. The troughs of emotional and physical inertia had gradually grown longer over the years. The brief flickers of mania, during which Sal's libido became frighteningly aggressive, were mercifully short. Even the plateaus were negligible. He'd often wondered if, during her moments of hypomanic madness, she'd ever succumbed to any illicit sexual impulses.

This wasn't an excuse. This was Scott searching for a reason as to why he could find himself half-naked on Trev and Josie's living room Axminster with her bare-breasted and riding him. It's not that it was the first time that Scott had lost time; it was that it was the first time *in years* that he had lost time.

He'd forgotten what it felt like to forget. He'd forgotten what it felt like to come round in the potting shed at the bottom of his garden with tagged items that he had no money to buy; items that even if he did have the money for, he would never have bought. He'd forgotten what it felt like to shake his head and find himself on the bus on his way to an unknown destination for an unknown purpose. He'd forgotten what it felt like to walk out of a public toilet in a venue that he didn't recognise to be hailed by a companion that he didn't know. He'd forgotten what it felt like to pretend to understand what the stranger was talking to him about. And always there was this malingering sense of guilt, the weighing-heavy feeling that came with each desertion of his senses. What did he do in those lost hours? How far did he go? What would come back to haunt him?

During his University years he had booze and drugs to fall back on to explain the misplaced time and atypical behaviour. He was pissed, or tripping; having a drunken blackout or an acid flashback. He'd almost blended into the morass of dope and drink steeped students whose conduct was not unlike his own.

But then he met Sally and the more time he spent with her, the more he felt like he was coming together. The shadows of himself, that always seemed to hover one stride behind him, stepped into line. He felt whole. Complete. Here. The lost hours became fewer and farther between until they were little more than the occasional moment of absent-mindedness, a day dream here and there, the odd memory lapse. As acuity and clarity flourished so the guilt withered, no fertile ground to be found in being present and correct.

Until Josie. Until he came to that afternoon with Josie grinding him. He'd caught himself *in flagrante* and remorse descended the instant the afterglow of their encounter had subsided. He'd searched himself for the reason and only one came to him – because he feared he was losing Sally. And losing Sal meant losing his integrity; losing Sal meant losing time. In those lost hours he found Josie's arms, her breasts, her thighs, her pussy and being too traumatised and transparent to hide it he'd spilled his guilt-ridden guts to Sally as soon as he'd carried himself over their marital threshold. She hadn't believed his amnesiac account and why should she? He could barely believe it himself.

Sally broke that day. She didn't break down, she just stopped working. Like a watch that stops ticking when it's been cast from the wrist it calls home. She stopped. In an effort to bring Sally back, Scott had since given Josie a very wide berth. It was shutting the gate after the horse had bolted; he'd paid the ultimate price for his unwitting indiscretion, and was evermore to pay the dues.

He'd lamented that day many, many times. But he was as certain as he could be that Trev had never found out. Josie would surely live in mortal dread of Trev's invidious retribution, so he was certain she would have reserved her right. Why would Trev be giving his wife's carpet-burnt quickie so much business if he *did* know? And besides, he was sure Josie had beguiled many other frustrated married men since their brief tryst.

But if Trev ever suspected that Scott was amongst the number he was sure he would see his haulage sheds razed to the ground. And that, evidently, would be the very least he'd have to fear. He cupped his balls through his jeans pocket as if to reassure himself that they were still were they ought to be.

Scott attempted to lift the atmosphere. 'Crackin story, that is mate. I'll have to tell Kirk and Em that one.' He fluted a long beam of blue smoke, tossed the last ember of his cigarette to the ground and toed it with his trainer. It gave him an excuse to avert his giving-himself-away gaze.

'Em? She's that lass you hang out with down the Clover,

yeah?' Trev's top lip curled.

'Aye, that's the one.'

'You ought to have a word with her about her fuckin language mate. Can't bloody stand a woman that swears. Makes her sound like a fuckin slapper.'

Trev couldn't have been more wrong about Scott's privileged access to the school-mum community. He'd kept himself to himself, fearing that getting too close to a potential partner would expose him as a pretender.

Ever since Sally had left them Scott didn't fit. He was a square peg. As a full-time parent he didn't belong to the nuclear family clique, or even the single moms' sub-set. If becoming a new Dad had been an expedition to a foreign land without a map or a compass, then becoming a single Dad was like being jettisoned into the cosmos in a tin can. He didn't fit with his spontaneous single mates. He didn't fit with the established couples. It's as if, like Gregor Samsa, he'd woken up to find himself trapped inside a form he didn't recognise. He was stuck on his back, peddling against the air, trying to find his feet. And like Gregor, he sometimes wished that if he just lay still, closed his eyes and didn't move then maybe everything would just return to normal. So often he'd daydreamed about the comforting blanket of oblivion in which Sally had cloaked herself. If it wasn't for Jae, he was sure he would have joined her within its folds.

As his thoughts drifted inwards he reached into his pocket for his rolling tobacco and papers. He cast them onto the desk and was about to set to work crafting a fix when a screwed up scrap of paper diverted him. He unfolded the shopping list-cum-riddle that he'd tugged down from the kitchen corkboard.

'Cuckoo... Fuckoo' he read aloud.

He tried again to coax memories to the surface but they swam at a depth that was beyond the reach of his line. He pulled the office keyboard towards him; the evasive quarry required a more intensive method of fishing. Perhaps a virtual net would reap some results.

He tapped 'Cuckoo' into the URL address bar and hit the return key. Scanning the headlines he plumped for best ranking one, an article from *TwitcherWiki* entitled '*The common cuckoo (Cuculus canorous)*'. He skimmed the background blurb until a sub-heading caught his eye.

Brood parasitism

The cuckoo is a brood parasite, which means it lays eggs in the nests of other bird species. The cuckoo egg hatches earlier than the host's, and the cuckoo chick grows faster; in most cases the chick evicts the eggs or young of the host species. The chick has no example to learn this behaviour from, so it is assumed to be an instinct that is passed on genetically.

Scott's phone vibrated on the desktop, jarring him from his new found interest in ornithology. Emma Burton's comically jeering contact photo rapidly shook from side to side, morphing it into a diabolical grimace that made Scott shiver. She put him in mind of the demons from his favourite film *Jacob's Ladder*.

'You forgot didn't you Scotty? Ya dozy twat.' Emma's alter ego was not the only one to be feeling rattled it seemed.

'Forgot? Forgot wha—?'

'I bloody *knew* you would. I'm at Glazebrook. You're picking me up from the 10:35? Or you would be if you'd—'

'Remembered to put it in me flamin phone. Dickwad. Soz Em, I'm, on me way.' Scott grabbed his car keys and dashed for the door.

'You'd better be, I'm dyin for a slash. The friggin loos are locked.'

'Girls can't slash. You need a dick for that.'

'I've got a dick. I call him Scott. Shit for brains.'

'I resemble that remark' he said as made it out to the Land Rover and jumped behind the dash. 'I'm out of the door. Have your slash at mine. I'll fix you a brew when we get back.'

'OK. Just hurry up, I'm freezin me nuts off...' She hung up.

Scott turned the engine over. The windscreen wipers juddered across the dry glass. A sheet of paper had been tucked behind the driver's-side blade; it fluttered in the breeze.

'Not another bloody ticket.' He cursed himself for not noticing it before as he jumped out and snatched it before it took flight. It wasn't a ticket he perused, however, it was a flyer.

Do you believe in destiny?

Believe some things were meant to be?

Have yet to find your perfect mate?

Then it's time to make your *Date with Fate*

Find your perfect mate at <u>datewithfate.com</u>

'Christ Roy, that's rich, even for you.' He shook his head as he pulled off.

CHAPTER 4: CUTS ME UP

Scott looked like he wanted to kill Iain who had just pulled out of the farm estate, forcing him to pedal the brake. The Land Rover stalled. 'Cut me up, pillock.'

'So, remind me why you love that guy so much?' Emma's query was spiked with more than a shot of her customary sarcasm.

'My perfect tosser of a cousin? Try the fact that he lives and breathes and I have to share this miserable, shitty corner of the world with him. He's a prize bell-end.'

'That's hardly a rationale.'

'*Brood Parasite*' he said under his breath. 'Circlin like a vulture to pick over the bones of me own Da's business. Kickin a man when he was down. Cunt. Underhand, smug little cunt.'

'You were in a no good place mate, and with your Mum and Dad away… The estate could've - *would've* - gone under.'

'So could *I*. Like that twat would've cared. Klepto-flamin-crat.' He dropped his head and shook his tresses. 'Come the day, he'll be first against the wall.'

'Mmm.' She struggled to find a proportionate response. 'Well at least Roy's in your corner. If it wasn't for him you wouldn't even have *Move it*.'

'*Move it with McCabe* – the clue is in the friggin name Em. It wasn't his to give, it's my bloody birth right.'

'You could have lost Jae if he hadn't stepped in.'

'Ah, Uncle Roy's alreet' he sighed. 'I know I owe him, don't I just. It's the only reason I stomach his fuckwit of a son sitting where I should be. Twat.'

'Ooh, you're in a delightful mood. Anyway, you'd better cut that out if you're gonna start dating again.'

'Cut what out? And who said I was—?'

'The language.' Emma held up the *Date with Fate* flyer by way of a reply. 'Some women hate swearing. Believe me, I bloody know.'

'Screw 'em' he said under his breath.

'You wish…'

Scott shot her a glance like she'd just cut him up. 'I'm *not* starting dating again.' He snatched the flyer from her hand and tossed it into the foot well. 'That's just Roy's latest brainwave of a business venture. Shady as shite if you ask me.'

'Roy's back?' Emma said, retrieving the flyer and tucking it into Scott's jacket pocket. 'Well, maybe that's providence, nothing ventured…'

'Anyway Sal loved my profanity' he digressed. 'Sweary Scott she called me the night we met. Sweary Scott and Sexy Sally. "You can't write a dissertation about the work of Scorsese if you're—"'

'"Upset by a bit of language"' Emma finished, gazing out of the passenger window. 'Not all girls are as open-minded as Sally.' Her voice floated on the air, along with her drifting gaze.

A keening, stifled whimper brought her back to the moment. Its source was beside her, and himself.

'Mate?' She leaned in towards him. Tears were edging their way down Scott's cheeks. He blinked hard and covered his eyes.

'It's just... the stupidest things...' His chest hiccupped. 'You think you're getting used to it but... the longer it goes on Em, the more the years come between us, the harder it is to accept I'll never see her again. All those things about her I knew so well... lost. And I'm lost too, without her.'

'I know hon, I...' Her eyes misted; she knew. But now was never the time to tell him, any more than it was the time to remind him that still she needed the loo. She rested her hand on the bleached knuckles of Scott's fist, still clamped around the steering wheel.

'I hope you don't.' He sniffed hard. 'For your sake Em, I hope you never feel like this. Everyone else just gets on with life as if... it never happened. For me it's like no time has passed; three years lost. It's totally unbelievable.' He shook his head, gazing vacantly into the middle distance. 'It's still... *unbelievable.*'

Emma nodded. 'I know it is.' It was all she could think of to say: *I know it is.* Her chin dropped to her chest.

'At first people rally round, bring you home cooked meals that you've no appetite to eat.' He pinched the bridge of his nose. 'But after a while they feel they've done their bit. So they leave you to get on with it. That's when it hits you; when all the fussing dies down. *This is how it is.* Limbo. A lifetime in flamin limbo.'

Silence hung between them like an invisible confessional lattice. Emma closed her eyes and tried hard to suppress a pang of envy. She wasn't allowed the fussing. She didn't deserve it.

'I know some people think I should've seen it coming. But Sal's depressions came and went. The highs were always more difficult than the lows. Even at her lowest I never thought she would— I mean— why was this time different? When she had Jae? She had *Jae* for Christ's sake. Why would she do that?'

'I…' She felt for the keys in her lap and started to edge each one around the ring as if praying the rosary. As she breathed in she could smell the violets as if the paper were still pressed to her breast.

Scott seemed oblivious to his confidant. His reconciliation poured on. 'I've forgotten what it's like to feel content. The churn… the twitch… the ache… it never goes away. She left me with this. She left me…' He wrestled with his breathing.

Emma wanted to comfort him, but couldn't bring herself to look over. She passed the last key over the ring, opened her eyes and looked down at them. How many Ave Marias? How many would it take to make amends?

'No one else to share Jae with. No one else to laugh with at the end of the day at summat he's done or said. No one else to make sure those moments don't get lost in time. No one else… Just me and Jae. And he'll forget most of it…'

Emma closed her fingers around the key and swallowed.

'Have ever you noticed that your early memories are only made of the moments that were snapped in family photos?'

She nodded, obligingly. Not sure that she had.

'I haven't taken any photos of me and Jae since Sal left us. Selfies… I mean *really*? Sad, pathetic selfies.'

She reached across the divide and tenderly dabbed his face with her glove. 'You can't go on like this Scotty. Alone. You need to get back out there. Sal's gone. Her pain is gone. Yours lives on. And it'll live on in Jae if you don't move on with your life. You're the only one who can give that little man a childhood – if you rob him of that, will he thank you for it? She'd found her Divine Intervention. 'Even if you don't feel you owe it to yourself, you owe it to Jae.'

'To replace his mum?'

'To find happiness. Be a family.'

'And I should take relationship advice from Ms Confirmed Bachelorette?' A half smile twitched on his lips.

'Bachelor will do me just fine. And I'm not confirmed. I just have high standards.' Emma fished a tissue out of her pocket.

'Maybe I do too' he said looking at it.

'It's clean' she reassured.

'Ah... I dunno'. He unfolded the offering and held it to his face, inhaling deeply as if it were a lemon scented hot towel. The Turin Shroud formed around his nostrils. 'I'd not be much good for anyone just now.' The tissue danced the can-can.

'That's starting to sound more like an excuse than a reason, hon. It's time. You've got to move on.'

He resurfaced from his baptism by hankie and stared at the wiper-smeared windscreen. 'Jesus, that came out of nowhere. Sorry.' A reverent pause kneeled quietly alongside them and lost itself in reflection for a moment.

Then Scott remembered who he was supposed to be.

'Self-piteous arsehole.' His playful glint acted as a smokescreen for the ache behind his eyes. The corners of his mouth conspired, curling upwards like a cat about to lick its lips. 'I could do with a shag, I know that much. I'm so desperate I've been wining and dining my fist.'

'Praise the Lord, that's the Scotty I know and loathe.' Emma managed to look him in the eye.

'Or a blow job, I'm not fussy.' He smirked, turning the engine over.

'Oh God I needed that, I was bustin. I haven't felt this relieved since Adam finished the line work on my ankle tattoo. You down the Clover tonight?' She slurped at her tea gratefully, cupping it in her hands to thaw them as she surveyed the familiar disarray of Scott's office.

'Indeed I am. Charley'll be here around seven-ish to babysit.' His gums itched at the thought of a pint. He absent-mindedly rubbed them with his finger.

'Cool. I should still be capable of conversation by then' she said, running her thumb down the glass pane that shielded Sally's likeness from her touch.

'Capable of conversation? Like a few bevvies would stop ya. Give me a break Em, you're a gobby cow on the beer.'

'Love you too. Right, I'd better get gone. See you later hon. Thanks for the lift.' She fired an ironic smirk his way.

Seeing Emma sat at his desk took Scott back to happier times. It was here that his wife had first introduced her student to him. She'd put Scott in mind of the Parisian girls in the 1960s French films that Sally lectured about. High cheek bones, boyish, cropped hair waxed to the side. Gamine but gangly. Emma was studying journalism and in an early ambition to become a film critic, had taken Sally's elective in Korean LGBT cinema. Poor Em had seemed genuinely shocked when Sal outed her as a dyke - her words - by way of an introduction. Scott wasn't. Sal had been on an upswing for a couple of weeks at the time and generally lacked candour when hypomania was bubbling under the surface. At first he'd paid superficial attention to his wife's suggestion that Emma could come and do some admin work for him. He was distracted by Sally's less than professorial hemline and the fact that she'd worn make up to campus that day. A familiar feeling of apprehension had bristled the hair follicles underneath his collar. Her erratic behaviour signalled the beginning of an unpredictable chapter.

Still, she was right. At the time Scott's shrewd business sense had seen the farm estate become a victim of its own success. The deli shop and cafe vied for more space, the petting farm had spawned more offspring, the self-storage units were almost running to capacity *and* the haulage side line was pulling its weight, Scott knew he'd needed as much help as he could get.

So, Emma became his Moneypenny and it was then that she and Scott's four years of dancing around the ring and pulling punches began.

And within a year Sally would be laid out.

He missed having Emma around the office, and lord knows he missed her timely texts reminding him of his diary commitments. Having seen out the last months of her degree earning her beer tokens with him, she had since very ably graduated from her studies and secured her debut as a staff copywriter for a Manchester-based IT magazine. Getting the latest hi-tech gadgets delivered to her door was a perk of her blogging rights. If he hadn't been such a Luddite he could have had several gratis phone upgrades by now.

They touched cheeks on her way out. Scott collapsed into his chair and sighed until he was empty. He picked up Sally's portrait, searched her eyes for reasons as he so often did, then gently laid her face down. Perhaps he should keep her in the drawer; try harder to move on. Perhaps Emma was right.

***

'Alright Scotty, what's the craic?'

'I… er…' Scott took a few moments to take in his surroundings. He seemed to be making his way up the lane towards the farm, which was just visible on the horizon line.

He looked at Roy, trying to pull him into focus. Then he looked down. His hands and knees were smeared with mud. Oh, Christ.

'I was... um... I was droppin off the van with Ash. Tracking needs looking at.' His lie might steer him into a pothole at some point, but right now it sounded plausible. He sucked in air to bring himself round.

'Hop in.' Roy smiled, leaning over the passenger seat and pushing open the door. 'Lordy, have you been crawling back on ye hands and knees or summat?' His voice was dark and earthy like treacle, steeped in Derry and thick from decades of chain-smoking.

'Ah... yeah... slipped over back there.' Scott assumed, wiping his palms on his jeans before climbing in. He sat for a moment looking at his hands, then at his feet; urging himself back into his body. As his senses settled on his surroundings he noticed that the car smelt bitter, like someone had just taken a caffeine hit from a cheap coffee machine. 'Thanks' he said.

'No bother – don't say ye owe me coz I've got a little favour to ask.' Roy always had little favours to ask. Some less little than others.

'Don't bugger about will ya? You've only been back five minutes.' He tried his best to sound casually cocky. 'Where'd you go for your circle jerk this time?'

'I'll mind ye to pay a bit of respect to ye old uncle' Roy said, raising an eyebrow. 'Was a business trip. Bucharest, to visit a supplier.' Then he added after a thought, 'Leather goods, dirt cheap.'

'Must be to justify the flight.' Scott said, looking at Roy sideways. He couldn't tell if his uncle was winking at him or suppressing his blinky tic.

'Ah, you know you're Uncle Roy, any excuse to visit a beautiful country. The trip pays for itself' he said, wiping the mist of his breath from the window with the back of his hand.

'G'on then spit it out, what's this favour?' He rubbed his hands together, noticing the prickling of pins and needles in his fingers.

'Need you to bid on summat – got to push the price up coz at the moment it's gonna go for a steal. I'll text ye the link. Ye might need to set up an account to do it but it'll only take a few minutes.' Roy crunched the gears and moved off.

'Aye, I can do that. Notin dodgy is it?' He shifted in his seat and used a cheeky smile to hide his unease, he was still adjusting to being back in the moment.

'Don't be saft. Got a load of camera bits and pieces I need to shift. Don't mither, if ye win it I won't make you pay. Just breaks me heart to see it go for notin.'

'What sort of camera bits and pieces? Anythin that'd be good for our Jae?'

'Nah, it's specialist stuff. Not for kids. I'm not lettin go of me classic gear, mind. Too many memories tied up in that, eh Scotty?' He shot him a glance then tapped Scott's knee with his gearstick hand.

Scott swallowed. He could smell his own staleness rising with the heat of his body, so he pulled at the neckline of his T-shirt and flapped it.

'You'll not remember then? That I was always snappin away with one camera or other. Aye, ye must?'

'Not really.' Scott shrugged, he could feel Roy's eyes twitching in this direction. 'Mind the road now Uncle Roy.' The lanky shadows of the birch trees rolled over them as they drove. They stretched languidly across the lane under the lowering sun; the sun that had been full in the midday sky a blink of an eye ago. He lifted the cuff of his jacket and glanced at his watch. Nearly four-thirty.

'Hey, what d'you reckon to the dating site? A goer?' Roy blinked-winked again as he turned off the lane and onto the cobbles of the farm car park.

'For me? Leave it out.' Scott quickly scanned the stationary vehicles to make sure the van wasn't evident. Roy didn't seem to notice.

'Nah, I mean good idea? A goer?' He pulled on the handbrake. '*Date with Fate*' Roy's hands hovered around an unseen crystal ball. 'Got to admit, it's got a ring to it. Ha. Get it? A *ring* to it.'

Scott shook his head. 'How the frig did you get involved in that?'

'Well, I'm not technically, just said I'd bung some flyers out in the farm shop. A boy of mine's doing all the technical jiggery-pokery for them. Mind you, if it takes off I might ask them if I can become a sleeping partner. Could be a ruddy good earner.' He rubbed imaginary readies between his fingers and thumb.

'Fattening your wallet off the back of the lonely and the desperate. Nice.'

The two men unclipped and climbed out of the car.

'That's a very cynical point of view you got there Scotty. What about helping people to find their soulmate?' Roy's blink-wink grew excitable.

'Don't make me laugh, since when did you ever do anything out of altruism?' He patted his jacket pockets for his fags and lighter. Empty.

'You talk like a man's not entitled to make himself a

living. There's people out there Scotty that have needs. These sites they just... ye know... bring 'em together.' He pressed his palms against each other.

'Maybe they could fix up that lad of yours. Might get him off my back if he had summat else to get a stiffy about.' He tried his jeans pockets. Just keys. Must have left his tabs in the office. Or somewhere else.

'Mmm... not much hope for Iain I'm afraid. I have tried Scotty, and it pains me to say it, but he's a bit of a lost cause on that front. Some men just don't have much...' he slammed the car door shut '... drive.'

'He can drive me flamin mad, so he can. Buckeejit.'

'Any more of that and there'll be less of it.' A flash of ire flickered in Roy's squint. 'Listen, I know it rages ye seein him lord it over your Da's business, but some day in the not-to-distant things'll right themselves. You'll get what's coming to ye.' There was no hint of a wink as he eyed his nephew.

'Not sure I like the sound of that.'

'*Due* to ye,' he said smiling, 'sorry, I meant due to ye. Give it time. And until then, don't be too hard on Iain, he can't help who he is.'

'No, that's your fault.' The suggestion of a smile skimmed Scott's lips.

'We're none of us perfect Scotty. But you'll know that now, being a Da yerself. We all understand our fathers a little more with hindsight.' His eyes found Scott's and fluttered on a blink.

'Better get back, before that son of yours starts scriking, or I give him summat to scrike about. Thanks for the lift.' He fist-bumped his uncle, wanting to appear at ease with himself.

'Bid it up Scotty.' Roy said with his thumb up, then he

turned and walked towards the farmhouse.

Scott stood for a moment and watched him enter through the front door. No, it wasn't easy seeing Iain lord it over the business, any more than it was seeing the pair of them staying in that house. Scott swallowed, trying to loosen the tightness in his throat. Then he turned and wandered towards his office.

Ping.

He pulled out his phone and swiped the glass with his thumb.

Roy: Here's that gear I need you to bid on:
Amateur_snapper/Cameras-Video-Equipment/715/en_1939726

Pausing outside *Move it with McCabe* he tapped the link. It took him to an e-auction page for a top of the range, semi-pro digital video camera, **CAREFULLY USED** as Roy had emphasised. The current bid was £2, 729.

'Bloody hell Roy, camera bits and pieces? You'd better *not* make me pay' he grumbled as he hit the *Make me an offer* button.

'Oi, McCabe. Penny for 'em?'

'Huh?' Scott resurfaced from trying to work out how to set up an account on the auction site. The source of the offer was behind him.

'Oh aye Jez. Alreet mate?'

'Struggling on Boss, tough at the top.' Jez winked, clucking his tongue against the roof of this mouth.

Jez was one of Scott's drivers. Off and on they had known each other for years. Since secondary school he'd skirted around the edges of mild criminality – he was the 'go-to' man for contraband. It had won him the dubious moniker of 'The Scrounger' after Hendley from *The Great Escape*. That was where the resemblance to James Garner ended; Donald Pleasence came closer. Some years ago Jez did a stretch and earned his HGV licence through an offender rehabilitation programme. The conviction was spent – Scott asked no questions so he was told no lies. He figured an old mate deserved a second chance.

'You after a gander at the roster?'

'More of a case of what I can show you, Boss. You got a minute?' The Scrounger shot a shifty gaze over his shoulder.

'Oh aye – what ya got?' Scott's casual inquiry couldn't mask his anticipation.

'Might be best if we stepped inside, Boss.' Jez nodded towards the office.

Scott wasted no time in ushering Jez through the door. He took the precaution of locking it behind them. 'So?'

'Clap your eyes on this little beauty.' Jez unfolded a flimsy leaf of silky, off-white cloth across the palm of his hand with the delicacy of a museum curator handling a priceless relic.

'Bloody hell, a butterfly?' Scott's eyes widened as he carefully lifted the highly restricted weapon from its courier's hands by the buffed metal, fold gate handle. He could see the blade nestling inside through its industrial, punch-holed design. It glinted as he brought it in for a closer inspection.

'Not just any butterfly my friend, but the queen of the gravity knives – a genuine Balisong.' As Scott was lost in admiration, Jez continued 'None of your sandwich-made shit that. Proper sturdy piece of kit – each handle is cast and milled from solid steel.' Jez's index finger hovered above the weapon, moving along its length with an airy caress. 'A kicker to prevent the inside of the handle coming into contact with the sharp edge...'

'Fuck me that is *gorgeous*.' The knife's handle was comprised of two narrow shafts of steel clasped together by a safety latch to protect the covered blade, giving it the appearance of a butterfly at rest. Scott flicked the latch off with his thumb, grasped the safe side of the split stem between his thumb and forefinger, then gave his wrist a sharp flick around to the right. The handle divided into two like its namesake flexing its wings, one half pivoting around the tang and hitting the back of Scott's hand. It revealed a razor sharp polished cutlass. Cupping the rest of his fingers around the conjoined hand piece he held the unsheathed dagger out before him.

'What an action that is mate, bloody poetry in motion' he said. For the time being all misgivings about his walkabout that morning were sliced from his thoughts.

'Aye, just look at the line of that swedge - and the spine - curved like the contours of a perfectly proportioned woman.' Jez was in his stride, a scouser by origin he had the gift-of-the-salesman-gab.

'She's a reet bobby dazzler mate. Where the blimmin 'eck did you get hold of this baby?' With another deft flick he brought to two wings of the handgrip back together again. He flipped and fanned the knife back and forth, amusing himself with his one-handed skill.

'Just back from the Philippines mate. You can buy these things from the bloody street vendors over there. Broad daylight, bold as brass. You'd think you'd died and gone to Heaven. Gettin it back 'ere was another thing though.'

'I'm not gonna ask.'

'I'm not gonna tell ya.' Jez rubbed his backside with both hands 'Let's just say that the hardware bolting me ole coccyx together came in handy again.' He winked. 'Should make slittin some little critters throat a bit easier, eh?'

'Bloody right – how much?'

'A ton to anyone else but, as you're a regular, and me boss, how about a bullseye?'

'You've got yourself a friggin deal mate.' Scott was already tugging at his wallet, battling its stubbornness to leave his back pocket.

'Nice one.' Jez nodded as he took the crumpled pile of notes from his patron's hand. 'I'll let you know if anything else rears its head. So to speak.'

'You do that Jezza – star job.' The pun was lost on Scott who was still flip-flopping the arms of the butterfly back and forth, flicking the metal latticework handles open and shut.

'Oh and, I know I don't need to say this, but keep it cleaned and oiled. And if porky pig comes sniffin around - you're on your own.' He made his way to the door.

'No worries mate – you're safe with me. 'Ere Jez, cop this.' Scott took a tab from his breast pocket, and darted it over to his partner in crime whose instincts gave him sharp reflexes for grabbing anything that was going for free.

'Ah, a tailor-made.' He sniffed, running it under his nostrils. 'Ciao boss.' Jez tucked the prize behind his ear and shot Scott a conspiratorial wink.

The tip of the steel blade tickles his eardrum. Pressure builds giving him barely a millisecond to grit his teeth and brace himself.

A sharp shove. An unholy explosion in his inner ear. An influx of pain so excruciating his tear ducts break their banks.

'Shut your little fucking mouth or I'll—'

'Jesus Christ.' Scott's eyes popped open to an upended view of the weekly roster. A shrill vibration was stabbing at his right eardrum. He sprung bolt upright, heart battering his chest wall, his stomach churning at the lingering mental picture of sticky, viscous fluid draining from his ear. He shook his head as if it would erase the sickening image like a dusting of aluminium powder over lines on an Etch A Sketch. The alarm he'd set to remind himself of afterschool club pick-up time was bleating, gaining in volume and agitation with every peal. Then the realisation dawned that he'd dropped off at his desk with his head on his phone.

He silenced it with a swipe of his thumb. His pulse was starting to recover from the sudden flush of adrenal hormones until he glanced down.

'Crap.' He'd been dozing with his hand still wrapped around the Balisong. If Iain clapped eyes on it, he'd waste no time dobbing them both in to the dibble. 'Jez would do his flamin nut' he said to himself, dispatching the smuggled steel to his desk drawer and rattling the key in the lock. Still shuddering from the visceral vision, he grabbed his jacket.

***

'Wehey fella – it's the weekend. Good day?'

'Yeah.' Jae said flatly, dragging his book back through the gravel.

'Good stuff. Any homework?' Scott picked it up and hooked it over his wrist.

'Nah.'

'Even better.' He grinned, raising his palm. Jae high-fived him, then took his Dad's hand as they strolled.

'Is Charley coming tonight Daddy?'

'Yep Monkey. She'll be round for tea.'

'Why does she babysit every Friday?'

'So Daddy can go out with his friends – you know Uncle Kirky and Auntie Emma.'

'Why?' Jae leapt over a single drain cover.

'Well sometimes grown-ups just need a bit of time with other grown-ups.'

'Are you going to the pub?'

'Yeah, to the Kilt an' Clover for a few beers. Like we always do.'

'Mrs. Bridden says that drinking beer is bad for you.'

'Oh does she? Well, she should know.'

'Why?'

'Never mind... just kiddin. Drinking *can* be bad for you but only if you do it too much, like eating too many sweets.'

'But sweets taste nice, beer is yucky.'

'How do you know?' He shot Jae a wry frown as his foot clipped a double drain. 'Toast' he said, winking at his boy.

'Daaad, that was a good luck one.'

'Oh, sh— sugar. Can I cancel out saying "toast"?'

Jae shook his head. 'Why do you drink beer?'

'It's good fun.'

'Why?'

'Well, erm... You know when I spin you around on the roundabout in the park and you get all dizzy and giggly? It's sort of like that, but for grown-ups – it makes us feel dizzy and giggly.'

'It makes me feel sick.'

'Mmm... well, that too. But Daddy doesn't do it that much do I? I mean how often does Daddy go to the pub?'

'Every Friday.'

'Every Friday. Exactly. Once a week – that's not too much is it?' Let's not tally the drinking at home.

'Why do you go out every Friday?'

'Friday nights are... they're tough Monkey.' He sniffed and gave Jae's knuckles a gentle squeeze.

'Why?'

'Just are. Hey tell ya what I'll get pizzas in, how about that?'

'You always get pizzas when Charley comes round.'

'Yeah. Every Friday. You like pizza though, eh?'

'These are people in the ground. Mummy is in the ground. This is Mummy.' Jae tugged at his Dad's hand, drawing them both to a halt. He was pointing to a small mottled patch on the pavement. Then he darted to his right.

'No… this is Mummy.' He designated a larger patch, more befitting of his mum's status. 'Is Mummy in the ground?'

Scott was well accustomed to Jae's repetitive lines of enquiry about his Mum and despite the way they made his heart ache, they made her still feel part of them. 'Yes but she's in the clouds too' he said.

'She's half in the ground and half in heaven. She's your girlfriend.' Jae often talked about his Mum in the present tense.

'My *wife*.'

'Oh yeah.' Jae gave his pedantic parent an unwitting

brush off. Still marking the sacrosanct spot, he said 'Say hello Sally.'

'Hello Sally.' Scott waved.

'Hello Mummy.' Jae waved too then squinted up at his Dad. 'Why are you sad?'

Scott's eyes shined with moisture and, as a single tear formed a haphazard runnel down his cheek, he replied 'Because I miss Mummy.'

CHAPTER 5: LOSING FACE

Emma was waiting for him in the car park of the Kilt and Clover pub, tapping her wrist and tutting. Scott shrugged as he trotted over to her side, tilted his eyes up to meet hers and said 'Do you wear heels just to make me look like a dick head?'

'No, you manage that all by yourself' she said looking pleased with herself. 'Get a haircut, loser' she added ruffling his fringe.

'Love you too Emsy. Fuck.'

'I'd rather not' she quipped as they made their way indoors. The pub was a traditional boozer, named after the origins of its half-Glaswegian, half-Belfastonian proprietor. For a freehouse it carried a disappointingly banal range of ales, alongside the obligatory Guinness, and boasted a beer-sticky carpet that threatened to rival the jaded décor and Celtic bric-a-brac for tackiness.

Scott stopped and patted the breast pocket of his combat jacket. 'Lost me friggin lighter again. I swear to God I put it here.' He popped the cigarette into his mouth freeing up both hands to frisk himself.

'Those things'll kill you matey.'

'Sumthin's gotta and I'd rather bring it on meself than get topped by Frank.'

'You seen him recently then?'

'Nah, not for a few weeks – will do tomorrow though. What joy.' He turned his back on his drinking partner and made straight for the bar. His nicotine habit was needling him for a fix. 'Hey Billy boy - you got any matches behind there?'

'Do I have a match? Try my arse; your face.' The landlord had the bulbous nose and waistline girth of one that had been sampling his own wares rather too much.

'Ha-de-bloody-ha.' A great publican Bill may be; a comedian he was not.

'Nah, sorry mate, apparently if we sell matches it might encourage people to smoke.'

'Christ's sake, nanny state. Can't I be free to kill myself in the manner of my own choosing?' The white stick pursed between his lips darted up and down, amplifying his cynical mumblings into a fully-blown protest. Still fruitlessly grabbing at his empty pockets, a white flare blazed under his nose threatening to set his floppy locks alight.

'You fiddlin with yourself again McCabe?' Trev held the flame just a little too close to Scott's face.

'Stone me Trev, you gave me a fright.' Scott breathed a sigh of relief and gratefully ushered his tab towards the fire.

'You can't smoke that in 'ere McCabe – outside now.' Billy shouted, like he was offering his regular out for a fight.

'Alright, alright keep yer knickers on.' A plume of purple smoke followed Scott, waving dismissively, as he headed towards the back door.

'Should a married couple be frank and earnest, or should one of them be a woman?' Scott threw his head back in mock hilarity, then realised he was the only one who found it funny. The emolliating, giddy feeling of alcohol seeping into his bloodstream was starting to take hold.

'Your gay jokes are so lame McCabe.'

'Oh get over yourself. It's one of me Mum's favourite jokes, that. Ain't that right Kirk?'

'So we know who's responsible for your enlightened outlook. Kirk – join me in raising a glass to Mummy McCabe.' Emma held her pint aloft.

'I don't get it.' Kirk chimed in. Kirk, or Jim Thorley as was his real name, was Scott's oldest friend. They had known each other since they'd used jumpers for goalposts and, being science fiction geeks at high school, the mantle 'Jim Kirk' had stuck. Kirk and Scotty: the original sci-fi bromance.

'Jesus, I don't know which I find more insulting, McCabe's cheap jokes or your blind eye. We don't just find 'life companions' and have 'close friendships' you know Kirk.' She took a hard slug of her pint.

'Steady on. I'm not that much of a cave man. I'm just a bit knackered. Was trying to fix Dad's PC until about two-o-bloody-clock this mornin.'

'Fix his PC? So now you're trying to make a bigot out of him too, eh?' It was all too easy. Goading Kirk into righteous indignation was one of Emma's favourite pastimes.

'Excuse *me*. You know there's no one that would like you to meet a nice young lady more than I would.' He feigned a pythonesque plummy accent.

'Why, so you could watch?' Scott fanned the flames.

'Bloody hell Scott, you've only got one thing on your mind haven't you? You know very well what I meant.' There was no suggestion of jest in Kirk's disapproval. Digs at Scott's prurience had occasionally been tossed his way ever since he'd confided his unintended infidelity to Kirk four years ago.

'And that very lady has arrived.' Scott deflected the accusation, nodding towards the bar. A brawny, robust member of the female darts team was growing impatient with the barman's pace of a snail. Behind a cupped hand Scott leaned in and murmured to Emma 'Yours.'

'Urgh. I wouldn't touch her with *yours*.' Emma glanced over the top of her phone, which she was using as a mirror to freshen her lipstick.

'I thought your type liked that kind of thing.' Goading Emma to righteous indignation was one of Scott's favourite pastimes.

'Yes, well of course the rest of *us* do. I'm the lone exception who actually finds the female form attractive. Remember what that looks like?' *Touché* was written all over her face.

'Ouch. Below the belt.'

'Believe me, I have absolutely no desire to get below your belt.'

To a degree Kirk was right. Scott did go through periods of having a one track mind. He'd not had sex for over three years. In a state of turmoil he'd spent a brief period in the early days of being a widower trying desperately to exorcise the pain of losing Sal by attempting to sleep around. His misplaced libido won him rejections from just about all of his once sizeable bevy of female acquaintances. He was humoured but was never successful. He'd wake up to find his only bed fellows were shame and humiliation. At the time he'd found himself in that threesome most Saturday mornings.

The female darts player, eventually served, was slurping from her pint as if she'd found a well in a desert. She carefully backed away from the bustling bar making way for one of Scott's previous brush-offs. Back then he thought Kat would be the grateful type. Pretty enough but pudgy with it. It turns out she was grateful – to Emma for rescuing her from a drunken, grieving, amorous fool. She'd lost weight lately, she looked good. She looked bloody good. He followed her with his eyes watching her shapely arse swish from side to side as she made her way back to her table. He imagined himself, trousers dropped to his knees, her naked butt sitting up and begging in front of him, his balls slapping rhythmically between her inner thighs… He nudged the head of his burgeoning erection with the base of his hand as if it would bring it to heel. Is this the effect of three years without a woman - getting a stiffy in the pub? Emma was right. Get a life boy. Get a bloody girlfriend.

His predicament wasn't helped by having to listen to a roll call of Trev's salacious encounters, as he stood at the bar.

'Ah bugger me did I ever tell you about that lass I picked up in Pillory Street when I was a cabbie?' It was a rhetorical question. Trev initiating a story was like a rollercoaster reaching the tipping point after a teasingly slow climb; there were no brakes, or breaks for that matter. 'Must've been just after chuckin out time at The Cat. This bird was on her own, totterin about on these fuck-off big heels, in a skirt that anyone else would call a belt. I tell you what for fuckin nothin she was rough as fuck. Even I wouldn't, I'm kiddin you not. Well, not in daylight anyway. When it twigged she was me bookin I thought "Ere we go Davies, buckle up for a rough fuckin ride", if ya know what I mean.' He winked and gave Scott a sharp dig in the ribs with his elbow, sloshing his beer overboard, and over Scott's white Vans.

Scott glanced down but knew that it was more than his trainers were worth to register disapproval.

'So she only fuckin gets in the passenger seat. I thought "Ey up, she's ridin shotgun, keep your eyes on the fuckin road Trev." Anyways she tells me where she's hoppin off and as I pull up outside this block of flats she suddenly announces "I've got no money". For fuck's sake, *I've got no money*. Christ it was only a six quid fare. I was fiddlin about with me meter thinkin I'll just write the fucker off; then she pipes up "D'you wanna take it out on that". Out of the corner of me eye I could see her knee pushing up against the gear stick. I'm thinkin "Aye, aye fuckin aye. If I turn round now it's gonna be winkin at me."'

'Deary me Trev, you didn't did you?' Another rhetorical question. Scott knew there would be little point in having to sit through this tawdry tale if not.

''Tween you and me I fuckin did. It was on a plate mate, what ya gonna do? Was the last time in a cab, though. Could've got in serious grief if she'd cried rape or summat.'

'Ya dirty get.' He feigned an envious smirk, knowing it was the reaction his companion expected to see. Frankly the thought of Trev nailing a plastered slapper in the front seat made him want to reach.

'Not 'arf as filthy as she was mate. Fuck me, in more ways than one, she was a proper minger. Had stingy wee and an itchy knob for days. Told the wife I'd trapped me prick in me flies and was too sore to screw. Bloody hell I'm tellin ya that was a close one.' He scratched his balls.

Scott was draining with colour at the thought of bedding Trev's wife after this cheap assignation. 'Think she suspected anything?' Dangerous ground McCabe.

'Nah, she thinks the sun shines out of my fat arse for some reason.' It was everything Scott could do not to let the thought *fat wallet* spring to his lips, as Trev tugged at his overstretched belt. 'Anyways Josie and I have an understandin.' He paused, eyeing his captive audience through his bottle-bottoms. '*I* do what I want and *she* does what I want.' He slapped his companion sharply on his left bicep. 'How do you fuckin like that? Heh-heh.'

Scott's face let slip a micro gesture of antipathy as he glanced at the offended limb.

'Another?' Trev pointed at Scott's empty glass; and without waiting for an affirmative, he waved a tenner at the barmaid like he was hailing a lap dance. Scott glanced at his watch, hinting at a getaway.

'Pint please duck.' Trev said, taking a pejorative peek at the timepiece that held Scott's wrist hostage. 'And one for Mr Flash Fuckin Harry over here.'

Ash, as Lee Ashley was known at school, was rangy, lean and lithe; almost feline such was the graceful precision of his movements. His gait was more like that of a dancer than a commercial vehicle mechanic, which is what he was. He didn't sit with his knees wide apart like most men, perhaps the well-endowed didn't need to. He sat with one lanky leg neatly folded over the other and with a cigarette, the one that reminded him he'd given up, balanced between the distal phalanges of his right hand and quivering with every twitch of his long, bony fingers like a funambulist's pole. His prodigious and outspoken sexual appetite, born no doubt of needing to assert his virility amidst laddish speculation about his sexuality, had earned him the reputation of having, and being, a big knob.

'Wonder if those two'll be licking each other's pussies tonight?' He nodded in Emma's direction, where the less than-steady-on-her-feet female darts player was hovering over her.

'You have a filthy mind Ash.' Scott had made a bee-line for Ash in order to give Trev the slip, who had been gearing up for another vulgar anecdote. Ho-hum.

'Don't tell me it doesn't cross yours.'

'Not Em's type.' Scott took a shufti around the bar. 'She's more Em's type' he said, gesturing towards a petite young woman, her dark hair tickling the waistline of her figure-hugging red dress. They watched as she bent her ear sheepishly towards one of a queue of underage lads who thought he might get lucky tonight.

'Christ, she's everybody's type' he said, ogling. 'Emma like-a-da-lick-a-da-lipstick-lesbian.' Ash stuck out his tongue and flicked it up and down. 'That's what I heard. Lock up your wives is what they say.'

'About Em? That's a joke, that is mate.'

'Apparently.' His benign cigarette nodded in agreement.

A shake of the girl's head crushed the boy's ego and sent him skulking back to a jeering posse of teenage speculators.

'Bollocks. Em's not scored in longer than me. And that's a friggin long time.'

'Whatever. Mind you, she's welcome to my wife. So long as I can video it for the wank duke box. You comin outside for a smoke?'

'Thought you give up months back.'

'I did. Got one of these now.' He opened his leather jacket and pulled out a silver tube, tugging on it with his lips and smirking with Machiavellian delight as the forbidden vapour escaped through a pop-eye gap in the corner of his mouth. 'It's a bloody gadget.'

'Don't see the point, meself. Talkin about gadgets - your place got any space to fit in tachograph job? Think one of mine's on the blink.'

'Aye, we can have a look-see. Smoke?'

'No I'm not on fuckin Faceless and I never will be. The people I want to stay in touch with, I have; the people I don't know anymore, there's a bloody good reason.' Scott had rejoined his friends at their customary table next to the central pillar of the lounge bar. His tongue loosened by inebriation, he was on a soapbox roll.

'Do you know the Chinese have this cultural concept called *Mian Zi* – it means 'face' and it stands for reputation; honour; respect. One of the worst things you can do in Chinese social etiquette is to cause someone to lose face – to pay them disrespect. No wonder they've banned shite like Faceless in all but a few square foot of Shanghai. Don't you think it's ironic that a country that could one day take over the world culturally forbids its people to lose face? And yet here in the West we're lining up to publicly disgrace ourselves through social media. Losing jobs over it? Losing relationships? Losing more than fuckin *face*.'

'How come you're the cultural attaché to China all of a sudden?' Emma attempted to halt Scott's tirade, initiated by her casual suggestion that he should raise his online profile.

'You can't teach Chinese film without understanding Chinese culture – Sal kindly passed that gem on to me during a pissed argument about my lack of respect for her.'

'Ah…' She lowered her eyes. 'Sorry mate, but I still think it's a great way to meet people, especially someone in your situation.'

'Nah, if you wanna parade yourself in a shop window and put a flamin price on your privacy and dignity, you be my guest. Me? I want no bloody part of it.'

***

Do you smoke?

'Nope.' Scott selected 'No way' from the *Date with Fate* drop down list, leant back in his swivel chair and mused on his 30-a-day habit as a deep draw on his cigarette excited its tip. 'Fuck it' he exhaled, 'I can make it through a meal without a smoke.'

Your relationship status:

Scott clicked the arrow next to the drop down list. His eyes surveyed the undesirable list of possible descriptors then fixed on the word 'Widowed'. He winced audibly as a shard of grief narrowly missed his heart and punctured his lungs. His chest caved. It felt as if breathing in would burn. Was he ready for this? He stared blankly at the crumpled flyer that Roy had left under his windscreen wiper. The tinkling ticking of his wrist watch marked time, as if it was tip-toeing around him. He braved taking in a lungful of fresh resolve.

'It's time.'

He chose 'Divorced', concluding that the truth would scare most women away before he'd even got their number. Scott sniffed hard and shuddered as he reached for his tobacco, pinched a moist clump, and cajoled it into a Rizla. He lit up. The comforting smell of smoked oak and the sear of the vapour as it parched his throat drew his focus back to the moment.

Do you have children? Yes, and they live with me always.

Add a photo: Remember: Your fate is in your face!

He toked hard on his smoke as if it would temper the onerous task of filing through memories to find a photo that didn't make him look like his wife had died. Where was his portrait in the attic? At 42 the palette knife of trauma, alcohol and Marlboro Red had coarsened his skin and dappled his hair with flecks of silver. Periodic insomnia had brushed half-moon shadows underneath his eyes. He used to be told he was cute. Jared Lito had been mentioned more than once. By himself mostly.

'I saw Jared Lito in a chip shop in Eastbourne once.' Kirk had claimed earlier that evening when Emma was telling Scott that he might be able to pull the fairer sex if he got a haircut and had a shave once in a while. 'He's got relatives there apparently.'

'It was probably Scotty' Emma had piped up, 'Was he wearing his slippers?' An awkward silence had thrown itself over the group like a fire blanket. Her quip, characteristically caustic as it was, related to an incident that occurred in the weeks following Sally's departure. Scott had been found in a state of confusion in the local chip shop wearing nothing but his boxers and his moccasins. He couldn't remember getting there, or getting home, but he did shudder with shame at the anamnesis, particularly the unconscionable thought of leaving Jae unattended. The fact that it hadn't been the first time, he'd left unspoken.

He let the thought drift into the past as the bite of the smoke hitting his throat brought him back to the present. Photos. Did he use his son as a date magnet? Do women go for seeing a guy with his kids or would it make his commitments all too real? He browsed through folder after folder of digital memories that he'd once taken care to sanitise – archiving most of his pictures of Sally into a rarely ventured to sub folder. Double clicking, scanning, hitting back, double clicking, scanning, hitting back, double clicking—

An arm's length selfie stopped him cold; one that had slipped his sickle. The three of them at a skewed angle, movement blurring the eventually-successful attempt at snapping baby Jae looking into the camera. Laughter peeling their lips wide. Sally looked happy, vibrant. And their little man had a heart-bursting smile.

He hit close. It shut him down. What was he doing? Why the hell was he doing this? The whole damned dating thing felt so contrived and desperate.

Nothing like the night he'd met Sal. He was twenty-six and lamenting being back in the parental fold following an unsuccessful attempt at severing the purse strings up in

Glasgow after graduating from University. He'd been trying to breathe life into the annual Rotary Club Yuletide party by hovering enough speed to reanimate the dead. Emerging from the toilet cubicle, he'd smoothed down his creased shirt, thrown the Gents door open with gusto and made his way back into the farm's Tithe Barn function room where his parents were making their seasonal contribution for the common good.

The multi-coloured beams from gyroscopic disco lights had danced and weaved around his head like a murmuration of starlings. Then a staccato snare beat, jangling guitar riff and piping horns made way for the iconic, grinding baseline of *Celebration*. Despite the insufferably predictable playlist the Billy was rising and Scott's fidgety hips were compelled to jiggle from side to side as his pupils widened to take in the scene. He'd surveyed the room, eager eyes scanning for women, intermittently locking onto them like a school-shooter's pistol scope looking for a random target.

The roly-poly, middle-aged Post Office master's wife came into focus, rhythmically pointing up and down, almost in time with the beat. Looking more *Hairspray* than *Saturday Night Fever* the cellulite on her chubby calves, revealed by her too-short hemline, wobbled and swayed counter to her steps like a fleshy damping pendulum.

Nope.

The painfully thin daughter of his father's best friend, her long crane-like neck and bowed head creating a swishing curtain of mousey, lanky hair making a vain attempt to mask her sizeable nose; only to cruelly unsheathe her prominent ears. She'd shuffled gormlessly from side to side, dancing the dance of a somnambulist.

Nope.

The gleeful, over-enthusiastic innocence of his nine year-old second cousin, with a face resembling a lurid ballroom dancer. Her golden hair piled high, crowning inappropriately scarlet lips, ruby cheeks and shimmery eyes which beamed with curfew-breaking delight as she waltzed hand-in-hand with his Uncle Roy.

Urgh.

The slender silhouette of a lone drinker at the bar nursing her complimentary Cava. Her brunette, glossy hair falling over her petite shoulders, laid bare by a sparkly, halter-neck dress that twinkled in the lights like a glitter ball. The gentle bumps of her vertebrae snaked hypnotically to the rhythm of the song, guiding his eye down her elfin figure to the sensual dip above the round of her trim, sashaying ass.

Yes please.

Unconscious of any volition, he'd self-assuredly made his way over, sliding up beside her like a ten-year-old on his knees at a wedding disco. His opening gambit had consisted of an amphetamine-fuelled dose of verbal diarrhoea. Yet despite the McCabe school of charm being in full flow, including him taking the rise out of her 'Mickey Mouse Film Studies degree', incredibly he'd been able to tempt her onto the dance floor.

'*Let the music play*, perhaps the DJ could be forgiven, eh Sal?' he laughed softly as he recalled her saying that her father was the new Grand Pooba Rotarian, or whatever it was they called themselves. 'Once a Moose always a Moose', she'd said. He remembered that because she had to wrestle her hand free of his to spread her fingers like antlers on either side of her temples. He didn't ever want to let her go.

She was smart. And she talked for Britain. And her eyes were huge, beautiful chocolate whirlpools of sweetness that the Augustus Gloop in Scott had just wanted to tumble into and never come back. He'd even thought she must have been whizzing too, but then mania was, as yet, an unknown to him.

Time had evaporated into adrenaline-fuelled effervescence that was only partly drug induced. The levity he'd felt in his heart had been unchartered territory. He'd never before given credence to love at first sight but that night he became its wide-eyed neophyte. At the end of the night flashes of blinding fluorescence burst through Scott and Sally's sanctuary like shafts of daybreak cast through fractured timbers of a zombie dawn. All around them the living dead had surrendered and ambled, ungainly and mindlessly, towards the barn exit. He still held the mental image of Sally pulling away and peeling off to join the exodus as if her body had been snatched. 'Hey sexy Sally. I've met the girl I'm gonna marry' he'd called after her. 'Go home. You're drunk. Or nuts' she'd said as she turned away. She didn't hear him add 'I am home. And I'm neither. Sexy Sally.'

From that night they were inseparable. Whether it was bracing endurance runs through the starved, hoary patchwork of the privet-lined Cheshire planes, marathon drinking sessions or chain smoking weed, they had tested their own and each other's limits. Just as Scott had laboured to adjust his naturally swift running pace to accommodate Sally, so she had struggled to train her sprinting thoughts to meet the stride of his.

The sex in those early days was incessant and urgent like they were trying to climb inside one another. Sally had inexhaustible energy. She was a dynamo who'd found stimulation at every turn of their tangential, early-morning pillow talk. Feral in the bedroom, Scott found her lack of inhibition incredibly rousing but somewhat intimidating. She'd roped him into kinky games that promised playful pain - the panderer to his every need one day; a pejorative bitch the next. The vacillations had given him vertigo.

Nothing was off limits with Sal. It was through her that

he'd learned that some women like it rough; that some women wanted to be hurt. He'd learned what 'safe word' meant, or rather safe *phrase*. It always amused him that she'd been a pedant for grammar even as she was suspended by rubber resistance bands from a pull-ups bar. 'Let me go' was Sally's safe phrase 'When I can't stand it anymore, I'll say "let me go". It'll keep us safe' she'd reassured as she implored him to whip her with a nylon skipping rope.

After those first fervent weeks Sally withdrew, failing to answer his calls or come to the door when he'd ventured over. He'd wracked his brain trying to figure out what he'd done to make her turn him away; why she would have had such a sudden and complete change of heart.

He waited some time for her to return and when she did he'd barely recognised her. Conservative clothing masked a fuller figure, and her coffee-almond eyes were clouded and hooded. She was calmer, easier to be with in some ways, but less vital and alive.

But Scott was already caught on the line and would stay hooked for every flip-flopping twitch on the thread that Sally's changeable moods would bring. If she was to be a slave to her unappeasable limbic system, then so was he. Still, at least the line that flexed between them held him firm; kept him here; stopped him from slipping the hook and sinking into his own murky depths.

So he'd wait patiently, helplessly even, until she'd won her internal battle of wills and sexy Sally reappeared to reel him in into her once more. It was a pattern Scott would become accustomed with over the years, but one that he would never get used to - that a barely perceptible lift or drop of her brow would signal a change was looming. Loving Sally, he would gradually come to accept, was like loving more than one person. And he was never truly sure which one was real, or which one he loved the most.

It's what had made them such a perfect match.

To even think of slicing Sal out of a photograph, like it would somehow enervate unhealed wounds, Scott knew he was a better man than that. So he reconciled himself to leaving Jae out of the picture, literally. One thing at a time.

He moved his attention to some more recent snaps. Himself and Kirk raising their beer jugs in The Clover - a boozy experimental reflection in the aged pub mirror, their squiffy, gurning faces distorted by its seeping glass. Could you make out the fag packet on the table in the background? Sod it. Not exactly the most favourable likeness, he searched for something less freak show; more wholesome and rugged. A shot lensed by Emma catching him in a flattering light leaning against one of the trucks in the yard, legs crossed, hands pushed deep into the front pockets of his jeans. It gave his physique a sculpted triangular profile, his face a deceptively youthful charm, complimented with a genuine smile. It was natural, sunny, perfect.

And rare because Emma always delighted in shooting Scott from the least bewitching angle possible. She must have been in a forgiving frame of mind that day, or had momentarily forgotten that she was supposed to make him look ugly and stupid.

Occupation:

Whatever he chose it would be misleading. He wondered if there was one of those websites just for women who wanted to date farmers: itshowyouploughthefield.com, Ivegottwentyacres.com, tractorthroughyourhaystack.com. Enough with the Wurzels already, Em's voice rang in his ears. 'Self-employed' would have to suffice.

Interests:

Oh surprise, surprise, trapping and butchering small fury animals wasn't on the list. Neither was brandishing illegal blades. Glenn Close gave bunny boilers a bad name. 'Watching horror movies'.

Scott continued to select one-line particulars from the options offered by the *Date with Fate* profile builder, planing the jagged edges off his individuality and carving a neat totem that could be packaged up for mass consumption:

Ethnicity: White (Celtic, northern and fuckin proud of it.)

Body type: Athletic and toned (Skinny frigger; smoke too much, eat shit all.)

Eyes: Blue (Cobalt windows to my dark, disfigured soul.)

Height: 5' 11" (OK 5'10" - bit short, in fact I come up short in lots of respects, but another inch might make me a Bigger Man.)

Faith: None (Neither 'Catholic apostate' nor 'Lost all' were proffered.)

Drink: Social drinker (Anti-social neurotic without a drink; oppositional egotist with one.)

Favourite read: One Flew Over the Cuckoo's Nest (Practically an autobiography. Truth is I never read: Don't have the concentration for books; Don't have the stomach for the news.)

About me and what I'm looking for:

I'm an embittered, guilt-ridden cynic whose wife hanged herself because I was too self-absorbed to keep it in my pants. Like most men I'm a total fuckin narcissist with the emotional intelligence of a thirteen year-old. Most of the time I don't even know who I am. I'm conflicted, maladjusted and unstable. I can feign being sociable but when all's said and done, I prefer to be alone. I'm not lonely, I don't need you. But my son does. If it wasn't for him I'd already be six foot under from a sustained and heroic campaign of self-annihilation. He's the reason

I live and breathe and the only person I'll ever truly love.

I'm looking to fill the fuckin huge void left by my dead wife. Ideally a clone, minus the bipolar disorder. Nobody I've ever met comes close, not even a little bit. I'm likely to unfavourably compare you to her every day, in every way. If you're looking for love, look elsewhere: that don't live here anymore. But I'm sure I can go through the motions, for the sake of giving my son a Mum and to keep my mates off my back. For some reason they think it's a good idea for me to share my despair and all round fucked-upness with someone else. It'll damage you as much as it's damaged me. And my dead wife.

But if you fancy a fuck, I'm your man.

Scott triumphantly planted a full stop at the end of his purging, crossed his arms over his chest, slouched back and admired his work.

Then, with the backspace key firmly depressed, he watched the hungry cursor eat his catharsis letter by letter. He typed:

I'm an easy going single parent in my early forties. Like many people of my age (...) I like the good but simple things in life - a country walk followed by a well-deserved cask ale in a proper (not wine bar) pub. Great company, good conversation, a lively debate, watching the footie, putting the world to rights. Once in a while, I'll confess, the "just the one" turns into an impromptu session followed by catching the beer scooter home... That said, being a family man, I'm just as happy with a decent (scary) movie and a bottle of Chilean red – but preferably not on my own!

I'm a physical guy who likes to get away from it all in the countryside, camping out, cooking over a real fire and getting off-road on my mountain bike. I also love swimming and am in the early stages of training for a triathlon. I'm a firm believer that a healthy body means a healthy mind. But everything in balance – life is for enjoying yourself too!

I'm looking for an honest, down to earth girl who isn't afraid of the fact that I have a kid and understands the limitations that places on my spontaneity - despite the desire to be. If you're inspired by the simple things in life and are looking to share good times in the hope of finding something special, then I'm your man.

'Bugger me. Never thought I'd write fiction. Full of surprises Scotty boy.' He clicked *Publish your profile* then swiftly shut the desktop down before he could retract it.

And with that BestBet7 was born. A disingenuous profile, befitting of half-baked intentions and false hopes.

CHAPTER 6: WATCH THIS

Saturday

'Daddy, what's this?' Jae threw the inquiry through the open living room door. It cut through Scott's customary morning haze like the beam of a fog lamp.

'What's what sweetheart?' He twisted a tea towel into the bowels of a china mug as he sauntered up the short hallway from the kitchen.

'This black stuff?' Jae was standing next to the stunted coffee table holding what would have been a perfectly square lump of cannabis resin were it not for one rounded corner that had been rubbed smooth. It could have passed for an innocent piece of Fimo but its partners in crime broke its cover - tobacco debris, peeled cigarette husks that resembled discarded banana skins and king-sized Rizlas. The paraphernalia of skinning up littered the glass table top. It took Scott a moment to register the scene.

'Oh Jes—' The mug hit the laminate floor and shattered. Panic flooded his brain sweeping away any lingering tendrils of fug. 'Give that to Daddy, Jae.' A pointless demand given that he'd launched himself across the sofa and snatched it from between his son's fingers.

'Sorry Daddy, I didn't—' The forcefulness and of his father's reaction was tugging at Jae's bottom lip.

'It's not your fault Monkey. I'm sorry, I didn't mean to scare you.' How did he explain this? 'It belongs to one of Daddy's friends.' Did it? Where the hell had it come from? He put it to his nose in the hope he was mistaken; the musky, patchouli perfume of recently softened block was palpable.

'What is it?' His boy persisted.

'It's... er... it's stuff that plumbers use to plug up holes in leaky pipes. I had to get a guy here last night to fix the heating. He must have left it behind. It's just not too good for you if you touch it and then put your fingers in your mouth – that's why I got worked up Jae. Sorry, I just didn't want you to try to eat it. In fact you'd better go and wash your hands.' It was an excessive, fumbling explanation that would have spelled dishonesty to anyone but a six-year-old.

As he spun his yarn he surveyed the room, looking for any clues that he may have had company last night. A vintage leather trench coat had been cast over the arm of the sofa, it said more 'Reich' than right - he'd not worn it for years. He stepped back into the hallway. Sprawled across the front doormat, a pair of retro para boots had been discarded - a trophy from his card-carrying, demo-stomping student days. As he drew closer he could see they were caked with fresh mud and lay next to a disembowelled squirrel.

'Jesus Norman.' Aside from the fact that Scott was the last person to need a lesson in hunting, he was more preoccupied with his own boots than with his cat's offering. He couldn't recall leaving the cottage last night and would never leave Jae alone. Knowingly. Scott pulled at the brush on his chin and shuffled back into the living room.

'What's up Daddy?' Jae's angst was like an emotional barometer, the unease in the air was palatable. He'd frozen to the spot and, having not heeded the instruction to wash his hands, was instead vigorously rubbing them up and down the front of his Ben 10 hoodie.

'Oh, er, nothing Monkey, I just thought I'd lost something.'

He put the truth into protective custody. Well-meaning

parental deception didn't count as lying, he told himself. But who was he lying to? His brain may be baked from getting stoned so often in the past, but he knew too well that this alone would not account for his dire lapse of memory, or explain the fact that the only clues as to the company he was keeping last night, belonged to him. Pin pricks of cold dread sprung from his pores as he hovered over the detritus on the table top, catching his reflection in the glass. He thought for a moment that he saw the ghosts of other eyes shining back at him, echoes of his likeness who licked the chops of a memory that he couldn't taste. He shrunk away from the image, repulsed by this feeling of shapes shifting within him; of not being alone in his body.

Scott busied himself clearing away the remnants of a misspent night; whose misspent night he couldn't bring himself to dwell on, and he had no time to lose if he was to remove the evidence before Frank arrived. He couldn't risk his brother-in-law suspecting that he was dabbling in drugs again. He'd vowed never to touch narcotics, unless prescribed, since almost losing his mind, and his boy.

Besides which, Frank had served in the Intelligence Corps; situational analysis was second nature to him. Scott's hands were still shaking as he sprayed the coffee table with polish and buffed it.

Knuckles rapped like machine gun fire against the front door. For some reason Sally's big brother never used the bell; Scott presumed it was because he was angry and needed something, or someone, to take it out on. Frank always seemed to be angry, especially with Scott. He still held him solely responsible for Sally's demise and never wasted an opportunity to remind his non-blood-brother of his rancour.

Scott breathed deeply to steady himself before making his way up the hallway. He needed to keep his composure intact if he was to brazen it out with Frank. He edged the door open.

'McCabe.' Frank always addressed men by their surnames; the tell-tale legacy of an ex-military man.

'Frank.' Ever the undisciplined civilian, Scott rebuffed the tradition.

Frank had worked in counter intelligence. His particular expertise had been in mitigating cyber threats. In his more paranoid moments Scott had convinced himself that Frank had plundered his computer files whilst he'd been temporarily detained by the local Mental Health Trust. If he'd been looking for erased proof of an affair his mission would have been thwarted – it had been too brief a dalliance to have yielded a data trail. Still, if he were to scan it today it might have provided some genuine fodder for his already low opinion of his sister's widow. Scott didn't need the spectre of Frank hovering over him to make him feel guilty for his recent foray into online dating.

'Jae? You ready? Uncle Frank's here.' Scott tossed the announcement over his shoulder, making sure to maintain eye contact with his brother-in-law. At six foot three and with an inspection-ready turnout topped with a services-regulation Number One, Frank may have cut an imposing figure but Scott refused to be visibly ruffled by it.

Jae dawdled up the hall dragging his P.E. bag along the floorboards behind him.

'Got your Gi?'

Jae nodded.

'Your belt?'

He nodded again.

'Come on then young man. The Sensei awaits.' Frank

bellowed the order, trying to make sound like an invite.

'Sen*pai*.' Jae said, with little trace of soldierly respect.

'Senpai, yes, right. Well, Nanna and Grandpa are keen to see you too. It's been a long time.' He eyeballed Scott.

'Have a good time fella.' Scott dipped down to hug his boy.

Jae clung to his Dad and wetted his cheek with a kiss. 'Love you Daddy.'

'Love you too Monkey.' Over Jae's shoulder Scott stared at Frank. His eyes said *Fuck You*.

Her lithe, athletic body writhed in discomfort as he yanked her arms behind her back, binding them at the elbows with bondage rope. He pulled the cord down and forced her spine into an unviable arch as he wrapped it multiple times around her ankles. Then he looped it between her feet to separate them and interlaced the ends together to form an elaborate slip knot which he pushed tight. She let out a muffled yelp, stifled by the ball-gag that forced her mouth wide.

Hog-tied and lying on her side the ripple of her muscular belly glistened with oil as he set to work winding another braid around the bulbous spheres of silicone stuffed under the skin of her otherwise dainty chest. With her tits deformed and protruding like zeppelins, forced proud by several loops of the rope, the torturer fastened it tight and retreated to a hand-crank operated winch at the back of the room. A burly, bearded, middle-aged man dressed in overalls, he rotated the handle, hoisting the girl up by her breasts towards the warehouse ceiling like a mechanic jacking up a car.

She squealed and thrashed like a pig about to get its throat slit as her strangulated boobs, stretching under her weight, turned puce.

The mechanic reached for his power tool, a long shaft with an industrial strength vibrator taped to one end – the type designed for deep-muscle body massage rather than stimulating the delicate, erogenous tissues of the clitoris. He twisted the dildo into the exposed fleshy parts between her legs with all the panache of a service technician taking a spanner to a stubborn wheel nut. She let out a throttled scream, flailing around on the rope trying to steer her swollen, beaten up pussy away from the instrument of torment, enduring another in a series of forced multiple orgasms that were by now more agony than ecstasy.

'Don't know why I watch this shit' he said to himself, twenty-seven minutes into the video. The girl had withstood every imaginable act of brutally-executed oral, vaginal and anal penetration and Scott had diligently sat through all of them. It seemed at times that genuine terror registered in her crassly painted eyes. She was barely legal for Christ's sake, thank the Lord he hadn't had a daughter.

He wasn't even convinced that he found it arousing, but whatever compulsion lead him to using hardcore S&M, on this occasion it had at least served to distract him from thinking about who had been skinning up on his coffee table. He'd swept those thoughts under the rug along with the leftover blims of hash and flakes of tobacco - an art that he was well practiced in when confronted with anything that he couldn't comprehend. Or couldn't cope with.

The routine post-coital interview with the star now rolled. She was swaddled in a cosy bath rope and giggling her way through the deconstruction of her victimisation whilst rubbing shoulders with her erstwhile torturer. Scott tapped his mouse with his index finger as if dismissing the ash from the end of a cigarette. The browser tab closed, taking with it the X-rated search engine. It revealed an open message in his mail box, and the source of his taboo viewing material:

Ey up boss. If you liked the last little gems I sent then you'll love this line up.

Watch this: <u>TripleXtube.com/hogtie</u>

Pretty tame stuff but I can hook you up with better shit than this. Just give me the nod. Delete this mate – you never know who is else watching.

Jez

'Tame? On what friggin planet is that tame, Jez?' He hurriedly closed the message then took care to erase his browsing history as if clearing his cache would somehow clear his conscience. Frank would have a field day. The screen fizzed briefly then died. Scott shook the mouse; it didn't rouse. He shook it again; nothing.

"Fucking fucker's fucking fucked... Fuck."

Scott glanced at the ticker weighing heavy on his wrist. The hour of braving Sally's parents approached. The thought made him cringe, even more so than usual whenever looking his tasteless time-keeper in the face. The garish monstrosity had been a fortieth birthday gift from his parents, less than a year after Scott had found Sally hanging. He'd still been tender to the touch from his mental meltdown. His emotional exoskeleton had been pinned and plated back together by drugs and do-gooders, callouses had formed around the fractures, but the fault-lines they left were vulnerable to breach. His fortieth could have passed without marking for all he cared; he'd never believed he would make it to that age anyway. But he had, nevertheless, tried to mask his contempt for life for the benefit of those who loved him.

At the time Peggy and Seth McCabe had made a sojourn from Malaga for a few weeks and had been staying at the farm, helping Scott to re-adjust to domestic life. They'd rallied round moving boxes of belongings from the farmhouse into the cottage, ensured Jae was settled in at his new day nursery and eased Scott back into daily routines.

In Scott's absence Seth had brought Peggy's nephew Iain

in to oversee the farm estate, whilst he himself provisionally stepped into the role of holding the reigns at *Move it with McCabe* while Scott had convalesced. With a degree of frustration that Seth found difficult to hide, he had gradually handed them back over to his struggling son in the hope that it would help him to man up.

'Time ticks on Scotty. Life ticks on.' His father had said as Scott prised the jaws of monogrammed jewellery box open like a vet trying to inspect a cat's teeth. And almost as if a gust of cat breath had hit his nostrils it was all that he could do not to visibly wince when he saw what was inside. His father's analogy alone, borne of the pull-yourself-together school of empathy, would have made him loathe the offering, even if it were remotely to his taste. So he not-so-gratefully accepted the watch which, he'd later discovered, he had Uncle Roy to thank for. Roy sourced it for Peggy from one of his many internet contacts. He was like the Delboy Trotter of the online marketplace, the only difference was that his suitcase full of booty was virtual.

Scott had stared at the gilded grotesquery in the box, knowing he was expected to drape it over his wrist and wear it with pride. He'd lost weight though and it ungracefully slipped to one side, half-langered. The lose fit had been Scott's the perfect excuse to slip it off and feed it to the open jaws of the chronograph case, just managing to snatch his fingers free of its snappy maw. No honeymoon phase for them – Scott and his new timepiece were always destined to have a fractious relationship.

And now it was telling him that it was time to leave.

***

Jae bounded over and launched himself up into Scott's arms. 'Daddy, Daddy I did my kata right. I got my third stripe.'

'Yeah? For orange belt? That's brilliant Jae. You'll be up for the next grading then, eh?' He squeezed his son around the waist and swung his floppy legs from side to side.

'He did really well. We watched from the cafe.' Angela bent down to pick up her grandson's bag, more in an effort to avoid Scott's gaze than to be helpful.

'Thanks Angie.' There was a tenderness in Scott's tone as he took the drawstring sack from his mother-in-law. However much Sally's mum doubted his integrity, she was one of the few people on the planet who still felt the loss of her daughter as deeply as he did. They shared an unspoken moment of 'Sally would be so proud' whilst watching Jae step through the kicks and parries of his kata.

'How's Carlo?' Scott scanned the capacious entrance hall behind her checking the arcaded, frosted-glass doors for signs of life.

'Working.' She half-smiled. It struck him as so Italian that Angela should respond to a query about her husband's wellbeing with an elusive comment on his whereabouts. Either that or her intuition told her that Scott was really asking if Carlo was home. He acknowledged her shrewdness with a respectful nod, still eyeing the middle distance. Angela might have noticed Scott's visible relief had she not been so absorbed by her grandson's street fighting antics.

Carlo Capote was an exceptionally private man with an officious and aloof manner that had been passed down to Frank. 'Working' was code for any number of possible pastimes or shady dealings that Carlo may have been involved with, especially given that he had all-but retired. If a self-made businessman ever truly retires. Carlo had been in demolition; swinging wrecking balls ran in the family.

Sally however had been cast in her mother's mould; warm and beautiful with a Mediterranean allure that came alive in her big, soft, bovine eyes. Angela had aged gracefully, she was the forward projection of what Sally could have become.

Scott ventured to speak. 'Well… I guess we'll love you and leave you.' He chanced slipping his arm around Angela's shoulder and ushered her towards him. In the absence of her menfolk she responded in kind, relaxing into the hug and rubbing his back with her palms.

'Jae is such a lovely boy, he's a credit to you Scott' she whispered, as if the walls might have ears.

'Thank you' he breathed, giving her a gentle squeeze. 'Thank you Angela.' Pulling back their eyes met for the first time. Hers were shiny with dew.

'You take care now Angie.' Scott rested his hand on her cheek.

'You too, both of you. Don't leave it so long.'

'I won't, I'm sorry.'

Angela returned the knowing nod.

'Say bye-bye to Nonnina, Jae.'

'Bye Nonnina.' Scott fixed Jae with his eyes, raising his eyebrows. 'Oh - I love you Nonnina.'

'I love you too sweetheart' she said, stooping to hold him close. 'Very, very much.'

As they turned to leave a hefty shadow shifted in the aperture of the front door. Scott pulled it open only to come face-to-chest with Carlo.

'McCabe.'

What the fuck was it with the men in this family?

'Carlo.' Over his father-in-law's shoulder Scott clocked

Frank making his way up the path. Perfect. Grunt *and* Swill. To Scott's surprise Carlo's stern expression quickly melted into a broad smile.

'So I hear we have a fighter on our hands.' He bypassed Scott as if he wasn't there. Frank stood in the doorway preventing him from making a nimble getaway. No sign of defrosting in his ice-cold demeanour.

'Come here son and show me what you got.' Carlo struck a karate stance. Jae promptly pulled a perfect roundhouse kick, cracking his Grandpa in his arthritic knee. 'Ooh, steady on karate kid.' Carlo withdrew, vigorously rubbing his leg. Scott stifled a chuckle.

'Jae, you need to learn some discipline. Karate is all about respect. You OK Dad?' Frank lurched to his father's assistance leaving Scott the perfect gap to slip through. He grabbed Jae's hand and pulled him away, hurrying him down the path as the little man shouted his retort:

'The Senpai said it was all about how to break somebody's leg.'

Good boy Jae. You tell 'em.

CHAPTER 7: FIGHTING THEM OFF

'Watch this.' It catches the light.

'Watch this.' Left. Right. Catches the light.

'Ten. Nine. Eight.'

Left. Right. Ruby light.

'Watch.' The face catches the light. 'This.'

'Seven. Six. Five.'

Ruby light. Fire light. Red light.

'Four. Three. Two…'

Red light. Red night.

'One.'

Red tights.

Out of the darkness.

Out of the red night.

Red tights.

Tight. Tight.

Wednesday

He clawed at his neck. He gulped for air. He gulped again, unable to swallow the sense of something pressing against his windpipe. Palpitations in his chest and knots in his stomach bore witness to the phantasms that raided his sleep and sought to throttle him. He could barely recollect them now, their likeness had slipped away, but the tightness in his throat told him they had paid him a visit.

He pushed the quilt down; even that weighed too heavy across his gullet. *Globus hystericus*, as Dr Leftwick had termed it, graced Scott with its presence in the early hours of most mornings. 'I'm not suggesting you're hysterical. Globus is a very common symptom of stress' he had said in an attempt to reassure. It did nothing to alleviate the suffocating discomfort Scott felt when it struck.

It wasn't a fear of the life being squeezed out of him that haunted him in these indigo hours. The thought of eternal nothing was a comforting damper to the bone-shaking ride of life, pot-holed with grotesque flashbacks and half-forgotten sensations. It was a fear of the life he woke up to that pulsed in his temples.

He tried to acclimatise himself to the duty of living by checking off the items on his mental to-do list: make Jae's packed lunch; remember to take his PE kit out of the drier; call the school; ask Kirk to fix his bloody computer; download drivers' data; get tachograph recalibrations organised; call safety inspectors back...

The tally of the day's tasks simply acted to amplify his anxiety. Swallowing hard again, he resolved to haul himself from beneath the sheets. The need the shake this uncanny feeling was one of the only things that compelled Scott to arise each morning.

That, and the little boy standing at his door.

Jae was kneading his sleepy right eye with a knuckle. He winced, forgetting that it was sore.

'Come here sweetheart.' Scott folded back the quilt and tapped the mattress. Jae shuffled over and tumbled in, curling up his legs. Scott tucked himself in behind his son and stroked his cheek. With each calming caress, the muscles in his own neck loosened.

'Don't worry lovely, Daddy'll sort it.'

***

Kirk was leaning over Scott's home computer untapping the last screw in the back of the hard drive casing. 'At fight?'

'Yep.' Scott hovered close by hoping that if his mate did eventually get the damn thing working again it wouldn't fire up the smutty site he'd last been looking at.

'Jae? Fighting?' Kirk rattled the shell gently from side to side to ease it off.

'Yep. Had the makings of a reet good shiner when I picked him up yesterday' he said, rubbing the side of his face.

'That's not like Jae.' Kirk squinted at the exposed computer components and pulled his glasses down from their resting place on his forehead. 'What's that all about do you reckon?'

'Dunno for sure – need to speak to his teacher. Jae said a lad in his class had been put in isolation. He wouldn't tell me anythin else about it. Just sat there and shrugged his shoulders every time I tried to ask him. I'm not very good at this stuff. Sal always…' the sentence died on his lips. Kirk momentarily stopped what he was doing and nodded.

Scott cleared his throat. 'I think it's this lad called Josh.'

'You wanna get to the root of that mate. Josh you say? Little turd.'

'Exactly. Anyways matey – talkin about gettin to the bottom of it, what do you think it is with this?'

'Well your monitor and lead are fine – work no problem when I hook them up to my laptop' he said, nudging the various card slots in the back of the tower.

'So why can't see anythin when I boot it up then? Was workin fine one minute then the next, dead as a Dodo.' Scott mirrored Kirk's inquisitive expression, like he had a hope in hell of making a diagnosis.

'Nah, it's not dead mate. The hard drive's firing – you can hear the fans. Loose connection maybe. I don't build any old crap you know. It'll be summat simple.' He jiggled a mass of knotted cables. 'Bloody mess this is mate, let's untangle this lot for a start.'

There was a lull in the conversation as Kirk tinkered with various cables and card slots.

'Yeah, so I dunno.' Scott broke the silence. 'I dunno what to say to help Jae.' He pushed his hands deep into his pockets like he was scouring them for the answers.

'Tell him how you handled bullies when you were his age.' Kirk grimaced as he wiggled a stubborn card out of its groove.

'Can't remember being his age.'

'Can't remember? You mean can't remember much?' He turned and sat back on his haunches.

'Nope. I mean can't remember anythin. Notin.' Scott's hand flat lined in the space between them.

'Mate, you *are* prone to exaggeration sometimes. You must remember bits and pieces. Who the hell doesn't remember anything?' He examined the liberated component.

'Me. I don't. Like this soddin computer.' Scott tapped the tower with his foot. 'You try to fire the memory up and you see eff all.' Speaking in the second person somehow felt appropriate given his alienation from himself.

Kirk frowned sceptically, 'Well *this* I can fix. It's the

video card. Buggered. I've got a spare – I'll pop over later and replace it.' He carefully slid the cover back over on.

'Cheers mate. I'll see you right for a pint or two. Can't be doin without this thing just now.' He patted Kirk on the shoulder.

'What about us? Do you remember us becoming mates?' A fleeting hint of chagrin glanced off Kirk's question.

'Just – I remember you showin up at our school. Probably one of the first things I can think of. Remember trapping with you and me Da, what age would we've been when we started doin that?'

'We were ten when I joined Edge Lane Primary, couple of years older when we started headin out with your Dad. That's mental mate, I can't believe I never knew this before. What about your family, your Sis?'

'Sweet Fanny Adams. A vague picture of her in senior school uniform. I've seen photos of me as a nipper but none of 'em ring any bells. It's like lookin at someone else.'

'Berserk... Alright then, well if you weren't bullied, I mean can't remember, I'll tell Jae how I handled bullies at his age.'

'Ran screamin from 'em like a girl?'

Kirk frowned. 'I held my own. I was *The Worm That Turned*.' He thrust his chin aloft and threw a defiant pose.

'Yeah, well I'm hardly gonna have ya sit down and have a manly heart-to-heart with Jae about how you used to hold your worm. The how-we-grow chat is a few years away thanks Kirk.'

'Har-har. Very funny. What *is* your plan then?' Kirk tapped a beat across his palm with his screwdriver.

'Gonna take the little fella camping at the weekend – see

if I can't get him to open up.'

'Trapping already? Is he a bit young?' He zipped up his tool pouch.

'Well I figure if the father-son chat doesn't take his mind off the little shits at school then slaughtering the cast of Watership Down just might.'

'*Nice...* Mind you, never did us any harm, did it?'

Scott gave a quick wave as his old friend pulled away in his telecoms van. His phone was harassing him.

'Mr McCabe? Jae's father?' The No Caller ID clearly knew him better than he knew her.

'Aye, aye.'

'Ah, hello Mr McCabe, it's Miss Brad—'

'Scott.' Pulling the front door of the cottage shut he turned to make his way back to the *Move it* office building.

'Of course. Scott, it's Miss Bradshaw. Head of lower school at Whiston Primary.'

'Ah, reet. You beat me to it, I wanted to talk to you.' He stopped and pulled the collar of his jacket up around his ears.

'Yes, good. Erm... Scott... Jae's behaviour has recently taken quite a turn for the worse. I'm sure you're aware of the scuffle he was involved in yesterday?'

'He came home with marks on his face – 'course I'm aware.' He shuddered as if a trespasser had crossed his grave.

'Right. And I'm also receiving feedback that he's being disruptive in class, distracting other children, back chatting the teacher, refusing to sit still, that sort of thing. I think it's time we all sat down together and had a chat. See if we can get to the bottom of this.'

'I thought you had? Didn't another lad get put in isolation? 'Bout time too. I've been complaining about him gettin bullied for a couple of weeks now.'

'Indeed, in fact both Jae and the other boy were put in isolation. We take bullying very seriously Scott, especially physical aggression. But having been in these situations many times in my twenty years of teaching, it's often a case of one child's word against the other, I'm afraid.'

'Oh, is it?' His ornery hackles started to bristle.

'Without empirical evidence to say either way we have to assume that—'

'Fuckin knew it. You people make me—'

'Scott, I really don't—'

'Mr McCabe.'

She composed herself. 'I understand Jae is attending holiday club next week. I can meet with you first thing on Monday before he goes in.'

'Yeah I'll come to your meeting, but don't expect me to lay on your doorstep and paint welcome across me forehead.'

'I don't think—'

'Do you know what? I don't care what you do or don't think. You know Jae's history?'

'Yes, of course, I was—'

'Then you should know better. Set the meeting up. I'll be there. Good fuckin day Miss Bradshaw.' He hung up.

'Unbelievable. Unbe-fuckin-lievable.' He tossed a pre-made roll up into his mouth and lit it, toking on it with vitriol before blowing out a lungful of pent-up frustration. Still cursing under his breath, his phone vibrated against his thigh as he crossed the courtyard.

Parentmail: Meeting with Ms Bradshaw. Monday 25th Oct, 08:30.

'K'arrf.' His dismissed the dispatch. 'Patronising bitch.' He was wedging it back into his jeans when it chimed again. Thinking he'd failed to sack it properly the first time, he was about to swipe its face to shut it up.

Date with Fate: SamiLuvsSkis has been looking at you. Login now to get chatting.

'Bloody hell, a hit.' Within seconds it pinged again.

Date with Fate: CupcakeKate has been looking at you. Login now to get chatting.

And again.

Date with Fate: NightOwl95 has been looking at you. Login now to get chatting.

'Flippin 'eck, it never rains...' He grinned, not realising that his apparent, out-of-the-blue popularity was due to him strolling back into the office's Wi-Fi zone. He quickened his pace, scooting across the cobbles, eager to find out more about his glut of new admirers.

'Scott.' His uncle's voice stopped him in his tracks. He spun round to see Roy with his arm draped around Jez's shoulders. As he approached he noticed that his driver looked ashen and jittery.

'Just the man, wanted a word with you Jezza.' Scott said conscious that Jez was avoiding eye contact.

'You lads pick up later. Scott I need you for a minute.' Roy slapped Jez on the back. Jez seemed to understand and dismissed himself.

'Don't go too far Jez – you're on a job for Trev later.' Scott threw after him then turned to Roy. 'Since when have you pair been so thick as thieves?'

'Ah, just passin the time o'day. Anywayz – I wanted to ask, how did ye get on with the dating site. Good eh?'

'He looked like he'd shit himself.' Scott watched Jez break into a canter, heading for the exit gate. 'He'd better bloody come back.'

'You know the scallywag, probably up to no good. He'll be back. So, the dating site?'

'Oh, yeah, well only just got started on it really but funny you should ask 'cause I've just started to get a stream of hits from it.'

'Told you boy – trust your old Uncle Roy to sort you out. It's based on a secret algorithm apparently; the only site of its type to use this specific technology–'

'Alreet Roy, spare us the sales pitch, I'll let you know if it's any good.'

'You'll get plenty of what's comin, you mark my words.' Roy winked. 'You'd better get gone then, lad. I'm not one to stand in the way of cupid's arrow.'

***

'Jayzuz, I sound like an arsehole.' Concluding that he must have been half juiced when he updated his profile, Scott read aloud to himself:

Think of me as a post-modernist – a pastiche of a 1970s footballer I may be on the outside, but on the inside I'm an anarchic philosopher – questioning the world through the filters of scepticism and irreverence.

'Christs'sake, did I really write that?' No surprise that they were looking, but not clicking.

Scott set about applying the law according to Occam, before his late night ramblings could inflict more damage on his already poor showing in the 'wink' rankings. With razor drawn, he sliced and shaved, sculpting a leaner, more loyal likeness. He strummed his fingertips against the desk; they were itchy for action but he had no idea where to start. Then it occurred to him to start with the place that everybody looks for answers. He Googled *Dating opening lines*.

VirtualDating.com came to his rescue, although he did question the wisdom of a site supposedly dedicated to romance having initials that sounded like a sexually transmitted infection. Nevertheless, in lieu of any better ideas, he implemented its guidance.

> **Bestbet7**: Hi SamiLuvsSkis. Well, I imagine no prizes for guessing you're happy when you're on the piste. Are you a black run girl, or more of a bunny slope babe?

So far removed from his natural disposition – or his comfort zone, Christ knows where he would take the conversation from there. Then he noticed that CupcakeKate appeared to be online.

> **Bestbet7**: Cupcakes? Sweet. So what would win your cupcake war, dark chocolate brownie or Victoria sponge?

Sweet? Sick-making more like. He waited a while to see if she was tempted or turned off. He slumped back in his chair. Turned off it seemed. He tried to make good.

> **Bestbet7**: Radio silence... Don't blame you that was a lame attempt. Sorry, new to all of this...

Scott decided to ply his borrowed wordsmithery elsewhere.

> **Bestbet7**: So what does a night owl do at night? Clubs, gigs, binge-watching box sets, yoga?

Sami the ski lover turned from amber to green. He tried another stolen strategy.

> **Bestbet7**: Hey Sami. It's your lucky day, you've just won a free trip to anywhere - where would you go?

Desperate. Embarrassing. No response.

Feeling like a curb-crawler loitering in the shadows of Cheetham Hill's red light district, he concluded that these trite pick-up lines made asking '*how much?*' sound positively seductive. He gazed out of the office window musing on why Jez would be sending him porn videos; another in this recent series of misplaced moments. He glanced at his watch. Speaking of the devil, Jez had better friggin show for his shift before Scott needed to pick Jae up.

While he waited he tapped *Today's mates* with his cursor. Six thumbnails revealed the latest potential matches that the dating site's algorithm deemed perfect. Each mugshot had a 'Save' button underneath it. Is that what these girls are looking for? Someone to surf in and rescue them? Is salvation what *he's* looking for? He wished there was a button he could click to save him from himself.

None of them appealed. Too old. Too young. Too fat. Too thin. Too mousey. Too brassy. Two fuckin heads. Bloody hell, this thing could seriously dent a man's self-esteem. He decided to define his own criteria. Hitting the Search tab he set a preference for women within a 25 to 45 age range and a 20 mile radius. He crossed his fingers as he clicked *Find my fate*.

This time the matches scrolled off the page and even at first scan he could pick out some genuine stunners peppered amongst the hopelessly optimistic. The pouting selfies, low cut tops, visible lace bra straps and flashes of cleavage took him back to his first time browsing the window displays in Amsterdam. He felt tingles of exhilaration as he surveyed the offerings.

He was drawn to raven-haired ChattyLass27. First he perused her pics. Her main profile photo had been taken from a high angle. Her arched eyebrows and sucked in cheekbones overstated her sex appeal. Digital filters, it transpired, had made her look deceptively cute. The less manipulated images in her gallery afforded tell-tale glimpses of a second chin and a complexion that suggested more porcine than porcelain. Still, not one to be deterred by some womanly curves he persevered, flitting his eyes over her headlines.

A buoyant personality, as the username suggested. Nothing to fear there, she'd be good at filling the awkward silences. Twenty-seven transpired to be her age. Perfect. Ish. Likes to go clubbing – well, gigs would play better for him these days but he could dust off his dancing shoes.

Oh shite, she's a God botherer. Sod that. That's a deal breaker.

By contrast the wind-swept, fresh-faced glow of Finn2bwith bore more promise. Even on closer inspection her first impression looked like an honest reflection of her unaffected prettiness. Her storyboard of photographs made good on the promise pitched by her pseudonym: Cat Woman striding across the finish line of a super-heroes-themed fun run; shrieking with terrified delight as she clings to the uppermost hand grips on a perilously sheer climbing wall; knocking back golden tequila shots with a throng of girlfriends; locking eyes with the camera lens, sun kissed and with sea-salted rats tails, reclining into the shoulder of a cropped out... somebody.

He glanced over her monologue – not because he needed any more baiting, the pictures alone deserved the wink that he had just shot her way. It all made pretty safe reading. Likes a drink (tick), likes tomboy movies (tick), fun-loving but looking for more (tick). Teensy bit heavy on the action adventure to be a match made in Heaven, but here on Earth she had mates who could blaze those trails with her.

As he was reading Scott realised he was being given the green light – literally - she had just jumped online. Had his wink tempted her to come out to play? Coincidence perhaps, but in the spirit of *carpe diem* he started to draft his opening gambit.

Bestbet7: Hello Finn2bwith – how's the craic?

'Bloody hell, that sounds like I'm asking about her flamin fanny.' He hit Delete.

Bestbet7: Hi there Finn2bwith. Like your username! You really do look like fun to be with so I figured it would be great to find out if you really are.

'For Christ's sake McCabe, what the frig is that?' He pressed and held Delete.

Bestbet7: Hi there Finn2bwith. Great username – you really look like fun in your pics, but I sense that you're also looking for more than just 'fun' – I get that. Me too. It's tough trying to get the right balance between coming across as 'good time' but not too shallow.

Anywayz from where I'm sitting you've hit the sweet spot, if you get what I mean. It would be fun... ha... to get to know you a bit better.

Is Finn your name BTW? Short for Fionnuala? Just curious to know if you're Irish. I'm Scott – but I'm not a Scot. I'm not making sense either.

Drop me a line if I haven't totally confused you...

Sx

Scott sat pondering on whether giving an 'x' to a girl you don't know is too forward or whether it was acceptable cyber-flirting protocol. He decided to delete it – better to be safe than scary.

His 'pick up Jae' alarm called time on his musings. A no-show by Jez. Bollocks. The last minute, back-up logistics would have to be dialled up en route. He gathered up his keys and his phone and made his way to the door. A chime in his pocket stopped him.

Finn2bwith: Hi Scott – thanks for getting in touch.

Yeah I'm Finn, but not Fionnuala – short for Finnley. I think it's Scottish actually, but I'm no Scot either. Not really sure where my parents got it from – probably some dodgy 80s TV series. They loved all that murder mystery stuff.

What you said is right, it's difficult to make yourself sound 'exciting' but not a total adrenalin-junkie-alcoholic-one-night-stander! I'm none of those things BTW... well, not all of those things anyway ☺

I would suggest meeting up this week but God has given me spots and a cold. Retribution, no doubt, for being a faithless little heathen. Plus I'm on that ridiculous alcohol-free-Stoptober tip. The sanctimonious phase of this is well and truly over - now it's just plain tedious, but I'm determined. I guess I might be able to face meeting without Dutch courage though... if you'd like to.

Would be good to chat. Send me your number?

Bugger me.

***

His phone shuddered and surfed across the kitchen table. He didn't recognise the number. Glancing down the hall he could see the flickering shapes cast by the TV set bouncing off the walls. Jae squealed with laughter. *You've Been Framed* had him captivated; he'd inherited his father's tendency towards *schadenfreude*.

'Come on, come on, come on. Be cool now Scotty boy.' He hit the green receiver icon.

'Hello? Scott McCabe speaking' his voice crackled. He held his hand over the phone to clear his throat. 'Or trying to speak.'

'Hi Scott, it's Finn. How you doing?' Was the tremolo in her casual query down to nerves or the phone network?

'Fine, thanks.' Deciding that it was reciprocal apprehension on the other end of the line, he added 'Well apart from the fact that me heart's thumpin and me stomach's in me mouth right now.'

'Me too, it's really odd calling people you don't know to arrange a date...'

'A date? Yeah I'd love to. Just thought I'd bite your hand

off for that one before you have chance to change your mind.' He guffawed, not quite meaning to.

'You're not backward in coming forward. Well I guess there's not much point joining dating site if you're not gonna go on a few dates.'

'Indeed, indeed. So, well, let's cut to the chase then Finn – when would suit you?' Better keep this short, before he gave himself too much rope.

'Well if it's OK with you I couldn't face you this week – not with this face.' She snorted, probably not meaning to either.

'Faithless little heathen, that was well funny. To be honest Finn that works brilliant for me - I'm taking me kid away for a couple of days this weekend. I could get a sitter the following weekend? If the thought of me needin to get babysitters doesn't turn you right off already…' He braced himself for an awkward silence.

'No don't be silly, you said in your profile. That'd be fine, the weekend after. Saturday?'

'Fantastic. I'll come over to Sale – you can take me to your best night spot.'

'Great. I'll book us a table and send you a link. See you a week on Saturday then.'

'Lookin forward to it Finn, really I am. Ta-ta for now.' He sat staring at the phone as its screen dimmed, then died. Bloody hell. A date.

His eyes wandered around the kitchen and settled on the fridge. He made his way over, pulled it open and grabbed a cold beer. Well-practiced at teasing tins open with one hand, he'd soon liberated its contents and was taking a slug. He slapped the door shut. It jostled an array of novelty magnets that fixed a haphazard jumble of life's detritus to its surface –

Jae's school planner, notes to self, just-in-case business cards for odd job men and two photos of his boy at after school club dressed as a diminutive Darth Vader.

His gaze rested on a drawing Jae had brought home that evening. Bold felt-tip lines framed a box-shaped dwelling topped with an acute-angled triangle. It posed as a backdrop for two stick figures levitating over thick stalks of grass. They were hand-in-hand; one tall, one short. 'Daddy' scrawled above tall. 'Jae' above short. A sheep-like cloud hovered above, enshrining another figure, reclining into its fluffy cradle. 'Mummy'. This was by no means one of a limited run, Jae often brought these sketches home. Their style was typical of child younger than Jae's years, but the colours were less so. High contrast, dark and light with the odd splash of crimson, not the standard primary overkill. Scott knew the pictures spoke volumes, but he wasn't skilled in their tongue.

On the other side of the house were two more figures also hand-in-hand, both short like Jae. A little boy and a little girl. 'Peta' above him, 'Red' above her. Red was drawn in red.

Scott planted himself onto the folding wooden chair and placed his beer onto the table.

'Peter; Peter…' He cast his mind back. *He's my friend. He comes out when we're here.* 'Ah, Jae's imaginary friend.' He tapped his chin with his phone. Red unnerved him. He distracted himself by tapping into his messages in case he'd missed a follow-up from Finn. The received texts were listed by name. His eyes were inevitably drawn, like rubber-necking a traffic accident, down to Sally's.

With Kirk's help he'd diligently transferred some of their precious exchanges from one phone to another. Still yet he couldn't bring himself to delete them; they kept her alive. Some served to remind him of the other selves he'd been in his previous life. They kept him alive too. He skimmed through them, pausing on one that he had sent after a sleepless night.

> I panicked last nite. Woke up and couldn't work out where I was...without u...didn't know u 5 months ago...now I can't live without u. Sxxxx

How could he have known then that he would have no choice but to live without Sally? That, as he listened to Jae gleefully chuckling along with the canned laughter in the living room, he would have no choice but to *live* without Sally.

The shrill ting of an incoming text stunned him back to the moment. The shadows of his former life receded slowly into the dim corners of his mind as he pulled focus to the present.

> This is the place: Casa Don Matias
>
> See you a week on Sat, 7:30. Finn x

He was about to tap a response but was interrupted by another incoming text.

> **Date with Fate**: NightOwl95 has sent you a message. Login now to get chatting.

Despite his vow to chat to one girl at a time, his flattered ego wouldn't let him resist. He thumbed the *Date with Fate* app.

> **NightOwl95**: Before I block you I have to ask – just what kind of fucked up game are you playing? No, forget it. I'm blocking you so don't bother replying.

CHAPTER 8: HOW?

Saturday

Jae jiggled around on the cobbles, shivering against the early morning frost as he obediently handed over one of the small copper plates he was fanning between his fingers like a pack of cards. Scott took it and scribbled a number and initials on its dulled surface.

'What are you doing Daddy?'

'I'm tagging these cages Jae - so I, and anyone else who finds them, know they're mine' he said, gesturing for his lad to deal another tag.

'Why do you do want to catch rabbits in a cage?' Jae looked perturbed.

'Well, I enjoy it for one thing.'

Jae scowled. He paddled the air with his copper plate distraction.

'When I say enjoy I mean, you know, it's what I used to do with my Dad. It's taught me a lot of skills. I'm good at it.' His son didn't look convinced. 'But seriously fella, people that have farms like Grandad have to – it's the law.' He threaded a thin braid of wire through the trap tag and twisted it around the handle of a cage. 'Too many rabbits damage crops and that makes farmers angry... and poor.' Scott looked up. 'You remember Peter Rabbit eating all those lettuce and beans in Mr. McGregor's garden?'

Jae nodded, his fringe licking his forehead from gusts of dew-laden air as he fanned himself with his unseasonal invention.

'Mr McGregor tried to catch him, right? Well that's what Daddy's doing.'

'But we won't be at Grandad's farm, or in Mr. McGregor's garden.' Jae always resorted to pure logic at times of protest.

'Nothing gets past you eh buddy?' Sarcasm – always ready with a mature rejoinder. Scott internally berated himself before adding 'No, you're right, we'll be on Will's land, Monkey. I'm doing him a favour and getting paid at bit for it, which always helps. Plus I get to keep any rabbits I catch to sell... or eat.'

Jae grimaced, pulling a standard issue 'yucky' expression.

'Aaaand...' Scott ignored the reaction and elbow-nudged his son in the ribs, 'you and me get to go camping for a couple of days.' He winked, hoping it would make the prospect of dead bunnies palatable.

'Poor bunny rabbits. Does it hurt?' This was going to need more than a nudge and a wink.

'Nah, it's actually very humane— I mean very gentle. The cage doesn't hurt the bunny.' He slapped his son gently on the back of the shoulder – more to signal the end of the conversation than anything else. 'Right, that's it sweetie, all of the cages tagged. Thanks for your help. Your next job is to get any stuff together you want to take.'

Scott had agreed to mop up the last of the rabbit population that lingered around Will's winter wheat crops - a good neighbour and just-surviving farmer. In return he and Jae would be sharing a very civilised double mattress in Will's rather stylishly renovated gamekeeper's hut; a timber-constructed Victorian shepherd's wagon complete with shabby-chic decor and a wood burning heater. No stove, however, the compact living space couldn't accommodate culinary endeavours. That didn't faze Scott, he preferred to set his own fire for cooking, plus it offered him the opportunity to share some survival skills with this boy.

Jae looked down at his feet then, after attempting to carve a divot in the frozen turf with his trainer toe, turned and sauntered across their modest patch of lawn. Scott watched him drag his heels into the garage and through the adjoining door to their cottage.

'Christ, this is going to be fun.' Scott sighed, his breath condensing into a cloud of water vapour. As he lifted the tagged cages one by one into the back of his Land Rover, he was starting to wonder if Jae really was mature enough for this father-and-son bonding trip.

Dismissing the thought, he threw in a backpack containing some trapper's essentials: gloves to mask his scent, spare wire for fixing cage doors, a catchpole, three sharp knives of various lengths and grinds, a pair of serrated butcher's shears, plus a small cleaver. Next he hoisted in his portable fridge freezer. No outdoor-loving, four-by-four aficionado would be without one, especially not one who would have to stow butchered rabbits until they returned. Finally he hauled his well-seasoned cast iron Dutch oven on board to accommodate those lagomorphs that wouldn't be making the return journey.

He heaved shut the back door of his 1968 Series II beauty, patting her aluminium flank as a cowhand would his trusty steed. He rustled around in his combat jacket pocket, grabbed the garage key fob and thumbed the remote. He watched the door descend. The stable door was closed. Time for the horse to bolt.

***

Scott had timed their arrival to coincide with the sun's postmeridian descent. His plan was to observe the ring-fenced crops by torchlight before putting Jae down for the night, then he would return in the darkness to place the traps. Once their bedding and supplies had been offloaded into the gamekeeper's hut, he tested his flashlight, took Jae by the hand and lead him through the nettle and bramble strewn undergrowth towards Will's field. They found the perfect vantage point and hunkered down.

'Why do we need to hide here Daddy?' Jae's voice was muffled by his egg sandwich, but Scott was still concerned the noise might render their hiding futile.

'Shhh, sweetheart. Try to keep your voice down. I want you to help me do a very important job' he whispered.

'Why?'

'Because I need to know how many bunnies there are. Do you think you can help me count? You're good at counting aren't you Jae?'

'Huh-hum.'

'OK, so I shine the torch along the edge of the fence and you count every time you see a bunny.' As they waited the sun dipped down behind the trees and without warning shrouded them in darkness.

'There's one!' Jae pointed, lurching forward. Two eerie pinholes of red eyeshine fixed them both in a paralysed stare.

'Shhhh, quiet sweetie. We don't want to scare them off. OK that's one, keep looking.' They waited in silence. Jae tried to grasp the idea of keeping still and quiet but twitched restlessly. Gradually his rustling settled down as rabbits started to appear.

'Two... three... four... five... there's lots Daddy.'

'Good boy, keep looking.'

Jae continued to log each appearance as shadows darted and flitted through the torch beam. The steady stream of Lepus were spilling out from a gap in the hedge row. Will's suspicion about the location of the harbourage was bearing fruit. They huddled together in the bluey-blackness, Dad cradling his boy and rubbing his chilled legs to prevent the rimy air from distracting him. Jae was so engrossed in his bob-tailed tally, he'd not registered the cold. The activity gradually slowed until they had been sitting staring at swaying wheat without visitation.

'Twenty-eight Dad.' A fleeting flicker split the beam.

'Twenty-nine' Scott turned to Jae and winked. 'OK Monkey, I think we have it.'

'Have what?'

'Now I know how many cages to put out and where. Chilly?'

Jae involuntarily quivered. He nodded animatedly.

'OK sweetie, let's go and get warm.'

The fire licked around the base of the pan as the simmering water within started to give up its heat to the night air. Jae sat swaddled in a thick, tartan blanket, transfixed by the orange tendrils lapping around the cracking logs, as pockets of gas popped throwing embers into the blackness like tiny fireworks.

'Hot chocky?' Scott shook a sachet of instant comfort. He tipped its contents into the plastic lid of the thermos flask, dissolved it into the boiled water, cooled it with milk then placed it into Jae's cupped hands.

He repeated the process for himself, burrowed his

enamel camping mug into the soil at his feet, then returned to dicing duty. A small pile of carrots, apples and turnips were being reduced to rabbit bait.

Jae, still spellbound by the flames, sipped tentatively at the edge of his beaker. Shadows danced across his face, camouflaging the dark circle of bruising that was jaundicing his right eye. Their unspoken contemplation was occasionally punctuated by the hissing and snapping of the camp fire and the intermittent dull drubbing of steel against wood.

'How did Mummy die?'

The word sliced the peace clean through. Scott froze like a rabbit snared in torchlight.

How?

He sat dumbfounded, bush knife poised. The wooden board slipped from his knees, clanking clumsily against vegetable pot. Jae had never asked how. How did he explain *how*? How could Sal have *left* him to explain how?

'How...' His thoughts slid their cover as the blade fell from his hand, almost spearing his foot.

'Yes... how did she die Daddy?' The dappled light from the fire caught the arc of a single shining tear as it ebbed down Jae's cheek. It broke Scott's trance.

'Jae, sweetheart, come here and sit next to Daddy' he said softly, unfolding his arm. Jae crawled over to his father and nestled into the waiting embrace.

'Jae, you knew that Mummy was poorly didn't you?'

Jae's head bobbed up and down.

'Well the kind of illness Mummy had, it wasn't like the kind of illnesses you and I get.'

'Was it an illness only girls get?' Jae's six-year-old logic rationalised a sickness that boys didn't seem to suffer from.

'No, fella, it wasn't like that. I mean it wasn't an illness of her body like a cold or a tummy bug. It was an illness in her mind.'

'Like a headache?'

'Erm... sort of... it certainly caused a lot of pain. It's hard to explain sweetie, but it was a sickness that affected the way she felt and behaved.'

'Did it change how she felt about me?'

'No, Jae, no, never. It affected how she felt about herself.'

'Did she kill herself?'

'Jesus Jae, where the f— where did you get that idea from?'

'A boy at school said my Mum killed herself because she'd had a loser like me.'

'Oh good God. That little shi— No, no, no lovely boy. Your Mummy loved you very, very much. More than anything.'

'So she didn't kill herself?'

'Jae this might be very difficult for you to understand. To be honest I still struggle myself, but Mummy thought we'd be better off without her... You won't remember this but after Mummy died I had to see a doctor for a while. To help me recover.'

Jae shook his head, wiping moisture from his upper lip.

'The doctor explained to me that Mummy did... what she did... not because she didn't love you, or me, quite the opposite. She loved you more than she loved herself.'

They sat in silence for a moment. Jae looked neither consoled nor convinced.

'This boy at school, he's just saying whatever he can think of to be cruel, Monkey. He doesn't know a thing. Bullies say shi— stuff like that because they want attention. I'll sort him, don't you worry. No one will ever say anything like that to you again Jae; no one.'

'How did she kill herself?' How was becoming the new why. Scott had to gather his thoughts before he could respond. Jae looked up at him, sniffing and catching his breath.

'OK sweetheart. Listen, I had to go to this meeting about how Mummy died. It's called an inquest and they have them when people... sometimes, when people die. I had to sit there and listen to the police and doctors describing everything about how...' He stopped and shuddered, losing himself in the memory. 'It really didn't help me Jae, I wish I'd never been. I don't want you to go through that. It's enough to know that Mummy is gone, and that she loved you. But we still have each other.'

'I can't remember Mummy.' He blurted it out like he was confessing to shoplifting; like he had been holding it under pressure; like saying it out loud might mean she was never really real.

Scott ushered Jae's head towards his shoulder, folded his arms tight around him and rocked him side-to-side.

'Are you going to die too?'

'I'll never leave you Jae. Never.'

'Can I have a new Mummy?'

He sat gazing at his little boy, kissed with the aura of firelight orange; bundled up in his sleeping bag like a new-born. Drifting off into blessed sleep. Blessed boy. An oppressive wave of guilt washed over him. He'd been so lost in his own pain all this time, so self-indulgent with it, that he'd failed to see what Jae needed most.

Scott rolled a cigarette, touched its tip to a flame, then drew on it deeply. He didn't know how long he remained in silent appreciation of the still life before him, vaguely pondering whether the cons of moving Jae to another school outweighed the pros. But he did have the resolve to do one thing when they returned. He'd give the dating a fighting chance.

Time to get to work. He tossed the stub of his tab into the fire, scooped up his precious cherub and transferred him to the wagon's sleeping quarters. Locking the door he threw the backpack of pre-prepared bait over his shoulder.

'Twenty-nine rabbits. Nine cages. Three trips.' Scott stretched his hands-free lamp over his head and twisted the wheel to turn it on. It flooded the back of the Land Rover, blinding him. He turned it again to narrow the beam. The floating blotches burnt onto his retinas started to die back, revealing the tools of his trade. He tugged a well-worn leather glove onto each hand, pushing the soft hide down between each finger. Looping an old belt through the handles of the first three traps he buckled them together, hoisted them clear of the ground and lolloped his way towards the border of the meadow.

Creatures scattered as his bobbing light approached. He tilted his head down to survey the damaged crops and rabbit droppings along the edge of the fence. This is the place. He continued along the field's perimeter until the erosion of the crops started to lessen. This would be his furthest pitch. He dumped the cages on the ground.

'Right yer little buggers, *The Year of the Angry Rabbit* is over.'

He freed the first cage and wedged it into place, grinding it back and forth to ensure purchase. If a rodent hovered at its entrance, it might otherwise tip over and prematurely trigger the door. Throwing the bait bag to the ground, he grabbed a handful of sweet smelling enticement and scattered it in and around the opening. Then he set the mesh door carefully onto the treadle arm and left the cage braced to trap.

He took the next cage and paced out ten footsteps back in the direction he had come, dropping a piece of bait with each step. He repeated the bedding in and baiting with this and the remaining cage before making his way back to camp. Two more trips and his job was done. By morning he should have a veritable warren and Will's pest would be ready for slaying, savouring or selling.

Tired and aching, Scott kicked dirt over the smoking embers of nature's stove and climbed the three steps up to the door of the cabin. He edged it open. Jae was sound asleep, nose-to-nose with a one-eyed, soggy-eared polar bear. He crept around the cramped, dimly-lit space and divested himself of his body warmer, pullover and jeans.

He wriggled down into his own bag and snuggled up to Jae on the double sleeper. Propping himself up on his elbow, he stroked his son's soft, silky hair. He basked in the moment, watching the rise and fall of his little chest, listening to his gently panting, shallow breaths. His eyeballs flicked from side to side under their hoods. He was dreaming. Happy dreams, Scott prayed. He tenderly stroked Jae's eyelids hoping to calm whatever visions were passing beneath them, then kissed his forehead and turned out the light.

'Night-night Monkey. Daddy loves you.'

A contented whine escaped as a deep sigh swept across Scott's pillow and dusted his face.

'Luff you too Daddy.'

Sunday

'No, I don't want to.'

'It's just to make you look pretty for the picture. You want to look pretty don't you?'

Shapes move across the shaft of light cast by the open door. Huge, tall figures they look to him. Huge, tall menacing figures casting gangly shadows that slither long the floor and climb the wall. Pushing the door wider. Two men facing away. A smaller, sylphlike figure wrestling with too many creeping hands. Broad, dark shoulders and sturdy legs obscuring his view. Arms tugging and pulling at vermilion woollen tights.

'No, stop it. I don't want to.' The girl's voice urgent now.

'Stop it!' A gut reaction. A Pavlovian plea resonating inside his head. A gut reaction that gives him away.

Heads shoot around. Faces shrouded in the night. Can't make them out.

A rough hand clamps his mouth. Another squeezes his neck. The repugnant smell of old leather. Crackling, wheezing breaths in his ear. A rasping, malevolence.

'Shut your little fucking mouth or I'll rip your little fucking tongue out.'

'Mummmmphh. Mummmmmeeeph.' Stifled pleas paralysed by pressure.

The two men peel away. He sees her now. Her face is familiar. Lips slowly mouthing a desperate appeal. A deep, drawling tone at odds with her years.

'Daah-deeh.'

Her face is familiar.

Out of the shadows the aggressors crawl. Closer. Close now; bearing down on him. Their vicious, twisted mouths spitting silent threats.

Grabbing his shoulders. Shaking him.

Smothered screams morph into the screeching of steel against steel.

'Daah-deeh. Daah-deeh.'

Terrified eyes pull focus. Blurred features sharpen.

She has Jae's face.

The girl has Jae's face.

'Daddy, Daddy.' Jae shook his Dad as hard as he was able.

Jolted free from his tormenters, Scott's strangulated screams rasped through his dry larynx. Still three years old. Still held by the throat.

'Daddy, wake up. You're making scary noises.'

'Stop. Stop it.' Dawning consciousness liberated Scott's voice.

'Daddy, you're being scary.'

'Oh God.' With a start he pushed himself up from the pillow, forcing himself back to the physical world. Pitch blackness offered little assistance or comfort. His heart bludgeoned his ribcage.

'Oh God.' He glanced across the bed and felt for the bumpy form of his son's body. Relief started to warm his synapses. He patted Jae's sleeping bag as much to reassure himself as his boy.

'It's OK Jae. Sorry. Daddy had a bad dream. Go back to sleep now.'

'You were making scary noises.' Jae's voice trailed as he rolled onto his side, pulling polar bear close. Drowsiness was already claiming his memory of the night terrors.

Not so Scott. He stared wide-eyed, his breaths hitching in his throat, as he scoped the cabin for recognisable shapes. His head was splitting. Rubbing his eyes sore, he smacked his tongue, tacky with congealed saliva, against the roof of his mouth. The cloying, resinous aftertaste of dehydration laced his breath with sickly sweetness. He felt along the bedside shelf. Empty. He must have forgotten to take his customary glass of water to bed.

Jae's breathing slowed and settled into a regular rhythm. Scott slid open the side zipper and swung his legs out of the sleeping bag. Planting his bare feet, they made contact with something rough and calloused. He pushed his foot across the floor boards. The object scraped along with it.

'What's—?' Combing the floor with his fingers, he felt for his phone. He groped its surface searching for the standby button. The night lit up as he pressed it, bringing the screen to life. Large illuminated numbers boasted the early hour. 04:27. 'Great.' He angled it downwards.

His foot was resting on a trapper's glove. His glove?

He rewound through his recent memories, picturing himself throwing the gloves on top of the backpack and slamming shut the rear door of the Land Rover. Was that muscle memory? Had he brought them into their weekend retreat without realising?

He swiped the face of the phone and tapped the torch icon. It flared like a camera flash, shrinking his pupils. He squinted, waiting for them to acclimatise, then swept the intimate space with the light. Something glinted on the small coffee table; then again on the return journey.

'Ach, dopey twat' he said, berating himself for leaving his water out of reach as he shuffled over to it.

He picked up the empty tumbler and put it to his nose. Acrid petroleum vapours seared his nostrils, giving way to the feint, stale scent of peat. He rummaged around for its source. His hand caught a bottle that was squatting under the table, almost knocking it over. He grabbed it, lifted the rim of its neck to his lips and tipped it. A trickle of hot, spicy liquor dribbled onto his tongue. Whiskey. However much had been in there, it had been drained.

The tumbler had company, his bush knife sat beside it. He had never left knives out with Jae around. He re-traced his actions after chopping the bait. He could swear it had been sheathed and returned to its holster in the back of the Landie.

The glove, the whiskey, the knife. Backstabbers all three of them, colluding with the hunk of hash and the cryptic cuckoo note to betray him to himself. How much time had he lost this time? Enough to put the knife to use.

Freshly carved lines were scored into the wooden surface of the table. His forty-two year-old eyes failed him at near distance. He tilted the phone-torch, affording closer scrutiny. It said:

KEEP US SAFE

What did that mean? A message to himself? Shush. Keep quiet. Keep him and Jae safe. Confessing to losing time would be confessing to losing his mind; tantamount to losing Jae; forever to lose himself in an endless bad trip.

No. Shush. Keep quite. Keep us safe.

There seemed little point in returning to bed. Attempting to sleep again with poltergeist etchings and haunting visions dancing across the inside of his lids would have been to no avail. Plus Scott needed to retrieve the cages and deal with any incarcerated inhabitants before Jae was up and about.

He pulled on his discarded clothes, grabbed the miscreant gloves and braced himself against the bitterness of the predawn frost. He trudged out to the field where, even from a distance, he could see jumpy silhouettes in the nearest cages. One by one he retrieved the traps, wrestling with the shifting weights en route back to camp. Twenty-two rodents had made the one-way trip across the cage thresholds. Not bad.

He wrenched open the back door of his four-wheel drive. Scott had called in various favours to get the wagon fixed up for survival without an electricity hook up. Along the side wall he'd rigged up his portable freezer. Powered by three car batteries sourced from dodgy scrap metal dealer he knew through the trade, they provided enough juice to run it for a day or two. He squeezed a pair of crocodile clips onto one set of terminals. The freezer shuddered into life.

Scott then constructed a makeshift slaughterhouse behind his truck, underneath a tree with conveniently low hanging branches from which he could hang his quarry. He unfolded a small table and on it he laid out his instruments: A steel bar, a razor sharp skinning knife, a sharpening block, some kitchen shears and his small cleaver. He felt his wrist, unclipped the clasp of his watch and slipped it off, laying it next to the tools.

Next to the table he positioned a stool on which he placed a large bucket of water drawn from a nearby cattle tap. Underneath the lynching branch he placed another large pail to catch spilled blood and viscera. Then he made a loop out of a strong nylon cord and threw it over the lowest branch. Feeding the loose lengths through the loop, he pulled them tight. The end of each was then fed through a rubber plate, creating two small nooses for the rabbits' rear feet.

The cages creaked and squeaked behind him as the distressed bunnies clambered over each other. He threw a tarp over them – they didn't need front row seats for the Thumper Chainsaw Massacre. Scott pulled on his latex gloves and tied an ankle-length rubber apron across his front. He braced himself. For a nimble-fingered butcher like Scott, field dressing a rabbit would only take a few minutes but, with so many, it would still be a messy and tiring job.

He pulled back the edge of the tarpaulin, unclipped the hatch of the first cage, grabbed a buck by the loose skin of its neck and lifted it out. Scott's preferred mode of killing was the 'broomstick method'. He held rabbit down on the ground, and put a bar across the back of its neck, wedging it in place with the toes of his boots. He then sharply yanked up the hind legs. The neck snapped with ease.

He picked up the floppy body and hung it by the hind legs. Taking the sharp knife he severed the ligaments around its neck. A red jet sprayed across his chest then settled into a steady trickle, splashing his boots before finding the waiting bucket below. He finished the job by crunching through the cartilage with the kitchen shears, pruning off the head to let the rabbit bleed out.

He chose a small, keen knife and cut the skin around the hock joints, flensing it from the muscle with short gentle strokes. Making an incision from one hind leg to the other, he carved through the fatty tissue that glued the hide to the meat. He then grabbed the fur around the thighs and peeled the skin down over the body as if taking off a sweater.

He tossed the pelt aside. With the cadaver still hanging he took the blade and sliced up from sternum to pelvis, opening up the trunk. The innards spilled out, liver and kidneys hitting the bucket with a bloody splosh. The intestines swung side-to-side like a giblet lasso. With a single slice the remaining organs fell, squelching against their companions in the tub. Scott reached down inside the chest cavity and swept it with his fingers to make sure it was clear before letting the husk down from the gallows.

He washed the carcass in the cold water removing remnants of hair and soil before casting it into the freezer unit. This he repeated with masterful dexterity for twenty-one of the creatures, sluicing down his tools, apron and boots and sharpening his implements as he went. Rabbit number twenty-two would be tonight's dinner.

He started by removing the front legs, not being attached to the body by bone they were easily liberated. Then he lay the rabbit on its side and ran the knife along the loin edge to the ribs. He filleted the meat off the ribs then turned his attention to the hind legs, gently cutting along the pelvis up to the ball-and-socket. Gripping each ankle he then bent them both back to pop the joints. A quick slice around each saltatorial leg freed them from the torso. He took his cleaver to the spine and severed it, slamming it down with his palm. Returning to his shears he pared off the ribs and chopped the loin into small pieces. Finally he trimmed them with his sharpest blade to remove remnants of silverskin and sinew.

He glanced at his watch. Seven thirty-three. Over two hours of gutting game had passed so instinctively that he'd zoned out. Impressed with his throughput, he bagged up the pelts, hosed down the tools and surfaces and dismantled his abattoir. He was exhausted as he threw his gloves and apron into a bin bag then swapped his boots for a less blood-stained pair. Just enough time, he hoped, for forty winks before roping Jae into preparing the stew.

With the fire blazing Scott climbed the steps of the hut to fetch the breakfast utensils. The lumpy mass under Jae's sleeping bag was shifting. Knotted curls were the first thing to make an appearance, standing proud like an air plant on a bonsai log. An arm wriggled free and swept the wiry tendrils away from his squinting eyes.

"Ey up fella. Hungry?' Scott was well practiced in the art of brushing fatigue aside. Survival skills of the single parent.

Jae peeked at his Dad through slatted eyes as if he were a stranger. 'What's that on your face?'

Scott rubbed his cheek and glanced down at his hand. Dried blood mixed with sebaceous skin flakes were smeared across his fingers. He stroked his beard, a tacky string of springy sinew attached itself to his forefinger. 'It's nothing sweetheart – bit of bacon fat. Come on, I've got brekkie on the go.' He picked up the skillet and spatula from the coffee table.

KEEP US SAFE

He shuddered, vowing to heed its wisdom, or its warning.

'Get yourself dressed Jae. I'll see you outside. Wrap up.'

Scott had been busy chopping what remained of his baiting vegetables as Jae chomped his way through a bacon sandwich, oozing red with sauce that he licked from his fingers.

'OK fella, when you're done there come and help me chop the rest of these.' Jae grunted and shuffled over, taking the paring knife from his Dad. Scott settled him down on a fishing stool in front of the camping table. Jae hacked away at a peeled carrot, splitting it into inedibly large chunks.

'Mind your fingers Monkey.'

Meanwhile Scott lifted pan of bubbling water from the fire and poured it into the Dutch oven. He'd taken the precaution of bedding the rabbit pieces down at the bottom of the dish and camouflaging them with sprigs of herb and crumbled stock cubes before Jae had entered the fray. If his son saw the dismembered game he'd refuse to eat it. Scott poured in the water swamping the kill with a muddy soup.

'Great stuff Jae. Chuck all those veggies in there now.'

He helped Jae to usher the cubes of carrot, potato and turnip off the chopping board and into the swim, placed the lid on the oven then nestled it into a pre-dug hole in the ground. Taking his shovel he scooped up a pile of hot coals from the morning fire and buried the pot under the embers.

'Sorted. Right fella, let's get our stuff and go and get ourselves some adventure.'

The boys shook off the night time spooks over a long, bracing hike through the bracken-littered trails of the woods, by way of a medieval archery contest, dinosaur bone hunting and slain giant climbing.

For these few hours Scott forgot his forgetting; he forgot the company that he kept inside; he forgot his haunting dreams and the pressing sense of guilt that forced the breath out of his body when he woke.

For these few hours they were everyman and his boy; they had a warm embrace to go home to; they had carefree small talk and flights of fancy in life affirming surroundings. They had fresh air to breathe, blood pumping through their veins and laughter in their hearts.

For these few hours Scott forgot that he doesn't do selfies.

CHAPTER 9: SHIT FOR BRAINS

Monday

If Scott had wished that the night-time terrors were the only cause of rude awakenings in his embattled life then the sight of a livid Trev Davies leering across his desk first thing on a Monday morning was to give him nasty start.

'Fuckin waste o'space. You can tell the little shit from me that I'll skin him alive when I get me hands on him.' Trev thumped the desk sending Scott's tea sloshing over his paperwork.

'Trev, what can I say? My reserve drivers were all on other jobs. I left a message.'

'A message. You pullin me pisser? What am I, some fuckin bird you just stood up? Christ on a bike. This is fuckin business. *Prick.*' The plexus of booze-broken capillaries leaking across Trev's bloated face looked fit to flood.

'I've got a good lad on the job today, Trev. He'll see you right.' Contrition following a screw up was Scott's least savoured part of the job. Especially when it wasn't his screw up.

'Two days bloody late. Where the fuck were you all weekend? Shoddy fuckin operation. Time is money, McCabe. Time is fuckin money.'

'This one's on me mate. Least I can do. It won't happen again.' Jez had cost him dear this time, but still he'd fair better if Scott caught up with him before Trev did.

'It'd better fuckin not. Christ all-fuckin-mighty; you losin the plot again or what?' Trev made a pistol of his fingers and tapped it against Scott's forehead, 'Don't fuck me again.' Pistol still cocked, he blew Scott a plosive kiss.

'It's all under control mate. I won't let you down.' Scott's phone chimed on his desk. A glowing calendar prompt invited him to his appointment with Jae's teacher.

Saved by the school bell. For the time being at least.

***

Scott sat with his arms folded across his chest tapping his foot on the soft felt carpet. The bright blue cushioned seating and low level tables in the primary school reception area made him feel like Gulliver in Lilliput; a rare glimpse into what it must feel like to be unusually tall. Jae sat next to him swinging his legs to and fro. He gnawed at his knuckles.

The all-too-familiar apprehension of sitting outside of the Head's office simmered beneath the surface of Scott's indifference as he glanced at the brightly-coloured bunting that hung across the top of the reception booth. It bore the school's values.

Be nice to each other

Everyone included

Learn and grow together

Observe the rules

Never give up

Give it your best

''Kin joke' he said under his breath. The trite sentiments did nothing to placate his combative temperament.

'Mr McCabe and Jae?' Miss Bradshaw appeared. She

looked joyless.

'Yup.' He and Jae rose to their feet. 'OK fella?' Scott placed his hand on Jae's shoulder. Jae looked up, he looked frightened.

'Please come this way.' The boys followed her as she made the short walk through the corridor and down a ramp and into her office. Her desk was messy, piled high with papers and pastel-coloured cardboard folders. The beige one on top bore Jae's name.

'Sit yourselves down.' She picked up the folder and gestured towards a low circular table with squat plastic chairs arranged around it. She sat and opened up the folder as if she was going to refer to it. Scott sat himself closest to the Head of Year and tapped the seat next to him, winking at his son. Jae obliged.

'Now, Jae, you know why I've asked you and your Dad to come in today don't you?'

''Cause I had a fight' he said without pausing to take his knuckles out of his mouth.

'What we want to do, Jae, is get to the bottom of why the fight happened. Do you think we can do that?'

Jae nodded, still chewing.

'Do you think it's all right to fight with your friends?'

'He's not my friend.' The knuckle was withdrawn in defiance.

Scott smiled. 'Too bloody right.'

'Mr McCabe, please. OK Jae, do you think it's all right to fight at all?'

'He said I'm gay.'

'He did?' Scott's smile dropped as he turned to his boy,

'You never told me that bef—'

'He said I'm gay because my Dad is my Mum.'

'Well, that's obviously not…' Miss Bradshaw's chair squeaked as she shifted her weight.

'Why didn't you mention this before Jae?' Scott said.

'You get upset Daddy. I didn't want you to get upset anymore.' The wells at the corners of his lazuline eyes started to spring.

'What else did the little sh— so-an-so say? Tell Miss Bradshaw Jae.' Scott slapped his palm on the table.

'He said my Mum killed herself…'

'Really—' She squirmed.

'…because of me.'

'And then tell her what happened. Tell her how you got—'

'Is that when you hit out at him Jae?'

'I didn't hit him, I tried to—'

'Tell her Jae.' Scott's volume rose. They both looked at him.

'Tell her.' He spun to face Miss Bradshaw. 'He grabbed him by the throat.'

A crinkle appeared between Jae's eyes. 'Daddy, he didn't—'

'He grabbed him by the throat and told him to shut his little fucking mouth. He grabbed him right by the fucking throat.' His hand was around the teacher's neck, squeezing hard, pinching the glands behind her ears. He tightened his grip until her face started to darken and bloat. She clawed at his fingers trying to prise them open. Gasping for words;

gasping for air.

'Mr McCabe, please can we let Jae tell us in his own words.'

Scott lurched backwards, his eyes frantically ricocheting around the room. They came to rest on Jae who had paused mid-sentence and was back at work nibbling his knuckle. Then to Miss Bradshaw who sat with her forearms folded before her on the table. Composed and professional, she nodded towards Jae.

'What happened after he said those things to you Jae?'

'I'm sorry, I don't know what just—' Scott hadn't heard her. He was busy scrutinising her neck for red marks. Nothing there but a loosely-tied, chequered cravat.

'Mr McCabe, are you all right?' she said, touching his arm.

'I don't know what I was...'

'You were just saying that this boy grabbed Jae by the throat but that's not what we understand. Jae, is that what happened?'

'No. He punched me. I tried to punch back but I missed and everyone laughed.' He hung his head. Drops of water fell onto the table from beneath the tresses of his fringe.

'I see. Well rest assured Jae that I shall be having strong words with Josh and his parents. Are you OK Scott? Would you like a glass of water?'

'No, I... What happens now?' What just happened then?

'Given the serious nature of what has been said I will be recommending a three day exclusion for Josh. That's the first step. If it happens again it could lead to further exclusions.'

Scott nodded conceding the moral high ground. His

episode in the twilight zone had left him spinning and in no state to question her judgement.

'And Jae I hope we will see an improvement in your behaviour too. No more messing around in the classroom. Deal?' She smiled.

'Deal.'

'Is that J-A-Y as in the bird?' The half term holiday club co-ordinator didn't wait for Scott to respond; she'd already written her version of his name on the blank sticker.

'No, it's J-A-E, as in the South Korean film director.'

She looked at him blankly.

'His mother's obsession; Jae-dong Cha.' Scott's top lip was moist from his funny turn. He wiped it with the back of his hand, then wiped his hand on his jacket.

'Oh. I see.' She binned her first effort and started to scribe of a fresh one. 'I'm afraid that foreign stuff is lost on me. Can't be doing with all those subtitles. Your Mummy must be very clever Jae.' She cocked her head at him, causing her second chin to swell like a goitre.

'My Mummy died.'

'Oh, I... I'm sorry.' She eyed Scott apologetically. He shook his head and raised his palm.

'Well, it's a lovely name and we can't have it spelt wrong now can we?' She adopted an especially patronising tone as she pressed Jae's name to his chest. 'So we're open til six-thirty – what time will you be wanting to collect Jae?'

'Can I come with you Daddy?' Jae hadn't let go of his father's hand. His eyes begged Scott not to leave him there.

'Daddy's got to work sweetheart. You'll be OK, you'll

make lots of new friends.' Then, addressing the play leader, he said under his breath 'It'll be six-ish.' He felt as though he was throwing his son into the lion pit.

'Come with me Jae. Now, what do you like doing? Drawing?' She untangled his hand from Scott's.

'No.' He pulled it away and started to gnaw the calloused flesh on his middle knuckle.

'Card games?'

'Nah.'

'How about Lego?'

He removed the raw, slobbery knuckle. 'I like Lego.'

'Perfect. Come on, I'll show you where the Lego boxes are.' This time he let her take his hand and guide him towards the back of the room. Glancing over her shoulder towards Scott, she mouthed 'He'll be fine'.

He wished he could be so sure.

***

'Alright Ash. How's it hangin?' Scott slouched in the chair opposite the praying mantis that was Lee Ashley, plucked the ready rolled cigarette from behind his ear and tapped the end down onto the edge of the desk.

'Slightly to the left mate, yerself?' Ash pulled his aluminium vaping mod from the breast pocket of his grease-smeared, once-green overalls and sucked on it.

'Listen I need to pick your brains about this digital tachograph system. Still trying to get me head around it.' Scott wiggled his Clipper free from his jeans and thumbed open its flip-top head.

'Can't do that in here mate.' Ash winked, his vape hissing like a threatened feline as he imbibed from its tip. 'What's the problem?' He fired a vapour ring across the table. Scott pierced it with his finger and smirked, returning his tab to its ear-hook.

'I've been running my first download from the driver's smartcards and the vehicle units, which I seem to have done right. So I'm trying to work out what the data is tellin me. There's this analysis software, but I—'

'They don't make it easy do they mate? Does the software supplier have any demos on their website?' The vaping liquid gurgled and whistled through the pipe as Ash disappeared behind a white cloud.

'There's a manual and I went to one-day training thing, but that was weeks ago. Buggered if I can figure it out now.' Watching Lee and his silver cylinder was making Scott itch for a smoke. 'Give us a blast on that mate.'

Lee wiped the mouthpiece with an oily rag and handed it over. Scott took it, placed his fingers along its neck and played it like a penny whistle. The vapour singed his throat, forcing a dry, rookie cough.

'Technology ain't your thing is it buddy?' Lee laughed and swiped it back off him. 'Got the SD card on you?'

'Aye, was hoping you'd ask that. Got it right here.' He flipped open his wallet and teased out the card.

'OK, let's shove into our machine and have a look-see.' Scott edged round the desk and hung over Lee's shoulder. 'Right, so you see this folder? That's where you'll find the data from the vehicle units and your drivers' cards.'

'That bit I managed to work out. Just need to check with you that I'm readin it right.'

'What's on your mind?' The vape rattled as Lee inhaled.

'I've got a feeling one of me drivers is fuckin about but I'm not sure if it's deliberate.' Scott wafted the air. 'We're new to this system – it might just be an innocent mistake. Just need to make sure I'm understanding the data before I challenge him.'

'What's your suspicion?' Lee's angular features cut through the dissipating mist.

'I think he's fiddling the tacho somehow - driving without putting his card in the VU, or using the wrong card slot after switchover. Maybe so he can make miles off the record.'

'Ecgh. That you don't need. OK, so you can compare the VU data with any individual driver to see if it tallies with what he's supposed to be doing. The VU data will tell you when the vehicle is being driven without a driver card. Here for example – *driving by an unknown driver* - that indicates the vehicle has been driven with no card.'

'Right, gotcha. That's dodgy for a start.' Scott tapped the silver tube; Lee acquiesced.

'So then the card data will tell you the period of time each driver's card was inserted into the VU – obviously this should be the whole time they are on a job, even if they're not driving.'

'Obviously.' He drew in the vapour, this time managing not to gag.

'Right, so you can look for periods of movement on the VU where there shouldn't be any. Then run the VU data and card data side by side. Like this – vehicle diary and driver diary. You can see the card in-out times on the driver's card – see?'

'Sod you Jez. He should've been recording there.' He took an agitated toke then handed the mod back to its owner.

'Like you say, could be accidental – dirt or damage to the card might screw with the VU. But either way, you wanna get on top of it mate. The DVSA don't look too kindly on ignorance or sloppiness. If the card's kaput he needs to be printing out every journey and getting a new one, sharpish.'

'The last thing I bloody need is for the fleet to be grounded.'

'Or worse. I'd have words.'

'I would if I could get hold of the dodgy get. He's done a bunk.'

'Get your drivers to print out their own data every week – that'll keep 'em on their toes. Another thing you might wanna think about is a fleet tracking system, uses GPS - you'll know exactly where your vehicles are all the time.'

'With only five curtainsiders? Jesus Ash, one thing at a time mate. This thing's doin me nut in as it is.'

***

He threw his keys onto the office desk and fumbled in his back pocket. Teasing the SD card out of his wallet he studied it, tapping it against his palm, as if looking at its surface would give him fresh insight.

He fired up his computer, pushed the card into the slot on the card reader, then made his way over to a small workbench in the corner of the room which acted as an altar to the Lord of the Brew. He clicked the kettle on and shovelled a heaped teaspoon of coffee into a tarnished mug bearing the dribbled-stained crest of Manchester United. The boiling kettle prompted the Pavlovian responses of drowning the grains, stirring in a large sugar and sloshing in the milk. He was about to take his first sip when a light tapping at the door turned his head. Iain didn't wait for Scott to greet him before making an entrance.

'Trevor Davies has been on the phone giving me flamin earache.'

Yeah not so bad cousin, how are you? 'That's Trev for ya. Argy twat.' Scott tossed the comment over his shoulder before taking a strident swig of his coffee.

'That argy twat is your best flamin customer Scott. Ever heard of the phase 'the customer is always right?''

'Keep yer knickers on Iain, I'm on it. I let him have a complementary load this morning.' He kept his back towards Iain, partly because looking at him made him feel green around the gills. Iain was too tall for his weight. His bowed shoulders gave him a concave chest which pushed his hips forward. Topped with a thinning, greasy barnet, droopy pockets of flesh for eyes and a rosacea-riddled complexion that made him look older than his forty-seven years, Scott knew just by looking at him that he had wandering hands whenever there was a fair young lady in reaching distance.

'That'll cost us. You gonna pay for that? What about the driver? What the flamin heck happened it him?' His breathy, high-pitched voice grated against Scott's ear drums. He could hear Iain licking his lips as his over-productive saliva glands got excited at the prospect of bollocking his younger relation.

'Why don't you ask your Dad?' Scott turned slowly, tracing his cousin's movements as Iain slithered towards Scott's desk. He craned his tortoise-like neck to peer around the PC screen. The VU data folders sat on the desktop.

'What's this?' he said.

'I told you, I'm on it.' Scott stood upright and square-shouldered, mainly because he could. He took another audible sup from his mug.

'You'd better be. I want to know what our drivers are

doing 'round the clock. We paid a flamin fortune for this new installation Scott – this shit should not be happening. I hold you personally responsible. Clear?'

Fuck right off. 'For the third time, I'm on it' he said, thrusting his chin skywards.

'Weekly reports from now on. First thing Monday.' His head meandered towards the door followed, in lateral undulations, by his torso and legs.

Scott lit a ciggie, waited briefly, then followed him. He watched Iain shambling from the building then he scurried up to the exit, quietly unlatched the door and peered out. Iain was half way across the courtyard and about to climb into his freshly polished Jeep Wrangler when Roy emerged from behind it.

Iain looked like he was boasting his managerial heroics to his father, pretending to square up for a fist fight. A once upright man, his cousin had shrunk over the years, Scott attributed that to the soul being sucked out of him. Karmic retribution. He'd be damned if he hadn't been stood at the Crossroads making his pact as a younger man. Fuck of a lot of good that had done him, Satan had clearly come early to settle his Red Book. Iain looked like a dead man walking.

Scott mounted his Land Rover and turned over the ignition. He could see the two men momentarily stop chatting and look over. As the engine coughed into life he stamped on the clutch, thrust it into gear then slammed his foot on the gas as hard as he could. He careered towards them. Iain's smug expression warped like a Halloween mask into wide-eyed terror as he lost his bowels. With a bone-crunching thud, a satisfying spatter of foamy blood sprayed across the windscreen.

He came to, drained his tab and cast it to the floor. Through the last flute of smoke he could see Roy put his arm around his boy as they strolled off towards the farm shop.

'Come the day.'

Tuesday

'Bren?'

Her pixelated face was sliced off below the nose. Her chin was moving, neck muscles flexing, but no sound issued forth.

'You on mute?'

'Oh holy crap I always do that.' She burst into life, adjusting the angle of her web cam to centre herself. 'How ya doin lil Bro?'

'Christ you're soundin more like a yank every day.'

'Hey, no crazies here. Anyway, how would you know stranger? Not heard from you in an age.'

'Aye, soz Sis. Been a bit of a mad time. You guys OK?'

Brenna's husband appeared in the background. 'We're good thanks buddy. How's sunny Man-ches-*ter*?'

'Alright Nate, not so sunny as it goes. In *Cheshire* that is.'

'Chesh-*ire*, Man-ches-*ter*, whatever, buddy. Bet you don't got your first snow? Just startin to come down here. Gonna be a goddamn cold winter, even for Ottawa. Thirdee below by Christmas they say.'

'Bloody hell, makes me shiver just thinkin bout that Nate. Explains the silly hat.'

'Ha-ha, yeah, needs must. Listen, it's good to see ya but I gotta run. Enjoy shootin shit with Bren.' He sloped off into the dim, impressionistic backdrop of their study.

'Bye honey.' Brenna called over her shoulder. 'Ah, alone at last. So how *are* you doin Scott? How's Jae?'

'Not so good Sis. Been some trouble at school. Total head fuck that was.'

'Why?'

'Some little twat told him that Sal killed herself. Christ Bren, I just totally lost my shit at the school. He asked me *how*, Bren.' He searched his sister's face like she had some answers. '"How did Mummy die?"'

'Oh Jesus, Scott. That is toadally fucked up. Whadid you say?'

'I sort of side-stepped it. Told him his Mum loved him and it wasn't his fault.' He looked away and took a deep toke on his almost dead tab. 'Just took me back Bren. Took me back to that bloody inquest. Christ, they might have well have been handin out a parkin ticket for all the sensitivity they showed. Thirty minutes I was in there Bren. Thirty fuckin minutes. And then out. Off you go. You go and deal with it now like a good boy.'

'That's messed up. I just don't know what to sa—'

'All because she didn't leave a note. Thank Christ I was out at the fair with Jae. I tell you what Bren, if there hadn't been so many witnesses they'd have tried to pin something on me.'

He tried to make eye contact but her eyes tilted down towards his image on her screen rather than looking into the camera lens. Either that or she was diverting her gaze on purpose.

After a pause she said 'I've... I've been writing for a while now Bro.'

'Writing? Yeah? What sort of writing?'

'Poetry.' She swallowed.

'Jeez, you know me Bren I'm not much of a reader. Especially not poetry, but good on you Sis.' He was grateful to have a diversion from his brooding.

'You don't get away that lightly Scotty. Got it published baby Bro, I've mailed you a copy.' She held up a slim volume to the camera. The cover carried a Baconesque painting of a smudged and distorted face behind a bold white title. *Shush: Out of the silence.* An anthology by Brenna Dumais. 'Not a major publisher' she continued, 'it's a charity actually. *Gateway*, based out of Toronto. They support…' Her voice trailed away. 'Anyway, should be with you inside of two weeks.' She lowered the book to reveal a pensive smile.

'Blimey, looks pretty intense Brenna. I'll give it a go Sis. Can't promise I'll understand it but I'll give it a go.' He tossed his burned out cigarette into the ashtray then glanced up. Were her eyes shining?

'So while we're bearing our souls I guess I should tell you, I've got a date.'

'A date? That's fantastic. Who with?'

'Well sort of a blind date really, from a dating site. Her name's Finn. She looks pretty.'

'Aw, Bro that is just great. I really hope that works out for you Scott. Just take it slow. Treat it like meeting a new friend.'

He nodded.

'Speaking of friends, how's Jimbo?'

'Kirk? Same old Kirk. Attacks life with all the gumption of geriatric waiting to die.'

'You wanna get him on your dating site.'

'Nah, he wouldn't want to lower himself to my level...'

***

He stirs from sleep, swatting the air. Something brushing his face. Wafting his face. He swats again. His hand finds something. Something thin, bony. A foot.

Legs dangling over his face. Red legs suspended overhead, disappearing into the darkness. Into the black hole.

'Let me go.' A rising, lyrical wail.

'Let me go. Let me go.' A lyrical, haunting wail.

'Let me down.' A haunting, beseeching wail.

A plume of powder; then a dead weight thumps his chest. Skinny red knees stab his shoulders, pinning him to the spot.

'Let me down.' A rasping hiss, gravelly with mortar dust.

'You let me down.' A spitting, rasping hiss. Head cocked at an impossible angle. A rubber garrotte eating into rotting neck muscle.

'You let me down.' A grating jeer. Cold, stiff fingers clawing at his throat. Squeezing his throat.

'You...'

Bulging red eyes. Blood red and wide. Blood red and wild. Necrotic flesh. Fetid breath.

'Let me down'

Fetid, suffocating cadaver breath.

'YOU'

Scott jolted from sleep and lay panting on his back, his heartbeat hissing in his ears in the pitch black of night. The mournful weeping of an infant's entreaty still ringing in his ears.

'Why did you let me down?'

He shook his head to rouse himself. Shifting shadows bled into the black, cross-fading with the familiar outline of his bedroom furniture. He lay in the dark with his eyes wide open, too scared to risk drifting back into the clutches of the succubus.

That face; that face so monstrous yet so familiar. That face that morphed between identities as is only possible in dreams. That face that morphed between the spectre of his late wife and the sweet little girl in the red tights.

Wednesday

Emma slouched back in the office guest chair and crossed her large feet on Scott's desk so that they almost toppled his monitor. He barely registered it.

'Did you know...?' She paused to check if he was listening; her friend was no multi-tasker especially when one of those tasks involved technology.

'G'on.' He made noises in the right places but Scott was absorbed in whatever it was that he was looking at on-screen. He periodically uplifted his eyebrows and scratched figures down into a series of post-its.

'Did you know that the hacking technology exists that can cycle through 350 billion password guesses per second?'

'No, I did not. Fascinating.' Another eureka moment lifted his brow followed by hastily jotted down notes.

'That means in less than six hours it could figure out all of the passwords in a typical business system.' She slurped her coffee for emphasis.

'Take a bloody sight less in my case – all me passwords are practically the same.'

'Reduce that to *five seconds* once quantum computing becomes a reality.' Emma put down her mug and whipped out her phone, then she busied herself tapping its screen.

'Quantum what? Aye, remember Quantum Leap? Used to love that series.' Scott stopped clicking and looked up. 'What I wouldn't give to be Sam Beckett. Imagine that Em? You look in the mirror and you see a member of the opposite sex lookin back?' He grinned sheepishly. 'Oh... you already do.'

'Screw you Scotty. Do you want me to babysit or not?' She toed the back of his monitor with her boot in retaliation, then returned to patting the screen of her handset.

'Hey, feet off the gear' he said, slapping her foot. 'Wonder what happened when he played with himself. When he was a woman, I mean – did he still have a dick?'

She rolled her eyes. 'I fear for Jae. I really do. But not as much as I fear for you - with a predictably easy to crack password like this.' She turned her screen round to reveal that she'd hacked into his *Date with Fate* profile page. She tapped into his favourites. 'And these girls are well out of your league. Good taste though, matey, I'll give you that.'

'Bloody hell Em, get out of there. That's me private business.' He swiped the air. 'What gives with the specialist subject anyway?'

'Writing a blog piece on hackers.' She pocketed her phone. 'Thinking of calling it *Size Matters*' she said, holding her hands out like an angler boasting their latest catch.

'And you make out like *I've* got it on the brain...'

'You have a password of seven characters, a hacker could guess it within milliseconds. Make that ten characters and you're talking months.'

'Oops. Always did fall on the short side.' Scott swigged

his coffee. Emma wriggled her little finger.

'That's the least of your worries matey. How many scraps of paper have you got lying around with your passwords scribbled on them?' She leant forward and tapped on his post-it pad. 'That is the number one biggest security threat to your business right there.'

'You know me Em, if it ain't written down it's gone.' Scott started to arrange the post-its into a sequence.

'You and your bloody notes.'

'Notes... yeah, bloody notes.' He eased himself back into the chair and stroked his stubble with his palm. 'Bloody notes.' Scott's pupils started to bleed into the blue, the way they do when a person stops fixing on something tangible and starts to drift inwards.

'Hello? Earth calling Scott?' She rapped the desk with her empty coffee mug. It gave him a start.

'Oh. Soz Em. Just thinkin about something I said to Bren the other day. I was tellin her about Jae asking me how his Mum died. The inquest. The no note thing.'

'Ah, the no note thing.' She placed the mug down, leaned back and locked her long fingers across her midriff.

'Why do you think... I mean, why didn't she? There was note paper out on the table like she was going to, why didn't she? Why don't I have any answers, Em?'

'I dunno mate...' She studied the steeple she was making with her forefingers, feeling his eyes on her, and tried to ignore the phantom fragrance of violets that seemed to rise with the heat of her flaring chest.

'Flaming irony is I've got every answer to 'how'. Not that I can share any of it with Jae. I've got every gruesome detail if I want it - the pathologist's report, the inquest report, the police fucking report. But why? *Why* did she...?' He started to scrawl concentric circles on the top leaf of the notelets.

Emma's head jerked up as something occurred to her. She tried subtly to cast her eyes over the objects on her friend's desk. 'I just...' She stopped mid-sentence distracted by her search. 'Matey I just don't know what to tell you.' No portrait. Sally's photo was gone.

'I know, Em. Just thinkin out loud. I know you can't give me any answers. Sometimes it just helps to say it. Pisses on the fire before it takes hold.' Their eyes found each other. The corner of his mouth attempted a smile.

'Scotty, while we're on the subject of notes, I've been wanting to ask you for some time...'

'Aye?'

'You know when we found you and Jae in the house before you were— before you went into hospital.' She paused to temperature check his reaction.

'Sort of... I mean, I'm not sure I knew much of anything when all that kicked off, but what of it?'

'There were pieces of paper everywhere, old envelopes torn up, scribbled with notes. They were all over the floor, like confetti. They said some odd things like 'Where are you?', 'We need you', stuff like that. Did *you* write them?'

'I dunno Em, I suppose I did. I mean if I didn't who did?'

She shrugged, but held her gaze like a non-directive counsellor might.

'I don't like to think about that time. I don't remember much and I prefer to keep it that way.' He avoided her eyes, scoring the pad with his biro.

She picked up Scott's *Things to do today* notebook and

skimmed it. 'Come to think of it they didn't all look like your handwriting, but some did.'

'Honestly I can't remember. That useless twat of a therapist they put me onto asked me about that. I really don't... it was all chucked out by the time I got home.'

'As long as I've known you you've left yourself notes on the fridge, sent yourself texts, set alarms, password reminders... shit for brains.' She smiled knowingly. 'But these were different. They weren't memory joggers, they were, messages.'

'I don't remember writing them. Shopping lists, I remember writing some shopping lists, but notin else.' He rubbed his eyes. 'I mean I was grieving, I guess I was trying to write to Sal or something? I dunno.' Then after a pause he added 'I get weird flashes of things – I think they're dreams but sometimes I'm not sure. Not sure if something's real or not.'

'Really? What kind of things?' She leant forward, then instantly regretted it.

'Ah, probably acid flashbacks.' He checked himself. 'That's what I told the therapist – had 'em for years, just random images and feelings – the residue of too many bad trips.' Scott's shifty body language ran contra to his dismissive tone.

'You know I'm here Scott. Day or night. You know that, right?'

'Right. And *here* is where I need you.' He grinned. 'At six-thirty on Saturday night.'

CHAPTER 10: COME AND GET IT

Saturday

'Nice watch.' Her smiling eyes, puckered lips and upraised eyebrows bore a playful twist of sarcasm.

Appearance: Petite, blonde hair, blue eyes. Age: 32. Married? Never. Kids? None. Smoker? Occasionally. Religion? None (thank fuck). Best qualities: Outgoing; Loyal; Open. Interests: Running and red wine. My idea of a great date is: Dinner with Scott McCabe.

OK so he'd embellished the facts with a bit of wish fulfilment, but in every other respect Finnley from Sale seemed to do her *Date with Fate* profile more than enough justice.

Scott eyed the ridiculously ostentatious timepiece that had slipped its cover as he reached for his drink. It was at odds with his casual denim shirt and chinos. Its '*head turning*' gold link strap certainly did '*captivate attention with just one glance*' but rarely in the way its designers had intended. This coupled with a skeletal-view of the movement, embellished with tiny gem stones, gave him the appearance of a darts champion that had splashed his winnings on the most expensive and tasteless wrist adornment he could find.

'Ah, this.' He shuffled uncomfortably, tugging at his sleeve, trying to manoeuvre it back over its bulky edifice.

'A present from me Ma and Da. Why on earth they thought I would want a f— a friggin great brassy reminder of the passage of time on me fortieth I'll never know. I wear it out of duty. They look for it in photos, can you believe?' He laughed; she joined him.

'You have a curious accent. It's kind of similar to how people speak up here but there's something different, a lilt of—'

'Lilt? Lilting is for southern...' Check yourself McCabe. She's no local girl. 'I was born in Derry. Me folks both still have pretty broad accents. They moved here when I was about three. Don't remember living over there but they had a farm that straddled the border.'

'Really? That must have been intense.' She ran her finger around the rim of her glass.

'Dunno, I guess it was. They got out before—' Bit heavy Scotty, ease back. 'Anyway some of the family followed them over. Settled here.'

'You said photos? You don't see your folks often then?' She was sharp.

'Retired to Spain five years ago. Jammy bas— beggars. Still have a farm shop and stuff here though. Oak Grove?' He paused to see if she recognised the name, then when she didn't he said 'It's named after Derry, the farm. Our piece of the homeland.'

'Any brothers or sisters?'

'A sister, older. She's in Canada. Went there to study, met a guy, never came back.'

'Wow, family all over the place then?'

'Yeah – is it me aftershave or summat?' He chortled, pretending to sniff his right pit. 'That was your cue to disagree...' He winked. 'How about yourself? I detect a lilt in your accent too.' A mischievous smile lifted one side of his mouth.

'Ha-ha. Fair play. I'm from Surrey. Only been here a few

weeks. Dad died three years ago, Mum's met a new man. It just felt like time to move on to pastures new. So...' she paused reflectively, 'I applied for a job and here I am.'

'How about siblings?' He mirrored her line of questioning.

'Only child.' She nodded, ruefully it seemed to Scott. 'Anyway being new to the area I figured this internet dating lark would be a good way to make new—' she adjusted '... meet new people.'

'And here we are.' He raised his glass in proffered cheers, she reciprocated. His hand was sweating so he placed his drink down on the chequered table cloth of the traditional tapas restaurant, and gazed distractedly at the huge paella dish that hung on the wall next to them.

'So your profile said you're divorced. How long were you married? If you don't mind me asking.' She curled a lock of hair around her finger. What does that signify? Is it the same as playing with your earlobe?

'No, that's OK. We were only married a short time, but we were together twelve years. This year would have been our fifteenth—' Scott stopped himself, remembering where he was. 'Sorry that's probably more information than you needed.'

'Well, you've done better than me, four years is my record' she appeased.

'Yeah, we didn't do too badly. Had our ups and downs.' He lost himself for a moment dwelling on his turn of phrase. 'My single mates took to calling all us couples by a Hollywood nickname, you know, like 'Brangelina'. Didn't they just take the—' he paused, thrice reminding himself not to swear. 'Well, let's just say they called me and Sal 'Scally'. Har-dee-bloody-har.' Did bloody count as swearing?

Finn dissolved with laughter. 'Scally? I get it. That's funny as fuck.'

Oh thank Christ, she swears. Scott was a little stunned by this seemingly sweet girl's incongruous profanity but relaxed into his seat. He could be himself. He'd been giving that self a hard time all day trying to practise minding his Ps and fuckin Qs. He leaned in and cradled his red wine glass. Sipping at the brim, he took a moment to drink in the view. Finn's pretty face was framed by soft golden curls that teased the edges of her upturned mouth. She was hunched forward slightly, her plunging neckline affording the briefest glimpse of a delicate cleavage. Her sapphire eyes were wide with anticipation, pupils expanding in approval. Scott felt a brief tingle of arousal. Don't balls this up McCabe.

'Sorry, shouldn't really be talking about my ex-wife on a date. Bad protocol.' He slapped himself on the wrist, smarting as his watch bit back.

'Nah, that's OK, I asked. We all have a past.' They both leaned back in their seats to make way for the waiter as he placed an array of garlic-infused dishes before them. 'Where is she now?'

'Gone.'

'Gone?'

'Gone away, I mean. Abroad. Australia. New husband.'

'Ah, that must be really tough for your son, his Mum being so far away.' She nudged one of the dishes aside, edging her glass closer to his.

'It is hard; it's been very tough on the little man.' Scott's expression was in danger of aching too much. Then he perked up, struck by what Finn had said.

'My son? How do you? It's not in my profile. I know I said I had a kid but I didn't think—'

'You know, you told me in one of your emails. Quite a long email actually.' The corners of her mouth curved upwards coyly. 'You have a six-year old son called Jay I think it is?

'I'm really sorry Finn, this sounds really bad... I don't recall—'

'And you're trying to teach him how to hunt small game' she finished, seeming proud of her powers of recollection.

'Weird, I must have been pissed or summat. I honestly don't remem...' Scott pulled at the collar of his shirt as a surge of heat flared up beneath it.

'Face it, you're a piss head' she said, teasing. 'I thought you were a bit chattier than usual that night. I can forgive a little forgetfulness, so long as it's not because you're confusing me with another woman.'

'Another woman?' His brow creased. '*Oh* I see what you mean. No, no,' he said, waving his hand. 'I promised myself that if a situation looked like it had legs I would only have a conversation with one girl at a time. I don't think my poor forgetful brain could cope with more than one woman.' Scott made light of his embarrassing amnesia.

'So I look like I have legs, eh?' She smirked invitingly.

Scott pretended to inspect the goods under the table. 'Looks like you have very good legs from where I'm sitting.' And what he wouldn't give right now to get between them. Did his eyes give away his amorous intentions? He hoped so.

Finn's smile bloomed to fullness. The email faux-pas was apparently forgotten. Scott seized the opportunity to change the subject.

'OK so this is a bit corny but I've seen it on a TV dating show so, what the hell. What do you look for in your ideal date?' Brace yourself to get shot down in flames Scotty lad.

Finn, still grinning, responded 'Well, let's see... Tall, devastatingly handsome – obviously - and doesn't take himself or life to seriously.'

'Ah, I'm not the tallest I'm afraid, and I—'

'Two out of three ain't bad.' She shot him a wink as she playfully wrapped her glossy lips around her fork.

Bloody hell, she's giving him the come on. Scott could feel himself flushing as his composure crumbled.

'Oh, and being a fitness freak works for me. You said you do triathlons?'

Oh god, so close to the finish line...

'Training for one' he corrected, swallowing hard and glancing around the bar. 'Actually if you want the truth.' He flicked his eyes back to meet hers, 'It would kill me to run for the flamin bus. The only one of my limbs that gets any kind of work out these days is my right arm.' He picked up his glass. 'Read into that what you will...'

***

'You're not just here for sex are you?' Finn said, shrinking back into the cushions of her sofa.

'Absolutely not.' Scott leant forward and pressed his lips against hers. She melted into the moment, submitting to the pressure of his searching tongue. He pushed his hand inside her bra trying to tease her breast from its pocket only to find his fingers wedged between her smooth skin and a resistant silicone bladder.

'Aaaahhh…' He dangled the chicken fillet aloft. 'I'm not the only one who tells porky pies.'

'Sorry, Mother Nature just needed some help. They're

only little.' She blushed, crossing her arms across her chest.

Scott tossed the sac aside then gently eased her arms back down and removed the other one. 'You don't need these.' He moved closer, kissed her behind her ear, pulled the front of her bra down and tucked it under her pert breasts. 'They are fuckin beautiful...'

He wrestled his jeans up to his waist and went to buckle his belt. 'My belt...' He looked around the room.

'Oh shit.' He felt a flush of embarrassment as he retrieved it from the bed post above Finn's head. He glanced down at her. She lay on her back with her head twisted to one side, arm positioned at a fractured angle over her head. She looked like road kill. He smiled to himself. She let out a gentle sigh and awkwardly untangled herself as her eyes flickered open.

'You're up?' She managed.

'Gotta fly – babysitter, sorry, didn't want to wake you. Totally lost track of time. I've really got to get back, but it would be great to meet up again.' It was almost a question. She smiled sweetly as she watched him grab his jacket and leave.

Scott took the stairs from her first floor flat two at a time. Once outside, he bounced down the steps to the pavement like his legs had springs. Little fishes of excitement fluttered around inside him, darting between his chest and his tummy.

Then, part way down the street, he stopped...

Finn had just shouldered the door to her flat shut behind her when she heard a vibration thrumming on her bedside table.

Her phone was lit up against the indigo hue of the early morning. She bound over to it.

'Scott? Mmm, you're keen.' She felt a twist of excitement as she tapped the incoming text.

Hi Finn. Think I left my watch in your flat.
OK to come and get it? S x

Smiling inwardly, she pictured the moment he'd slipped it off then slid his hand up her dress. She scanned the visible terrain, lit by a shaft of light cast from the bedroom. No trace of it, or none that she could see. She tapped back, trying to camouflage her dismay as nonchalance.

Don't see it. You're welcome to come and retrace your steps.
Can't disappoint Ma and Da. Xx

She made her way down the stairs to the ground floor, hoping he would take her up on the offer. Pulling down the front door catch, she yanked the stubborn oak free of its frame.

A searing pain shot through Finn's inner ear. The force of the blow from the hefty door, as it smashed her on the side of the head, burst her ear drum sending an excruciating pulse of white noise between her temples. Reeling from the blow she stumbled, teetered, then swooned. Felled like a fighter hitting the canvas, the back of her skull cracked against the unyielding terracotta floor.

Semi paralysed, she vainly jerked her neck, desperately trying to create enough momentum to hoist herself up from the slabs. But as the viscous treacle of failing consciousness oozed in to smother her synapses, she had the briefest of dulling moments to register the dark figure descending down on her and the sickening mustiness of mildewed leather as it closed over her nose and mouth.

***

Scott threw his jacket onto the chair in the hallway. It landed lopsided, with one sleeve flung over the armrest. Road kill. Well, at least that's what it reminded him of. He smirked as he tentatively tapped open his living room door.

'Em? Really sorry, didn't mean to be so late…'

CHAPTER 11: THE BIS HAVE IT

NOVEMBER 2016

Tuesday

Scott clamped his desk phone between his shoulder and his ear as he rushed to input the last of the drivers' data into his belated weekly report.

'You OK?' Emma's concern rang tinny on the other end of the line.

'Yeah, sure. Well, as OK as I ever am when Iain's on me bloody case. Why?'

'It's... you know. It's the first—'

'What, the first date I've been on? Hardly reason to be traumatised Em' he said tutting and poking at the keys.

'No, hon. I mean it's the first... The first of November.'

He stopped tinkering.

'Oh. Fuck.' He deflated, slumping into his chair.

'Scotty, I'm sorry mate, I shouldn't have—'

'It's not your fault. I'd...' He covered his eyes.

'Scotty, do you want me to—'

'I'd fuckin forgotten Em. I'd *forgotten*.' His throat clenched. He swallowed a ball of muscle like a boulder-sized pill. Emma paused, waiting for him to recover himself. 'Oh God. As if I didn't feel shitty enough about dating again as it is. How could I?'

'Mate, don't beat yourself up. Isn't it a positive thing for the anniversary to slip your mind? Doesn't it mean you're moving on?' She tried to cajole him into a glass-half-full interpretation of his memory lapse.

'Moving on. Who am I kidding? What the hell am I doing?'

'Christ, I wish I hadn't reminded you. Come on matey, you're doing the right thing is what you're doing. It's *exactly* what you should be doing. Anyways, how did it go?' She tried to steer the conversation into a more superficial space. 'I was too knackered to do the post-mortem the other night.'

'I dunno, I thought we hit it off pretty well. She seemed keen.'

'Great. Seeing her again?'

'Not sure... I'm hopelessly out of practice at this shit. Not heard from her.' Any sense of joy had deserted him.

'Have you tried to contact her?'

'Yeah, once or twice. Notin back.'

'Did you...?' She left it hanging, knowing he knew her well enough to fill in the blanks.

'Yeah.' He suddenly didn't feel as proud of breaking his three-year cherry as he thought he would.

'You did? Fuck a duck McCabe, I thought you'd be frigid.' Emma seized the opportunity to drag the tone kicking and screaming into the terrain of banter.

'Me too.' His head bobbed up and down like a dashboard toy. 'Thinkin about it that might be why she's gone quiet.'

'Doesn't like little dicks, eh?'

'Har-har. Nah, I mean I think the sex was, you know, a bit 'playful''

'Playful? Oh, right. Ya dirty tart.' Then she said after a pause 'What d'you mean *I think*?'

'Bit pissed, bit hazy – reckon I must have got carried away with enormity of the moment.'

'Don't flatter yourself' she ribbed, then eventually conceded that he wasn't in the mood for jesting. 'So playful equals player, right?'

'I'm thinkin, yeah maybe. Maybe that's the impression I gave. Shame. I liked her.'

'Fall back.'

'What?'

'Fall back. Don't be too keen. Women love a player and I reckon you've played it perfectly. She'll come runnin. I reckon.'

Friday

The pub was bristling with after-work drinkers already well lubricated from skipping dinner in favour of the amber liquid. Scott craned his neck as he caught a glimpse of Kat making her way to the door. Sod it. He'd missed her again.

'You slept with her? Kirk almost showered Scott with beer spray.

'Slept with who?' Scott said, still lingering on thoughts of Kat.

'I can see it all over your face. Bloody hell, Emma wasn't pulling me plonker then?'

'You know very well, Kirk, she wouldn't pull any bloke's plonker. But thanks Em for broadcastin me private business' he said to no one.

'Christ, Scott you don't waste any time do you?' If he wasn't chiding, it was as near as dammit.

'She was pretty, what can I say?'

'You could have said let's wait for the second bloody date at least.' He was chiding.

'Oh stop being such a flamin prude Kirk – you would've.'

'I bloody wouldn't.'

'Well I bloody did. So.' His raised hands said *leave it*.

'OK, here's one for ya.' Emma appeared from behind a wall of punters with three pints locked between her splayed fingers. Scott was inwardly grateful for the shift of focus. He avoided Kirk's eyes, musing over her outsized, unladylike hands.

As if she'd read his thoughts she declared 'Once a barmaid, always a barmaid'. She deposited the pints on the table without spilling a drop and sat down, striking a tomboyish pose with her legs akimbo. 'Right.' She slapped her hands over her knees.

'G'on.' Scott nodded towards her. He loved Emma's conundrums.

'So this is a question psychologists ask murderers when they're trying to assess whether or not they're psychopaths or they just committed crimes of passion.' She locked eyes with each of them, gauging their interest.

'OK. A woman goes to a funeral where she meets this guy. He seems to be there alone, like she is. They get chatting and over the course of the afternoon she falls madly in love with him.'

'Bit fast' Kirk said, shooting a meaningful glance at Scott.

'Yeah, yeah, whatever, that's not the point.'

'What *is* the point then?'

'The point is... the following week she murders her sister: Why?' The boys looked at each other over the rims of their pints, Scott's sins of the flesh now usurped.

'And it has to be your gut response' she added, before it was too late. Scott already looked pleased with himself.

Kirk offered first: 'Er... because she found out her sister was going out with this guy?'

'Good guess, but you're not even close' she said, grinning.

'Because...' Kirk searched his memory bank of murder mystery plot lines. Scott still looked smug.

'...because her sister *wanted to go out with* his guy?'

'Nah, nah. Totally wrong track.'

'Oh sod it, I bloody hate these—'

'It's because she wants to go to another funeral.' As soon as it was out there it felt to Scott like the angle-poised lighting that leered over pub picture rail had swooped round to finger him.

'Scott, matey, are you serious?' Her smile melted. 'Like, that is *really* your first thought?'

'Yeah. So? She meets someone at a funeral; She wants to meet them again; She needs to make another funeral happen.'

'At the expense of her sister's life? Jesus.' Kirk turned inquisitor. Emma shook her head.

'What's the big flamin deal?' He held his palms aloft.

Em cleared her throat. 'That's the answer psychopaths give.'

Kirk had made his archetypal early departure, claiming he had to clean his fridge the following morning; or iron his socks; or some such lame domestic chore. Kirk always had a middle-aged, vacuous excuse for retiring early. Emma entertained the theory that he was either Cinderella or an after-dark prowler. Scott and she, on the other hand, had drank until the death before stumbling out into the bitter night.

'Come on Em, help me out. If you weren't a dyke would you fancy me?' Scott tried to suck in his cheek bones and draw his drunken, putty-like features into a modelesque pout.

'Scott, you've got an Adam's apple, a square chin, hod-carrier's shoulders and you desperately need a shave.'

'So exactly what you lot look for then, is that what you're saying?'

'Fuck off McCabe.' She couldn't help smiling. 'When will you get it? I fancy *women*; women that look like women.'

'Oh come here Emsy, you know you love me really. Give us a kiss.' He leaned in with his lips pursed searching for a smacker.

'Not if you were the last man standing.' Emma spied her opportunity to step aside and, without a target for his affections, Scott unceremoniously hit the deck.

'Oh... you're not standing. Ha-ha. Now that is funny' she giggled.

Scott made a vain attempt to get ambulant then resigned himself to the pavement. 'Ah, fuck it.' He swatted the air.

Emma softened at the sight of her best friend crumpled in a heap like a discarded sack of charity shop clothes. She extended her hand. 'Come on you, let's get you home to that little man of yours.'

'That's no way to talk about my dick, just because you're a dyke.' Scott pealed with laughter seeming perfectly happy with his roadside resting place.

'That's it, twat - you can find your own way home.' She shoved his leg with her boot. 'Sod it, if you can't beat 'em, join 'em.' Emma said as she lay down next to him on the damp tarmac and belly laughed.

'Seriously though Em', he said as their jollity subsided, 'how are you gonna find a bird if you don't like lesbos that look like lesbos?'

'Urgh. If you had any idea how much I *hate* that term.'

'I do... Where's the fun if it doesn't wind you up?'

'You really are on top cunty form tonight, McCabe. *Lazerbeam* if you don't mind' she paused, reflecting on her dilemma. 'I know, you're right though matey, there's a total dearth of skirt. Why can't more gay women look like girls? Fuck it, I fancy *girls*.'

'Must be why me, you and Kirk hang out together. You're the only people I know that have been single as long as I have.' He turned to her. 'What happened to that bird you were seeing when we first met? You were all loved up then. Why did that go down south? If you'll pardon the expression…'

'It was complicated. She was already hitched. To a man.' Emma studied the sky and swallowed.

'So Ash was right?'

'Right about what?' She propped herself up on one elbow.

'Lock up your wives, he said.' He made a circle with his thumb and forefinger and poked his tongue through it.

Emma tactically ignored him and chose a suitably glib response 'Ash can fuck off. I can't stand curious bloody straights. Go and waste someone else's time. Give me a dedicated bisexual any day of the week.' She grinned.

'Maybe I should try that market? Women are always telling me I'm pretty. Or cute. Or some other emasculating attempt at a compliment.'

'Piss off and find your own territory mate. The bis are mine.'

***

Kul4abeer: No I'm not. What sort of creepy question is that?

The message alert roused him. He lifted his chin off its resting place on his chest, the slither of dribble hanging off it was dangling dangerously above his keyboard heading for the gap between the B and N keys. It jarred him to wide-awakeness. He foiled its progress with the back of his hand.

'Oh Christ...' He shook his head, wiping his hand on his jeans. The words on his monitor came into focus. He glanced at his watch. Two thirty-eight am. He could barely remember paying Charley for her customary Friday-night Jae-watching. *Did* he pay her? He grappled with his back pocket to free his wallet. Nothing but shrapnel. Balls, he'd been overzealous with the tip again.

He stared at the incoming reprimand, struggling to make sense of it.

'No, I'm not... *what?*'

Scrolling upwards through the thread of exchanges between Bestbet7 and Kul4abeer, the full horror dawned on him.

'Oh good god, you didn't. You bloody piss head.' He

gawped at his pervy query about the recipient's sexuality, hinting at a three-way. He clicked through to her photos to see if the situation was worth recovering.

His jaw dropped. She was exquisite. He hastily tapped away at the keys praying his tanked up alter-ego hadn't totally screwed his chances. Face it McCabe, this was going to take a bloody miracle. He had to think quickly before she moved onto a more suitable... suitor.

Bestbet7: I am so sorry you received those last few messages. Really I am. I'd just nipped out to make a brew and my roommate came in from a party. He thought it would be funny to join the conversation. Me less so. Please ignore that. I'm not really a bad lad.

Her online presence indicator glowed green. She was still there. He waited to see if the three dots that told him she was replying appeared. They didn't.

'Sod it. She's blocked me. What a total twat.' He drummed his fingers on the desk. They made their way to his tobacco pouch. He rolled himself a white stick and tossed it into his mouth. The cocked Clipper flamed its tip.

He inhaled. Still no sign. Exhaled. More drumming.

'Fuck it.' He slumped back in his chair and gazed at the ceiling, draining the remainder of his tab in brisk, desperate tokes. As he rose to his feet he twisted its nose into the overflowing ashtray. It triggered a small avalanche of old fag butts and stale ash.

'Bollocks.' Using a cupped hand he ushered the rubble over the edge of the desk into his palm then made his way out into the kitchen. He'd just about reached the door.

Ping.

The incoming chat chime rang though his desktop speakers. He stopped dead in the doorway.

'*Please...*' He dashed into the kitchen, dumped the ash in

the bin and rinsed his hands. It was only now that he realised his hangover was kicking in. He kneaded his throbbing temples then yanked open the kitchen drawer, grabbed an unsheathed blister pack of pills, popped a couple into his mouth and necked them. He dashed back to his desk.

Kul4abeer: OK, I'll let you off this once. Tell your mate that if he ever decides to do online dating he seriously needs some lessons in making a good impression.

Yes! Perhaps she liked the look of his photos too, enough to be forgiving. Scott planted himself back into the desk chair eager to capitalise on his deceit.

Bestbet7: Is that before I've throttled him or after? Haha ☺

He tried to sound as frivolous as possible.

Bestbet7: Like your username. Do we have a love of beer in common then?

He sat back, clasped his hands across his midriff and waited for her response.

Where are the three dots? Gimme the three dots. It felt to Scott that old father time had spun the jog-shuttle wheel to the slow-mo setting. Each second that his ticker tocked by rang between his ears like a funeral toll. Had his miscreant missives delivered the deathblow to this assignation? Perhaps only now she was reminding herself of what he looked like. Perhaps his carefully selected portfolio wasn't so appealing after all.

The three-dotted bubble burst into life, blinking on and off in sequence like a traffic light. Red; Amber; Green:

Kul4abeer: Actually I prefer wine. I guess I thought it was a clever play on words. My name is Kulbir :-s

Get in. We're on.

Bestbet7: Ha – you're smart too. Hello Kulbir. I'm Scott.

Kul4abeer: Too?

Bestbet7: As well as being breathtakingly lovely ☺

May as well go in all guns.

Kul4abeer: You look pretty cute yourself, Scott.

Play nicely now. When they are this beautiful, they're excused.

He grabbed a spent envelope cowering at the back of his desk and scribbled the date, time and venue on the back of it. Then, knowing himself too well, he thought it wise to add '*Kulbir*'.

That had been a very narrow escape, one that had sobered him up fast. Still, the thought of a threesome with such a seductive bird had put him in the mood for some light, or not so light, entertainment. Clicking to kill the *Date with Fate* browser tab, his business email inbox was revealed. The conversation with Kulbir was apparently not the only one he had blacked out in the course of. There was an unread reply from Jez. Convenient.

Soz boss. Had to shoot thru. Bit of biz from a couple of years back caught up with us. I am sorry tho. Yuv been gud to me. Didn't want any of this shit to look bad on you so you cud say Im doing you a favour. I said Id see you right tho. If you cant find a bit of wot tickles your fancy in this lot then "the scrounger" is loosing his touch! skintradexv7dig5x.onion

Ciao boss. Delete.

Jez

Bemused, he clicked the link. A new browser tab popped up and buffered briefly whilst it redirected, then a dialogue box appeared, prompting him to download a player. Almost without volition he clicked 'Yes' and as he did so a spinning icon appeared. It looked like an onion shedding its layers. When it stopped spinning a page started to load and, image by image, *Skintade* revealed itself. It carried an array of labelled thumbnails set against a deep red, textured backdrop that looked like it had been splattered with glossy paint. Aside from the fact that the women depicted were half-naked, blind-folded and chained, it had many of the hallmarks of a dating site. That is until he started to peruse the titles: 'Breath Play Blonde', 'Skinny and Skinned', 'Slow Burn'. Different, even for a porn site. Intuitively, he hovered his mouse over the first image, anticipating that he'd be given an enticing animated preview. A flicker-book of stills flashed before him. Pretty blonde. Plastic bag. Bulging eyes. Blue face.

He whipped his cursor away. Pretty Blonde returned. Laying his hand on the mouse, he paused. He felt his heart throbbing as the rest of him switched polarity between being attracted and repelled.

'What kinda twisted shit is this Jezza?' Twisted or not it had stirred his curiosity. He pushed his mouse. The cursor landed on the showcase of a bony dark-haired girl. It sprang into action like it had been shot with adrenaline. Suspended. Whipped. Flayed. Skinned.

'Fuck that.' He axed the browser with a flick of his finger, unaware that the onion had pinned itself to the taskbar at the foot of his screen.

It had roused a yearning for something, though, something closer to his threshold of assent. He scrolled up through the message thread with Jez, back to the hardcore link he had previously emailed, the one that hadn't yet made it into the trash. The idea of it now seemed tame in comparison.

Pretty tame.

Within seconds he was skimming the *Hogtie* thumbnails, hovering his cursor over them to see if the animated highlights were tempting enough to draw him in. Then he spotted one that was.

'Can't beat the hog-tie. The trappers favourite.'

He clicked and reclined.

Saturday

'When are we going to the fireworks?' Jae bustled past Scott through the front door and into the hallway, stumbling over the shopping bags, oblivious to the tussle his Dad was having with them.

'Er... dunno Monkey. Let me get this lot into the kitchen and I'll check the flyer.' Scott was knackered. His eyes itched from lack of sleep; his arms and legs felt starched. In all honesty the last thing he felt like doing was standing in a freezing cold, soggy field watching a bunch of damp squibs. And as if the local *Whiston's Got Talent* show wasn't bad enough, he didn't feel in the mood for the fireworks either. Still, it was Will's benefit do. He needed to show solidarity with his fellow farmer.

He off-loaded the carriers of groceries into the compact kitchen; threw the perishables into the fridge, kicked Norman's water bowl sending its contents across the floor and cursed. Then tried to remember where he'd left the leaflet that had been posted through his letterbox a few days earlier, much to the delight of Jae. The multi-million pound display pictured to sell the event had sent his lad into orbit. A little expectation-managing might be in order.

He pulled open the kitchen drawer, knowing it wasn't there. He wandered out and checked the pile of unopened mail on shelf by the front door, knowing it wasn't there either. Then he made his way over to his computer desk where a crumpled envelope, or rather the note scribbled on it, caught his eye.

Kulbir

He grinned. His sore eyes and aching limbs were soothed by its promise. It had been worth the early morning vigil. Clocking the date, time and venue of their meeting, he pulled thoughtfully at the tufts on his chin. A buzzing sound rattled him from his daydream. The small tower of desktop drawers that sat beside his PC was vibrating. It buzzed again, louder this time. He snatched open the bottom drawer. Nothing. He rested his hand on the surface of the stack. It tickled with every quiver.

Then it struck him.

His hand trembled over the top drawer. He didn't want to open this drawer. This particular drawer. His heart sent a flurry of beats through his chest and a flush of saliva to his gills.

It can't be. Can't be. Doesn't make any sense.

He edged open the drawer that held Sally's old phone.

Bzzzzzzzz

He slammed it shut, clamping his hand over his heart. The dampened buzzing sounded again. He had to look. Swallowing hard, he inched the drawer out. It clattered against the base with every peal. He swallowed hard and grabbed the device, turning it slowly in his palm. It felt bulky and heavy and of unfamiliar proportions. He rolled it onto its back.

It stopped. A red dot had appeared over the message icon. He felt sick. One shaking finger poised over the thumbnail. Then it fell like a guillotine:

Why are you doing this to us?

He dropped it like a hot coal. It clanked against the desk, bounced and hit the floor face up. He stood looking at it. The glow on its surface faded. It lay there in wait. He didn't want to provoke it, so he stood stock still wondering what to do, letting his heart settle into a steadier rhythm. Then he plucked it off the floor between his thumb and forefinger, as if it were harbouring a virulent contagion. Tossing it back into the drawer, he closed his eyes whilst pressing and holding the standby button.

'When is it time to go Daddy?' Jae appeared at his elbow.

'Oh God. Crikey Jae, you made me jump.' Saved from contemplating the impossible, he slapped the drawer shut.

'When is it Daddy? When can we go to the fireworks?' Jae was tugging at his jacket sleeve.

'Sorry fella. Right, here it is. Six o'clock matey.' He tried his hardest to sound unperturbed. 'Let's see, what time are we on now?' He glanced up at the top drawer and nudged it, checking it was shut; that the dormant poltergeist wouldn't be disturbed. Then he flipped his wrist over.

'Blimey it's five-twenty already. Betta fly Monkey. Said we'd meet Em and Kirk at quarter to.' He didn't convince himself with his forced levity but it seemed to fool his son.

'Come on Daddy. Come on let's go.' Jae was now pulling his father towards the living room door.

'OK, OK. Give me two ticks. Gotta lock the cat flap so Norman doesn't get herself scared witless.' Scott made a brief diversion to the kitchen, grabbing a six pack of beer from the discarded shopping. Something told him he was going to need some anaesthesia this evening.

'You alright mate? You look like summat from the *Walking Dead*?' Kirk's blithe concern confirmed Scott's failure to brush off the phone portent.

'Yeah, I'm fine.' They clanked beer tins. 'Just a bit knackered is all. Crap nights' sleep.'

'Few of these'll see you right.' He took a swig. 'Tell you what, that bloody bonfire is way too close to those overhead cables.' Ever the health and safety officer, Kirk was the harbinger of an altogether more earthly doom.

Scott surveyed the muddy meadow. Will's old scarecrow was tethered to a dining chair at the apex of a mound of broken furniture, old pallets and doctored tree branches, awaiting the torch. Burly men in biker jackets and distressed combat trousers were wrapping up the sound checks on the stage, awaiting the torture. At least that's how *he* anticipated the vocal delights of the local stage school.

'Alright losers.' Emma jumped them from behind, swiped the tinny from Scott's hand and guzzled from the brim.

'Oi, get your own.' He protested, but only half-heartedly, as he twisted one of his beers from its plastic noose and passed it to her.

'Hi Auntie Emma.' Jae squealed, beside himself with excitement at the prospect of the annual sacrificial burning.

'Hi Monkey Man. How's my favourite little Guy Fawkes then?' She scooped him up and gave him a bear hug. 'Wanna get on Kirk's shoulders when the fun starts?' She sniggered; Kirk was oblivious but Jae caught on and started to giggle.

'How's your bum for spots, Scotty?' She spun round to face him. 'Oh. You look like shit.' Ever ready as she was with a confidence-booster.

Scott hunched his shoulders. 'Late night.' He slurped at the hole in the top of his can.

'Ooh... more action?' She eyed Jae cautiously, realising he would know little of his father's nocturnal activities.

'Maybe.' He couldn't resist a smirk. 'Next Saturday – you on?'

'Sure count me in. Anything to help out me old buddy. What time do you need me?'

'Six-thirty OK? That'll give me time to squeeze in a bit of

Dutch courage.'

'Do you hear that Monkey Man? You and me gotta date – next Saturday, six-thirty - you're mine.' Jae cheered and galloped up and down.

'Why's that? What are *you* doing next Saturday McCabe?' An unmistakeably terse and charmless interjection punctured the jolly atmosphere.

'Frank.' Scott nodded, his smile falling away. He wasn't about to justify the interruption with an answer. 'Didn't think this was your kind of thing. Can't keep away from me?'

'Don't big yourself up McCabe. I've got better things to do than to stake you out.' He scanned the scene as if he were the hired security.

Jae stopped, leaned back and gazed up at his uncle like he was trying to scale the elevation of a skyscraper. He said nothing.

'Well, as much as I'd like to stay and enjoy your little party I have places to be. Paint the town red next Saturday McCabe, whatever it is you have planned.' A mere glance from Frank felt like a cross-examination to Scott, there was no inflection of well-wishing in his words. He turned his back as Frank sloped off to join two dark figures of similarly bulky proportions.

'Mmm... I see what you mean. He's certainly, enigmatic.' Emma followed Frank with her eyes as his sinister form shoulder-budged its way into the shadows.

'Enigmatic? He's fuckin insane is what he is.'

CHAPTER 12: ALL ABOUT THE PHOTOS

Saturday

It wasn't Scott's choice of venue. The high, domed ceilings from which hung ice-drop chandeliers above glass tables contrived together to create a hollow, impersonal acoustic. Every now and then the grating drag of steel across slate pierced the hushed undertone of the other diners' conversations. The place made him feel overstrung and overexposed.

'Kulbir. That's a beautiful name. For a beautiful lady.' His inner cool cringed. How the hell had that slipped out?

It was true though; Kulbir was stunning. Long, shiny locks of blue-black hair tumbled down to the tiniest waist Scott thought he'd ever seen. Her huge, purple-brown eyes, artfully emphasised with sweeping Cleopatra lines, were framed with luscious lashes. Her flawlessly smooth, caramel skin looked sweet enough to eat. She was way too young for Scott. But he wasn't lying to himself – tonight was all about the photos. Christ he didn't care if she could barely string a word together, he just wanted to look at her all night. Well... maybe a little more than just look.

'So how come a gorgeous girl like you needs to use a dating site?' Jesus, what is this – cliché Tourette's? Scott decided to put his glass to his mouth in an effort to stem the flow of chance-busting comments.

'I work long, unsociable hours I'm afraid. It's really difficult trying to meet someone, you know? I had to swap a shift to make it tonight.' She shrugged.

'A shift? Right... so you work in a club or a bar or something?' OK, a bordering-on-intelligent question at last. Scott was starting to adjust to her awe-inspiring beauty and settle into conversation.

'I'm a junior doctor.'

'A doc—?' Beer caught in his throat. Bloody hell, she's a scholar. A damned sight smarter than him for sure. Scott's inner cool now closely resembled a little boy in school shorts sitting on his hands, his bony legs swinging over the edge of an oversized chair. Bruised knees? Bruised ego more like. He coughed into his napkin, trying to rescue his dignity.

'Wow, that's impressive.' Impressive? He may as well just be done with it, drop to his knees and hail her perfection. 'I mean, that must be really hard work' he said, dabbing the corners of his mouth. 'I'm really sorry, I'm not normally this socially inept. It's just, I have to say it, you are possibly the most beautiful woman I've ever met.' There. Good night and good luck.

Kulbir's tired expression melted into a smile that could advertise toothpaste. 'Thank you' she acknowledged modestly, 'that's a lovely thing to say.'

'If somewhat unoriginal, I'm sure.' He held her in his gaze, trying to look like a serious contender. 'OK, I'm over it now' he said, slapping his hands down on the table. The noise broke the tension like a pin to a balloon.

She giggled and played with her garlic bread. 'So what do you do? You're self-employed right?' Changing her mind, she settled for taking a sip of wine instead.

Scott decided to have some fun. 'I'm a football coach.'

'Oh right. So how come you're self-employed? You're not tied to a club?'

Might have been dangerous, attempting a ruse with a

clever bird. Scott needed to think on his feet. 'Nah, I'm an Executive Coach. A Consultant Coach.' He paused to see if it meant anything to her then, encouraged by her lack of response, he continued 'I get contracted by various clubs to advise other coaches. I work with all the top North West teams.'

'That explains the expensive watch' she said, nodding towards the monstrosity clinging to his wrist.

'Ah, yes, that. Working class lad made good – hence the poor taste.'

Kulbir's smirk suggested she was starting to cotton on. 'So you're loaded then?'

'Was. Not anymore.' He rolled an olive around in his mouth trying to harass the flesh off the stone.

'How come?'

He swallowed, stone and all, then composed himself for his denouement:

'I spent a lot of money on booze, birds and fast cars. The rest I just squandered.' She was surely too young to remember Bestie.

'Ah, now your profile name makes sense.'

OK so she's not too young. Maybe she was closer to his age than she looked.

'My Dad is a big George Best fan.'

'Your *Dad*.'

A white cloud billowed out into the night air; too vaporous to simply be the smoke from his cigarette. Rueing his decision not to bring a jacket, he shivered against the chill and pulled his phone out of his jeans pocket. He was about to tap the

Streetcabs thumbnail when he noticed an alert on his *Date with Fate* app. Too curious to leave it for later, he patted the logo with his thumb.

You have a new message from Finn2bwith.

Balls. Now she gets in touch.

Finn2bwith: You said you wouldn't speak to any other girls while I still had legs.

He fingered a rapid-fire reply, keen that Kulbir wouldn't catch him in the act.

BestBet7: Hey Finn. You went quiet on me. Figured you'd met a better fate. How's things?

'I *knew* you were a smoker.' She was at his right ear. He spun around.

'Oh Jesus, you scared me outta me skin.' Scott quickly pocketed his phone. The tone of Finn's indictment had made him feel jumpy. How could she have known he was seeing another girl? He shrugged inwardly; he was a bloke on a dating site for Christ's sake, wouldn't that much be obvious?

'Mind if I have dibs on that?' Kulbir stole the tab from between his fingers.

'Thought you doctors were supposed to be healthy.' He happily relinquished it - a guilty-pleasure shared is a guilty-pleasure halved.

'That's the funniest thing you've said all night. Sixty-hour weeks if we're lucky; grabbing sleep where we can find it; not stopping to eat then shovelling in crap when we do. We're too busy keeping other people healthy.'

'Doesn't look like it's done you too much harm.' He looked her up and down, then winked.

A coy pout puckered her freshly glossed lips. 'You *should* quit though' she said, piping a stream of smoke over her shoulder as she handed it back to him.

'Don't think I could. In 1992 I gave up women and alcohol' he paused for comedic effect, 'It was the worst twenty minutes of my life.'

***

She lifted his wine glass out of his hand and placed it alongside hers on the kitchen table.

'Come with me.' Her burnt violet eyes beckoned him.

Scott couldn't take his eyes off her; his pupils swelled with intent as he unclipped his watch and slipped it off. He didn't need telling twice. She grabbed him by the belt buckle and sauntered backwards pulling him with her towards the bedroom.

Once there he took the initiative and pushed her onto the bed. On his way past her dressing table he'd swiped a chiffon scarf draped over the mirror. She lay with her legs dangling over the edge of the mattress. He straddled her with his knees, then leaned in to wrap the scarf around her eyes, easing her head up to tie it tight at the back. Her confident demeanour started to slip; she seemed anxious. He bent down and whispered in her ear.

'Don't worry. It's just a bit of fun.'

She jumped as she heard the snapping of a leather strap quickly followed by the jangling of a buckle. Then Scott was lassoing her wrists and manoeuvring her up the bed towards the pillows. He wrapped the belt around the aluminium bed frame and tied it tight.

'What are you doing?' She began to squirm.

'If I told you, that would spoil the surprise. Just relax.' He adjusted the blindfold to make sure she couldn't peek beneath it.

He slipped off the bed, tugging at his jeans and boxers. They fell to the floor. Then he was up beside her again placing one knee either side of her shoulders. She could feel him hard and smooth nudging her lips, coercing her mouth open. He started to slide himself in and out, rubbing himself up and down her tongue; pushing himself into the back of her throat. He groaned.

She tensed, trying to pull her wrists free. The belt held them tight. She gagged and coughed, forcing him out. A string of frothy spittle flopped down her chin.

'OK. Your turn.' He made his way down her body, unbuttoning her shirt. He loosened the fastening on her silk skirt, slipping it down her honey-bronzed legs, hooking her lace underwear with his fingers. They were both discarded. Then he positioned his knees inside her legs, forcing them wide. He pushed up her bra. Her fretful twitching and twisting aroused him.

He licked her mulberry nipples, biting them hard. She sucked in air sharply. Tracing his tongue all the way down the midline of her torso, he slid it down and deep. She started to moan and writhe. Her salty-sweetness flooded his taste buds. Her breathing quickened. He pressed on, clawing her buttocks, and pushed two fingers up her asshole. She squealed, arched her back, then shuddered.

'Oh *Jesus.*' She gasped.

He got up, straddled her again and pushed the blind fold back.

'Nice?'

She nodded.

'I've got something else for you now.' He licked his lips, wanting her to watch.

He wet tips of his fingers and started to stroke himself,

slowly at first but then harder and then faster. He pushed up onto his knees, flexing his ribcage, arching his back. As he rose to his peak he let out a belly-deep grunt and exploded over her, squirting across her chest and hitting her face.

'Oh!' She shrieked in surprise as Scott sat back on his haunches. He was breathing in short, shallow gasps. Tilting his head backwards, he closed his eyes. He held himself like that for some time.

Kulbir tried again to free her wrists but her arms wouldn't respond.

'Scott? Please can you untie this now? My arms are dead.' Her pleas were spiked with distress. She waited as he sat between her splayed legs; head still angled towards the ceiling. His breathing slowed.

'Scott? Are you *awake*? Scott can you untie me please.'

'Ah.' He shook his head as if stirring, sat upright and peeled opened his lids. The ink drained from his eyes, as in washed the blue.

'Oh God. Sorry Kulbir, I was gone there for a while. Are you OK?' She was glistening with his cum. Suddenly awash with post-coital shame, he slid off the bed, grabbed his boxers and pulled them on. Then he untied the belt and rubbed her wrists.

'Sorry, are you hurt?' Concern softened his tone. 'Wait there.' He darted off into her bathroom and promptly returned with a pack of face wipes and a toilet roll. Kulbir was easing herself up onto her elbows – the feeling returning to her arms.

'Here, let me clean you up.' He gently mopped his ejaculate off her sternum and belly, handing her a few sheets of toilet paper to pat herself dry.

'Thanks.' She pulled her bra down to cover herself and

started to button up her shirt. He sheepishly retrieved his belt from the bedstead, pulled on his jeans and slipped it through the loops around his waist.

'Kulbir, this sounds really, really bad, but I have to head off.' He was pushing the metal bar through a well-worn hole in the leather. 'I promised my sitter I wouldn't be back at stupid o'clock tonight. Can I call you tomorrow?' Scott's erstwhile cockiness took a back seat, he felt caddish and self-conscious.

'Sure, no problem. I understand. Really.'

Was it his paranoia or was she pacifying him? 'OK. Listen, you are a *beautiful* girl. You really are. I'd love to see you again.' He stroked her face.

'Me too.' She tapped his hand.

Scott thought she didn't look convinced. It felt appropriate to get out of there and leave her to it. He strolled out into the hallway and called a cab. Peering back around the bedroom door, he saw that Kulbir was still sitting on the edge of the bed looking a little startled. 'Tell you what, I'll wait outside. Let you get yourself to bed. Thanks for a great night.'

'You too.' One side of her mouth twitched.

Scott clicked the door shut behind him and made his way out into the street.

Her phone trilled fretfully from its forsaken place on the floor. Still sat on the end of the bed, she bent down to pick it up. The glow from the display bathed her face.

> Hi. I'm really sorry but I think I left my watch in your kitchen. Is it OK to pop in and get it? Sentimental value... S x

'Oh, great.'

Forcing herself to move, she leant over and pulled a dressing table drawer open, grabbed a pair of checked flannel pyjama bottoms and pulled them on. She made her way through to the kitchen hoping to find nothing. She was in luck, no sign of it.

> Sorry can't see it. Sure it's not in your pocket?

She stared at the phone; a small, grey, pulsing bubble told her he was composing a reply.

> No, I defo don't have it. Sorry, is it OK to come and check? Might be somewhere else...?

She huffed as she padded down the entrance hall, dropped the chain and yanked at the door catch.

Before she had chance to pull open the door it burst towards her, slamming against her forehead. She stumbled backwards, butting up against the wall of the narrow hallway. Black clad arms reached for her, trying to clutch at her throat. Kulbir thrashed her head from side to side attempting to dodge the grasping, leather-bound claws, but her long locks conspired against her. The assailant grabbed a fistful of hair and twisted it around gloved fingers, snapping her head backwards towards her spine.

She braced herself to scream but try as she might she couldn't force the air through her throat. Another glove folded over her nose and mouth. Adrenaline was flooding her veins, dizzying her brain and clouding her vision.

Kulbir glimpsed a split-second glint of ice-blue eyes as a balaclava swooped towards her and an explosive crack on the bridge of her nose put out the lights.

CHAPTER 13: BABY, BABY, BABY

Monday

Kirk rolled the Nokia N8 around in his hands 'Where was it?'

'Right there. Top drawer. Where I've always kept it.' Scott's eyes motioned towards his living room computer desk as he rolled a thin sausage of tobacco around in a Rizla. It refused to co-operate until he licked his finger tips to gain better purchase.

'Bloody hell, haven't seen one of these in years.' Kirk examined the stumpy silver handset like it was a museum piece. 'Bloody awful platform. Good camera though if I remember rightly.'

'Would it hold charge after all this time?' Scott tried not to look nervous as his friend looked around for the power button. He assisted nevertheless, 'Underneath' he said, the word vibrating through the tube of tissue paper pursed between his lips.

'Right, let's fire it up and see.' Kirk pressed the standby button and waited for it to flare into life.

Scott flicked the wheel of his Clipper and lit the tip, trying to appear nonchalant.

'On the typical smart phone, you'll be lucky to get more than two or three days of standby, but if you switch it off completely then it shouldn't be draining the battery at all. You might get a little residual leakage but nothing to worry about.'

Easy for you to say, Scott kept to himself. Kirk was so absorbed in his technical consultancy that he hadn't noticed

Scott getting twitchy.

'Ah, there you go. It's got some juice.' He started to tap around the interface. 'With this everything's accessed through the Menu key.' It brought up a screen featuring a number of apps. He tapped an icon that looked like a lakeside scene on a sunny day. 'Crikey mate, there's still some photos on here.'

'Lemme see.' Scott craned his neck over his taller companion's shoulder as he opened up the photo album. 'Blimey, that's when we were making a diary of the Monkey.'

Kirk scrolled through a series of pictures of Sally in almost exactly the same posture every time, turned sideways with one hand resting on the top of her abdomen, the other supporting it underneath. The first few showed the barest swelling to her belly but gradually a mound appeared, then a bonafide bump.

'This one's a video.' Kirk had tapped the play button before Scott could tell him not to. Sally burst into life swivelling from side to side. She looked pink and bright. Her eyes were wide and she licked her lips so that they were shiny.

'This is the Monkey at twenty-seven weeks.' She bowed her head down to her belly saying 'Hello baby' then made a nuzzling sound. 'Baby-baby-baby.' She looked up, into the camera lens, and said 'Say hello Daddy.'

'Hiya Monkey.' Scott's voice boomed through the camera's on-board mic. 'It's Daddy here.'

Kirk fumbled with the on-screen controls and paused the scene. 'Shit, sorry, I didn't think.' It froze on Sally with her head tossed back, laughing. He hesitated before closing the video. It reverted to a tiled view of the photo library. The thumbnails displayed selfies of the three of them, Jae as a baby dressed in various Babygro's, several pictures of him as a toddler at different stages of being ambulant and a candid shot of Emma sipping from a coffee mug.

By the time Kirk had closed the app Scott had turned away. His head was bowed, a plume of smoke was jetting towards the floor.

'Must be tough reliving those memories.' Kirk stared at the carpet.

Scott sighed expelling another lungful of smoke. 'You don't know the half of it mate.' He had been replaying a scene in his head. Sally around twenty weeks pregnant, unmedicated and manic. Pacing like a caged tiger as she clawed at her belly professing that she'd never wanted to keep the baby. *Baby-baby-baby*. She'd trapped him in the bedroom, wedging herself between him and the door, as she erratically skipped from one unfinished thought to the next. He'd got every gun she had that night. Sitting, muted by fear for his unborn child, whilst Sally dismantled their history, piece by piece: every thoughtless act; every misplaced word; every well-intended mistake; every character flaw; every crime he'd unwittingly committed. Every lost opportunity that had passed Sally by. A five-hour outpouring without pause until, having exhausted herself with the reckoning, she had slowed, slurred and slouched. Eventually, in the diffuse, dirty light of dawn, Sally's eyes had drooped shut and her head had fallen to her chest. Scott had been awake all night by the time he'd managed to settle her on the bedroom floor and call her doctor. His eyeballs had grazed against the inside of his lids as if Sally had one-by-one stuck pins in them in penance for his sins.

A surge of moisture made his eyes sting. He rubbed them, sniffed then turned to face his friend.

'Well, I think we can safely say it works.' He shot Kirk a wry smile.

'Sorry mate.' Kirk briefly made eye contact.

Scott raised his palms. 'It's OK. I asked you about it. Can I just have a gander at the messages before I put it back where it belongs?'

'You sure you want to?'

'Yeah, it's fine. Got most of 'em on my phone anyway. Just want to check summat.'

Kirk surrendered the device and sat down in the swivel chair at his friend's PC. Scott tossed the stub of his dead rollie into and already full ashtray then disappeared towards the kitchen studying the phone.

He went into its menu and selected the envelope icon. He tremored over the inbox, not sure that he wanted to look. He closed his eyes and let his finger fall. When he opened them again he saw that the last message came in at 17:16, 05/16. It was a single line:

Why are you doing this to us?

The name next to it wouldn't compute: Scott.

'Fuck me.' He came over light-headed and had to plant himself in the kitchen chair. Not wanting to believe what his eyes were telling him, he pressed the standby button to dismiss the screen. He took in a long deep breath, then he slowly let it leak out. This called for a drink. He pocketed the phone and grabbed two tins out of the fridge. Trying to look composed, he sauntered back into the living room. Kirk was tapping a rhythm out on the desk with a biro pen.

'All right mate? You look a bit peaky.'

'Aye, just thirsty.' He handed Kirk a tinny.

Kirk was first to pop his can; a sharp *phsst* quickly followed by a scrape of tearing tin. Scott's followed in quick succession. Only the babbling noises of gulping and swallowing broke the silence. A loud *ping* from Scott's back pocket pierced the air. His stomach clenched. It was the only muscle that moved.

'You sure you're OK?'

Scott could feel himself draining of colour. He pulled the Nokia from the rear of his jeans and pushed the standby button. He groped around for the Menu. The array of app thumbnails appeared. No updates.

'Ah, dozy twat. Wrong phone.' The words tumbled out, surfing a wave of relief. He quickly shut his wife's phone down before it could taunt him again, opened the drawer and dispatched it to its wooden box. Then he pulled out his own phone. A *Date with Fate* message alert was dissolving into the shadows of the dozing screen.

'Aye Kirk, fancy a bit of window shopping?' Time to lighten the mood.

'Bout time you got some double glazing in here mate. It's brass monkeys.' He crossed his arms and rubbed his biceps to labour the point.

'Christ, tell me you're not *that* literal.' Kirk's blank expression told Scott that he was. 'The dating site you plonker – someone's just eyed me up. Fancy havin a look?'

'Thought you went out with some bird the other night?'

'I did. Don't think I'm her type though. Givin me the cold shoulder – next.' He jostled his buddy with his elbow. 'Come on, we might find some totty for you.'

'You slag. What would Sal say if she saw you carrying on like this?'

'Steady on Kirk, what are you my flamin conscience or summat? Jesus, I mess up one time. Aren't I allowed to move on?'

'Sorry mate, you're right, I shouldn't have said that.' Kirk held his palms up 'Change the subject.'

'Change the bloody record more like.'

'G'on then, let's see what these heifers are like.' Kirk made horns with his fingers at each of his temples and scraped the floor with his foot, baying like an Ox.

'That's the attitude.' Scott rolled his eyes. 'Let's look at it on the PC – you get a better view.' Scott leant across Kirk and clicked shortcut on his desktop. He logged in and checked his inbox.

Finn2bwith: Don't leave me hanging around.

'Ey up, looks like she's keen.' Kirk said, reading the message over Scott's shoulder.

'Weird. *Weird*. Can't work that one out mate. Every time I message her I get nothin back. Then out of the blue some cryptic comment. Dunno – back burner for now. Look at this one though. CheriBrandi - looked but didn't touch.'

'Whassat?' Kirk looked utterly dumbfounded by the number of women Scott had added to his favourites.

'She passed me by buddy' he said, pointing at the subject line, 'This update tells me she checked me out but moved on. Flamin foxy though.' He wasted no time in clicking through to CheriBrandi's profile.

'Jeez. She looks a bit wild mate.' Kirk shrank back from the screen.

'You say that like it's a problem.' Scott clucked his tongue against his palette then clicked the message icon. 'She ain't gettin away that easily. Come on Kirk, you're good with words, help me get this one on the line...'

Kirk excused himself and left his friend to it. Having reeled CheriBrandi in, Scott was feeling emboldened by his new-found prowess in the art of seduction and couldn't resist lingering on the *Date with Fate* site to browse the delights and delusions of the other window displays. None were as tempting or as risqué as Cheri, though, she was a vixen. He was about to sack the idea and make his way back to the office when he noticed the onion icon on his taskbar.

He drummed on the mouse as he internally thumbed through his recent activities in an attempt to place it. He felt a twist in his belly as the memory clicked into place.

Jez's email; the *Skintrade* site. As far as shop windows go they don't come much more lurid than those. They made Cheri look pretty tame. There it was again, that phrase: *pretty tame*.

His stomach simmered as he moved his cursor down and hovered over the onion. Why would he look at that shit? Why be taken in by it? But then, why not? It'll all be effects and make-up, consenting adults playing grown-up games. Fancy dress for those brave enough be their darker selves. Who doesn't want to do that? Even if the play does get a bit rough. They'd have their safe words; they'd know when to say '*Let me go*'. Sally had taught him that.

He hit the onion with his arrow. A blue circle appeared next to it and started to spin as if it were a key revolving the barrel of a lock. It flickered and stopped like it was having second thoughts, then resumed its spinning. It was giving Scott time to reconsider. It had scared the living crap out of him last time. It looked so real. Watching the blue circle spin was hypnotic, though. Like a fish lured by the twisting feathers of a fly, it drew him in as the net was closing around him. His eyes glazed.

Skintrade snapped him out of his daze. Window by window the girls were displayed. His stomach lurched. It was more hardcore than he'd recalled. It was dark and raw; bruises and blood; flesh and fear. He could smell the sweat and semen, taste the metallic taint of rare meat.

He tried to turn away but his eyes refused to obey. This

site gave rubber-necking new meaning. Rubber tubing knotted tight around the neck and wrists; a rubber mask pinching at the throat; rubber chokers, rubber gags. He swallowed as saliva pooled at the back of his mouth.

He hadn't noticed on his brief flirtation with it before that there was an alpha-numeric code under each image, single numbers followed by the suffix LTC. The more brutal the image, the larger the number. Some kind of ranking system? Views? Ordering references? Then a flashing banner at the top of the screen caught his eye: *New Flesh* it boasted, 'click to see the prick teasers'. He clicked.

A row of freshly added thumbnails appeared. They looked like grainy VHS cover stills from banned video-nasties, similar to those that he and his friends had traded at school. Snuff. That's what they used to call it. Is that what this is? Or pretending to be? That was surely an urban myth to grab headlines and pull in punters. Now it's found a new platform, and new purveyors with more sophisticated technology that render fantasies as if they were reality. The effects may have been hokey back in the day, but they sure as hell weren't now. Sure as all hell.

This line up had a theme: the collection was called *Hanging around*. It featured three teasers: a redhead, a brunette and a blonde, all brassy and synthetic. Man-made. The freeze frame of each showed them in various states of molestation, faces battered and swollen, disfigured beyond recognition. Barely human. Each had a garrotte around her neck. Scott felt a surge in his stomach as he tentatively pushed his cursor towards the blonde, knowing that when it reached the hot spot, the image would lurch into life. He wrestled with himself, wanting to look, but wanting to turn away. The follicles on his top lip prickled with cold sweat, he felt pressure in his throat and a sickly sizzle in his midsection.

The Scott who wanted to look grappled the mouse from

his hand and pushed it over the girl.

Noose tightened. Zoomed out. Stool kicked. Neck snapped.

Bile unloaded into his mouth, burning his throat. His vision bleared with the strain of containing his guts. He thrashed around the interface clicking randomly. He wanted to spit out this baleful bait, to rip the poisonous hook from his flesh. In his rush to kill the browser his cursor skated over the brunette long enough to see her dangling, broken legs jerking and twitching.

With his cheeks bulging with revulsion, he bolted towards the bathroom.

***

'You got her?'

A voice from aloft, in an echo chamber.

A lone dark figure standing on the bed; his back to the door; cradling something in his arms.

'Let her go.'

It's dark. No light. The lights are out and it's dark. He edges closer, trying to see round the bulk of the black shape blocking his view. He can't see. It's dark and his view is blocked.

'Ready? Three; Two; One.' A whirring sound. A lash of a lasso.

It flops through a hole in the sky. Flops down into the man's arms. Floppy. Lifeless. He lays the form down.

Now a glimpse. A glimpse of red legs. Vermillion red legs.

'Got her?' The voice from the heavens booms.

'Got her?' It goes impatient.

Red legs. Small red legs. Too small. Too small to be grown up.

'I've got her.' The man starts to fumble. Tugging at clothing. Pulling and tugging.

The form lies there. It doesn't flinch. Lies there and lets him.

'Stop it!' Unable to keep in it.

'Leave her alone!' Unable to keep watching.

Then her eyes are open. Her head turning towards him, locking him in a lifeless stare. Her mouth moving.

'Why are you doing this to us?'

Then he's grabbed from behind. Grabbed and grappled to the ground. A giant's boot held to his throat, squeezing his Adams apple; squeezing; wheezing.

A head looms in. Dark. Faceless. Huge. Eclipsing all else. It snarls at him.

'Shut your little fucking mouth or I'll rip your little fucking tongue out.'

Scott's eyelids sprung open like a reborn victim of the undead. His heart burst against his chest wall. He strained for air. Every breath he reached for burned his stomach-acid-skinned throat.

Forcing himself back into his body, he lifted his head from the pillow and looked around. A twisted, tormented face wailed at him from across the room; a blurred freeze-frame of thrashing, blind panic, and underneath it:

The most frightening thing about Jacob's Singer's nightmare is that he isn't dreaming.

CHAPTER 14: STHPEAK SSSOFTLY LOVE

Saturday

The dim lighting and blood-red clotted gloss that was daubed over the interior walls of Kipps Wine Bar created a feeling of being back inside the womb. A seventies-style leather settee pulled Scott into a deep bear-hug, coercing him into its arms and folding him in on himself like an unborn waiting to be delivered. Everything about the place lulled him into an intimate embrace. Or rather it made him hot and claustrophobic.

Lack of sleep had left him feeling edgy and wired. As he waited for CheriBrandi to arrive he twitched and flinched as people bustled by, as if ducking imagined blows. The deep sofa, forcing him to recline, exaggerated his unease, so he pushed himself forward and perched awkwardly on the edge of the cushion.

He started as a waitress appeared at his side offering table service. He ordered his second drink, relying a little too heavily on beer to tempt him into a sociable mood. His eyes flitted between the doorway and the bar in case he'd missed her entrance.

The irony of this prospect struck him when she eventually made her appearance. She had on a Day-Glo orange basque and a skin-tight, black satin pencil skirt that was laced up at the back. It dusted the top of her knee-high, muscular biker boots that wielded spiked harnesses around the ankle. Her hair was crimped and scraped into a ponytail at the side like a 1980s pop star. It revealed the left side of her skull which bore a buzz-cut carved with tram lines. The more hirsute half of her head was a peacock display of vivid violet at the roots dissolving into electric blue before fading to a steely grey at the frazzled ends. This particular colour combination was more flamboyant than anything he'd seen on her profile. She didn't seem to be wearing a jacket on this bitter November night, but she did have on a backpack adorned with rubberised spikes that made it look like she was giving a piggyback to a hedgehog. She was Manga personified.

He instinctively ducked back into his seat and watched her as she briefly checked out the bar area then made her way to the counter. She tugged a bulky vaping device from what looked like a shoulder holster and toked on it, artfully – and rather blatantly Scott thought - shooting a rapid-fire cascade of smoke rings into the air. It was then that he saw she was wearing fishnet fingerless gloves. Under the harsh LED ceiling spot lights of the bar area he surmised that she was older than her camouflage suggested.

She leant over and ordered; handed over her card and then waited whilst the bartender busied himself with some kind of alchemy. When she emerged from the bar she was carrying a large jug of hazy pinky-red fizz decorated with green leaves. No glassware, just two large, bright yellow straws bent over the rim.

He braved a wave. She clocked him and swaggered over brandishing her purchase.

'Hope you like Thangria. Sorry, sssangria.' She planted the jug on the table and slid down into the sofa next to him.

'Aye, I'll give anything a go.' He consigned his half-finished pint to the floor. Sweet speech impediment, he thought, maybe her brazen appearance was a shield.

'Maln after my own heart. Thith ith new, ssstill teaching myself not to lithsp.' She stuck her tongue out and waggled it up and down. It was split down the centre and the two halves curled up around her top lip like horns.

Just about every fleshy part of her head was pierced with studs, and some of the gristle too; her eyebrow, each cheek, the tragus bumps in each ear, the skin above the jawline, and her chin. She had a bar through the septum of her nose with small spikes on either side. Underneath all the metalwork she was very attractive.

'Here you go.' She reached for the pitcher and angled one of the straws towards him, taking the other into her mouth. She sucked on it seductively, not taking her eyes off him. He tentatively sipped at his; the intimacy of sharing the drink made him feel uneasy, but at least it was in keeping with the overbearing ambience of the place. He tried very hard not to look directly at her cleavage, which was difficult because her breasts we hoisted up under her chin by the basque and squeezed together as she clutched the Sangria jug.

'I love this plasth. Feels like you're sssitting inside sssomeone's ssstomach.' After a pause she said 'Go on sssay it – thaths easy for you to sthay.' She threw her head back and laughed. She had gold-capped front teeth.

Scott reciprocated, not being able to resist a giggle. The booze and her gregarious presence were starting to calm him.

'So you wouldn't tell me much online—'

'Nah, I hate all that sthmall talk shit. Ha. That word I can sthay.' They both snickered as she eased the slightly lighter bucket of booze onto the table. 'Bethst way to figure out if you like a guy ith to meet him.'

'And what's the verdict?'

'I'd already be outta the door.' She tugged on her e-cig and kissed a cloud of vapour across to him. It smelt familiar, reminiscent of a past life.

'You didn't wink at me...' He winked.

'Didn't think I'd be your type. Glad you messsaged me though.' She smiled an innocent smile, but the sibilant quality of her speech put Scott in mind of Kaa from Jungle Book. Her hypnotic, reptilian contact lenses and forked tongue colluded.

'Is Cheri your real name?' May as well start with the basics.

'Itth Cheryl, but everyone callth me Cheri because of thisss.' She presented her right arm then shifted round in the seat, pulling her ponytail away from her neck. A huge stylised red and black cherry blossom tattoo crept up her arm and over her bare shoulder. 'It goesth all the way down my back and over my butt' she boasted. 'The Japaneez believe cherry blossoms represthent the beauty and fragility of life.'

Scott stuck out his bottom lip and nodded. 'Very impressive. Looks great.'

'And they call me Brandi because of thisss.' She pivoted round to show him the bicep of her other arm with a branding of two Japanese symbols one above the other. 'This one meansth *love*.' She pointed to the one nearest her shoulder. 'And this one underneath meansss *pain*.'

'Holy shit. Excuse my French but *bloody hell*. How painful was that?' He rubbed his arm.

She playfully pushed his aghast chin up with her forefinger. 'It's a third-degree cauterised burn. It hurt like a bitch. And I have a high pain threshold. Smelt like Sunday dinner too, but I love it.' She traced her figure over the raised lines of the scar tissue. Scott started to feel well and truly out of his depth.

'You got any tatsss?'

'Nah... Never liked the thought of—'

'Needleths?' Never had a problem with them mythelf.'

As she raised the vape to her mouth again he noticed that her tattoo licked around her right arm with tendrils creeping across the tender skin on her inner forearm.

Even in this light it hadn't completely disguised the feint marks that were dotted around the junction of veins clustered near her elbow crease like a colony of dead ants. He wondered how much of the past tense was insinuated in her use of the word 'had'.

'That vape smells like skunk.' He breathed in, relishing her second-hand steam as if he were one of the Bisto kids.

'Wanna know a sthecret? Mate of mine's a bit of a chemissst. Figured out how to draw the THC out into vape juice. If anyone asthks, it'sss just another funky flavour...'

'Clever.' He tried to mask his growing trepidation with a casual tone.

'Fuckin geniusss more like. It'sss very mellow. Want sthome?' Wisps of vapour licked her upper lip as she caught it trying to escape and drew it up her nose.

'Haven't touched it in years... I'll stick with the Sangria, thanks.'

'That'sss odd...'

'Not really – few too many bad trips, got me in a bit of bother few years back. Got to keep me head together these days. Booze and fags'll do me.'

'No, I mean it'sth odd you say you haven't touched it for yearsss, unless you were trying to impresss me when we spoke.'

'Spoke...?'

'You were ssskinning up and complaining that resssin is so hard to come by these days. Prefer ssskunk anyway mysthelf...' She reached for the jug again and pointed the straw at him.

'You sure it was me you were talking to?' He leant in and drew hard on it, gulping down the sweet, musty liquid.

'What you trying to sthay?' She smiled and arched a banana-barred eyebrow as she paused to take a sip. 'I know we both like a toke but my memory is better that yoursss by the sthound of it.'

'I must've been makin a rollie...' The comment was a decoy whilst he cast his mind back to the morning he'd found the gear in his living room. Had he been calling Cheri that night?

'So you *were* showing off. It'sss OK, I'm flattered. You don't have to be too cool for sthchool.' She closed her lips around the straw, then withdrew and added 'Maybe I can tempt you later.'

'Ooh, you have been out of the game for a while' she said, giggling, as she folded her hand over his.

A tingle of fear had stirred behind his ribcage and was rising like a twister through his chest, pumping a rush of adrenalin through his body and filling his eyes with fireworks. Grabbing her knee was a reflex response to steady himself against the tidal surge.

'What is it?' He managed to say as the wave began to recede. Experience told him he needed to put up his psychological breakers fast if he was to weather the eye of this storm. Man up McCabe.

'A little Molly. Just a *teensy* bit. You don't need much of thissstuff.'

He pressed his fingers into her thigh, bracing himself for another tsunami.

'Just surf the cressst, you'll be fine. The rushing sssettles down after a few minutesss. Then you'll feel fuckin brilliant.'

He'd passed off the bitterness of their frenzied kiss as the citrus aftertaste of the cocktails. Now he was grappling with conflicting impulses that glanced off the walls of his brain like a 1970s Binatone game. Chagrin at being duped, flushes of elation and spikes of sheer panic all competed with each other for the high score.

By the third uprising, though, he was learning the rules of engagement; mastering the art of catching the shoulder, gliding across the peak and coasting down the open face of each wave. She was right, it felt fuckin brilliant. He was reeling now, enjoying a fast, smooth ride; the swells were smaller and the ocean glassy. Rolling strobes of light and a thumping bassline conspired with the crystals to bring him up and ease him down. Explosive bursts of arousal jump-started his synapses as he looked around the bar. He felt an overwhelming warmth radiating from the strangers jostling around them; a transient, body-hopping allure that passed from one to another compelling him to reach out and stroke every one of them.

To a passing observer he and Cheri were two loved-up clubbers getting in the mood. They huddled together, passing the vape between them, blowing clouds into the crowds; entwined legs beating out the rhythm of the ambient dance tunes. Pawing each other like juveniles, they kissed passionately until, too restless and turned on to stay put, and with more than one entreaty to 'get a room', they rose to their feet and danced their way out into the street.

***

Cheri's bedroom was like an extension of the bar - dark, warm and visceral. The brushed flock crimson and black wallpaper was punctuated with a series of heavy, pewter-effect moulded picture frames bearing ornate gothic twines, leaves and grapes. They showcased monochrome, sadomasochistic prints of rubber-clad women with impossibly synched in waists and heaving bosoms – one wearing a leather hood with a hasp and shackle padlocked over the mouth, her arms and legs bound behind her in a hog-tie; another with her legs splayed wide, suspended in a sling from a metal frame; a third pictured from the rear, strapped over a bench and with bloodied welts across her fulsome buttocks.

An enormous bed dominated the room. The bedstead was scaffolded from iron, opulently fashioned into ecclesiastical arches that resembled stained-glass windows. It was draped in black satin and behind the headboard hung rich, red velvet curtains.

They tumbled through the room, lips still locked and fell onto the mattress, sliding across its sheer surface. Every touch sent an orgasmic shiver through Scott's body. He frantically unlaced her basque as she uncoupled his belt and whipped it out from the loops of his jeans. He caught it and snatched it from her hand all the time kissing her hard and rough. Having liberated her breasts he moved to fasten his belt round her wrists, she squirmed free giving him chase.

'I can do better than that' she said as she made her way to the head of the bed.

Saying nothing he crawled behind her, clawing at her urgently. Undeterred she rose up to her knees and drew back the velvet curtains behind the iron gothic arch to reveal two rings bolted into the wall; fixtures for a pair of bondage straps and cuffs. Scott tossed his belt to the floor, unclipped his watch and set to work tethering her outstretched arms.

They took it in turns to work on each other, Cheri guiding Scott through her box of tricks – spikes, probes, whips and clamps – pleasures he'd not indulged in for many years. The Ecstasy raced through his bloodstream and whilst the swash and backwash of the surf had calmed to leave a shiny finish, it had still gifted him an iron-clad hard on. He was inside her now and so achingly close to peaking when she said.

'Put your handsth round my throat.'

He tentatively obeyed, placing his thumbs either side of her wind pipe and giving it a gentle squeeze.

'Harder.'

He faltered and relaxed his grip, teetering on the cusp of passion and reason.

'*Harder.*' Her ophidian eyes commanded and begged him all at once and he was so close now that he pressed his palms together, increasing the pressure with every drive of his hips. As he heard her retch and wheeze to a climax, synesthetic slashes of colour and light exploded before Scott's eyes. He raised his lids in time to see the bulbous, bifurcate tips of her viper's tongue darkening and quivering.

'You're gonna need thisss to hold your jeanths up. Unlesth you want the world to sthee the marksss on your asss' she laughed, dangling Scott's belt over the threshold of her unlatched front door.

'Ah, thanks. That was fuckin *wild*. Or wild fucking. Either way I had a great time.' He hooked it from her fingers, stood on her doorstep and started to thread it back through his waistband.

'Me too. Alwaysss good to meet a kindred sthpirit. Til next time.' She waggled her fingers.

'Good luck with taming the lisp.' The door was shut with the last syllable still hanging in the air. Scott shrugged, tossing a pre-rolled fag into his mouth. Hunched against the cold, he turned and bounced down the pavement. The tarmac felt spongy under his feet as made towards the cab rank that they had passed earlier in the evening. He'd lost all sense of time, lord knows how late it was.

Cheri had almost reached her back kitchen when a series of staccato violin shrieks heralded an incoming text. She glanced at the phone only long enough clock the first few words:

Think I must have left my watch…

Then fired off a rapid reply:

I love a bit of kitsch but that fine specimen you can keep.

Strumming the door frame with her talons, she fleetingly glanced over each surface for the truant timepiece. Failing to spot it she sighed, pivoted around and half-heartedly headed to the door. She tugged it open.

A dark form lurched at her, grabbing her by the throat and pushing her up against the wall; leather-clad hands clamped around her windpipe. She clawed at their fingers, breaking off two black polished acrylics.

'Get your fuckin handsth off me you freak!' She gagged on the words, scratching at the hood that masked her assailant's face. Scrambling to release the grip, she tried to beat the arms with her fists and tug at the sleeves.

The strangler squeezed and squeezed until a crimson stain blotted her vision, affording her just an instant to register the glint on their wrist before the red bled into the black.

***

He clinked two tumblers together next to her ear. She jerked up at the sound of the bells and prodded the face of the phone that was lying on the floor next to her dangling arm.

'Eh? What's—' She fumbled with the device, still dazed.

'Night cap Emsy?' Scott sloshed around the amber remnants of a half bottle of single malt.

'Oh... Christ, what time is it?' She wiped the tacky corners of her mouth with the back of her hand then combed her fingers through her hair to tame a quiff fashioned from being wedged between two sofa cushions.

'Join me for one?' He started unscrewing the cap.

'Egch, I dunno. Got the car. Plus I've, like, just woken up – I'm not at the stage where I need a drink first thing *just* yet.' She rubbed her eyes and pushed herself up onto her elbow.

'Suit yerself.' He poured a liberal measure for himself and took a slug.

'What bloody time is it McCabe?' She was coming to, as was her naturally feisty disposition.

'Only one forty-five.' He pulled back the sleeve that covered his watch to verify his claim, but didn't look at it.

'Only...' She watched him grimacing as he took another nip of whiskey.

'Reality is merely an illusion, caused by lack of alcohol.' He grinned a joyless grin studying the golden light refracting through his glass like an aficionado at a tasting.

'Ooh, you're in a good mood. Shit night?' She swung her legs round to peel herself upright.

'Fuckin crazy night actually. Nah, just feelin a bit fucked up. Hell, what's new?' His eyebrow lifted.

Emma eyed Scott from across the coffee table.

Something was different but she couldn't quite put her finger on it. 'Dunno. You tell me – what *is* new?' She studied his face. His eyes, that's what looked different. They were dark. Too dark. They were all pupils and no iris. 'You OK matey?'

'Yeah, just...' The maudlin phase of coming down was starting to kick in. Scott knew too well the inevitable pay back for his intoxicating evening with Cheri; that it would not be worth the hours of self-deprecating anguish that was to come. 'Sally always loved Oban.' He swirled the tincture around in his glass. 'It would have been her birthday tomorrow. Well, *today*, now.'

'Oh Jesus. You're right, I'd— Sod it, in that case...' She swiped the bottle from the table and glugged a decent double into the empty tumbler. 'To Sally.' She raised her glass and waited for Scott to reciprocate.

'To Sal.' He chinked and they both swigged at their drinks. 'Feel like a total shit now. You won't *believe* the evenin I just had.'

'I can take a good guess.' She held his eyes with hers. 'Don't get involved with that shit again Scotty. You'll have me to answer to if you do.'

''Kin hell. You can tell?' He pulled out his phone, opened the camera and switched it to selfie mode. Even with the softening effect of the low resolution lens he could see that he that looked wired.

'I know you. Don't fuck up. Do *not* fuck up.' She swallowed the dregs and planted her glass on the table top to add an exclamation mark. 'You look like shit, by the way.'

He smirked a sarcastic thanks. 'Don't worry, you don't have to break me friggin balls. It was a one-off. Hardly anytin. Just got carried away.' Then he whispered 'Asshole.'

'You said it.' She leant down and picked up her phone

and keys.

He drained his glass and poured another. She sat and watched him rocking side to side, slurping at his drink. 'I worry about you matey. You gonna be OK here tonight?'

'Yeah, yeah. Told ya, I'm fine now. Just feelin a bit shite. Couple more of these and I'll hit the hay.'

Emma rose to her feet, pulling on her jacket. 'Only if you're sure. Don't stay up all night Scotty. You know Jae'll be up with the larks.'

'You g'on. I'm dandy.' He got up too and gave her a hug. 'Thanks Em. Y'know... f'everytin.'

'You get more Irish when you drink whiskey.' She pecked him on the cheek.

'It's Scotch.'

'Whatever. Laterz loser.' She had already turned to the door, waving with the back of her hand.

'Laterz lezzer' he said, giggling to himself.

'I heard that' she hollered from the hall just before he heard the front door clicking shut. Then the key rattled in the lock and it creaked open again. 'Oh, almost forgot' she shouted from outside, 'That parcel on the table was stuck in your letterbox. Might be something important.' The door clunked again.

Alone with himself he clipped his phone into the speaker docking station. 'If I'm gonna feel sorry for meself, may as well do it properly.' He opened up the music app and scrolled through the song titles. 'There you are Andy me ole mate.' He tapped the title and slouched back against the base of the sofa. Within milliseconds of closing his eyes the baritone key strokes and soaring violins made his head swirl, so he opened them again and started to mime the words to *Speak softly love*.

The love theme from *The Godfather* had been his and Sally's first dance song. He reeled up the memory on his sensory sprocket-catchers. It flickered through his lenses, every spin and twirl; the feel of the chiffon against his palm as he guided her around the dancefloor, the lavender scent in the dip of her collar bone as he moved in close, the giddy joy of moving as one.

'I'm sorry, Sal. I'm sorry I'm such a fuckin let down.' Tears came now, spilling over his cheekbones and into his beard. He knew this is where the song would take him before he'd pressed play, he'd been there many times. The saltiness of the cleansing almost tasted good. He swayed as he did the night he held her and drank in the memory of her perfume.

His faltering voice joined the crooner as he belted out the impossibly falsetto crescendo. Holding on to the note drained him. Holding on to the moment sucked out his soul. His life was still hers. He slumped down, empty, and grabbed his drink, swigging the fire water like it was a flagon of ale. Dizzy with dredged up delirium he decided that was enough flagellation for one night. He hit the 'shuffle all' button.

His music selection must have fallen prey to a host of drink-and-download decisions. Some of the opening beats and riffs that appeared were not even familiar to him. He tapped skip a number of times then gave up and just let the phone serve up its random selection; listening to choices he'd made in a past life, in a lost time, by a different self. It spooled up a retrospective of archived moments: the record shop where he bought his first seven inch after a week of starving himself to save up his dinner money, the ballad he had played ad nauseam to indulge his broken teenage heart, the track that helped him to lure Sally onto the dance floor that New Year's Eve. He was about to skip that song when it faded into the background. A loud '*ping*' rang out through the speakers. He unhooked the handset from its perch. A *Date with Fate* message banner was displayed across the screen.

Kul4abeer: Why did you cut me dead?

'*Kulbir.* Jesus, I didn't think she was…' He rolled a cigarette and lit it before responding.

BestBet7: Hi Kulbir. I didn't think I had. Did try to contact you but… no reply. S x

He tapped 'send' then took a draw on his fag, looking for the instant message bubbles that would tell him she was up for a chat.

Nothing. He tried again.

BestBet7: I'm sorry about leaving abruptly that evening. Would love the chance to make it up to you. S x

He waited a few minutes, sucking the life out of the rest of his ciggie. Nothing.

'Ah, fuck it.' He docked the phone in the amplifier and let the music play.

He wedged the dead fag butt into the piled up ashtray. Next to it lay the package Emma had brought in. The Air Mail stickers and Canada Post stamp were enough to tell him who the sender was without taking in his sister's return address. He picked it up and tugged at the seal on the jiffy bag. Inside was *Shush*, a slim paperback book with a brief note which simply read '*Let me know what you think. Love ya Bro. B xxx*'

He bent the book between his little finger and thumb and fanned through the pages from the back like he was riffling through a flip book. The rapid-fire series of titles that danced before him played like rotoscope of Brenna's thoughts and feelings. One title *Red night; Red light* piqued his interest but he moved on, feeling the hairs on his arm prickle with unease. He flicked a few more pages and perused the lines of *Borderland state*.

Only one way to go
You can't go down

There's nothing there
But a hole
A massive hole
A hole like a wall
A hole like a tunnel of light
Light splits and breaks
Breaks into lines
Lines of fire
Shoot and shift
Shift and connect
The Tetris effect
Pushed together; locked together
Can't move; can't speak
Mind awake body asleep
Where is the hand
The blessed hand
That leads me out of
No-man's land

His flesh crawled with centipedes of subliminal stirrings. He tried to grasp at the memories as they scuttled beyond his reach, but his powers of literary interpretation were wanting at the best of times, even without the whiskey and serotonin fatigue stymieing his sensibilities.

On the opposite page *Shadow people* beckoned to him.

Darker than night
All gravity; no light
Always inside me
Always behind me
Drawing me in
Drawing me down
Weighing me down
Making me drown
Making me choke
Making me baulk
Saying don't talk

The shadows behind his own eyes were rousing and shape-shifting; ghosts of the lost hours sensing their calling. He slapped the volume shut. Then he noticed a dog-eared corner just a few sheets in from the front cover. He fortified himself with a fresh tot of liquid courage before reading the titular stanzas of '*Shush*' that his sister had marked for him:

Shush, don't say a word
Shush, I'm going to record
Shush, your pretty little head
Shush, and lay here on the spread

Shush, it's just for you and me
Shush, it's just a game for thee
Shush, your pity little head
Shush, until the day you shed

Shush, tell him to be quiet
Shush, tell him not to cry out
Shush, your prissy little head
Shush, until the day you're red

Residual traces of MDMA jump-started his senses, jabbing him with sharp spears of panic. Hot blood flushed his face; flooded his chest. Fingers clawed at his neck and scratched his eyes. Red flashes. Red thrashing. Red legs. Little red legs. *Leave her alone.* Breath brushed his cheek; musty leather and stale coffee. Pressure on his throat; pressure in his temples. *Stop it.* He needed air. He got up suddenly. Blood drained to his feet. Lightening arced between his eyes. He stumbled, lurching forwards. His shins caught the edge of the coffee table. Sprawling across it, his tumbler hit the floor. It shattered and speared his palm with shards of glass. A clipped, English-accented girl was stalking him through the speakers, accusing him of being a scank, accusing him of fucking some slut. He tried to push himself upright. His bloodied palm slipped on the polished glass of the table, slapping the wind out of his chest. He looked at his hand, blood oozed from the gash. He pressed his thumb into the stigmata and struggled to his feet. Thumping footsteps getting closer... the doorbell chiming... thudding on the front door... his phone is ringing... smashing glass...

'And now you're going to die.'

'Who—? Who's there?'

Flailing from side to side it dawned on him that the sounds were coming through the stereo. He scrambled across the floor to his phone. It sat there staring at him blankly like a raven on its roost. He grabbed it, hitting the skip button. It wasn't his music. It was a South Central rapper revelling in rhymes about snapped necks and bloodied butchers knives. *Shut the fuck up.* He stabbed at the phone's sardonic face. It started to bleed, red clots smearing its surface. It wasn't his music. It was a voice as smooth as silk, lyrically slicing his windpipe, taking his last breath. His fingers slipped across the glass, scrubbing through the tracks. It wasn't his music. It was a rapid-fire vocal assault. A blackout. Coming to. Covered in blood. Dead bodies. *Shut up!* It wasn't his music. It was fucking with him. Trying to find the stop button. The same words over and over. 'I must have killed 'em. Killed 'em. Killed 'em.'

Shut your fucking mouth!

CHAPTER 15: KNOCK ON WOOD

DECEMBER 2016

Thursday

'Daddy, who would win out of Brock Lesnar and CM Punk?' Jae tried to stand still whilst his Dad, lunging awkwardly, fiddled with his school tie. The wound in his palm was stinging under its dressing.

'Brock Lesnar... err... he's that big guy isn't he? Weighs three hundred pounds?'

'Two hundred and eighty-six and he's six foot three. He's called *The Beast Incarnate*.'

'The Beast... How big is this CM Punk?' Front tail too short, back one too long. The tie had the upper hand. Scott groaned, pulled the knot apart and, after kneading his sore Life Line, started again.

'He's one hundred and ninety pounds and six feet tall.'

Jae was being jostled from side-to-side by his Dad's grouchiness. He smiled an apology. 'Lesnar hands down then fella – he's got the weight, height *and* the reach advantage over Punk.' He paused, sinking back onto his hindquarters. Weighing up the odds on WWE fighters at the same time as mastering the Windsor knot was too much for his sleep-deprived brain.

'Yeah but actually CM Punk *did* beat Brock Lesnar. It was in a brawl before SummerSlam twenty-thirteen. He hit him with a camera.' Jae brought an imaginary, and evidently unwieldy, studio camera down onto Scott's skull.

'Ah, well that's cheating.' He parried the blow, knelt up

again and resumed the struggle with his red and grey striped polyester nemesis.

'He was being *smart* Dad. He put Paul Heyman in a wheelchair too.' Jae struck several more blows with the make believe weapon.

'Who's Paul Heyman?' Sharp pains started to needle his knee caps. He threaded the wide end of the tie up under the noose around Jae's neck.

'Brock Lesnar's advocate.'

'Advocate? That's a very grown up word Jae' he said, pulling it down through the front loop.

'It means he talks for him.'

'Advocate, right…' He patted his son's chest. 'OK, we're there.' Not exactly fit for a Duke but a presentable effort.

'Brock Lesnar needs someone to talk for him 'cause he's got silly high-pitched voice. Paul Heyman used to be CM Punk's advocate but he left to go to UFC.' Jae sat down and pulled back the Velcro fastener on his grazed black shoe.

'Who, Paul Heyman went to UFC?' Scott hoisted himself up off the floor, lamenting staying down there for so long. His knees had locked.

'No, CM Punk did.' He pulled the Velcro back again, then smoothed it down, then pulled it back again, then smoothed it down. He was just about to do it again when Scott placed his hand over it to say *that's enough*.

'Does CM Punk have a silly high-pitched voice too?' Scott gave his legs a vigorous rub.

'No. They were just best friends. Brock Lesnar is in UFC too. Would Connor McGregor beat Brock Lesnar?' Jae put on the other shoe, this time without the fun and games.

'They're in totally different weight classes Jae.' Scott turned towards the back kitchen, not sure whether he should be proud of that fact that his six-year-old was a fan of cage fighting.

'Yeah, but Connor McGregor can beat up *anyone*. Can't he?' Jae jumped up like he had springs for legs.

'He's a fu— flamin legend, but even he might struggle with a three hundred pound guy.'

'Two hundred and eighty-six.' Jae started to assault his middle knuckle with his top front teeth. Having lost the two lower ones he resorted to scraping it.

Scott re-emerged with Jae's lunch box and foisted it onto the already full backpack, squishing down the PE kit. 'Fingers fella' he said, nodding towards Jae's gnawing. 'You OK? Anything worrying you sweetheart?' He considered getting back down on his knees again but thought better of it.

'It's spelling test day.' The attack on the digit intensified. 'I forgot.'

'I see. You'll have to knock on wood then, Monkey. If you've got any knuckles left.' He bent double and rapped his own on the hard floor. 'Well, laminate.'

'Why do I have to knock on wood?' He took his hand out of his mouth and mimicked his Dad.

'It's for good luck.'

'Why?'

'Dunno. Good question. Let's Google it.' He pulled his phone out of his back pocket and tapped the phrase into its browser. 'OK here goes:

Knock on Wood: An old Irish belief that you should knock on wood to let the little tree people know that you are thanking them for a bit of good luck. There's also a belief that the knocking sound prevents the Devil from hearing your unwise comments.'

Scott lifted his eyebrows as if to say *fancy that.*

'Is the Devil real?' It seemed that the wood knocking had done little to allay Jae's fears. The middle joint was back in its rightful place, being subjected to more gnasher-grating.

'Well, *I* don't think so. If you believe in the Devil that means you have to believe in God. And I don't.' He grabbed Jae's coat by the shoulders and held it open like a matador's muleta.

'Does that mean you'll go to hell?' Jae pushed an arm down each sleeve.

'Is that what Nonnina would have you believe? No Jae, it's all mumbo jumbo. Daddy's not going to hell.' Not just yet, anyway.

Fierce thudding on the front door threatened to avenge his nihilism. Perhaps Saint Nick had come for him.

'Who's that Daddy?'

The doorbell clanked abruptly. Then again. Then more thudding.

'I dunno fella – haven't answered it yet.' Scott shuffled up the hallway. 'Whoever it is *they* can go to hell at this time of the morning' he said under his breath.

'Mr McCabe?' More thudding and clanking. 'Answer the door please. It's the Police.'

'All right, all right.' He slid the safety catch off and pulled the door towards him, peering around the edge. 'Keep the noise down please, my son is inside.'

'Who's that Daddy?' He heard from behind him.

'Just a moment Jae. Go and sit in the kitchen, just a moment.' He turned back to see that two black leather wallets bearing the warrant cards of Michael Woods, Detective

Inspector, and Dawn Wilmington, Detective Constable, had been thrust through the gap.

'Open the door please Mr McCabe.'

Scott inched backwards, taking the door with him. The two plain-clothed officers hovered at the threshold.

'We need you to accompany us to the station sir. We believe you may be able to assist us with a current inquiry,' said the one carrying Michael Woods's ID. He was older, shorter and plumper than his female colleague.

'What, now?' Scott was trembling. He moved his hand away from the door latch to conceal his shakes.

'Yes please sir. I see you have your son here. Is it possible for you to make arrangements for someone to take him for a few hours?'

'A few *hours*, he's supposed to be at school. I can see if his Nanna will take him.' The thought of explaining this to Angela made his blood run cold, but she was his only option at this time of the morning.

'If you would please sir. We'll wait out here, unless you'd prefer us to come in?' Woods craned his neck towards the kitchen. Wilmington shuffled up behind him.

Scott's brain was spinning in his skull like a gyroscope, but he knew he had to think straight. The last thing he needed was Iain seeing plod on his doorstep. Did they *want* to come inside though? Have a good look around without a search warrant?

'No. That's fine. Wait there, I'll make the call.' He clicked the door shut. Dark shadows remained behind its head-height frosted aperture.

Then he opened the door again. 'What's this about anyway?'

'We'll discuss that with you when we get to the station.' Woods turned his back and nodded to Wilmington who was now in the yard surveying the out buildings.

Scott shut the door and leant against it trying to compose himself. He hastened back into the kitchen scouring it for his mobile. Jae was sitting on his hands in the wooden chair next to the sludgy dregs of his morning cereal, swinging his legs to and fro.

'Sweetheart, Nonnina might have to take you to school today.' His hands were shaking so badly he could hardly scroll down through his favourites. Reluctantly, he tapped the instant dial for Angela Capote's mobile.

***

He drummed on the Perspex shield that surrounded the Desk Sergeant. The officer didn't look up at Scott but continued to study his screen, clicking with the mouse occasionally and holding his hand up to put his charge on hold. Scott waited, looking at his feet. When he looked up again the Sergeant was there at the window.

'Do you know how long this will take? I need to get back to work.' Frankly work was the last thing on Scott's mind, he just wanted the torturous suspense of not knowing what was going on to be over. He patted his watch face as if that would speed up the proceedings.

'They'll be with you shortly sir. Please just take a seat.'

That seat had already been a front row ticket to the booking of two pubescent entrepreneurs who had broken into a pub cellar and started to fill their non-insured van with crates of bottles; a verbally abusive drunk who had hopelessly failed the roadside drink-driving tests during the morning rush hour and stank of faeces so badly it made Scott retch;

and a late middle-aged woman with memory failure who had been found wandering the streets in her too-see-through nightdress with mud and blood-encrusted bare feet where slippers should have been.

Scott's phone alerted him to an incoming bulletin. He pulled it out of his jacket pocket and hoped the *Date with Fate* news flash was going to brighten his day. Two new messages.

CheriBrandi: You put me in a box

This girl was trouble. If to say so was stereotyping her, then so be it. He had avoided contacting Cheri since she set him up on his joy ride. She made him nervous. He didn't read beyond the subject line.

Kul4abeer: Just because you're a farmer doesn't mean you have to slash and burn.

Why would she say that? Aside from the fact that he had tried repeatedly to make amends and to arrange another date with Kulbir, he was pretty sure that the farm had not cropped up in conversation. He mentally scrubbed through soundbites of their dinner date, trying to recall.

'Scott, sorry to keep you waiting.' Detective Constable Wilmington interrupted his deliberations. 'The duty solicitor has arrived so we're ready for you now. This way please sir.'

She led him through a rabbit's warren of corridors. Within moments he would have struggled to find his way back to the reception area without a SatNav, not least because he still felt like a rabbit himself, frozen in the spot light of the law. Whilst Warrington police station was an elegant, if imposing, example of stately, red-brick Edwardian architecture on the outside, on the inside it had all the hallmarks of a publically-funded institution that had seen many a scuffle. Chipped grey paintwork, smeared and scuffed skirting boards and grubbily grouted subway-style tiling all attested to beauty being only skin deep. The further they ventured into its belly, the more drab and dingy it seemed to get.

They rounded a corner into a corridor lined with solid steel, royal blue doors sporting eye-height, letter-box style windows with sliding shutters. A right turn took them into another passage, this time flanked by numbered beech-veneer doors. Scott's eyes smarted as the sharp glare from a strip light pierced the gloom. One of the doors was wide open. He squinted as he followed the lanky policewoman into the interview room. In direct contrast to the vaulted arches and baroque crests that adorned the exterior of the station, this small, stark room was perfectly square. It had an off-white Formica table up against the wall with four black, ribbed-plastic chairs around it. On the table top was a gunmetal recording device that looked a little like an old, bulky domestic CD player except that it had four disc drawers, each with its own LED timecode display. On top of it was a small set of teak-stained stationary shelves containing different coloured forms. There was a single disposal plastic cup of water in front of the empty chair nearest to the wall.

The sight made him want to lose his bowels. He felt a pang of empathy with the drunk driver.

Woods was sat facing the entrance in the chair next to the machine. Diagonally opposite him was a baggy, thick-set man with poorly-groomed salt and pepper hair. He was dressed in an ill-fitting shirt that was straining at the shoulder seams and would have been white had it not been laundered to oyster. It matched his skin, which glistened with moisture and diffused a sulphurous odour suggesting a penchant for garlic-rich cuisine. A beaten up, tan leather case was resting on the floor next to his loafers. Scott recognised him as someone he'd seen out of the corner of his eye when he was checking his messages near the duty desk, but had mistaken him for a felon.

Woods looked up without moving his head and

motioned with his watery green eyes for Scott to take the seat opposite. Wilmington took her place next to Woods. The Constable's temperate expression, lean physique, russet-brunette hair and bolt upright stature gave her the look of an English Pointer.

'Scott McCabe; Nick Young - duty solicitor.' Woods conceded a bob of his head towards the oyster man.

Nick rose to his feet and as he did his waistband relinquished its grip on his shirt, exposing a hairy pot belly. 'Hello Mr McCabe. I'm here to act as your advocate throughout this interview.' His voice was baritone and bronchial.

'My advocate...' Scott's banter with Jae that morning seemed like a lifetime away.

'My advice is impartial and completely independent of the police.' Nick grinned, revealing nicotine-rimmed teeth, as he extended his palm. Scott looked down at it. His fate could be held in this clammy shell. Sensing he needed all the help he could get, he clasped both hands around Nick's then dragged back the chair next to him and slid into it. He thought about knocking on Formica; the Devil might be eavesdropping.

'You can consult your counsel in private if you wish to. If so we will pause the interview.' Woods had his shirt sleeves rolled up to reveal his burly arms, bristling with an apricot down. They were resting on a closed case file. The fingers of his sturdy, freckled hands were clasped together in front of him. 'There's a coffee machine down the hall. Let us know if you need refreshment or a comfort break.' He flipped open the folder then promptly shielded it with his orangutan arms.

'I'm OK thanks.' Scott realised that he was sitting on his hands. He shuffled side to side to release them and held them together in his lap. His fingers were twitching and his gums itched for a cigarette.

Woods leant forward and pressed a button on the face of the recorder. The digital timecode displays bolted off the line and sprinted neck and neck. 'This interview is being recorded and is being conducted in an interview room at Arpley Street, Warrington. I am Michael James Woods, Detective Inspector 2514 Cheshire Constabulary. Constable Wilmington would you introduce yourself.'

'I'm Dawn Erin Wilmington, Detective Constable 9032 Cheshire Constabulary.'

'Thank you. Mr Young?'

'I'm Nick Young, Solicitor with Young and Foster.'

'And you Mr McCabe, your full name, address and date of birth please.'

'Scott Thomas McCabe.' He dislodged a frog from his throat. 'Number two Tied Cottages, Oak Grove Farm, Holcroft Lane, Glazebury. I was born on September twenty-fifth, nineteen-seventy-four.'

'Thank you. The time if we can agree it is eleven-twelve am and the date is the eighth of December two-thousand-sixteen.' Detective Inspector Woods paused briefly to allow his three companions to confer agreement. The Constable and the Solicitor said in well-worn unison 'Agreed'. Woods, with an air of impatience, waited as Scott peeled back his left sleeve and tilted his watch face towards him.

'Yes, twelve minutes past eleven.' He glanced up and caught the DI studying him. Woods's complexion was the pallid colour and gnarled texture of root ginger. If he weren't so short he'd make a good Thing, Scott distracted himself with the thought.

Woods sniffed. 'At the conclusion of the interview Mr McCabe I will give you a notice explaining exactly what will happen to the CDs. Do you understand?'

'Yes.' He wished he did.

'You do not have to say anything. But, it may harm your defence if you do not mention when questioned something which you later rely on in court. Anything you do say may be given in evidence.'

'Am I under arrest?' The caution shot a bolt of panic through his forehead.

'No Scott. We're looking into a matter that we think you might be able to help us with.' Wilmington half smiled. She's the *nice cop* then.

'Know this bloke?' Woods held up a mug shot. Despite it being a few years old Scott instantly recognised the dappled complexion, weaselly eyes and thinning pate.

'Should I answer?' he said turning to the duty solicitor who was reaching into his case for a breeze-block of a laptop.

'Can you tell us the nature of the investigation?' Nick opened the cover of the device, shocking it out of its slumber. He took out a glasses case and slipped on a pair of petrol station readers.

'We believe that one of the men that drives for Mr McCabe's haulage firm may be involved in criminal activity. The caution is purely a formality in the event that we need to use any evidence in court.'

'Against Mr McCabe?' He started to tap on the keys.

'He's the driver's employer. We need to establish whether he has knowledge of these offences, or indeed if they are in collusion.' Woods was matter of fact.

Nick nudged his specs down to the bridge of his nose and looked over them at his client. 'I'd advise you to co-operate Scott. But you can decline to answer any of the questions put to you. You just need to think about how that might look in court should it ever come to that.'

Scott gave his counsel a wide-eyed nod.

'The photo. Recognise him?' He pushed the Polaroid across the table.

'It's... Jez. Jez Steele. He drives for me.' Resignation infused his tone. 'But I'm presuming you know that already.'

Woods didn't flinch. 'Apt name.' He leant down under the table and hauled up a dusty black sports bag. He reached inside. 'Seen these before?' He placed an oily cloth parcel on the table. It clanked as he slowly unwrapped it to reveal an array of prosecutable blades. A Balisong butterfly, flick knife and belt-hidden knife were amongst their number. Scott owned their twins.

'Oh right. So *that's* what this is about then.' He unclenched his jaw. 'Listen, I'm aware that Jez is into this shi— stuff, but I've no idea where he gets 'em.' He scrutinised Woods's glassy eyes wondering if every word he uttered was self-incriminating.

''Course you don't.' He remained expressionless but his brow twitched.

'I've never seen 'em, mind.' Scott's heart beat started to pulse in his ears like ultrasound waves.

''Course you haven't. I mean, why would you? They're not the sort of knives that trappers use are they?'

Scott gulped. 'No... That's right. I *do* have knives, yes, but they're all legal. Purely for my work. I mean, hobby.' Wilmington clicked her biro and scribed something into her notebook. Is hesitation body language for lying?

''Course they are.' Woods paused but held his gaze. 'Four years and an unlimited fine for each and every one. Think about that for a moment.'

Scott tried to swallow again but his throat was arid. He reached for the water. Nick was all the time flitting across the keyboard with his fingertips, blowing out gusts of garlic.

'You said *then*... "That's what this is about *then*."' Wilmington piped up. 'What did you think this was about Mr McCabe?'

Scott sat with his mouth open for a moment looking at the Constable. 'Er... well, Jez has… he's been a bit unreliable, lately.'

'Hardly a criminal offence Scott.' Wilmington digged at him with a pointed stare. She was reneging on her nice cop promise.

'He's fucked— sorry, messed me around. Let me down on jobs. I think he's been driving off the radar.'

'Off the radar?' she needled.

'Off the tachograph. Not clocking all his miles.'

'And what makes you think this?' Woods joined in.

'The data on his smartcard and the VU doesn't add up. But, it might be—'

'Sorry to interrupt.' Woods leaned forward. 'Can you say that again in English please?'

'Ah, yes. We've not long since changed over to a digital system. All our drivers have these smartcards with their unique ID on them. You insert the card into the tacho which is also called the vehicle unit - the *VU*. When a card is put into the VU it logs the time that driver clocks on and the hours and activities he does on each job, even if he's not actually driving – like, he might be at rest, or loading, or unloading. Then it logs when the card is removed, which he should only do at the end of his job.' Scott mimed the card in and out actions, mainly because it made him feel less anxious to do something with his hands.

'And why do you say the data doesn't add up?' For the first time Woods registered interest in what Scott had to say.

'Well, I'm no expert at analysing the data, still gettin me head around it, but I reckon he's taking his card out and making miles off the record. Notin ridiculous that will spin a job out for days or anythin, just, I dunno, just miles here and there.'

'And where exactly are these miles "here and there". In what locations?'

'I dunno. It's not a GPS system. All I can see is if the vehicle has been driven without a card in the VU.'

'We'd like to take a look at that data Scott. It could be material to our inquiry.'

'It's all on an SD card. You can only view it with the card reader and the right software.' He kicked himself under the table.

'Well, we can play this one of two ways. You can let us have the kit voluntarily' Woods paused for effect. 'Or we can confiscate it, if we have cause to believe that Mr Steele is involved in criminal offences. Which we do.'

'You want me to bring it in *here*? But I need—' The scene where he explains the missing tech to Iain was playing through his mind.

'Or if you prefer we could come and seize your entire computer system.' His tone was knowingly nonchalant.

Scott's face was suddenly cold, he felt his colour drain like a river level dropping after its banks had burst. His mind kicked over the rocks lining his memory banks to unearth the squirming clew of taboo fantasies that were born of his dubious, non-work-related browsing.

'No. No, my business would fall apart without it. I'll bring in the card reader.' He wondered if they'd noticed the film of perspiration on his top lip. 'What do I do if the DVSA springs a spot check?'

'We'll inform them of our investigation. They will probably want to pursue their own lines of inquiry.'

'Oh Jesus, they could ground the fleet...'

'To be frank, Scott, that could be the least of your worries.'

'What do you mean? I was going to report—'

'That's for you and the DVSA to tussle about.' He waved his hand as if wanding away a fly. 'No, what I mean is that if it turns out that any of your vehicles have been used to commit a serious offence you may be looking at criminal charges yourself.'

Scott was stunned into speechlessness.

'Exactly what is the nature of the serious offence you're insinuating?' The solicitor stepped in. Not before time in the opinion of his client.

Woods addressed his response to Scott. 'Well, we suspect our Jeremy here has been a naughty boy. A very naughty boy... Have you heard of modern slavery, Scott?'

His heart slammed up against his chest wall like a train that had lost the rails and found a granite bank. 'Sort of, I mean the girl... woman... at the recruitment agency gave me a leaflet. About the signs to...' His head was reeling. 'Can't say I've read it cover to cover but—'

'You may want to. We have reason to believe that Mr Steele may be involved in people trafficking. What we are interested to know is: is he a lone wolf?' There was something about the question that suggested Woods already knew the answer.

The tapping on Nick's keyboard amplified and became more frenetic, as did the scratching of Wilmington's note taking.

'I dunno what you're talkin about. I told you what I know.' He swept the stubble around his mouth with the back of his hand.

'These scumbags, Scott, they snatch to order. Lonely hearts columns, escorting websites, internet dating...' Woods eyed him intensely 'Easy prey.'

'I told you as far as I'm aware he's just been—'

'And when they've been drugged, beaten and raped into submission,' Woods continued, 'their ordeal is streamed online for paying punters with the sickest of appetites. Some way to become an internet star, eh Scott?'

Oh Christ, please don't seize the computer. 'I swear, that's all I know.' He wished he had a God to pray to.

Inspector Woods sniffed sharply. He dropped the photo into the open file and closed it. 'OK, let's park that for a moment – if you'll excuse the pun.' His comment was as devoid of humour as a black hole is of light. 'Let's return to the matter of the blades.'

Scott squirmed in his seat. He could deny the abduction allegations all day long and still pass a polygraph. The knives, on the other hand, sliced too close to the bone.

'Has Mr Steele ever offered to bring prohibited goods into the country for you or anyone else at the depot?' The sentence didn't rise at the end like a question was supposed to.

'You don't have to answer that if you need to consider your position, Scott.' Nick stopped typing and looked up over the rims of his specs.

'No, no, it's OK. I don't have anything to—'

'Take another look at each of these weapons Scott – because that's what they are. Lethal weapons. Weapons that could be used to, oh, I dunno, intimidate someone? Threaten to slash their pretty face if they don't do what they're told? You know, that sort of thing.' The detective was turning up the heat and it felt like stepping off a plane in Vegas.

'Jez... he had pictures of knives he was flashin about, on his phone. But not the blades themselves.' Scott could feel the follicles in his scalp ooze like groundwater springing through an aquifer.

'So you knew about them then?' Woods had handed him a spade and marked out the hole.

'No— I mean, only that he had an interest, they were internet pictures.' Oh shit, did that sound remotely convincing?

'Internet pictures. Make a note of that Wilmington, Mr Steele liked to share internet pictures with Mr McCabe.' That hole just got bigger. 'So you've never seen Jez carry any of these items about his person or in his cab?' And his eyes were saying *keep digging*.

Scott shook his head.

'Speak up please sir.' Wilmington motioned towards the recorder.

'No' he said, trying to sound assertive.

'You've no idea how he might have brought such items into the country?' I said *dig*.

'I... I've told you what I know.'

'Scott, we understand you're an upright guy. But believe

me it won't look good for you on the trafficking charges if you've been shown to be lying about the knives. Juries don't like suspects who tell porkies.'

The word 'suspect' hit him like a dose of salts. He would have reached for the cup to quench his raging thirst were it not for the fact that the ripples in the water would betray his somersaulting stomach. He gawped at the Inspector and said nothing.

'Are you lying about the knives, Scott?'

He couldn't speak, his jaw fell.

'Scott?'

'I've told you what I know.'

The four of them sat in silence whilst the LED stopwatches split each second like tiny razors slicing through the tension.

After what felt like an achingly long impasse, Woods slapped his hands down flat on the table and slowly sunk back into the chair, not once diverting his jaded glower from his interviewee. Scott could tell those eyes had seen things that no man should see, nestled as they were within deep pouches of weariness. The only sound was the pitter-patter of Nick completing a sentence.

'OK. We'll call it for now. We'll send someone over later to pick up the SD card and reader gadget.' He waved his hand in the way people do when they mean to say *thinga-me-bob*. 'Interview terminated at twelve-twenty-six. Interview is exactly one hour fourteen minutes in duration and the date is still the eighth of December two-thousand-sixteen.' He pressed the stop button and the timecode numbers froze in their tracks.

'Make a note of the recording ID number please Dawn.' His junior officer obliged, scribbling the details in her book before flipping it shut.

'Can I go now?' There was a beseeching bent to Scott's tone.

'You can, but don't stray too far. We may need to speak to you again.' Woods took the master disc out of the recorder and handed it to Wilmington who sealed it in an envelope and placed a label over the seal.

'Sign here please sir.' She passed the package to Scott and held out her pen.

Scott obliged. It felt like he had forgotten how to write, the pen slipped across the paper making a mark that bore little resemblance to his usual signature. Wilmington pushed the envelope across to the solicitor who made his own scrawl on it.

'Can I use the bathroom?' Scott felt like a school child asking teacher.

Woods was labelling the other copies with an indelible marker. He didn't look up. 'Dawn, show Mr McCabe out will you?'

Scott felt dazed. He let Wilmington usher him towards the door before realising he had failed to thank the solicitor. He turned back, they exchanged a perspiry handshake and agreed a follow up call. Then he was out into the dimly-lit corridor. After being in the poorly-ventilated interview room the air felt fresh as it hit the moisture on his brow. Scott inhaled until his lungs felt sore. They walked a few yards then Wilmington reached around him and tapped the door of the gents.

'There you go sir. I'll wait out here.'

'Thanks.' Scott didn't need to relieve himself, he just needed to regroup.

He went over to the basins and ran the tap. Cupping his hands under the running water he splashed his face, then shook it dry. He tugged a couple of green paper towels out of the wall dispenser and dabbed his forehead and cheeks. He stared at himself in the mirror as he dragged the coarse tissue down over the brush on his chin. God he looked dreadful. And full of dread he was. Fuck knows where all this was going to lead. He breathed in as deeply as he could through his nose, then released the air through his mouth. He repeated that three times, feeling sick, but telling himself with each out-breath that he could do this.

He pressed his palm to the aluminium push plate on the door and eased it ajar, just in time for him to overhear Woods's parting words as he left his young colleague in the corridor.

'Let's keep a close eye. This one knows more than he's letting on.'

Scott darted back into the toilets before Wilmington spotted him. He waited a few moments then breezed through the door as if emerging for the first time.

***

He climbed out of the taxi into the courtyard; eyes everywhere as he slapped the door shut. He watched it pull away then sized up the scene. Customers were filtering in and out of the automatic sliding doors on the side of the farm shop clutching Oak Grove Farm carriers and hessian bags-for-life. A self-drive hire van was pulling up to the security gate that led to the *Store it with McCabe* lock-up units. Two mums with pre-school children were choosing ice-creams in the diary annexe. The haulage sheds were shut apart from one which housed one of the smaller curtainsiders, the front of the cab was yawning and Wes, one of Lee Ashley's callout mechanics, was examining its tonsils.

He scrutinized the scene for anyone who might have been a plain clothes copper and for Iain – if he'd spotted Scott arriving back at the farm he'd be on his case for sure. No sign. He stood for a moment, heart pounding, wondering where to start. Then he pictured the Balisong blade sitting in his desk drawer like a snitch waiting to squeal. The office.

Scott scooted across the cobbles pulling his keys out of his pocket. So close to the edge of panic, he tried to force the key into the keyhole. Had Iain changed the lock? He tried a few more times then looked at the offending Yale. It wasn't even the right colour.

'Fookin eejit.' The correct key popped the door open. Dashing over to his desk, he riffled through the bunch to find the one for the top drawer. He yanked it open. The blade skated across its base clunking against the front upright.

Glory to god. He breathed out like he'd been holding his breath since the cab pulled up. The rest of his collection was in the cottage. He'd deal with them when he'd sanitised the office. He fired up the PC hard drive whilst he flitted about lifting the edges of folders and documents... where was it? Then it came to him, he checked the mail shelves and found the blue PVC cash bag that he used for banking. He unzipped the tamper-proof zip lock and dropped the knife in. He zipped it, then turned his attention to the computer.

Three different browsers were loaded onto the office system, each one optimised for the various software programs that he used daily. They all needed cleansing. One by one he went into the settings and cleared the cache. Within minutes his browsing history was... history. He went on to clear all of the temporary files, cookies and any other superfluous data that was clogging up his C-drive. The dialogue boxes tracking the cleaning process seemed to leaf through files for an eternity. He drummed his fingers on the desk praying that

Iain wouldn't stick his greasy beak around the door before he was done.

At last the reboot prompt appeared. He suspected that the police would be able to retrieve everything, but that was no reason to advertise his proclivities. He'd worry about the implications of deleting the files if he was ever questioned about it. Kirk might be able to work his magic and make them disappear for good.

Satisfied he'd done all he could to make his working desktop at least *appear* squeaky clean he grabbed the cash bag and made a hasty retreat to continue his housekeeping at the cottage.

As he crossed the yard again his head spun left then right constantly surveying the visible terrain for spies. He reached his front door, burst through it and slammed it behind him. First he bolted up the narrow staircase and flew into his bedroom. He pulled a wooden box out from under the bed. A souvenir from his gap-year days in Thailand, its lid was carved with an intricately rendered scene of two lovers seated in a swing under a giant Catechu tree. He pulled it open. Its red velvet interior showcased two flick knives, a Japanese cut-throat razor and a hidden blade masquerading as a belt buckle. He scooped them up, unzipped the cash pouch, chucked them in and locked the seal.

Next to see to his home computer. He knew what he had to do for peace of mind, but it was with reluctance. He logged on to *Date with Fate*. Skimming the help section, he looked for guidance on how to get rid of any trace that he'd been on the site. He read the section on archiving a profile. Not enough, he needed to completely eradicate it. He clicked links that led to links that led to more ways of keeping your profile on hold.

Fifteen minutes into browsing he found it.

Sure you want to leave us? Here's how to delete your profile.

'Jesus, about friggin time. These bastards don't wanna let ya go.' He turned on his printer and when it had finished doing whatever it is that printers do to juice up he hit the print button. Then he clicked the profile icon to open his home page. Unable to resist one last check of his inbox in case he'd garnered a new love interest, he scanned the recently received subject lines.

Dec 8th: Kul4abeer: Just because you're a farmer

Dec 6th: CheriBrandi: You put me in a box

Nov 26th: Kul4abeer: Why did you cut me dead?

Nov 21st: Finn2bwith: Don't leave me hanging around

It read like a stalker's phrase book. 'Christ. A bunch of flamin nutters, the lot of 'em.'

A compulsion hit him. It hit him with the same inner conflict he had when the urge to rubber-neck hard-core porn struck. Before he excommunicated himself from the site, he had to know.

He opened up a new browser tab and typed in Cheshire Police. The Home page looked bright and welcoming, two bobbies on the beat – one male, one female – smiling as they carried out their good-humoured community relations. Brightly coloured boxes advertised the various areas of operation carried out by the constabulary. His eyes skirted over them, stopping on the orange box in the lower right of his screen. The *Missing Persons* category was represented with an iconic illustration of a person with a question mark inside its head. The question was in his head too – was this a good idea? He clicked anyway.

The page was full of blurb heralding the dedication of the force to finding aberrant loved ones. He ignored it. He was looking for photos. A large purple box labelled 'Find Missing People' caught his eye. The arrowhead of his cursor became a pointing finger as he hovered over it, he paused to breathe before pressing the left mouse button. It sprung a new tab, linking to an external charity site. On the right of the page was a grid of passport photos headed 'Help Us Find'. His breathing was shallow and quick as he skipped over an array of faces – a rosy-faced middle-aged woman, a carefully preened teenage boy, a business-like forty-something man, a smiling schoolgirl with her hair in bunches. His stomach turned thinking about what might have become of them, but selfishly he felt relieved that they were all complete strangers. Underneath the photo roll-call was another heading 'Recent Posts'. The Twitter feed had no pictures, just a stream of pleas for lost friends and relatives to get in touch.

#Nicola, 41, missing from Stockport since 24/9. We can listen and help you be safe.

#Jaden, 12, missing from Crewe: Pls call or text.

Pls RT #George, 58, missing from Staffordshire since 18/10. George, we're here for you.

He dry-retched.

#Finnley, 32, missing from Sale since 2/11: Finn, pls get in touch with Mum.

The skin on his arms and neck prickled as the follicles stiffened.

It couldn't be. Must be a different girl with the same name.

But how many women had he ever met with that name? His eyes were drawn to the date. Just a few days after his date with Finn. He remembered that because Emma called him about it on November first, the anniversary of Sal's death. He remembered it because he'd felt guilty and ashamed for forgetting. He remembered it because he'd felt like a total shit.

He clicked to return to his *Date with Fate* inbox. His chin dropped to his chest. Thank the stars for that. The last communication from Finn was date-stamped November twenty-first – weeks after this bulletin. An unlikely coincidence then. After a few calming huffs into his ribcage he raised his head and was about to shut the site down when he realised that each missing person's name was a hyperlink-highlighted hashtag. Presumably a drill-down to more information. There was only one way to be certain that he'd jumped to conclusions.

He clicked on Finnley's name.

Her glowing smile, soft fair curls and laughing blue eyes filled the screen.

Oh fuck oh fuck oh fuck. Hammers pounded the inside of his ribs. No, Jesus Christ, no.

It was the same picture she'd used as the main attraction on her dating profile. The first picture he'd seen of her. The one that had drawn him to her. Underneath the picture there was a number to call. On the edge of hysteria he toggled back to his dating profile. His eyes traced the subject line of her last message to its date. Definitely November twenty-first. A whole three weeks after the Twitter post. He ran a search for Finn2bwith.

No matches found.

Why had she contacted *him*? Why him instead of her family? Had she sent one last message then run away? To start a new chapter somewhere else? With someone else? Had she taken her profile down right after she'd sent it? Should he get in touch her Mum? No, that would implicate him in her disappearance. Should he call the charity with an anonymous tip-off? What would he tell them? What did he know?

If Scott had moments ago been reluctant to end his love affair with the dating site, now he was desperate to dump it. Still trembling he whipped the step-by-step instructions out of the printer and set about following them.

A foreshadow of dread swept over him. He paused and

stabbed Kul4abeer into the search box.

No matches found.

'Jesus fucking Christ.'

CheriBrandi

No matches found.

But the messages? They're messaging? *How*? Scott was dizzy with questions he couldn't answer. But there was one question he had a resolute answer for.

Are you sure you want to permanently delete your profile?

'Yes I bloody do.' He tapped the OK button.

Barely breathing, he watched BestBet7 disappear forever. He shook his head as if it would help his thoughts to settle. It scattered them like the flakes in a snow globe. He had to get his head together; had to finish the job. He set to work clearing the browser caches as he'd done in the office, ran the disk clean up and hoped that all traces of his online antics had been wiped. The onion sat silently on his taskbar as he stared at the screen in disbelief. Was this all some kind of waking dream? Had these girls been real? Was this fucking nightmare *for real*?

He had to get a grip; had to tie up one more loose end.

The blue cash wallet jangled as he picked it up. The contents of this alone lay claim to a twenty-year stretch. He sprinted out of the living room and through the door adjoining the garage. He popped the catch at the back of the Land Rover and climbed into trailer, pulling tarps and tools out of the way in his search. The shovel was hiding under a yellow and indigo McCabe tartan picnic blanket that Sally had gifted him. Without sentiment, he tossed it aside and grabbed the handle. He climbed out and then circled round to the driver's door, chucking the spade into the passenger seat. He had just raised the remote-controlled garage door and turned the engine over when he saw Iain attempting to canter over to him.

'Oi, Scott! Where the flaming hell have you been all day?'

'Go fuck yourself, Iain' he hollered through the open window as he wheel spun it out of the garage and towards the exit gate. He looked back to see his cousin fist pumping the air and mouthing obscenities. Scott gave him the two-fingered salute and pummelled the accelerator.

The unforgiving suspension pounded and rocked over the pothole strewn lanes. Scott's eyes flitted between the rear-view and wing mirrors. He looked over his shoulder, covering the blind spot. No one was around. He listened for the humming of other engines. No one was following.

The clumped, soily fields that stretched out either side of the road glistened with the first dew of early evening frost. Sepia light strobed through the trees and hawthorns that lined the muddy patchwork of meadows. The sun was low in the sky, blinding him as he swung round a sharp bend. He slapped the visor down with his left hand. His sleeve rode back to reveal his watch. It was five past three. Jae.

'Shit.' He yanked the steering wheel and pulled over into a passing bay and, for the second time in a day, speed dialled his mother-in-law. She answered like she'd been waiting for it.

'Angie, I'm so, so sorry to ask this again but *please* can you pick up Jae? Still got a few things to see to then I'll be over.'

'Of course Scott, I can do that. Is everything OK?'

'I'll explain later, thanks Angie.'

'I think you'll need to.'

He didn't have time to fret about what that might mean. He rung off and shifted the stick into gear, checking over each shoulder again before pulling back onto the scabrous tarmac. His eyes darted from mirror to mirror. After several more hairpin bends the road opened out into a Roman stretch as far as the eye could see. Up ahead he could make out his destination, Dingle Woods at the edge of Lump Brook Valley.

To his left he came upon the clearing where a criss-cross farm gate met with a style at the start of the woodland walk trail. He pulled off the road alongside the gate, grabbed the cash bag and shovel and dismounted the cab.

He stopped and swept the surrounding area. Still no sign of anyone. A crackling of branches behind him made him spin. The critter that had caused it was shuffling off through the undergrowth. He crouched down and stared through the thorny hedgerow, but the smoky light of dusk veiled the interloper. He straightened up and pulled open the passenger side door; felt along the shelf under the dash and grabbed his torch. He twisted it into light and set off along the footpath that ran along the perimeter of the field. It snaked off into a spinney of birches, ashes and oaks.

After a few yards he stomped across a narrow footbridge, not much wider than a scaffolding plank, that ran over deep crack in the earth once carved by a brook. He knew the spot he was heading for - the Queen - a huge Beech tree in the dip of the valley next to a wooden picnic bench. It was a landmark that he and Jae had lunched beneath many times. The behemoth had seen the turning of two centuries. Its immense, twisting trunk and creeping roots made it look like a mythical beast hoisting itself out of the earth by its tentacles. He reached the colossus and stood in awe of her for a few moments.

Taking ten paces to the left to clear the reaches of her roots, he kicked aside the broken twigs and shrivelled bracken tendrils that festooned the bed of the woods then started to dig. The ground was cold and hard but he managed to chip away a divot large enough to slide the head of the spade into. The surface frost gave way to damp earth and the excavation became easier. After a short while he'd chiselled a burrow deep enough to hide his booty. He dropped the cash bag into the hole, shovelled the soil back over it and patted it down as hard as he could. He speared the ground with the shovel then he covered the spot with twigs, punk and woody pulp. Sweating like a glass blower, he wiped his brow with his sleeve, steadying himself against the handle of the spade.

Then he strolled back over to the Queen and pressed his palms and forehead to her craggy trunk. Craning his neck heavenward, he prayed for watchfulness under her outstretched arms.

How many secrets could she keep, this majesty of the woods? One more, he hoped. He looked at his pale hands against the bark, formed a fist and knocked three times on wood.

***

Throwing his spent rollie into the bush he rapped his knuckles against the heavy oak door. He blew out the last toke of smoke in quick, sharp gusts, fanning it away with his arm. When there was no response he thumbed the doorbell.

Muffled voices approached from behind it, punctuated with the odd excitable squeal. Angela was still giggling when she opened the door.

'Hi Scott.' Her smile dropped as she looked him up and down. 'You look tired.'

'Thanks, you're looking great yourself'. He ruffled his fringe then pecked her on the cheek.

'What's all this about Scott. Jae said the police came round.' She stroked her Grandson's hair as he buried himself in the small of her back, then peered sheepishly around her waist at his father.

Scott sighed. It wasn't Jae's fault he'd let it slip. He didn't know which was more morally reprehensible – lying to the police or asking his six-year-old to keep a secret.

'Ah, it's sumthin-a-notin. One of the lads has been up to no good is all.'

'Why did they take you in then?'

'Yeah McCabe, why did they take *you* in?' Frank's voice boomed as he emerged from a side room off the capacious hallway. Had his ear been pressed to the door?

'Witness statement – they're takin them from a few people. Just routine.' He shrugged.

'Plain clothes? They don't make routine house calls.' Frank had evidently given his nephew the third degree. Jae cowered behind his Nanna.

'You know the filth – always ready to make a crisis out of a drama.' It felt to Scott like he was back in the interrogation suite.

'Tell it to the judge McCabe. If you've been up to something I can find out.' Frank sidled up behind his mother and crossed his thewy arms over his equally muscular chest. Scott bored through his brother-in-law with his eyes. His stare said *shut the fuck up*.

'Come on sweetheart. Grab you stuff, let's get home and have some tea.' He tried his best to sound every day.

Jae scuttled off and returned with his backpack and coat. Angela eased them over his arms and, as she guided him towards his Dad, she mouthed 'I'm always here.'

Scott nodded, eyeballed Frank then took Jae by the mitten. They made their way out hand-in-glove across the huge expanse of herringbone brickwork outside the Capote residence, past a Range Rover Autobiography, a Mercedes C Class coupe and a Fiat 500. Jae was looking at his feet as they approached Scott's beat up four-by-four.

'Is Mummy in the ground?'

'She is sweetheart' he sighed.

'But she's in the sky too?'

'Yeah, she's up there looking down on us.' After this day, he hoped to God she wasn't.

'She's half in the ground and half in heaven.'

'Yeah something like that.' The passenger door grumbled as he pulled it open.

'Where is she in the ground? Is she everywhere?'

The question took Scott by surprise. Not because his son wanted to know where his Mum was, but because he was suddenly aware that he'd never been to visit Sally's grave; not since the day her remains had been buried.

'No sweetie, she *is* somewhere. Somewhere I haven't been to for a while.' He jerked the seatbelt free from its hook, wrapped it around his boy and clipped it down.

'Can we go there? Can I see Mummy?' Jae spun around and looked his Dad in the eye. He was twinkling with anticipation.

'I'm afraid you can't see Mummy Jae. Mummy is gone.' He rubbed his eyes hard, he felt drained.

'But I can take you to where she is.'

CHAPTER 16: WHERE?

Saturday

He popped the iron bracket that clipped together the heavy, bitumen-stained oak gates, and gently swung them open. A meandering, shingle path lead up to the quaint medieval church. They stood there for a moment; Scott stalled crossing the threshold. He rested his hand on the gate post to steady himself and noticed they had been erected in memory of Lesley Evans who had graced the earth from 1904 to 1996. At least she'd had a good innings he supposed. Everything in this place was etched with loss. He imagined the icy bite of the December air could well have been attributed to the presence of so many lost souls, held in limbo by the grasping skeletal arms of the naked oak, birch and sycamore trees that surrounded the Holy site. Despite the sun's celestial rays streaking through the mesh of branches, Scott's heart was already feeling a familiar, onerous pull towards his diaphragm.

St Peter's boasted a proud history, being the oldest surviving Catholic house of worship in the region. The original limestone bell tower and the conical wizard's hat of a steeple were beautifully preserved. A once diminutive chapel building had been periodically supplemented over the generations with flint-encrusted extensions to accommodate a larger chancel, sanctuary and vestry. Whilst Scott loathed all things ecclesiastical he had to admit that the age and heritage of it alone inspired awe.

He braced himself and took Jae's hand. They strayed from the gravel path and started to respectfully weave between the headstones. Scott steered Jae along the edges of the, sometimes barely visible, burial mounds. He shot glances over each shoulder, trying to shake the feeling that shadows were shifting and flitting between the trees. Perhaps a deer. Perhaps his imagination. Perhaps in a parallel space-time continuum someone was stumbling onto *his* grave.

A distant, haunting tune wafted towards them on the breeze, sound waves surging and receding with each gust of wind. They veered to towards the source, picking up the perimeter path and ambling alongside its crumbling dry stone wall. Scott recognised the eerie minor key strokes of a lonesome piano ringing in hollow space; its only companion an unmistakably theatrical wailing as the singer questioned whether there was any *Life on Mars*. The notes floated on the zephyr as if the spectres of the lawman, and the wrong guy that he was beating up, were rising from one of the crypts.

Strings swelled melodramatically as they approached a rather inadequate looking cement-splattered, silver plastic ghetto-blaster. Scott jolted Jae to a halt. The speakers rattled, struggling to do justice to the operatic histrionics. A spade stood wedged in an open bag of cement next to a bucket of water and a mixing palette. Fresh render oozed from the gaps between the stones in the wall. He glanced around. No sign of life, in the most literal sense possible. He could still smell a whiff of the Bowie fan's exhaled tobacco smoke. He strained to see around the edge of the church, then back behind him, the way they had come. No one. The still life gave the ghoulish impression of an absconded grave robber having been caught in the act. Scott shivered.

They left the path and started to dodge between the memorials, Scott's head flitting from side to side, scanning the names. The graves were in varying states of repair. Some sported fresh flowers, strimmed edges or lovingly tendered bedding plants. One or two even boasted modern family photos and hand written letters carefully wrapped in weatherproofing sleeves, updating long gone relatives on new arrivals to the family, the stretching limbs of latter-day toddlers and the marriages and offspring of those who were too young to date when last seen by the loved ones laying in rest.

Other burial places were ramshackled. The hoodlums of passing time had rendered them voiceless – acid rain had eaten pock marks into aged stone and overgrown brambles obscured what was left of the eulogies. Those that would have been the caretakers, themselves now in the ground. No one left to preserve their dignity whilst they slept. Time rendered all of the graveyard's occupants equal, from the most modest marking of the spot to flamboyant sepulchres that reunited familial generations. Time was the ultimate leveller.

Scott's throat tightened uncomfortably in the presence of so much bereavement. He'd kept his own buried in an unmarked vault. It had been his experience that when grief is fresh others prefer you to hide it; as time passes they expect you to. So he had largely obliged. Now, as they made their way through to where Sally lay, he felt the mortal loss of so many. Amongst the reverent tributes to loving memory, being called to rest, or falling asleep he was struck by a more contemporary-looking epitaph, a marble tablet embossed with bold black letters:

LOVING AND KIND WITH A SMILE ALWAYS

UPRIGHT AND JUST TO THE END OF HIS DAYS

SINCERE AND TRUE IN HEART AND MIND

A BEAUTIFUL MEMORY LEFT BEHIND

Randall Richards and his wife Mary lay together. He'd passed in 1938 aged 59; she in 1971 aged 90. Thirty-three years. She'd waited to be reunited with him for thirty-three years. He glazed over and tried not to divulge his sorrow to his boy. *Til death do us part* had no meaning to Mary; her wedding day pledge extended to the life hereafter. It made Scott realise that it wasn't only the loss of Sally he had mourned these last three years; it was the loss of himself. Would she have called him 'Sincere and true in heart and mind?' Would her faith in him have endured, had he been capable of making better choices? The thought lingered as they arrived by her side.

They stood hand-in-hand at the foot of Sally's grave. Jae studied the inscription, trying to sound out the words letter-by-letter.

'What does it say Daddy?'

Scott cleared his throat and swallowed, then he softly read aloud:

IN LOVING MEMORY OF SALLY CAPOTE

BELOVED WIFE OF SCOTT AND MOTHER TO JAE

OUR DEARLY LOVED DAUGHTER

WHO LEFT US NOV. 1st 2013

AGED 34 YEARS

MAY YOU FIND EVERLASTING PEACE

His voice faltered.

'What does 'be-lov-ed' mean?'

'Ah-hem. It means we loved her very much. *Love* her.' He silently chastised himself.

It hadn't been Scott's choice to bury her in the grounds of Angela and Carlo's church. He would have preferred to mark Sally's passing with a plaque at the crematorium but his in-laws had insisted, and paid for the privilege. Even though their Catholicism had all but lapsed, they held the residual belief that Sally may one day be forgiven for taking her own life if she were buried on consecrated ground, clinging as they did to the more forgiving tenets of the Catechism for its palliation of her sin. His protests had fallen on deaf ears; that it wasn't Sally who needed to be forgiven; that she didn't hold with those bullshit ideals. At the time it was too easy to ride roughshod over his wishes. And Sally's, it seemed.

'Is Mummy asleep?'

'Sort of.' Scott's contribution had been the closing sentiment. Sally had rarely enjoyed peace of mind on This Side. He genuinely hoped, if his heathen lack of conviction to the idea of the Other Side proved to be misguided, that she will have found it now. 'Do you want to give your picture to Mummy?' Scott rubbed his son's shoulder.

'OK.' Jae flung his Spiderman backpack to the floor, unzipped it and pulled out an A4 plastic wallet containing his latest artistic interpretation of the bridge between Heaven and Earth. As was the case in most of his compositions Jae and Scott stood outside the house, holding hands and hovering above the green brush. Sally was nestling into her cloud. In this version, though, there was a sweeping line joining Jae's other hand to his Mum's.

'What's that fella?' Scott pointed to the umbilical.

'That's my Spidey web. I'm splinging it so I can fly up and see Mummy' he said, in that matter-of-fact way that children do when they are explaining the magical way that they see the world.

'*Riiight.*' Scott said with a well-worn inflection. 'That's very clever. Mummy will like that. And who are these two?' He pointed to two small stick figures that Jae had drawn standing behind his father.

'That's Peter and Red. They miss Mummy too.'

'They do? They knew Mummy?' He pondered briefly on

whether Jae was too young to conjure up imaginary friends when his Mum was still with them. 'Well… OK then.' He signalled to Jae to give the drawing to his Mum. Jae placed it carefully on the bleached gravel and dragged an empty stone-effect rose bowl over the top edge to act as a paperweight. The corners of the picture fluttered in the breeze making it look as if the stick figures were edging closer to one another.

'Is that pillow for her head?' Jae said, pointing to the headstone which had been crafted out of granite to mimic an open prayer book.

'It would be.' It slipped out before he could stop himself.

'Would be? Why? Isn't Mummy here?'

'You know that the important part of Mummy is her spirit don't you?' Scott squatted and rested his elbows on his knees. Jae copied him.

'Her spirit?'

'Yes, that's the part that floats up into the clouds.' He pointed to Sally in Jae's sketch.

'Into Heaven?'

'That's right.'

'What about the rest of her?'

'Well, some people are buried. Others prefer to be cremated. That means made into ashes. In a fire.'

'A fire?' Jae jumped to his feet. 'Why?'

Scott wondered briefly how this revelation might be made manifest in future artworks. He turned to face his son and closed his palms around each shoulder.

'It was what Mummy wanted Jae. It didn't hurt' he said softly. 'She had already gone to Heaven. This grave is… it's somewhere that we can come to when we want to remember her. She's already gone. She's *safe*.' He straightened up, rubbing his knees.

They stood in quiet contemplation.

Scott broke the silence. 'Shall we go and light a candle for Mummy?'

It took both hands to turn the large wrought iron ring that unlatched the solid oak, arcaded door; a surviving testament to the durability of medieval craftsmanship. It opened out into a compact anti-chamber pathed around the edges with slabs of stone which surrounded a large black granite homage to a predecessor of the current custodian. The grave stone for this age-old cleric was carved with a Latin obituary and dated 1317; it covered almost the entire floor space so that visitors were forced to walk over it to reach the inner sanctum.

The door to this was ajar. Scott slowly pushed it open. For some reason he did everything slowly and quietly when he was in the house of God, even though it wasn't his God. They walked through an oatmeal-coloured stone arch and stood at the base of the flint tower that had once hailed the church's presence from a distance. It had a high vaulted ceiling lined with curved dark oak beams and facing them was another stone arch, the mirror image of the one they had entered through, which led to another small annexe that was home to the confessional.

To their left was the back wall of the church, the tallest stretch of chalky render which boasted a striking and incredibly well-preserved mural depicting a Middle Ages imagining of the consequences of earthly sin.

Scott had poured over this purgatorial scene many times in the past when he'd been obliged to attend family christenings, weddings. Funerals. It was an elaborate method for putting the fear of God into a peasant's soul and was no doubt very effective at safe guarding – or correcting – moral character. He'd perused the amateurishly produced literature next to the collection box so often that he almost knew it by heart.

The painting was divided into four quadrants, each depicting a different tableau. To the lower left a huge demon with the face of a gargoyle pitchforked sinful souls into a fire pit. Around the inferno, waiting to be dealt their fate, were skinny, naked figures representing three of the seven deadly sins – Sloth, laying on its back; Gluttony, drunk on wine and Pride, admiring her jewels. To the lower right were the other sins: Avarice, spewing money bags; Envy, clutching at a youth; Anger, brawling over a sheep and Lust, locked in a fervent threesome. Some were being cajoled into the flames; others were being roasted over the blaze on what looked like a rack of wooden spikes, carried by two cloven-hoofed goblins – one with the face of a dog, the other a cockerel.

'Is that like the fire Mummy was burned in?' Jae looked so mortified he was gulping back tears.

'Christ, no Jae. This is all a load of bull— baloney.'

'Why?'

Scott couldn't answer that so tried diversion instead.

'Mummy's up in the clouds isn't she? Like those up there.' He gave Jae a squeeze as he pointed to the apex.

The two quadrants at the top were populated by lighter souls, being guided towards a celestial saint by airborne angels. On the left, an emissary of God was placing souls into the pan of a counterbalance scale to ensure their consciences didn't weigh heavy. On the right, and in the spirit of the Old Testament, the principal angel was feeding the devil to a serpent, forcing him into its open jaws with a long pointed staff.

In the centre, running up the entire height of the piece, was a many-runged ladder. On the lower slats bodies slipped, lost their grip and fell into the clutches of the furies. Above the half-way level the figures climbed assuredly upwards, disappearing into a welcoming, white cloud at the pinnacle of the stairway.

The transport of man from sin to virtue. The ladder of ascension to God. The place where Heaven and Hell meet. The ladder of souls. Jacob's ladder. And at the foot of this ladder limbs were scorched. Limbs were peeling. Limbs were bleeding. Limbs were red. Legs were red. Red legs. Red legs with demons grasping, pulling. Little red legs kicking, flailing, being held, being pulled, being forced...

'Leave her alone' Scott yelled.

The demons stopped. They turned. They were looking at him. The gargoyle grimacing. The dog snarling. The cockerel cackling. They were coming for him now. Coming for his soul. A cleft hoof stepping out of the wall, landing heavy and huge on the stone at his feet, sending up a plume of dust. Charred flesh still hissing. Cadaverous arms reaching. Billowing with smoke, making him choke, making him wheeze. Talons swiping for him, catching his mouth, clasping his mouth. Flaking, shedding skin. Singed tissue pressed to his nose. The stench. The heat. Can't breathe. Nostrils flaring against his cheekbone. Searing his face. Squeezing his jaw. Rasping in his ear:

'Shut your little fucking mouth or I'll rip your little fucking tongue out.'

***

'Jesus baby Bro, you look like seven shades of shite.'

Good to know his sister hadn't thrown out her

Mancunian phrase book, even if she did have a transatlantic drawl.

'What is it with everybody tellin me a look shit all of a sudden?' He glanced down at the thumbnail video of himself in the corner of the screen. He was pale, drawn and unkempt. Everybody had a point.

'Because you do? Jokes aside Scott, you worry me. I was tryin to reach you on yer other username – how come you switched it out?'

'Oh yeah, sorry about that Sis. Just a bit of housekeeping you know, security and all that.'

'Did you get the book?' She was studying her screen, trying to gauge his reaction.

'I did, yeah.'

'So—'

'To be honest Sis I've only looked at it once. Sort of... creeped me out a bit.'

'It did?' She searched the web cam as if trying to meet his eyes. 'Why's that Scott?'

'Just... reminded me of summat.'

'What?' She leaned forward.

'I dunno for sure. Just made me feel creepy, like it reminded me of sumthin but I can't—' He shuffled in his seat.

She kept quiet, looking like she was torn between urging him on and treading carefully.

'I get these dreams, Bren. Nightmares. Least I think they're dreams; sometimes I don't know if I'm awake or asleep.'

'What's in these dreams?' Her eyes flicked from side to side.

'It's all mixed up. Some things are about Sal, about her hang…' He couldn't finish the word. 'But it's all mixed up with other stuff; stuff I don't—'

'Scotty, have you ever thought about talking to someone?'

'I talk to Em sometimes. I talk to you.'

'No I mean someone who can help you understand what it all means?'

'What, like a dreams interpreter or summat? Loada bullshit that is Bren.'

'No, I don't mean… I mean a therapist, psychologist, some who can help—'

'You think I'm going nuts, Sis, is that it? I just need a good fuckin nights' sleep is what I need.' He twisted the pads of his palms into his eye sockets.

'I see a therapist Bro – if I'm suggesting you're crazy than I must be too. It helps me. Helps me to deal with… To be honest Scott there's some things we need to talk about.'

'What sort of things?' He felt a growing sense of unease, like snakes sliding over each other inside him.

'It's, a lot of the stuff in my book, it's…' she struggled to find the words, 'it's stuff I don't want to kick up unless you have someone you can talk to.'

'I told you, I ta—'

'Someone professional.'

'A shrink? A flamin quack? Listen Brenna, I've got Frank and Carlo just lookin for reasons to declare me an unfit parent so they can take custody of Jae. Plus I've got Iain and

Roy hovering over each shoulder like a pair of vultures, waitin for me to screw up so they can get their claws into the rest of Da's business.'

'Roy's back? I thought he was away.'

Scott felt relieved that she'd suddenly changed tack. 'Yeah he's been hangin around for a few weeks this time.'

'*Uncle* Roy?'

'Don't know any others.'

'Scotty, why don't you and Jae come over here? You need a break. Get away. Come see us.' A sense of urgency bubbled beneath her thin film of calmness.

'Can't afford it Sis.'

'We'll pay your flights. Come on, book it. Stick it on my card. Shit I'll book it for ya.' She gave a twitch of a smile.

'I can't let you do that Brenna.'

'Yes you can. It'll give us chance to talk.'

'We're talking now.'

'Properly, I mean. Face to face. Not like this.'

'I can't Sis, I... I can't leave the country right now.'

'Can't leave the *country*? Waddaya mean, can't leave the country?'

'The police, they turned up here at stupid o'clock one morning last week and hauled me in for questioning. Give me a right bloody grillin.'

'Why? What for?'

'One of the lads that drives for us has been up to no good.'

'Anyone I know?'

'Steeley – you remember him from school? He was in your year wasn't he?'

'Steele... rings a—'

'You know, we used to say he was called Steele 'cause he was always on the pinch.'

'Oh, *Jezza*. Jeremy Steele?'

'The very same.'

'He always was a wrong 'un, that one. He works for you?'

'On and off... More *off* as it turns out.'

'What's he done?'

'Not sure. Some pretty serious shit.'

'But why does that stop you coming over? You're not under arrest are you?'

'Nah, but it's gonna look well dodgy me skippin the country after the pigs have asked me to stay put. Looks like I've got summat to hide.'

'We need to talk Scotty.'

'Listen Bren, just let me wait for the dust to settle. Then we'll be over there like shit off a shovel. I promise.'

CHAPTER 17: FLESH AND BLOOD

Tuesday

Roy popped his head around the office door. 'What's the craic Scotty lad?'

'Oh, aye Roy.' Scott shuffled the papers on his desk. He wasn't keen for his uncle to know what he was doing.

'Busy?' Roy's dodgy eye flickered.

'Oh just pissin around with numbers. Iain has me doin these soddin reports every Monday.'

'It's Tuesday.' Roy smiled.

'Aye, always is by the time I can be arsed to do it.' He dropped the spreadsheet with distain.

'Don't ye have some fancy electronic system for all that malarkey now?' Roy's eyes flicked over the contents of Scott's desk.

'Did have.' It slipped out before he could stop himself.

'What's that?'

'Notin… Brew?'

'Ye said "*did have*". What's that all about then?'

Scott sighed and started to craft a cigarette. He got up, sauntered as casually as he could past his uncle and flicked the kettle on.

'What's it all about?' He turned to Roy and lit his tab, squinting through the smoke. 'Good question Uncle Roy.

What's it all about?'

'Well?' Roy's eyelid stuttered.

'I wish I bloody knew. The pigs. They've got the friggin card reader. They seized it.'

'Oh aye? What's that all about then?'

It sounded like a question, but Scott wasn't entirely convinced. He drew slowly on his rollie, exhaling in a long, slow sigh. 'They think Jez has been up to mischief. Might get us into a bit of strife. Dunno yet. It's doin me nut in if I'm honest.'

'Iain know?' Roy said, rubbing his jaw.

'Bits and pieces. Not about the card reader. Tryin to get the report together to keep him sweet for now. If I give him what he expects to see, hopefully he'll ask no questions.'

'You did right Scotty, don't tell Iain just yet. He's enough on his plate with the rest of the businesses just now.'

'Oh, boo hoo, my heart bleeds' Scott said under his breath.

'You heard from Jez yourself lad?' Roy edged around the desk, pushing at the edges of the papers that were piled on it.

Scott eyed him from behind his smokescreen. 'No notin, not heard owt since he fucked off' he lied, some of his cards must be worth playing close to his chest. 'You?'

'Me what?' Roy looked up.

'You heard from him?'

'Me? Why would I hear from Jez? Hardly knew the man.' Roy's twitchy nerve made his eye flutter again.

'Knew?'

'Iain said he saw one of the wagons down by the quays

though. Two days ago.' Roy ignored his question and steadied his gaze. 'Thought it was you driving at first glance. So he said.'

'Must've been mistaken – I don't drive the wagons, as well he knows.' Scott threw his tab to the floor and killed it.

'Aye must've. Could it have been Jez?'

Scott shook his head. Then he shrugged. 'The pigs have got the card reader. And even if they hadn't, he wasn't using his flaming ID card.'

'Aye. Well keep me in the know, though, for now. Til we know what the craic is.' Roy made his way towards the door, pausing to take in a framed photo of Scott's sister, huddled up with Nate against a vividly unreal backdrop of golden, red and pink maple leaves.

'Beautiful picture, that.' He tapped the frame and turned around. 'How is she? Brenna?'

'She's good. They're good.' Scott nodded.

'Good. Aye that's what they say over the pond isn't it? Good. What ever happened to fine? I'm *fine*.' Roy's gaze lingered on the picture a little while before he said 'She was a bonny little girl was Bren. I'll never forget the day, few months before we came over here, when we were back home, Bren must've been four years old if a day.' Roy shook his head. 'She came running into the kitchen one day after school shouting *it's gone; it's gone*. We were like, what's gone Bren? *The road*, she said, *it's gone.*'

Scott's hands started to tremble, he occupied them with a Rizla and some fresh tobacco.

'We were right there Scotty.' He drew a line in the air with his hand. 'Almost split the farm in two. The borderland they called it.' His eyes grew distant as he cast his mind back. 'Broke your mother's heart to leave.'

'She never spoke about it.' Scott swallowed. His eyes stung.

'No. She wouldn't. There were streets, Scotty, that ye couldn't walk down. You'd go in one direction and there was just… notin. A flamin huge hole' Roy said, drawing an arc this time, 'the road just… dropped off the edge.' He looked up at his nephew. 'Gave a new meaning to one-way street. You wouldn't remember that though, I don't suppose.'

'Nope. Was too young. Bren might… just.'

'Aye. Bren might.' He tapped the photo. 'You're Ma begged me to come over here too, said she couldn't bear it if I stayed behind. She'd have never coped with the B&B alone for sure. You're Da worked long hours, you little 'uns ran her ragged. She'd have never been able to drum up the punters like I could. Ye remember us movin here, Scotty? Remember when the farm was a B&B?' Roy's eyes locked on Scott's like he was trying to see behind them.

'I… I don't remember much at all Uncle Roy. Not much at all.' Scott slumped into this office chair and picked up his papers as if intent on work.

'No. It seems. Like driving the wagon down by the quays?' Roy blink-winked.

Scott looked at him blankly.

'Seriously though Scotty, keep an eye on that. Forgettin tings. Ye don't want to go down that road again – the one that lead to your own black hole, if you'll pardon the pun.'

'When I lost it? That's what you're getting at Uncle Roy? When you had to step in?' He could feel his hackles rise.

Roy raised his palms 'Hey lad. I'm just lookin out for ye.' His voice oozed with balm. 'You know I'd do anytin for ye Scotty, yeah? You and Jae, ye me own flesh and blood.'

'Aye, I know that. I shouldn't—'

'Away wit ye now, I touched a nerve. It's I that should be sayin sorry. Ye just keep me in the know, mind?'

Scott nodded contritely.

'Forget this crap for now. Get out and have some fun. Get crackin on that dating site, meet ye self a nice gal.'

Scott placed the plate of beans on toast in front of Jae on the kitchen table then took out his phone and searched up some old episodes of Spiderman.

'There you go fella' he said as he propped the screen up on the phone's case.

'Does Spiderman eat beans on toast?' Jae said, spooning in a mouthful.

'Oh aye, Monkey, all the superheroes need their beans. You eat up now, Daddy needs to do something.'

Scott made his way into the living room and sat at his desk. The something he needed to do was to start getting his ass into gear ordering presents from Jae's Christmas list. The little man had written his letter to Santa weeks ago, mostly asking for wrestling and mixed martial arts memorabilia. Scott fired up the desk top and tapped 'Connor McGregor merch' into the search bar, then selected the images tab. A series of T-shirts and Christmas themed hoodies appeared. *Merry Christmas to absolutely fookin nobody* the fighter shouted from the page.

'My sentiments exactly, Connor.' Scott scrolled down through the images giggling at the thought of Jae turning up to Christmas jumper day at school sporting that little yuletide number. He didn't have the heart for Christmas shopping, though; he could be eating his figgy pudding behind bars for all he knew. His eyes wandered down over the optimised offerings, none of which were age appropriate. He sighed, resting his chin in his palm and stared at the white space between the pictures. The pixels started to wiggle and swim around each other like bacteria under a microscope as he mindlessly stroked the wheel on his mouse, scrolling endlessly through increasingly irrelevant search results. A movement on the bottom taskbar broke his trance. A green glow around a loading icon.

'Sweet Jesus, I forgot about you.' The onion finished dancing in circles and sat coiled like a viper. His heartbeat stuttered as he hovered over it, as if it might leap from the screen and strike him. He right-clicked hoping to tame it; hoping that the shortcut menu would offer a quick and painless way for him to neutralise it. The onion had other ideas though. The quick links it offered him were to be anything but painless. Instead it tempted him in with his recently closed pages. *New Flesh*.

He'd hit the target before he'd even pulled the arrow back.

Slashed and Burned it flaunted as the theme of the update. Three new thumbnails, this time looking as though they might be the same girl: dark skinned, where skin remained, and with long, raven-black hair which was matted and tangled and obscured her face. 'Cut her dead', 'Slash fiction' and 'Slow Burn II' were the titles of the trilogy and the LTC codes underneath them ranged from single to double-digits, rising with each instalment.

He clicked on the centre frame. The 'Slash fiction' page loaded, playing a continual loop of the teaser.

A hood over her head, naked from the waist down, some sick bastard stripping the flesh from her leg, blood leaching from her limbs.

He drew breath and winced, putting his hand to the screen as his stomach rolled over. Spinning the dial on the mouse, he flicked the scene out of sight. Underneath it there was a brief description. 'For those who like to get under the skin: 7 LiteCoin'. A 'Buy it now' button sat alongside 'Register' and 'Sign in' options.

'Daddy, can we watch it on the big telly?'

Scott's his heart surged as he resurfaced. He spun in his chair to see Jae standing behind him, holding the phone.

'Holy sh—' He felt woozy and sick with the bends, like he'd been yanked back from the black depths of *Skintrade* before he drowned.

'Can we Daddy? On the big telly?' He said with a bean-juice Joker grin.

'Sure we can sweetheart' he said between breaths, 'Sure we can.'

CHAPTER 18: SHORT BACK AND SIDES

Friday

Christmas. The season of joy and goodwill to all. Scott's most dreaded time of year. And this year it was seasoned with a liberal sprinkling of added trepidation. Whilst no news from the police could be taken as good news, he was still twitching through each day on tenter hooks. Propping up the kiosk end of the Kilt & Clover bar, he counted the shrapnel in his palm. Perhaps he could imbibe a drop of that balsamic spirit yet. He glanced up to check his place in the pecking order.

'Ey up, didn't know you were workin ere.' Scott's chipper tone veiled the shame that made him want to fold in on himself every time Kat caught him looking. His mind mockingly conjured up hazy drunken memories of him lasciviously pouring himself over her in the dark days following Sally's departure. Why had that shame not been spared by amnesia? He'd never grown the balls big enough to apologise for his behaviour, he'd chosen instead to plead the lesser offence of having a wasted blackout.

Kat attentively handed some change to another punter and turned to face him. 'Oh wow, I didn't recognise you.' Her green eyes lit up like a traffic light.

'Ah, yeah.' Scott smoothed a palm over the back of his head. 'Em's always tellin me to get a fu— friggin haircut. Still feels well weird.' He rubbed the clippered nape of his neck as if dusting off some itchy, prickly hairs. The truth is that he thought a short-back-and-sides and a clean shave would play better in court should Jez's antics bring him before *that* bar.

'Beard's gone too, you really did take her advice.' She smiled.

He switched to rubbing his naked chin. Warmth radiated across his cheeks, partly because she was being friendly and he felt contrite; partly because she looked incredible.

'It was good advice.' She looked directly into his eyes. 'All you need is a newsboy's cap and you'd look like a *roight fookin Blinder*' she said, breaking into laughter. As she did the pink gloss on her lips caught a glint of the downlights in the overhead glasses shelf. 'Looks nice.'

Nice. Why did she have to say nice? Now he wasn't sure if it was a platitude or a genuine complement. Flecks of light flitted across the olive skin of her face and neck as the tinsel draped above them fluttered on the breeze of the air con. Its magical quality fixated him the way fresh snowfall does. He was almost feeling festive.

'You can see your face' she added after a slightly uncomfortable pause.

'And that's a good thing?' He hooked his right eyebrow. Given their history it was a valid question.

'Yeah, that's a good thing. You look younger.'

Perhaps it was a genuine complement after all. 'OK. I'll take that.' He grinned, scooping the ghost of his fringe out of his eyes as an amputee would scratch a missing limb.

'And what else will you take?' She motioned towards the beer pumps, her arm unfolding and sweeping across them like a magician's assistant unveiling a set of swords.

He resisted the urge to say 'You. Now. On this bar.' It seemed like his past indiscretions had been forgiven but better not push his luck.

'Pinta Boddies please Kat.' He didn't like Boddingtons,

but the pump was at the other end of the bar and Kat had a fantastic ass, wrapped in snug, dark blue jeans. She nodded obediently, turned and squeezed by Billy the Landlord, who jumped and squealed playfully as she passed, as if she'd pinched his bum.

'Jammy get.' Scott murmured as his gaze grew tendrils that snaked down the narrow bar after her and, like a dirty Mr Tickle, caressed her behind. She may have shed a few pounds but Kat was no waif. She had womanly curves, these days in all the right places.

He turned his attention to counting his small change, almost dropping it when a hefty shoulder barge landed as a customer wedged himself into a gap at the busy bar. He turned to admonish the jostler, only to find Trev's partially turned back in his face.

'Areet mate.' Scott gently nudged his elbow against Trev's chubby arm.

Trev turned and eyeballed the stranger through a squint. 'Fuck a duck,' he said after a pause to process, 'thought for a minute some ponce was tryin to get in me knickers.' He pushed his thick-rimmed glasses up his nose.

'Being the fine specimen of masculinity that you are Trev, I imagine they find it hard to control themselves.'

'What the fuck happened to yer head? Had a scrap with a John Deere or a bad case o'lice?' He was still eyeing Scott as if he were an imposter.

'You're all charm Trev.' Scott shifted uncomfortably under Trev's magnified stare. He cleared his throat. 'Mate, don't suppose you've heard owt from Jez have ya? He's gone AWOL. Again.'

'That useless piece o'shite.' Trev shoved his other shoulder up against another of the waiting clientele, giving him a jolt. Trev's bulldog expression silently asked the guy if he had a fuckin problem. 'As it happens I did have a word. Don't think you'll be hearin from that clueless cunt any time soon.' The other customer overheard him and shuffled away.

'Oh yeah?' Scott swallowed 'What did you say?' He was starting to wish he hadn't asked.

'Not so much what I said, more a case of what our Micky did. Difficult to drive with your arm in a sling. Heh-heh.' He punched Scott on the shoulder with less-than-friendly force. 'No weaselly little cunt fucks me about and gets off scott free.' He turned and pinned Scott with a hard glare. 'Put Barry on the job, he's a good lad.'

'Tell you what Trev why don't you come by the office and plan all the friggin logistics for me?' Scott refused to appear intimidated, even if he was.

'I'd do a fuck sight better job of it than you, ya dopey prick.' Trev craned his neck, trying to catch the eye of Kat. 'Christ, what am I, the invisible fuckin man?' He stuck his hand up and waved. 'New barmaid's a waste o'space and all. Nice arse though.' Failing to hail her, he tried a more vocal tactic 'Oi Billy lad, stick a pint on the end of the bar for us will ya? McCabe'll pay for it.'

'I will?' Scott looked at the coins in his hand.

'If ya tryin to fuck me the least ya can do is get me pissed first.' He slapped Scott on the back, enough to make it sting. 'Anyway, y'owe us a pint for gettin rid of that dickhead driver of yours.'

'Aye, you may have done us a bigger favour than you think' he said into his collar.

'Talk Monday, gotta new job for ya.' Trev cocked his forefingers and thumb like a gun.

'It's bloody Boxing Day on Monday.'

'And? I'll bring you a Christmas Box, how about that?' He pulled the trigger and left Scott agape.

Kat had finished pulling his pint and was making her way back over to him. She carefully lowered it through the beer taps and onto the counter, reaching out for his money with her free hand. The move squeezed her breasts together underneath her skin-tight black vest. The compulsion to look down got the better of him.

'Ta chuck, take for Trev's pint an'all. What does the 'E' stand for?' The cunning ruse to camouflage his ogling as an interest in her pendant also afforded him the opportunity to subtly explore the potential of a significant other.

'My name.' She tossed her curls over her shoulder. His vacant expression prompted her to add 'Ekatarina. It's Bulgarian… My Dad's Bulgarian.'

'Ah, that explains it then.' His heart was pummelling his chest. He shoved his hands in his pockets to disguise his jitteriness.

'Explains what?'

'Your Mediterranean beauty.' He gulped, trying to sound casual.

'Balkan to be precise' she chastised with a smile. 'But I'll forgive you.'

'Give us a pack of cheese an'onion too please Ekatarina.' He winked, partly to cover a nervous twitch in his eyelid. 'You working here full time now then?'

'Few shifts a week.' She bent double and plucked a packet of crisps from the box on the floor. He could have asked for Emma's favourite flavour, but where was the fun in asking for one kept at waist height? 'Just needed a bit of extra cash.' She emerged, tossing the crisps onto the bar. 'And a distraction.' She glanced over her shoulder, checking to see if anyone was waiting to be served. Or, it appeared to Scott, she made it look as if that's what she was doing.

'Distraction from what?' He risked reaching for his drink. His neck juddered as he dipped in the take a slurp. He felt like an adolescent trying to chat up his first crush. 'Sorry, tell me to fuck off.'

'Dickhead ex' she said, almost to herself, then turned back to face him. 'Do you still like a smoke?'

'Indeed. I'm one of the unenlightened.' Realising his ironic choice of words he added 'So to speak.'

'Give me a shout when you go for one. I'll see if Bill will let me sneak out for a quickie.'

'Hello? Happy Christmas' he said, laughing.

'A *ciggie*. Filthy mind.' She pouted then swung round making sure he got an eyeful of her fulsome butt. He stood at the bar long enough to let her know that he was watching then grabbed his drink and weaved his way over to Kirk and Emma who were resident, like pieces of pub furniture, at their usual table.

'Bout bloody time, my stomach thinks my throat's been cut.' Emma swiped the crisps from Scott's hand, almost taking his drink with it.

'Ey, steady on.' He sat down then raised his dripping pint. 'Greetings of the season.' Emma and Kirk grumbled, scrooge-like, as they clinked their glass rims against his.

'New admirer?' Kirk rolled his eyes as if to say *he's at it again*.

'Don't blame you matey. Kat looks fit as all hell these days.' Emma leaned backwards to improve her view of the bar. Kirk tutted.

'Bit short. Great backside though.' Scott winked and dug

his accomplice in the ribs. Kirk scored a hat-trick of disapproving gestures.

'Cheese and bloody onion? I *hate* cheese an'onion. Didn't they have any salt an'vinegar?' She begrudgingly tugged at the seal.

'Not on the bottom shelf they didn't' Scott smirked. He'd endured Boddingtons in the name of a good view, and if Emma had been there to share it, she would have gladly taken cheese and bloody onion.

'And here's me thinking you were losing your touch… You've not asked me to babysit for a few weeks' she blurted through a muzzle of crisps.

'Nah. Knocked the internet dating on the head. Bunch of flamin nutters the lot of 'em.'

'I told you not to go for that one that looked like Cruella de Vil. Christ, she had more metalwork in her face than that geezer from Hellraiser.' Kirk sipped his beer sanctimoniously.

'You're not wrong, buddy, she *was* a hell raiser.' He exchanged knowing glances with Emma. 'I was gonna block her but then I thought, sod it, I'm done with the whole bloody thing. Deleted me profile. At least I think I did.' He took a swig from his pint then quivered as if he'd gargled with vinegar. 'Kirk – is it possible to wipe files off your computer so that even the police can't recover them?'

'You been looking at those dodgy websites again?' Kirk chuckled, oblivious. Scott didn't flinch, but he could feel heat flush his face.

'Digital forensics are pretty sophisticated these days.' Kirk said, gearing up for a geek-fest.

'Digi-what?' Scott feigned indifference by forcing down another mouthful of insipid beer.

'Digital forensics. The police have specialists that analyse computers, phones, tablets, you name it. It's like digital archaeology. They have all kinds of diagnostics that can piece together what someone's been up to, even if some of the data's been deleted. They call it tracing a digital footprint. Clever stuff. Why do you wanna know?'

He nodded in approval at Emma who had shoved the foil bag under his nose, more to get rid of the offending snacks than to be generous.

'Ah, it's just to settle an argument I was havin with one of the lads. He reckons the police can recover anything. I said if I could find a way to prove him wrong I would. We got a tenner on it.'

'Well—' Kirk crunched, 'technically you can't stop the police from running whatever data mining tools they've got if they have good reason. But if you're smart enough—' he swallowed, 'you might be able to booby trap your system with a failsafe.'

'Failsafe? What's that when it's at home?' Scott waivered his turn as the crisps came his way.

'Failsafes are back-up tools that are installed to do something similar to what you're talking about – if your computer fails they keep critical data safe.'

'That's not what I need though… to *know about*, I mean.'

'Yeah, yeah, hold yer horses. Hackers can rig failsafes to do the opposite of what they were designed for. In other words, if the system fails – or if the booby trap is triggered – they encrypt all the data. Or hide it. Or corrupt it. Or permanently erase it. There's a number of ways to skin the same cat.' He gulped his pint as the salt hit his throat.

'Is it summat you could do?'

'Dunno. I'd have to do some research, but searching for

stuff like that can get your name flagged on all kinds of watch lists that I don't want to appear on. Bet Frank would know all about it.'

'No thanks. Frank would rather skin me than the proverbial cat. I'm not asking that tosser for notin. Still, I reckon you've told me enough to win me a tenner. Your next pint's on me mate.' Scott tapped his breast pocket to check for his Marlboro before getting to his feet. 'Can't drink anymore o' this pish. I'll get a round in on me way back.'

'Way back from where?' Emma was scouring the greasy lining of the crisp bag with her finger for the crusty remnants.

'I got a date. With a certain barmaid and a pack o'ten.'

'Bloody hell, Ron Jeremy, how many jonnies do you need?' She giggled as Kirk's eyes rolled skyward again.

'I wish.' Scott flashed a smile. 'Just gonna have a ciggie with Kat.' He pulled his jacket off the seat of his stool and headed towards the bar.

'And get some salt and bloody vinegar.' Emma hollered after him.

'Thought you smoked rollies?' Kat took the tanned tip of the cigarette that stood proud of the other suspects in the line-up.

'Bit of both. Depends on how self-destructive I'm feeling', he glinted 'easier to chain smoke tailor-mades.' Scott flipped the lid on his Clipper, spun the flint wheel and leant in towards her with the flame. They both lit at the same time. Out there under the moon, shivering in Billy's poorly constructed gazebo-cum-bus-shelter trimmed with fairy lights, the moment almost had a *Lady and the Tramp* romanticism about it.

'You're cold, here take this.' He slipped off his beaten up leather jacket and draped it around her shoulders. She assisted, accidentally touching his hand. He instinctively recoiled, not wanting to put her in mind of his latter-day, whiskey-and-grief-fuelled lechery.

'Listen, Kat.' He started to shake, not entirely because of the chill in the air. 'I, its long fuckin overdue, I know, but I'm really sorry for... you know—'

'Oh Jesus, Scott, are you *really* still feeling guilty because you got a bit fresh when you were drunk? Believe me, I've had much worse than that...' She paused, gazing at her Converse and rubbing the toes together. 'Much worse. You were having such a terrible time back then. I wasn't pissed off. To be honest I—'

'Please don't say you felt sorry for me.'

'No, it's not that, I was just... I was selfishly wishing it didn't take you to be plastered and bereft to find me attractive.' She kept her face lowered but raised her eyes. Her eye lashes sparkled with glitter like magic wands.

'I was being an arsehole. I'd lost control.' He shook his head.

'They say grief is the price you pay for love. You must have loved her very much.' Her eyes glistened and the end of her nose shone rubescent. Scott couldn't make out if it was the biting cold or something more.

'I was angry.' He tossed his smoke then studied his hands. Without thinking he curled the right one into a ball and folded the other over it. 'Still am sometimes.'

Scott turned to face Kat. He took the spiral of one of her brunette ringlets and curled it around his finger. Her pale green irises and dusky lure drew him back to the moment. He traced the profile of her cheek with his fingertips. 'What is it that Billy Crystal says in *When Harry Met—*' he sighed. "'What's the statute of limitations on apologies?'"

'About three years.' She twinkled, darting the firefly stub of her cigarette into the night.

'Ooh, I can just get in under the…' He leaned in and tentatively pressed his lips to hers. She melted into a long, soft, warming kiss '… wire.' Her pupils pulsed as he stroked her chin with his thumb and whispered 'I'm sorry.'

He put his arm around her and she settled into the crook of his shoulder.

'Tell you what it's bloody *freezing* with short hair. My ears are killin.' He laughed, puncturing the membrane of intensity with some archetypal superficiality. 'Was better off being a scruffy fucker.'

'I have to disagree. You look well—'

'Don't say cute.'

'I was going to say sexy.' She tilted her eyes up to his and caressed his earlobe. 'You look well sexy.'

'Ah, now you're gonna get me blushin. You're very sexy yourself Kat. Very sexy.' They kissed again, slowly and tenderly. A small ember of belief throbbed and flared in his chest. It warmed his blood, loosening the rime that had put his heart on ice for so long. Molten amber flowed through his veins and glowed behind his eyes.

They pulled apart and looked at each other without saying anything, both seeming to be blindsided by the potency of their connection. So they basked together in silence under the flickering lights.

'I'll bet Jae is excited about Santa coming tomorrow night.' Kat said after a few ponderous moments.

'Yeah, it's driving me nuts. I try so hard to be on it for

him but… it's such a tough time of year. Does it sound selfish to say I dread it?'

'I don't know anyone who doesn't. Let's face it, if your life is anything short of perfect Christmas is a total ball-ache.'

'Couldn't put it better meself. Bloody hate it if I'm totally honest. This year is *really* fucked up.'

Kat looked like she was going to ask why but then thought better of it. 'Perhaps we can cheer each other up.' She nestled into his neck.

'Ah, yeah, you need a distraction' he said, rubbing her shoulder. 'So how come you started work here then?'

'The Christmas money helps, but… mostly I didn't want to be home alone in the evenings. Wanted to be out of the flat, amongst people. It suits me just fine.'

'Anything you want to tell us about?' He cradled her in both arms, touching her forehead with a delicate peck.

'Not right now – long story.' She stroked his arm as it rested across her chest, tracing a figure of eight on it and nudging an object underneath the sleeve of his hoodie. She hooked up the edge of the cotton jersey. 'Wow, that's some bling.'

'Wear it outta duty.' He pinched the cuff with the thumb and forefinger of his draping hand and pulled it back over the gaudy plexus of dials on his wrist. 'Do you have a day job Kat?' His watch-bearing arm slipped down. He softly stroked the top of her leg.

'I'm a legal secretary for a solicitor's in town. Mitton Allock?' She reciprocated, resting her hand on his inner thigh. 'Hoping to train to be a barrister someday. When I can save enough for the course fees.'

'Clever as well as beautiful.' He moved in for another

kiss, this time pressing harder and gently probing her lips with his tongue. She let out a light moan. He pulled back gave her a cockeyed smile. 'Your lip stuff tastes good.' He tried to lick it off.

'Looks better on me than on you.' She smiled, drawing her thumb across his bottom lip.

'So what kind of law do you deal with?' He leant towards her and brushed her cheek with his.

'Most of it is the usual stuff' she whispered between kisses. 'Family mediation…'

'Mmm…' He enticed her with his tongue.

'… corporate crisis…'

'Oh Kay…' Kissed her nose and cheeks.

'… employment law…'

'That so…' Pressed his mouth to hers.

'… fraud…' she breathed, '…criminal law—'

'Criminal?' He withdrew a little.

'Yeah, everyone finds that one interesting. That's what I want to do.' She straightened up sensing he had tensed. 'You OK?'

The back door shot open and a shaft of yellow light, haloing a squat, rotund silhouette, spilled across the cobbled yard.

'Oi, Katy' Billy boomed, 'I'm not payin ya to sit on your arse all night. Nice arse though it may be, I need it back behind this bar.'

'I *haaaate* being called Katy' she breathed into Scott's collar bone.

'Aye, he's a proper, old-school, patronising perv is our

Bill.' Scott rose up guiding her to the door. As he took back his jacket he slipped his hand down over the seat of her jeans. 'I'll watch this lovely backside for you. Anyone gives you grief, you tell me.' He chanced one last peck on her lips.

Ping.

'Is that you or me?' She tapped her hip 'Ah, can't be me. Left it inside.'

Tugging the handset from his jacket pocket he clocked a small red circle hovering over the messages app. He tapped the icon as she turned towards the door.

Date with Fate: CheriBrandi has been looking at you. Login now to get chatting.

'Eh?'

'I'll stick my phone number on a beer mat for you' she said over her shoulder as she skipped back into the pub.

***

'Charley?'

He crept down the hall towards the quivering slithers of light beneath the living room door. High pitched shrieks gave way to the deep, throaty thrum of a bow scraping across the strings of a double bass. It reverberated through the floorboards with every purposeful step. Reaching the door, he pressed his ear to the stripped pine; a sound like shale running through an egg timer.

'Charley?'

He edged the door open. It ground out a testy groan. An array of DVD cases and discs were scattered across the hearth rug. On the TV set Janet Leigh's huge dead eye filled the screen. As the camera slowly spiralled backwards droplets of water rested on her lower lashes like tears. Charley was face down on the sofa, one arm draped off its edge with the hand flopped into a toppled bowl of popcorn. Her slack jaw mirrored the on screen victim.

'Psst. Charley.'

"Mother! Oh God Mother! Blood! Blood!"

She stirred. 'Oh God. What? Oh… my arm's gone dead.' She pushed herself up and sat back on her haunches, rubbing her numbed bicep back to life.

'Everything OK tonight?' He picked up the remote and paused the movie. The freeze fame caught Norman Bates recoiling in horror, mouth clamped with his palm.

'Oh yeah. Fine. Thanks for leaving out the box set of *Harry's TV Burp*, we watched the *whole* series.' She feigned delight.

'Sorry, the latest in a long line of obsessions. How you doing? Uni going OK?'

'Gagging for the Christmas break. This year is sooo much more intense than first year.'

'Ah, you're a clever girl, you'll cope.'

She unfolded her legs and massaged her feet. 'Jae was well hyper. He's sooo excited about Santa coming tomorrow night. Took me ages to get him settled.'

'Notin to do with the tonne of toffee popcorn of course.' He righted the bowl and used it to scoop up the miscreant pieces. 'Sod it, it's Christmas.' He winked, then threw one of the nuggets into the air and caught it in his mouth. 'On the subject of that, here you go.' He reached into his jeans pocket and shoved a crumpled pile of notes into her hand.

'You're pissed again Scott. You always pay me too much when you're drunk. And you're drunk every Friday.' She started to fan through the notes. 'You don't *seem* pissed though…'

'I'm not. Just a little Christmas bonus. Go and get yerself rat-arsed. At your age if you're not wantin chuck into your Chrimbo dinner you ain't tryin hard enough.'

'Wow thanks. Blimey you've changed your tune. Christmas was the work of the Devil before you went out. You sure you're not drunk?'

'Nah, just had a good night.' He gave her a smug smile.

'You? Having a good night without getting bladdered?'

'Call it festive spirit.'

'Call it meeting a new woman by any chance?'

'That obvious?'

Ping.

'Bet that's her now. I'll get out of your hair so you can get on with sexting or phone sex or whatever it is that you oldies do.' She put her fingers down her throat and gagged. 'Oh, I forgot' she said, rubbing his crew cut, 'I can't get out of your hair coz you don't have it anymore. Ha-ha.'

'Ged-out-avit ya cheeky fucker.'

She pushed her feet into her ballet shoes and slipped her arms into the sleeves of her parker. 'Happy Christmas Scott' she said, giving him a quick peck on the cheek.

He followed her out into the hallway. 'And you. Drive safe Charley.' He clicked the door shut behind his babysitter.

'Phone sex. *Eew*' he heard from the other side of the door. He shook his head and chuckled as she mumbled her way out into the courtyard. Plucking his phone from his jacket, a scrap of card came with it and fell onto the rug. He bent down and rescued the piece of beermat. The top layer of cardboard had been carefully peeled away. Kat's name and number were scrawled across its rough, exposed dermis.

'Mmmm. Phone sex.' He tapped the mat across his knuckles and flipped his phone over to key in the number. Emma's name was splashed across his screen. He swiped to read it:

Got you an Xmas pressie. Don't get choked up – it cost me nowt. You were outside for a long time…

He thumbed a quick reply.

You gonna tell me what it is or keep me in suspenders…?

He watched the grey bubble pulse.

Ping.

Give you a clue. I'm always telling you get a fuckin new one.

Haircut? Done.

Ping.

That thing you're always fiddling with…

Haha. You of all people ain't gonna hand me one of those ;-)

Ping.

Gross. Gonna keep you in suspenders then. You didn't answer my question.

What question?

Ping.

About tonight. Outside with Kat?

That wasn't a question.

Ping.

Now you're just being pedantic. I shall feel free to read into that whatever my dirty little mind wants to.

You do that.

See ya tomoz Em.

Ping.

Killjoy. I'll get it out of you tomorrow. Nite.

He'd wandered into the kitchen as he was texting. Dregs of single malt lay in the base of the bottle on the side. Grabbing a tumbler he syphoned it into the glass, stalling in the hallway to listen for any signs of movement upstairs. All quiet.

He strolled back towards his living room, dumping his mobile on the coffee table en route to the computer desk in the corner of the room. Bubbles of anticipation started to effervesce inside him. He threw the shredded beermat onto the desk and lifted the receiver of the landline. He looked at the keypad, breathed in deeply then flopped into the swivel chair. His finger hovered over the digits. He bolstered himself with a nip of Whiskey and keyed in Kat's number. Before he could think better of it, hit the call button. The call tone pealed through the earpiece. He drummed his fingers in time with its rhythm.

Click.

'Heh... hello?'

'Kat, it's Scott. Is it too late?' He grunted, trying to quell the quiver in his voice.

'Oh, hi Scott. No it's fine, I'm always wired after work. Just thought for a minute you might be someone else.'

'Someone else better or someone else worse?' He giggled.

'Sorry, didn't mean it to sound like that. I'm glad it's you.'

'I enjoyed tonight. It was really—'

'Nice?' She laughed.

'Yeah, nice. Very nice.'

'It was kind of weird, like, a connection. I wasn't expecting you to—'

'I wasn't intending to. Well, actually that's a lie. I wanted to kiss you from the moment I laid eyes on you.'

'You look great with short hair. You were… good looking before, but it really suits you.'

'Bloody glad I did it now. You around at all over Christmas?'

'Maybe, it's a bit full on, what with extra shifts at the Clover and fitting in all the family obligations…'

'Yeah, tell me. Got my folks coming over. Joy.'

'You don't get on with them?'

'I do, we just… don't see the world the same way. Let's just say my watch was their fortieth birthday present to me. It's like *that* level of not seeing eye-to-eye.'

'You wear it. I won't say well.'

'You don't have to. They're my folks. They mean well.'

'Listen, Scott, I have to go just now but call me again. This number – is it your landline?'

'Yeah, moby needs charging' he fibbed, for some reason not wanting to taint the purity of their connection with the shallow encounters in his inbox. 'I'll text ya when it's back up.'

'Please do. Night Scott.'

'Night Kat. Would be great see you again. Go for a walk sometime?'

'Yeah, that sounds… nice.' She snickered. 'I really want to see you too.'

Click.

Ping.

His handset was face-down on the coffee table. He moved to pick up but instead he grabbed the TV remote lying next to it. He dismissed Norman Bates's terror as if he were Arbogast rebuffing his innocence. The DVD player whirled to a stop. He flicked over to the TV. The familiar face of the regional newscaster was etched with earnest reverence. On the screen behind her appeared a smiling selfie of a young woman.

A bolt of white, blazing panic shot through his thorax like a bullet.

'The police are growing increasingly concerned for the welfare of twenty-six year old Kulbir Zafar who was reported missing by her family two weeks ago.'

'Fuck. Me.'

'Co-workers at the Warrington and Halton Hospitals NHS Trust raised the alarm after the junior doctor failed to show up for work. Police are making a fresh appeal for information regarding her whereabouts following the release without charge of a sixty-three year-old man and a thirty-two year-old man.'

The live broadcast cut to a VT of a stolid, middle-aged, sandy-haired detective with a glaucomatous cloud of cynicism fogging his eyes; the sediment from a lifetime of suspicion. Scott could still feel the cold film of sweat on his brow that DI Woods's gaze precipitated.

'Colleagues of Miss Zafar have told us she had arranged to meet up with a man, possibly someone she had met through an internet dating website. We are very keen to trace this man to eliminate him from our inquiries.'

'Fucking, fucking hell.'

He killed the TV and kneaded his forehead. Could Woods have suspected something when he questioned him?

Was the investigation into Jez a ruse? He struggled quell a rising undercurrent of panic; to resist being drawn into the eddy that was gathering speed behind his eyes.

His phone. In the silence it seemed that the *ting* of the incoming alert still rang in the air. Dread passed through him, cold like a ghost. He reached for his handset and flipped it over. A red circle hovered in the corner of his messages app. Swallowing, he tapped it.

Date with Fate: Kul4abeer has been looking at you. Login now to get chatting.

'Get the fuck—' He dropped the phone as if he'd been tasered.

Scott cradled himself, shuddering with the aftershock of the bolt. He rocked to and fro trying to lull himself calm, but with each muscle twitch a visceral freeze-frame flared before his eyes. Fleeting pictures pulled from his depths like particles of iron being drawn by a magnet. Rorschach impressions at first, but each image appearing more clearly than the last. His thumbs clamped around a delicate windpipe. His skinning blade slicing through tissue. Fistfuls of flesh. Flensing skin from muscle. Sinew and bone. A slit jugular. A deluge of blood. Red. Screaming. Red. Crying. Red.

His blood ran cold. He shivered hot. A storm of self-doubt rose and twisted inside him, thundering between his temples. Memories? Secrets? Nightmares? He squeezed his eyes shut and pressed his palms to his ears. *Stop it.* Holding it in. *Shut the fuck.* Can't let it out. *Shut the fuck up. Shut the fuck up.*

CHAPTER 19: UNDER THE SKIN

Sunday

Peals of polite laughter fell like pine needles around Peggy as she indulged in her annual rendition of Tree-Chocolate-Gate. One Christmas morning she and Seth had arose to find a three-year-old Scott perched quietly underneath the reaches of the conifer. A heady aroma of resinous-cocoa clung to the air like a badly concocted festive air-freshener. It was only when they came to share out the tree chocolates between him and Brenna that the source of the brown smudges on his cheeks and chin became apparent to his parents. Every confectionary delight that dangled from low hanging branches had been meticulously skinned of its foil and eviscerated. The empty aluminium husks were painstakingly sutured back together so that, to the inattentive eye, they looked whole again. For some reason the ritual re-telling of this banal tale had become McCabe festive folklore. He couldn't remember the incident, but he knew it inside out.

'He was a glic bugger, as we say. We couldn't *believe* it. I didn't know whether to feel pride or shame.'

'Ha-ha. You always were good at gutting things, Scotty lad.' Seth shouted the comment through the open door of the kitchen where the parents were sharing a seasonably early gin and tonic with Emma. Scott and Kirk were playing chair-Tetris around a drop-leaf table that was too small to seat them all. Jae was feeling the tree chocolates, just to make sure his Dad hadn't been up to his old tricks.

'Sod this.' Scott huffed.

'You got a bigger table anywhere?' Kirk was sat at one of place settings testing the elbow room. Norman wrapped herself around his ankles.

'Aye. In the office. Help us grab it?'

'Lead the way.' He took care to shuffle his legs free before standing, having stumbled over the Norman foot stool on too many occasions.

Scott unconsciously slipped a ready-made into his mouth as they made their way out. He needed some fresh air. Christmas made him feel boxed in. Always had. He stopped on the threshold and took a long toke on his cigarette.

'You OK?' Kirk blew a stream of vapour into the frosty atmosphere, whimsically recalling what it felt like to smoke.

'Aye' he lied, then thought better of it. 'Just Christmas. Does me nut in. It's life, Jim, but not as we knew it.' He fleetingly raised his brows, bled the fag dry in a single draw and tossed it.

'It's a tough time of year mate.' Kirk drew in his upper lip and nodded.

'It's worse than that...'

'You just gotta get through it. Make sure the little man has a good one.' Scott knew that Kirk's prim sense of humour wasn't worth testing with innuendo so he held his tongue.

'Yeah, you're right Kirk. I know you are. Thanks for coming over. I'd seriously lose it here wit' me folks if it weren't for you and Em.'

'You can return the favour tomorrow when mine are over.' He slapped Scott on the shoulder and ushered him across the cobbles.

The erratic whirring and clicking of the hard drive caught Kirk's attention as soon as they entered the office. 'You wanna shut that down, Scott. It'll overheat.' He made his way over to the desk, feeling down the side of the tower casing. 'It's bloody hot.'

Scott stood in the doorway. Something wasn't right.

'I didn't leave it…' His words evaporated as he studied the room. It looked like a facsimile of his office, like a double exposure in which everything was doppelgangered but fractionally out of sync. Papers had been slightly disturbed. Objects subtly moved. Or did it just feel that way?

He caught up with his friend who was, by now, shaking the mouse to bring the system to life. It responded slowly and when it finally roused from its sleep, asked for a password.

'Better shut it down, mate, before it does some serious damage to your motherboard.' He stepped aside and let Scott do the driving.

Sitting at the keyboard he had the same uncanny feeling of everything being strange in its familiarity. Familiar. Similar. But not the *same*. His eye was drawn to a hand-written note. It bore a scruffy hand, scribbled in a hurry, but it was his own.

Riverside

He rattled his brain trying to tease forward the memory that the note was intended to jog. Could be a pub. Could be a restaurant. Had he talked about meeting up with Kat there? A previous date maybe? He keyed in his password and tapped the return key. The *Date with Fate* logo leapt off the screen.

It took a few moments for him to take in the rest of the page. It was his inbox. He had received a despatch from a new affiliate, *MrMacabre49*. It simply read:

I know it was you.

'Holy crap.' In a lightening reflex he clicked the 'X' in the corner of the page to kill it.

'What is it mate?' Kirk spun around, he had wandered across the room to another desk and was sizing it up for seating capacity. 'You look like you've seen a ghost.'

Scott didn't reply. He clicked on the member's pseudonym, intending to block whoever the hell it was.

This profile has been removed.

'I deleted my account' he said to himself more than to Kirk. He clicked 'back' and scanned the inbox headlines. 'I *deleted* it.' None of the communications were dated beyond the day he was pulled in for questioning. Did he imagine the mystery contact? Shaking his head clear, he navigated back to his profile page and once again selected the 'Cancel and remove' button.

'Just when I thought I was out…' Kirk assumed a throaty, New Jersey drawl and grasped at the air with both fists '…they pull me back in.' He yanked them melodramatically towards his chest, then straightened up, intuiting that his friend had failed to see the funny side.

'Shut this goddamn thing down. Shut it down.' Scott poked around the desktop until, with a last gasping whine, the screen faded to black. He sat staring at it, his heart was beating so hard that his wrists throbbed.

'Will this one fit the bill Sir?' Kirk was gesturing towards the desk with a stained, crumpled tea towel from the brewing-up bench draped over his forearm.

Scott massaged his temples. 'Er, yeah. Yeah, that'll be fine. Let's get the fuck out of Dodge.'

His legs were restless. Sitting there watching his parents inundate his son with pricey gifts, his knees bobbed up and down like he was at a spinning class. He laid a palm on each quad in an attempt to quell his jitters, then reached for his beer. Alcohol should do the trick, if more chicanery was what he needed.

'Oh. That's very… generous.' One corner of his mouth lifted; he tried to disguise his displeasure. 'Say thank you to Grandma and Grandad, Jae.' Scott had been holding off buying Jae a tablet – if his boy's predisposition for bingeing on anything that mobilised the brain's pleasure sensors was akin to his own, having a kick about in the yard could well be a thing of the past.

'Thank you Grandma. Thank you Grandad.' Jae launched himself at each of his grandparents in turn, rhapsodic with his new gadget.

'You're welcome sweetheart.' 'Ah, you're a good lad.' They said in chorus.

'So have *you* been a good boy Scotty?' Emma reached into her bag and pulled out a small box, gauchely wrapped.

'Depends on your definition of good.' He winked as he took it from her. 'Ta Em, you shouldn't have.'

'I didn't. It's a freebie.'

Scott wrangled with the layers of Cellotape. 'Jesus, Em, Fort Flamin Knox would be easier to break into.'

'Sorry, I'm shi—' She glanced at Jae who was oblivious, busy as he was trying to download Minecraft with his Grandad. 'I'm crap at wrapping.'

'I know, I've seen the YouTube videos.' Eventually he liberated the gift from its tenacious sheathe. 'Bloody hell. Thanks Em.' He tossed the nearly new Samsung phone from one hand to the other.

'Someone's got to drag you screaming into the twenty-first century. It's been kicking around the office for weeks. There's new devices being released all the time so I don't think it'll be missed. Gave it a good review, this one.' She smiled. 'It's got a pay as you go sim in there for now – you'll need to do a sim swap if you want to port your number.'

'Port? The only port I know has a vintage and goes well wit cheese.'

'It means *keep* it, dozer. Sim's got twenty quid's worth of credit, coz that's just the sort of charitable gal I am.' She flicked her imaginary long hair.

'So that came as a freebie too, yeah?' He tossed her a sardonic grin.

'Something like that.'

'Huge screen' he said as he thumbed the power switch.

'Perfect for all those selfies you take with Jae' she said, smirking. 'Kirk…' Emma reached into her Santa's sack once more, 'this is for you matey.'

'Aw, cheers Em.' His cheeks flushed.

Scott left Kirk wrestling with his own tightly bound parcel as he excused himself and slipped towards the hallway. He nipped into the kitchen and replaced his empty tinny with a fresh one from the fridge.

'Oh, what? A Poke Ball charger – that's magic.' Kirk said with even more puerile delight than Jae.

Scott scuttled up to the living room door and eased it onto the latch. He shook his head and muttered to himself about how Kirk and Jae were on the same intellectual level, if that didn't belittle his boy. Then he sloped up the stairs to seek out some privacy, collapsed onto his bed and fished out the crumpled piece of beermat that he'd been transferring from one pair of jeans to another. Bloody hell he could barely read the number. While he could still make it out, he tapped it into his new handset and saved it under *Kat*. Then he hit the call icon. A shoal of forage fishes darted from their haven and flitted around his gut, glancing the walls of his stomach, as he listened to the dial tone ring out. He popped the ring pull on the beer and took four long, determined gulps.

His shoulders dropped. She hadn't picked up. Didn't recognise the number. The fishes slowed and let the ripples of the ebbing tide carry them towards a sheltered hollow. He took the phone away from his ear, thumb hovering over the red symbol that would end the call, and slugged on his beer again.

'Hello?' A tinny voice rang from the ear piece. 'Hello? Who is that?'

A fresh tidal surge flushed the minnows out from their sanctuary.

'Kat? Don't hang up.'

'Scott, I thought it might be you – so this is your moby?'

'Yeah. Well, a new one actually. Save the number, I haven't got a flamin clue what it is.'

'Chrimbo pressie? Nice. How's it going?'

'It's going. And you know what they say - if you're going through hell, keep going.'

'That's the spirit. Bah humbug.' She giggled.

'Wouldn't want to disappoint.' He laughed. 'Fact is I'm grinning like a Cheshire Cat just now. Having a fun time?'

'Yeah, lovely. I'm at my folks. My big bruv and his girlfriend are here. Getting to meet my baby nephew for the first time. He's adorable.'

'Aye, they are when you can give 'em back.'

'Don't give me that, I'll bet if anyone tried to take Jae you'd rip them limb from limb.'

'Huh, that's a whole other story, I may tell you sometime. Kids leave you vulnerable, you know? Well you probably don't but take my word for it.'

'Getting a feel for it with little Zak. He may not be mine, but he's blood.'

'Listen, how do you fancy gettin away for a couple of days when you're back? I got a mate with a great little camping lodge. Notin dodgy mind, you can bring your own sleepin bag. Just need to get away and well, there's summat about you that makes me feel… safe. Is that weird?'

'No. Not weird. Lovely. Sounds great – I'd love to.' She fell quiet and for a moment and Scott didn't know what to say, suddenly worried that he'd overstepped the mark. The rousing brass section of a fifties big band swelled up from the stereo downstairs and rescued him from an awkward silence.

'Ooh, is that Sinatra I can hear? Very festive.' She started to hum along.

'Ha-ha. That's crackin. Left me stereo on full whack. Ma'll be scrambling for the remote.' He'd forgotten what it felt like to laugh and mean it. 'You gotta love a bit of Frank at Christmas.' Scott drained his beer to bolster his courage then, with his voice meandering in the vicinity of the correct notes, belted out the chorus of *I've got you under my skin*. As if to underscore his embarrassment the last few words rang out acapella as the backing track ratcheted down a few notches. Ma had found the remote.

'You pissed already?' Kat was laughing with him, but her tone was laced with caution.

'Ah, maybe a merry little at Christmas. Great excuse to start early.' Scott thought he'd better allay both of her possible fears – that he had a booze problem, and that alcohol might be colouring his affections a shade too vividly. 'I dunno Kat, sober as a judge I still think you'd make me feel giddy.

Now that's just saft innit?'

'It's very lovely, as are you. Scott, I've got another call coming through that I have to take, but call me again. Soon.'

'I will, count on it. Have fun, beautiful.' As the phone rang off Scott squeezed the empty can so that it buckled at the waist. He smiled. Downstairs he could hear the low rumble of music and the hub-bub of conversation peppered with laughter and the occasional shriek of excitement from his son.

He made his way downstairs. As he did a nostalgic chord drifted up to him from the gap underneath the living room door. Distinctive, warbling twangs on a wah-wah filtered electric guitar. He pressed his ear to the pine.

'Ah, Terry Jacks, I love this one—'

'Now you're showing your age, Jim—'

'Puts me in mind of you boys when you were lads, skinning your knees. No doubt skinning your hearts too.'

Then he noticed a small, slim gift-wrapped parcel that had appeared on the doormat; the flap on the letter box still jammed ajar. Scott stooped to pick it up.

'Urgh, what a load of depressing crap—'

The package was artfully tied with novelty string, threaded through a glitter-encrusted tag.

'Emma's right, Jim put something else on. It's Christmas for goodness sake—'

'All right, all right, spoil sports—'

Scott straightened up and flipped over the card. It read:

You got under my skin

No name. No initial.

Kat's away, how would she have been able to slip something through the door when they were just talking? Maybe she'd stayed close to home after all; was planning to surprise him.

Chuckling to himself he pulled at the ends of the string and pushed his thumb under one of the flaps of gift wrap, prizing it open. He repeated the same at the other end of the box, always preferring to postpone the big reveal until the last possible moment. Then, running his finger down the seam along its back, he opened it to find inside a large match box - the type that hold cooks' matches.

'Well, she knows I like a smoke…' Scott shook it from side to side. It rattled but didn't rush with the percussive sound of peas inside maracas that you'd expect of matches. The object inside was singular. Tentatively he pushed one end of the box with his index finger to slip it of its cover.

The thing was a curious shape with a texture like the gelatinised, over-sewn parchment of art deco table lamps - thick, viscid and opaque. In the dim light of the hallway it looked like it featured a cryptic carving. No, not a carving; a relief. He plucked it out of the box to examine it more closely, cursing his latter-day need for reading glasses. Yes, it was a relief of some kind. A symbol. Chinese characters? Japanese?

This one meansth love.'

Her voice floated into his thoughts.

'And thisth one…

He stared aghast at the piece of skin lining his palm.

'…meansss pain.'

'Jesus-fucking-H-Christ.'

It fell from his hands. He teetered, throwing his back against the wall. A herd of hooves came galloping, stamping on his sternum, crushing his chest. He tried to suck in air. Speckles appeared before his eyes, then spread and congealed to form blotches. His knees buckled and bent, drawing him down the wall until he sat hugging his shins, swallowing hard to quell the queasiness that was churning his belly. Norman approached him warily, sniffing the crust of dried flesh. She shrank down onto her haunches, ears pinned back and hissed as if she'd seen a demon. A ridge of raised fur prickled along her spine and bushed her tail. She cowered further, issuing a guttural, rumbling drawl as she eyed Scott guardedly.

'Alright girl.' He moved to soothe her. She lashed out catching the back of his hand with drawn razors.

'Jesus Norman.' She darted back the way she had come. As the cat flap clattered in the back kitchen, he wiped his bleeding hand and took three long, deep breaths in through his nose, and blew them out. A cigarette would cauterise his lacerated nerves. He reached for the crumpled packet of tobacco in his back pocket. Despite his shakes the well-honed ritual took seconds. Unable to rise to his feet he cocked his Clipper right where he sat and lit it.

After a few quick drags he resolved to make an anonymous call to the police – he could use this phone, it's not registered to him, they wouldn't be able to link it to him. But they might trace it back to Emma's magazine publisher – get her in strife for giving stuff away. She could lose her job. He drew on his cigarette pensively.

Then it struck him. Maybe Cheri was making a twisted plea for attention. She was a nutter after all. Maybe she'd taken her penchant for body modification to another level. What was that new gruesome trend he'd read about? Body carving. That's it – she's got herself into body carving and sent him a trophy. Fucked up. She's one fucked up motherfucker.

He pulled himself to his feet, spat in his palm and killed

his tab in the puddle of spittle then posted it through the letterbox. He fanned the air with his arm then, realising the futility of doing so, opened the front door and swung it to and fro until the smell of stale smoke had dissipated.

Frisking his breast pocket for his new phone, he whipped it out and tapped into his recent calls. His lone contact was listed there. Their call was only minutes ago but it felt like an age. He hit the phone icon next to her name.

He didn't care if he looked too eager. He didn't need to hear her reassuring voice. He needed a solicitor.

CHAPTER 20: INTO THE WOODS

JANUARY 2017

Saturday

'A winter campfire, a half decent single malt and my arms around a beautiful woman. Doesn't get much better, it surely doesn't.' Scott gave Kat an affectionate squeeze around the middle and kissed the small of her neck as they huddled spoon-like under his unzipped sleeping bag. 'You warm enough?'

'Yeah, it's lovely.' She nestled into him. Her eyes danced with the lapping flames of the fire that Scott had set on their return from a day of scouting in the surrounding woodland. The crisp night air made her skin tingle and bristle, even as the warmth of the blaze and the mellow glow of contentment was ushering in a thaw.

She rubbed the back of his hand then slipped her arm from its cover, reached over to the tree stump-cum-occasional-table that held their drinks and passed one to him. Scott released his hold to give her some wiggle room. She shuffled around to face him, picked up her glass and tilted it towards him. Tear tracks of the golden liquor caught the firelight as they dripped down the side of her glass.

'Cheers Scott—'

'Cheers beautiful.'

The glasses rang out like the tines of a tuning fork as they touched. For all the sublimity of the moment it may as well have been a pitch-perfect, concert 'A'.

'Thank you for today, it's been magical. I know that

sounds corny, but it really has.'

'You're the first girl I've met that would call laying traps for rabbits magical.' He laughed and took a gulp of his whiskey. 'Still, it gets us a nice place to get away to. I've been promising Will I'd do a mop up of the pesky blighters for weeks.'

'You were right about the wagon, it's perfect.' She glanced up at the shepherd's lodge, their muddy boots on the steps leading up to the barn-style split doors, the lace curtains at the windows.

'Aye, not exactly roughin it. Only the best wit' me' he said, winking.

'I've learned loads today. It's kind of sexy watching a man do something he knows so well, especially something as manly as hunting' she giggled and batted her lashes, sipping seductively at the rim of her glass. 'So what happens to the bunnies when you catch them?'

'You'll find out tomorrow if you're game.' He baited her with a twitch of his eyebrows.

'I get a feeling I won't want to be the game in question.' She laughed harder, the booze was tickling her. She looked at him and offered her elbow. Scott hooked his arm through hers and they tilted their glasses and drank.

'You're game of a whole different kind, Kat. One I hope I've already won.' He leaned in and pressed his lips to hers. They melted into a long kiss, bodies cradled close and bleeding into each other. Scott's head became light as blood surged to his groin. He pulled back, wanting to slow the moment down. He stretched over her and reached for the bottle, unscrewed the cap and topped them both up.

'I may spare you of the gory details, but I said I'd dress a couple of rabbits for Jae's Nanna as a thank you for having him this weekend.' He took a nip of drink, 'God knows I *needed* this,' then knocked back a liberal gulp and winced.

'Scott...' The word curved up at the end, in that way that it does when someone is about to ask an awkward question, or an undesirable favour.

'Is this something I want to hear?' he said, rubbing his scalp.

'You don't have to answer this... But why do you need a solicitor?'

'Some trouble with one of the lads at work.' He didn't miss a beat but avoided her eyes.

'A *criminal* lawyer? For an employment dispute?' She dipped her head so she could read his face.

'Yeah. It's... not so much work-related. It's more serious than that.' His eyes flickered up briefly. 'Don't *need* one. Now I mean. I just wanted a number. Just in case.'

Sensing him close down, she slouched back and relaxed her gaze. 'OK, I won't pry.' Then she couldn't resist adding 'It wasn't for you then?'

'Just protecting my interests.' He nodded sheepishly, then artfully switched the polarity of the probing. 'So when we got chattin in the Clover before Christmas I got the impression that sumthin was up. I've picked up on it a couple of times. You mentioned an ex? Is this guy a problem I should know about?'

'Urgh. God. Yeah. Well sort of. It's why I took the shifts in the Clover. Lee put me up to it, said he could look out for me better if I was under his nose.' She contemplated the contents of her glass. Her long eyelashes cast slatted shadows, putting her cheekbones behind bars.

'Lee? What Ash? *That* Lee?'

'Yeah, Lee Ashley – you know him, I've seen you chatting to him before now.'

'Aye, we was at school together. He works on the vehicles for me now and again. It's not Lee you were seein?'

'No, God no. Lee's just a mate.'

'Is he heckers like. He'd be in yer knickers quicker than that.'

'Ah, Lee talks a good flirt but he's all mouth and no trousers. He's got a good heart has Lee.'

'So what's his deal in all this then?'

'I think he just feels, sort of, responsible…'

Scott bobbed his head to coax her on.

'It was Lee who introduced me, to Rob. They work together.'

'Rob? At Lee's place? What's he look like?'

'Your sort of height, bit stockier than you. Short dark hair, stubbly kind of beard…' Kat lost herself in reflection. '*Urgh.* Makes my skin crawl just thinkin about him now.' She shuddered and sipped her drink.

'Doesn't ring any bells. Does he drink in the Clover?'

'Nah, he doesn't drink. Met him at Lee's workshop.'

'Never trust a man who doesn't drink. There's always a reason and it's usually 'cause he's a nutter.' He raised his glass and drank as if to seal his credibility.

'Wish I'd had that advice at the time…' She rolled the whiskey around in her glass. Her tone had changed, she'd grown distant and sad.

The sight piqued his compassion. 'Kat?' He nudged her chin up with his finger. 'Tell us then, what's he doing? This

Rob guy.'

'I thought it was just a bit of fun, you know, not much more than a roll in the hay really.' She gulped before continuing. 'He's married… I didn't think he'd want anything serious.' As she glanced up, a quiver of contrition flitted across her eyes. 'Don't judge.'

'Ah, shite, we're none of us whiter-than-white on that score. These things happen.' He stroked her cheek.

'Sounds like you're talking from experience. Did *you*?'

'Just the once.' Then he added quietly 'Least I think it was.'

'Anyone I know?' Now she was turning the tables on him.

'I could tell you but I'd have to kill you.' He winked.

'Oh go on, I can keep a secret, I promise.'

He held her firmly with his eyes, 'You've really *got* to promise, seriously he'd fuckin skin me alive if he knew.'

'Who would?'

Scott drained his glass and promptly poured another.

'Trev…'

'Trev? Trev Davies? You shagged *Josie*?' Her incredulity instantly made him wish he hadn't let the single malt loosen his tongue.

'Don't remind me. Fuckin worst, most unbelievable thing I ever did.' He dipped his head and shook it, wishing he still had his floppy fringe to hide behind. 'Anyway, we were talkin about you.'

'We were.' Kat reached down into her rucksack and brought out a gold tobacco tin embellished with a bright green, iridescent marijuana leaf. Scott wondered why potheads always felt the need to advertise the fact that they were holding, but kept this thoughts to himself as she nimbly sealed two Rizlas together and rolled a neat trumpet of a spliff. The perfect gentleman, he had his Clipper aflame the moment she placed the long, tapering stick between her lips.

She took a lengthy, deep draw on it, held it down for a few seconds then blew out a plume of smoke as if to brace herself.

'Rob was the kind of guy who always wanted to know that you were there. Always checking up to see what you're doing, who you're with. Texted constantly and got arsey if I didn't text back right away. At first I found it flattering, all his attention. But after a while it got suffocating. I couldn't do a thing without him giving me the third degree. If I decided not to respond, just to get some space, he started to get personal – nasty. A couple of times he called me names – selfish bitch, tart, accused me of fucking other people. Which is *rich* coming from a married man.' She shook her head, put the joint to her lips once more and inhaled.

'I tried to break it off.' Purple, musky smoke escaped between her words. 'I thought I'd play him at his own game - threatened to tell his wife if he didn't leave me alone. *Big* mistake…' She held the spliff towards Scott.

'Nah, thanks' he said, waving it away, 'don't touch it.'

'Never trust a man who doesn't toke. There's always a reason and it's usually 'cause he's a nutter' she said, smirking.

'Fair point. G'on then, just a little toot.' He obliged, taking two deep draws in quick succession.

'He started threatening to kill himself. I ignored it, figured it was just another manipulative plea for attention.' Scott passed the joint back to her as he held the fumes in his lungs. 'Then he calls me one night from A&E, said he'd been there for hours having his stomach pumped. I just couldn't bloody believe it. It's not like we ever said we *loved* each other or anything.'

'So what did you do?' He blew out what was left of his toke, already wishing he hadn't held it down for so long. It was strong.

'I told him I didn't care if he killed himself. I told him to fuck off and leave me alone.'

'Good girl.' His head was starting to spin. He pressed the seat of his palm to his forehead.

'You OK?'

'Yeah. Lightweight. Told you I'm not used to it.'

'It's pretty mad skunk. Sorry, I should have warned you. It does mellow out after a few minutes though.'

'You must be flamin bulletproof.' His jaw tensed. The crackling of the fire ripped through his ear drums like rounds of gunfire. He tried to hide the jerk of his head as it caught him by surprise. To his relief Kat seemed not to have noticed.

'Anyway, so after that I got a stream of nasty texts. *Really* nasty. Violent kind of nasty. Got to the point where I was lying awake at night scared that if I fell asleep he'd break in and stab me in my bed.' Her hands had started to tremble. Scott pulled her close and rubbed her back, partly to quell the THC-induced tinglings of paranoia that were crawling over his skin like spiders. 'I spoke to one of the solicitors at work and they told me to report him to the police for harassment.'

'Aye, so they can serve and protect you, before the stalker strikes.' He jumped and threw his eyes over his shoulder. Was someone creeping around in the undergrowth? His rational mind struggled through the fug to tell him it was the cannabinoid-boosted sound of bristling branches in the thicket behind them catching a breeze. 'They're really proactive on domestics like that, the pigs.' He managed sarcasm despite the centrifugal draining of his cerebral fluid.

'Yeah, right.' She took another long drag on the skunk. 'But thankfully telling him I'd reported it seemed to scare him quiet. I got a couple of pleading, remorseful calls over Christmas. Well, voicemails. I've kept them just in case.' She paused and smiled sweetly, trying to lock his fogging eyes with hers. 'What happened with Josie then?'

'Long story.' He rubbed his eye sockets and said, almost under his breath 'Sally had bipolar disorder – you know what that is?'

'I didn't know that Scott, I'm sorry. It's some sort of depression, right?' She took a last blast on her spliff before tossing it into the fire.

'*Manic* depression. It's the Jekyll and Hyde of mental health problems. Peaks and troughs.' He made a sinewave in the air with his arm. 'It's not an excuse. I totally know what happened was bang out of order.' Blotches started to form and shape-shift across his vision.

His pulse quickened.

'Just telling you so… so you know where me head was at back then. Oh, God—' He closed his eyes and tried to tame the globules of colour that burst against the inside of his lids. Kat slid an arm around his shoulders.

'She was sectioned after a fucked up manic episode.' He rocked from side to side to the rhythm of the rushing tide between his ears. 'They increased her medication.' He fought to stop his thoughts from getting caught up in the weed. 'But instead of being stabilised, she was… *numbed*.' Like swimming against a strong undercurrent. 'Neutralised.' Like being pulled under. 'They said it was safer than… another crazy trip.' Scott paused for a beat and hummed, he clenched his jaw.

'How wrong they were.' He sounded bolder, colder. His eyes snapped open. They were as black and glassy as melanite. 'She became a Stepford wife. Compliant. Devoid of depth. Wearing the vacant, plasticised expression of an automaton. Deadpan. Smooth. Injected with emotional Botox—'

Kat was poised to cut in but didn't know how to. The dull grinding of tooth enamel that punctuated Scott's soliloquy grated against her inner ear like magnified cricket chirps.

'Light years away from the Sal I used to know. The excitable, fiercely intelligent PhD; the foul-mouthed, beer-swilling, opinionated fire cracker that had been my match, my soul mate, my better, my life. What did they do with the real Sal? Where are they keeping her? Is she still alive somewhere?' His eyes were trained on the middle distance, as if he were addressing an unseen audience from an invisible stage.

'Scott, are you—?' She shrank back.

'It'll ease your mind…' He interrupted and started to laugh.

'What will? Scott, what do you mean?' Kat felt edgy. The skunk was too strong.

'She *is* alive. In my subconscious. Night after night.' His volume rose and with it his enmity. 'Sometimes an angel stroking my fears away, telling me it's not my fault; sometimes a ghoul, wrenching my heart from my chest, striking fear of death - or life - into my atrophying soul.' His lids fell once more. His shoulders slumped then, after a brief hiatus, rose and fell softly as his breathing tempered.

'I'm sorry. I'm really sorry I asked.' She really was.

Moments passed to the sound of the crackling and popping of the fire until guilt usurped her unease; she shouldn't have prodded his hornet's nest of memories. 'I didn't mean to—'

'Didn't mean to what?' His voice broke low and hoarse. His eyes fluttered. The blotches floating before them condensed and evaporated. Focus returned, and with it the sapphire in his irises.

'I… You were…'

'Jesus, sorry Kat I think I bloody dropped off there for a minute.' He shook his head. 'That stuff is *strong*. Fuckin *wrecked*. What didn't you mean to do?'

'You were talking about Sally' she ventured.

'I was? Christ, talk about screwing your short term memory' he said with another vigorous shake of his head. 'If I said anything out of—'

'You said something about it not being your fault. That Sally comes to you and says it's not your fault. Is that what you think? Do you think you're to blame because of what you did with Josie?'

'I said that?' He sighed deeply and percolated the question. How could he tell Kat that he didn't remember getting naked with Josie? She'd no more believe him now than Sally did back then. After a few moments he spoke, soft and sore.

'Not *because* of Josie. Not directly. It's just… She didn't trust me after that.' He swallowed the saliva that was pooling at the back of his throat, stifling the urge to cry.

'The night I found her—' Choking back the swell, he rubbed his neck like he could feel the noose around it. 'The night I found her she'd seen a text from Emma on my phone. We'd been out. Bladdered. She must've… thought I was messin about.' He sniffed and pressed the cuffs of his sleeves to his eyes. 'Again.'

'Oh Scott.' Kat leaned forward and ran her fingers over the brush on his skull. 'Everyone was— we just couldn't believe it. When we heard about Sally.'

'I still can't' he whispered, leaning into her hand like a bunting cat, letting her touch drift down his cheekbone until she cradled his jaw. He buried his face in her palm and kissed her like he had found the wounds of his saviour.

'You said some… odd things. Just then. You looked. *Different.*'

'I did?' He raised his eyes to meet hers, still touching her hand with his lips like a deferent serf. 'Can't take my weed. Dickwad.' He laughed, sat up and planted a cheerful peck on her cheek. 'Whiskey… now that I *can* handle.' He poured another two fingers into each of their glasses.

'Come on, let's change the subject. We're here to enjoy ourselves.'

Her frown melted into a beatific smile, as radiant as the warmth from the flames. He cupped the back of her head in his hands and drew her towards him.

'The here and now' he whispered in her ear, 'that's what matters.' Brushing his lips against her cheek, he felt the tension her neck die away as he tempted her into a kiss with his tongue.

'Ouch.'

'What is it, you OK?'

'Your watch, it's caught in my hair.'

'Bloody thing. Sorry.' He unclipped the clasp, gently untangled it from the curls at the nape of her neck and tossed it into her open bag.

'Now, where were we…?'

'Game.'

'Fair game.' Another agrees.

'Just a game.' A third chips in.

'It's just a game.' The first insists.

'No. I don't like it.' A child's voice.

'I don't like it.'

'It's just a bit of fun.' He tightens the leather around her wrists.

'I don't like it.' A woman's voice. His woman's voice.

'Just a bit of fun.' He curls himself around her. Her wrists turn white.

'It hurts.' She tries to struggle. Can't move.

He folds himself around her.

Legs twitch. Legs kick. Legs thresh. Red legs.

'It won't hurt.'

He draws the blade. Slim blade. Sharp blade.

'It won't hurt.'

Red legs. Red legs threshing. Sharp blade.

'It won't hurt.'

Red blade. Red running. Thick and running. Thick, red and running.

His eyes sprung open. His heart bolted out of the traps. In the pitch black he could feel her cradled in the curl of his body, his arms around her waist, face buried in the curve of her neck. Left arm wedged under the arch of her waistline. He couldn't move it, it was numb. His right hand flopped around her belly, fingers folded around something hard, cold and wet. He rubbed their tips together, trying to breathe life into them.

They were tacky. Sticky. Resting in a thick, viscous fluid as it was pooled on the bed. *What the—?* He slipped his arm from under her, straining to focus in the darkness. Pushing himself up onto his elbow, he raised his hand before his face. A shaft of moonlight cast though the lace. Glinting on the steel. Fingers around the bush knife. Wet. Black. Dripping. *Christ all fucking—* Terror leapt to its feet, sprinting through his veins. *Kat?* She lay motionless. Pooling before her. Pooling before her, wet and thick. Motionless. *Kat? Kat—*

His eyes sprung open. His heart bolted out of the traps. In the pitch black he could feel her cradled in the curl of his body, his arms around her waist, face buried in the curve of her neck.

'Fuh… Kah…?' Scott stirred. 'Kah…?' He tried to form the words, forcing himself to rouse. He'd been here before, Kat lying spooned in his body.

He shook her shoulder. 'Kat? Kat wake up. Kat.' She stirred. She started.

'Wha…? Scott. What is it? What's going on?'

'Oh fuck.' He threw himself onto his back and panted hard. 'Oh f—'

'You had a bad dream?' She stroked his forehead. It was wet with sweat.

'A dream.' He processed the words. 'I had a bad dream.'

Sunday

'Poor things.' She glanced over her shoulder at the three brace of beheaded rabbits hanging in the back of the Land Rover. 'Thanks for not chopping them up.'

'Aye, they've bled out so it'll wait til I get back.' He finished cleaning the blade with a cloth, pulled off his gloves then tossed them into the wagon. Kat grimaced.

'Not exactly the most charming thing to do on a date, eh?' He smiled, leant over and planted a kiss on her cheek. In truth he didn't quite have the stomach for butchering this morning – the potent mix of too much whiskey, strong weed and a bad trip to the land of nod had left him feeling fragile. The thought of returning to reality after making an escape with Kat didn't do anything to contain his angst either.

He traced her cheekbone with his fingertips. 'Thanks for coming away with me Kat.'

'Thanks for being the perfect gentleman.' She smiled coyly. 'You didn't need to be.'

'Promised I would. I'm in no rush.' He moved in for a gentle kiss. 'You're summat special' he said, nudging her nose with his. Her green eyes glimmered. It felt to him like she could see inside him. He felt naked, but it felt good.

'And part of that promise is to get you home in one piece. You got everything?'

'Yep. Think so.' She patted her rucksack symbolically.

'What time's your shift start?' He glanced at his watch.

'Billy wants me there at four.'

'Bloody hell, betta get a wriggle on.' He turned the engine over and reversed, rumbling over the deeply gouged tire tracks furrowed by Will's tractor. They jostled from side to side, laughing like it were a fairground ride until they backed out through the open gate and found the comparatively flush tarmac of the lane. Scott jumped out quickly to latch the gate then threw himself back behind the wheel and gunned the accelerator.

'Can I ask you something?' Kat said.

'Dunno til you tell me what it is you want to ask.' He

flashed her a schoolboy grin.

'It's about something you said last night.'

'Oh aye. What's that then?'

'It's just—'

'What, sweetheart? What is it?'

'You said you thought Sally might have misread Emma's text… The one—'

'You don't have to explain which one.' His expression dropped.

'Oh God, this sounds awful…'

'Why would Sal think that? Is that what you want to know?'

'Yeah, sorry I just…' She cleared her throat. 'Have you and Emma ever been—'

'More than friends?' He started to laugh. She was jealous. 'No Kat. There's never been anything more between me and Em than a heap load of sarcasm and a shed load a beer.'

'Oh, God I feel so shitty for asking now…' She buried her face in her hands.

'Don't. I'm flattered. Honestly.' He rubbed her leg and added as an aside, 'That was the whole flamin tragedy.' He reached for a Marlboro from the open pack that was wedged into a plastic smartphone bracket suckered to the dashboard.

'I'm sorry, I shouldn't have brought the subject up.' She reached for his Clipper and lit up for him.

'It's OK' he inhaled. 'Really. I don't want any secrets between us.' He passed her the cigarette. 'You've nowt t'worry bout with Em.'

'Same here. *Nowt t'worry bout.*' She eyed him coquettishly

and took a draw on the tab before handing it back to him.

'Not even with this Rob?' He took a couple of decent drags but saved the last for her.

'He's history.' She yanked at the stubborn ashtray drawer, drained the last of the fag then stubbed it out, a little too enthusiastically.

They bounced along in comfortable silence for a few minutes before Kat leaned over and turned the switch on the radio. An irksome jingle jovially trumpeted the arrival of Danny Edge, Wire FM's mid-afternoon DJ; a man replete with irksome jingles and not-so-comedy characters.

'Too much blether and not enough music' Scott said and, as if to ratify his complaint, the DJ prattled through the opening chords to one of his favourite songs by way of a painfully farcical, zany conversation with a pre-recording. When he'd eventually shut up, Scott discordantly sang along with the Oasis lyrics he knew by heart.

He glanced at Kat and smiled, then returned his eyes to the road as he assuredly navigated the twisting country lane in the fading light. She watched him as he passionately mouthed the words to *Wonderwall* and gave his knee a gentle squeeze. His cheeks flushed at his own sentimentality. The DJ saved him his blushes by cutting in.

'Over to the news desk now for your three o'clock bulletin with Adrian Price.'

'Thanks Danny. The police are asking for the public's help in locating a missing trainee doctor last seen four weeks ago. A police spokesman said they are treating the woman's disappearance as suspicious. Detective Inspec—'

Scott spun the tuning dial so fast the knob almost snapped off in his hand. The cacophonous white noise of interference made Kat wince and cover her ears.

'Bad fucking news. It's all we ever get' he said to cover his swift move to silence the story. He killed the radio and attempted a smile, just as they were approaching the mouth of the housing estate that Kat called home. He pulled up outside her maisonette, but left the engine running.

'You want me to wait and drop you at the Clover?'

'That's sweet, thanks Scott but Lee usually picks me up on his way through. You'd better get those rabbits ready to take to Jae's Nanna.' She glanced back and scowled at them. 'I'm gonna grab a quick shower.' She picked up her bag and planted it on her knee.

'OK. If you're sure.' He leaned over and kissed her tenderly. 'See you in the week?'

'That'd be great. And thanks again Scott, I've had a lovely time.' She shouldered the passenger side door and slid off the seat. 'Bye.'

'Bye Kat. I—' He checked himself before he said too much. 'I'll bell ya.'

He watched her walk up the path then, as she disappeared inside, he ruefully put the Land Rover into gear. He manoeuvred around the cul-de-sac and was about to pull off.

'Ah, shit.' He turned the ignition off.

Ping.

'Christ Lee you're not outside already are you?' She knotted a towel between her naked breasts, pulled her pants back up and padded her way into the living room. She rummaged around her backpack for her phone. Her fingertips pricked on something sharp and metallic.

'Ouch.' She grabbed it and pulled it out. Scott's watch. 'That damn thing is determined to hurt me' she said to herself as she sucked a droplet of blood from the tip of her thumb. She retrieved her phone but by the time she saw Scott's name across the screen the front doorbell was chiming. She answered it and peered around the edge of door.

'Hi. Oh sorry.' He averted his eyes when he realised that she was wearing nothing but a bath towel. 'I think my watch is in your bag?' he said to the doormat.

'Just found it. Do you want to step in?' She pulled the door open and beckoned him inside. She held onto the towel as she passed him his timepiece.

'Thanks.' He took it, slipped it into his breast pocket, then grabbed her hand and pulled her towards him. He smothered her giggles with an ardent kiss. Their tongues locked as he pulled at the knot and let the towel drop. He cupped her breasts in his hands and pushed his face into them, pinching her nipples with his teeth, sucking at the firm flesh. 'God you're gorgeous.' He wanted to devour her, bearishly clawing her back with his fingers. She buckled at the knees. He grabbed her ass and pulled her hips towards his. She could feel him through his jeans, hard and keen.

'Scott' she whispered breathlessly. 'Oh Scott, I'd love to, but I have to—' He silenced her with his mouth, but kissed her softly and slowly.

'I know' he said, peppering her face and neck with kisses. 'I know beautiful. I'll let you go.' He bent down and picked up the towel, carefully draping it around her back and closing it over the swell of her chest. He stood looking at her, catching his breath.

'I'll see ya later. Thanks.' He patted his breast pocket and made to turn.

'You will' she said, stroking his shoulder.

Scott made his way out into the dark and reluctantly pulled the door shut behind him. 'Fuck *me*.' He rubbed his face as if he was splashing it with cold water.

Kat retreated to the bathroom and placed her phone on top of a small chest of drawers. She turned the dial on the shower. It almost drowned out the clang of the doorbell.

'Dammit. Not now Lee.' She grabbed the knot at the front of her makeshift toga and jogged back down the short hallway to the door. She could see a shadow through the frosted double glazing. It wasn't tall enough to be Lee.

The figure looked like they were pulling something from the inner pocket of their jacket and holding it up. It glinted as it caught the porch light.

'Scott?' She could swear she could make out the tune of Wonderwall being hummed above the rushing of the water. 'Scott, you're going to make me late…'

***

The brakes whined as he pulled up in the yard. He was thrown forward by the sudden stop and collapsed back into the seat. He must have negotiated the lanes on auto-pilot; he didn't remember a single turn of the drive. Closing his eyes he let out a deep sigh and collected his thoughts. Then he opened his palms and studied the blood on his hands. The cloying, gamy smell of dead flesh clung to his nostrils. He felt sick.

Reaching down he picked up the brace he'd thrown into the passenger foot well after leaving Kat's. The rest of the kill could wait, but these he had to dress for Angela. Stomach or no stomach.

Ping.

He smiled. Only Emma, Brenna and Kat had this number so there was a thirty percent chance that a certain Baltic beauty was thinking about him as much as he was her. He wiped his hands on his shirt before pulling out his phone.

It wasn't Kat.

It wasn't Brenna.

It wasn't Emma.

It was No caller ID and it simply read:

I know it was you.

CHAPTER 21: KEEP OUT

Thursday

> Hey beautiful, hope ur week is going well. Gimme a shout when ur free. Longing to see ya gorjus. S xxx

Scott strolled over to the window and twisted the blinds shut, snapping off the blades of sunlight that cut through the smoke in the office. He wasn't feeling very sunny. Three days straight he'd texted and called Kat, but she'd cut him as dead as he'd just cut the rays. He lobbed his phone onto the desk, wandered over to the brew bench and doused a teabag from the kettle. What was it with him and women? Just when you think things are hotting up, they go off the boil. He prodded the tea bag half-heartedly. The brew was as lukewarm as his love life.

Ping.

'At flamin last.' Tipping the tepid tea into the sink he dashed over to his phone with renewed hope that his thirst for Kat was to be slaked.

> Hey baby bro.

What felt worse, he wondered as his hopes were dashed, the disappointment itself or the dishonour of it?

> Hey Sis, how's it hanging?

Ping.

> I'm good Scotty. You OK?

> Ya know

Ping.

> Think about what I said

I do Sis, believe me

Ping.

I need you to do a favour for me

Shoot

Ping.

Do you still have a key to the farmhouse?

Might have…

Ping.

There's something in there that I need

He made his way along the well-worn clay path running the length of a brook that had once snaked its way across back of the tied cottages. The spine of a small wooden footbridge was just visible through the undergrowth, fashioned from a tar-stained beam by Scott's father many years ago. It had rested across the narrow banks of the stream, itself long since parched, for nearly four decades. His mother had often delighted in telling him of the Three Billy Goats Gruff game that he and Brenna used to play as children. Scott's Da and Uncle Roy would take it in turns to play the Troll, lurking under the oak, ready to pounce. His only sentiment for the game was more recent than that, of Jae the toddler clip-clopping across the timber and Scott squatting in wait. On the other side of the bridge was the garden fence at the rear of the farmhouse, accessible through a waist-high gate. He tip-toed quickly across the beam for fear of being caught, then stopped and scoped the garden for signs of life. All quiet, even as he studied the slabs of glass that walled the conservatory for any shifting shadows inside.

He unclipped the gate and scurried in a low crouch across the garden until he reached the sliding doors. Praying that Iain hadn't changed the lock, he tried the key that his uncle and cousin didn't know he'd kept. It popped the lock.

Scott waited to see if the noise had stirred any occupants before easing the door ajar and slipping through. He was careful to slide it shut behind him. A high-pitched beep rang out from beyond the conservatory. Crap, the alarm was armed. The touchpad was on the wall in the entrance hall, he had thirty seconds to get there before the company that monitored the system would notify the police. He scarpered across the tiles and through the door to the living room. The bleeps coming faster and more urgently now as he dashed through the home office that was once the dining room and out to the hallway. He tapped in the month and year of Jae's birth, in the hope that Iain had been too lazy or disorganised to change the code, mis-keyed the last number, hit clear and stamped it in again.

Silence.

He stood for a moment to catch his breath. The bannister swept upwards behind him. He could feel its presence over his shoulder as if it were possessed by the ghosts of his past, daring him to once more tread the boards to the summit. Enticing him to uncover its secrets. No matter what lay in wait, he said to himself, it could not possibly be any more fateful than that darkest of November nights.

He took a deep breath, turned and made his way to the foot of the stairs. As he looked up to the shadows obscuring the landing his legs turned to rubber, like his bones had been soaked in vinegar. Blowing his cheeks, he bolstered himself against the balustrade and once again mounted each tetchy tread. He paused briefly to test the air for movement, in case the creak of the floorboards had alerted anyone to his approach. Satisfied that he was alone, he took the rest of the stairs quickly, keen to shake off the portent of awaiting tragedy.

Once at the top he avoided looking to his left. Today his interest was not in the room he'd once shared with Sally.

Today his interest was in turning the clock back farther. Today he was to make his way, under his sister's instruction, to the room that he and she used to share when the rest of the farmhouse was taken with paying guests.

The door was shut as he approached. He twisted the doorknob and pushed it open, half expecting to see wall-to-wall posters of 1980s New Romantic male dandies, gazing down aloofly, covetously even, through heavily guy-lined, man-scared eyes onto Bren's hairspray and make-up strewn dressing table. Even during his years here with Sally he had rarely had cause to venture into this room, or rather had rarely the desire to. It felt like stepping through a portal to another time, one charged with static that caused the hairs on his arms to bristle. It was clear from the flat pack boxes, rolls of manilla paper, bundles of bubble wrap and tape guns that Roy was using it as his online auction store room. That and the whips, spanking paddles, cuffs and ballgags stacked on the bookshelves bearing Romanian labels. Hardly the leather goods that beautiful country is known for, Roy. Nothing of Scott or Bren remained. At least not to the uninitiated.

In fact even to those in the know it was difficult to see. But as he moved closer to the corner of the room, beneath the window where Bren's bed had once stood, he could just make out the join in the skirting board, several inches out from where the two walls met. Standing there he could imagine her bed, he could feel the presence of others around him. He glanced over his shoulder. Nothing but the bedroom door. He suddenly felt claustrophobic; the presence made him want to bolt. He took in air slowly to quell the urge to run. He was here for Bren. He moved to the corner of the room and knelt, wedging the slim paring knife that he'd come prepared with into the slither of a gap, and jemmied open a panel of skirting about a foot long. It came away quite easily with a little encouragement, revealing a hidey-hole in the cavity between the stud wall and the adjacent room. Bren would have had to crawl under her bed to stow her precious secrets here, and to this day it is where they had remained.

He crouched down to look inside and there it was. Bren's box. The one she'd asked him to retrieve. Inside it, she told him, was her earliest volume of poems and recollections. Her publisher was keen to issue a retrospective, written from the viewpoint of a child. Scott reached in and ushered it out. It was an old school-shoe box. Bren had taken a red marker pen to it. KEEP OUT it warned. TOP SECRET it claimed. Despite its highly classified status the only impediment to entry was a thick rubber band around its midriff, which time had rendered brittle and sticky. It fell apart under the slightest pressure.

Inside there were two dog-eared exercise books variously scrawled with similar caveats alongside ever-lasting declarations of love for Philip Oakey and David Sylvian. One of them was entitled *Bren's Poems*. Having already been perturbed by her more recent compositions, Scott was not particularly tempted to intrude on her adolescent reflections. He flicked briefly through the pages and couldn't help but notice, even at a cursory glance, that Bren harboured feelings of antipathy for someone, whom she only ever referred to as 'he' or 'him'. *I hate him. I wish he would die. I'll scratch his stupid eyes out.* A boy who had shattered her fledgling dreams perhaps?

A handful of Polaroids lined the bottom of the box, which over the years had bled their cyan dyes and faded to a muted reddish hue. A family group picture taken in their garden, in which a primary-aged Brenna wears the expression of a glum teenager, in advance of her years. Dressed in her school uniform, her scarlet tights glowing with the red shift of the print. In another snap she and a little boy are perched on each knee of a male relative, or perhaps a family friend, with a woman who bears a striking resemblance to their mother standing behind, smiling proudly. There were various other group pictures taken in or around the farm. They all had something in common. Bren had taken a compass needle to the face of someone in each picture. *He* had been scratched into oblivion. The pictures prompted no recollection. For Scott it was like looking at a stranger's family album, were it not for the fact the he recognised his big sister.

Scott sat looking at the photo of Bren and the little boy – himself possibly - sitting on a man's knee. He rubbed the score marks on the print with his thumb as if it would help him to excavate memories of who the faceless fellow would be.

The sound of a key in the front door snapped him back to the here and now. Quickly followed by it slamming shut.

'Would ye calm da fuck down, man. Aye, Iain's not set the flamin alarm again. Bloody eejit. He'll get me fleeced…'

Roy. Shit. Scott closed the box and tucked it under his arm.

'Eh? Don't be so saft man, we're solid. It's all good. Just calm the fuck down. Get away now.'

He could hear his uncle cursing to himself. He was alone. Only one set of footsteps, which grew softer as he strode into the belly of the house. Scott shuffled on his hands and knees out onto the landing. He could hear Roy running a tap then stomping back towards the front of the house. Scott prayed he was going out the way he had come in.

'Fuckin want a job done, do it ye self. Christ's sake' his uncle mumbled to himself. Scott crawled up to the struts of the bannister. Gazing down through the wooden bars into the hallway, he could see Roy loitering near the front door. He looked up.

Scott jerked his head back and held his breath.

'Iain? You here?' Roy hollered up the stairs and waited.

'Gonna see me fuckin fleeced, that boy.' He shook his head as he retreated into his home office. Scott could hear the sound of a desktop booting up, the melodic flourish of an operating system coming to life; Roy's footsteps moving to the window; the rush of the curtains being drawn; the tick of a desk lamp switch.

Under the cover of Roy's distraction he crept to the top of the stairs and butt-shuffled his way down step-by-step. Christ knows what he would do if Roy emerged as he was part way down. He stopped briefly, listening to the tapping of fingers on a keyboard. Quickly, he bumped down the last few steps and edged his way along the wall to the doorframe. He glanced down the hall. He couldn't leave the way he'd come in, that would mean scuttling past Roy and across the adjoining lounge. The back kitchen door, though, he could make it out through that if – please – it had the key in the lock. Peering around the door he could see his uncle sat with his back to him, dark against the glow of his screen, fingers tripping rapidly over the keys. Without looking Roy reached for his glass but instead of grabbing it he knocked it splashing to the floor.

'Ah fuckit.' He bent down to pick it up. As he did Scott caught a brief glimpse of his screen. It looked a little like the dating site he had used, but the girls it showcased looked more posed; more like an escorting site. They looked young. From this distance it was hard to tell if they were too young to be legal. Dressed provocatively and heavily made up, it was difficult to discern what age they'd pass for. And he could hardly point the finger at another man for ogling on-the-edge girls after some of the porn he'd perused. Roy pushed his chair back, grabbed the empty glass, cursed at the puddle on the floor and turned around. Scott threw his back against the wall. He could hear Roy's steps approaching him. Heading for the kitchen? To get a cloth? His heart thumped.

He could almost feel his uncle's breath against his ear.

Roy's phone trilled from behind him. 'What the flamin 'eck now?' He turned, striding back to the desk.

'Oh, fu—' Scott breathed. He quickly bolted past the doorway, into the back kitchen and wedged himself behind the door.

'Oh for cryin out loud, man. Stay where ye are. I'm on me way.' Roy was careful to shut down his system before scooping up his keys and phone and heading for the exit. 'Babysitter too now am I? Have to do flamin everytin.' Scott heard him mumble before the jarring thud of the front door shook the house silent.

***

'Hey Kat. You OK beautiful? Listen, if I've done summat to offend… just, well, just let me know sweetheart. Give me chance. Please. Missing you.'

He sat staring at his phone willing it to ring. It didn't, so he thumbed a quick text to his sister. Mission accomplished. He fanned the faded photos out across his coffee table. Who was it that Bren hated so much? Who is Mr Faceless? He knew he'd have to ask at some point; knew that's what Brenna was driving at, getting him to steal into the house on the back of some spurious tale about needing the box. She wanted him to see its contents.

But in order to see, he had to be willing to look.

And that way madness lies.

CHAPTER 22: MATTER OF TIME

Monday

Where is Kat? Why isn't she responding? Scott was starting to feel desperate. He kneaded his temples, trying to rub away the pressure that clamped the sides of his skull. *Nothing has happened. She's dumped you. Nothing more.*

The thought did little to console him, even if he supposed that the lesser of two evils – her casting him aside – were true. It took the absence of her this last few days to make him realise that he had fallen for Kat. Like, *fallen*. He felt safe in her presence, content in her arms. Whole. But with every day that passed without word it felt like he was desiccating; like particle by particle he was breaking up and blowing away. Just as he had felt in those days and weeks after losing Sal. Piece by torturous piece he was falling apart.

He glanced down through brimming tears at the Blackberry in his hand. The one he'd thrown against the wall; that had died along with Sally. The one that had been a knife through their hearts. Why had he left it there, where she would find it? *Why?* That fucking Blackberry.

He yanked open the drawer of the office desk, tossed the cracked and buckled husk back into its tomb and shoved it shut. He threw his head down onto his forearms and sobbed until his belly ached.

He hadn't gone into work that fateful day, but his thumping head and the oppressive atmosphere in the house hadn't provided much incentive to stick around the farm. Sally was preparing a lecture, sitting at her laptop at the breakfast bar. The light from it, he remembered, cast a ghostly, cyanosed hue across her face that had made her look even more lifeless than she had been of late. He'd sighed, pulled his Blackberry from his breast pocket and slid it onto the kitchen table.

She'd barely flinched, tossing a nonchalant glance at him over the rims of her readers before turning her attention back to her screen. The static charge that bristled between them stiffened the follicles on his scalp. Either that or alcohol withdrawal had screwed with his thermostat. He felt clammy and cold and the sour smell of stale booze hovered under his nose. His Blackberry rattled and moaned, sending vibrations through the pine. It caught Sally's attention.

He tapped its face, skim-read the message from Emma, hailing his staying power during last night's drinking session, and chortled to himself. Then he'd blithely wandered over to Sally and placed his hand between her shoulder blades. Her spine had rippled away from his touch like a cat that didn't care to be stroked. He withdrew his hand and glanced over her shoulder.

On her screen was a freeze frame of two young, beautifully pale South East Asian women caressing each other erotically, one touching her lips to the other's porcelain cheek. 'What's that?' he'd asked, hoping that showing interest would recover the situation.

'It's a Korean film called *In My End Is My Beginning*.' The factual tone and lack of elaboration in her answer had spoken volumes. He'd asked her to explain.

'As one door closes another one opens.' She'd looked at him sternly. 'It's about a woman who is heartbroken after her *cheating husband* dies in a car accident.' He remembered sighing, knowing all too well where this was headed, but he was wrong-footed by Sally's dispassionate composure. He'd been expecting a fight for burning the midnight oil. Instead

344

she told him the story.

'The other woman comes to beg her for forgiveness. They move in together and their love-hate relationship develops into a lesbian affair. So the other woman is the end and the beginning.'

As he left to clear his head in Dingle Woods for a few hours, the last thing she had said to him was 'Drive safely.' He'd often wondered what would have happened if he had perished that day and Sally had lived. With his end, what would her beginning have been? And with hers, what is his?

Kat.

He swallowed back fresh tears and fumbled with his breast pocket, pulling his Samsung free. His heart was thumping. He hit her name on speed dial. It rang out. He must have already filled her voicemail with his pleas. He dragged open another drawer and pulled out the bottle and glass that he kept there, sloshing a muscular measure of whiskey into it. He knocked it back in one and poured another.

Three sharp raps at the door stopped him pouring a third. Iain skirted tortuously over the threshold before Scott had opportunity to invite him.

'What the frig is this?' He tossed a large manila envelope at Scott who had surreptitiously placed the malt back into the drawer and eased it shut. Iain stood before Scott's desk with his hips thrust forward in a way that made Scott feel bilious. His tongue flicked over his lips like a snake testing the air for the scent of prey. 'Is that whiskey I smell? Have you been drinking?'

Scott wiped a droplet of the spirit from the corner of his mouth and stared at his cousin.

'What the frig is this?' Iain's bony finger nailed the letter to the desk.

'How the fuck should I know?' He snatched up the envelope, unravelled the string from its washer-seal and peered inside. Photos. Large format photo prints. He pulled them out. The black and white enlargements were mottled with grain that suggested a fast film had been used in low light.

'No postmark. No stamp. Is this *your* idea of some sick joke?'

'Why single me out? I'm sure there's plenty of admirers out there that would want to send you love letters, Iain. Popular man like you.'

The images showed an array of knives laid out on what looked like a work bench. The type of blades that a hunter would use for butchery. Dark smears dulled the steels.

'What is it? Is it summat to do with that ex-con you hired? I knew he'd be trouble. Do I need to get the police involved?' His voice quaked. It gave Scott a secret thrill to hear the fear in his vibrato. 'The note.' Iain slid over his shoulder. 'What the chuffin hell does that mean?' A mist of cold spittle peppered Scott's cheek. He made a point of wiping it clean with his sleeve.

'A note…' He fumbled around in the envelope. A post-it note was sticking to the surface of one of the prints.

Ask him what he's keeping at Riverside.

He peeled it free to reveal a close up of a skinned carcass. A slaughtered rabbit.

Riverside. A similar post-it note, bearing the same name, was sitting right there on Scott's desk. He used the photograph in his hand to obscure Iain's view as he shuffled the correspondence on his desk. He carefully moved a sheet of paper to mask it.

'Haven't got a clue.' Despite his feigned indifference there was truth in his response. He sheathed the photos and thrust them back at his cousin's chest.

'Call the coppers if you wanna. Means sweet FA to me.'

'Wipe that bastard's data clean. I want no flamin trace. I'm not havin his dodgy dealings come back on me.' Iain was all too aware of the banned blades that Jez and Scott had been trading over the past few months, but Scott said nothing. The fact that the pigs already had the drivers' data was something his cousin didn't need to know.

Iain licked his lips again. 'Do it.' He swivelled to face the door.

'Iain.'

The drawer was open. The Balisong rigid.

'What?' His head turned.

The blade hit. It split his brow. One droplet of blood trickled down his forehead and into the crease at the corner of his mouth before his knees gave way.

'One shot.' Scott pointed to Iain's forehead.

'What?'

'One shot. I did have one.' He smirked like a rebellious teenager spoiling for a fight.

'Get a grip Scott.' Iain turned and fishtailed his way out of the door, leaving it open.

Scott waited a few moments then pulled open the whiskey drawer, uncapped the bottle and took a swig from the neck. He pushed the papers on his desk aside and studied the post-it that he had hidden from Iain, written sometime in his own handwriting. Riverside… *why* had he made a note of that? *When?*

He picked up his phone and tapped the name into the browser.

Riverside Retail Park

Riverside social housing

Riverside bar & restaurant

Riverside school

Riverside skateboard centre

Riverside (Rock band)

The list scrolled on. His first hunch, that he'd scribbled it down as a potential 'first date' venue, held some credence. But that made no sense in relation to the note in the envelope: *Ask him what he's keeping at Riverside*. Ask who? Keeping what? He clicked through to the Riverside gastro-bar website and browsed the photos, but no bells rang. He shut it down, opened his contacts and hit speed dial.

'Kat, it's Scott. I've left messages... Give us a call. Please just let me know everything's OK.' Then he added after a pause, 'Even if you've changed your mind.' He hung up then immediately followed up with a text.

Kat, tell me to fuck off if you need to. I'll deal with it. Just get back to me. Please. S xxx

Why hadn't she worked her shift at the Clover on Friday? Had she missed any others since they got back?

Ash would know. And the wagons were due a safety inspection.

***

'Did you shag her? Go on give us the juicy details.' Lee's bony elbow gave Scott's shoulder a needle. 'Couldn't get a sniff meself.' He sniffed then crouched under the wagon's front grill to check the under-cabin engine was over the pit.

'Christ's sake Ash. I thought you were lookin out for her.'

'I was. I am. If you're looking mate, you can't help but see...' He sucked at the tip of his vape and grinned. He slapped the side panel on the cab with his huge palm like he was testing the loin of a thoroughbred.

Scott's phone vibrated against his chest. He looked down at his jacket but ignored it.

'Might be her now.' Lee tapped his vape against Scott's breast pocket.

'Nah, it'll be Iain tryin to find out what I'm up to. Twat.'

'How can you be so sure?'

'It's me old phone, use it for work stuff. Kat doesn't have this number.'

'S'good enough for me.'

'So have you seen her? In the last week or so?' Scott followed Lee as he worked his way around the vehicle, tapping the wheels on the roller brake tester with his steel toe-cap.

Lee stopped and turned around, 'Went over there to pick her up last week but no one home.' His façade of laddish banter liquesced. He pensively sucked on the vape. 'I figured she'd done a runner with you.' He shivered, either because the air in the workshop was bitter, or because his grave had been trespassed.

'Doesn't make sense. When I left her she said she'd get a lift with you.' Scott took out his tobacco and, ignoring the no smoking sign, quickly scaffolded a rollie. He offered the baccy to Lee, who waved it away with his vape.

His phone buzzed again briefly but he paid it no attention. He lit his tab and inhaled a lung full of smoke as if it would help him to deliberate. 'Is Rob about? The one she was seeing?'

'Nah. Told him to sling his hook a few weeks back.'

'Why's that?'

'Well aside from being a knob'ead, he started showing up here drunk.'

'Drunk? Kat said he didn't drink.'

'Fell off the wagon when things went tits up with her. Literally.' He grinned, leaning against the wagon.

'Bloody *knew* it. How'd he take it? When you sacked him?'

'Not good. Got a bit lairy so a couple of the lads chucked him out. Not heard owt since. Have you tried the solicitor's she works at?'

Scott shook his head. 'Thought you'd be more likely to know summat.'

'Rob was making a reet pain in the arse of himself before Christmas. That's why she went up to her folks' place.'

'You think he's hassling her again?'

'Dunno mate, but if he is perhaps she's laying low up there. I'll let ya know if she gets in touch.'

'Please. Cheers mate. Give me a shout if the wagon needs any work.'

'Aye, aye.' Lee saluted, strolled to the back of the workshop and started to wheel a mobile platform towards the truck as Scott made his exit through the roller doors. Spitting into his palm, he blotted the remnants of his rollie then tossed it into the hedge. He pulled out his phone. A new voicemail alert was splashed across its face. He swiped it fully expecting to see Iain's number. What he saw stopped him cold.

He swallowed. Is this a stalker? *Why* is this fucker stalking him? His heart stammered out a flurry of beats, then he chastised himself for being dramatic. It could be any marketing call, the bastards all withhold their numbers. Feeling emboldened by his own rationale, he listened to the voicemail.

'Mr McCabe. Detective Inspector Woods, Cheshire Constabulary. Called in at your yard at eleven o'clock this morning, that is, Monday January twenty-third. Mr McCabe further to our previous conversation we need your assistance in answering some questions. Please report to Warrington Police Station, Arpley Street at your soonest convenience and ask for me. You may wish to arrange for your own legal counsel to attend with you. May I take this opportunity to remind you that if you refuse to attend of your own volition it may reflect badly on you if a case comes before the court. Good day.'

***

'Resuming questioning of Mr Scott McCabe regarding case number 4315035/17. The time is sixteen-twelve and the date is Monday twenty-third January. We previously interviewed Mr McCabe on Thursday the eighth of December during which he confirmed that he is acquainted with Mr Jeremy Steele as a sometime employee of the *Move it with McCabe* Haulage Company and that he was aware of Mr Steele's interest in prohibited weapons. Is that correct Scott?' Detective Inspector Woods folded his fingers together and rested his hands on a pile of papers set out before him.

'For the benefit of the recording Mr McCabe has nodded' said Detective Constable Dawn Wilmington.

Scott glanced up at the corner-mounted CCTV camera then back at Woods's rheumy eyes. Which could see through him more?

'OK, let's try something different this time Scott. We're in receipt of some disturbing correspondence. From whom we do not know, it's been sent anonymously.' He paused and scoured Scott's face for any flickers of disclosure.

'Do you recognise her?' Woods turned over one of the papers. He pushed a large format photograph across the interview room table with his freckled forefinger.

Golden curls, auroral blue eyes and flushed lips that seemed to kiss a smile at Scott. The photo was more formally posed than any he'd seen on her profile, but Finn had an indelibly pretty face.

Scott looked up at the detective, searching his face for the connection. Woods gave nothing back. Scott turned to his legal representative, Mark Mitton, a sharp man in a sharp suit with an equally wounding hourly rate. Mitton smiled and nodded, silently affirming the advice he had given to Scott when he'd received his call.

'No comment.' Scott submitted.

'Does that mean you *do* recognise her and you're not telling us? Could look bad for you Scott if it turns out that you know this girl.'

Scott squirmed in his chair but said nothing.

'Recognise her now?' This picture he held face down like a casino dealer, flipping it at the last second.

Scott strained to make it out. It took a moment for his brain the register the badly exposed image. It didn't make sense. He pivoted the photo first left, then right trying to determine the correct viewing angle. Then he realised whatever, or whoever, it pictured was upside down. Hanging upside down.

He moved in closer as if it would help him to pull it into focus. A naked torso was slicked with dark paint. Blood? No. Raw flesh. Areas of the upper body had been artfully skinned revealing muscle and sinew. A long, deep gash ran the length of the trunk, spilling what was left of the innards. Melanoid, glistening voids swallowed the space that breasts had once occupied. The filleted orbs were displayed on a workbench in foreground of the frame, next to a black pile of steaming offal; a gruesome sacrificial alter over which the arms, partially stripped of tissue, hung either side of a bloated face. Blood dripped down its distorted contours, matting together her blonde locks into brown-red clumps.

'Oh, Jesus Christ.'

Woods's stubby finger drew his eye to some implements that were laid out on the bench in a grotesque parody of a surgeon's instrument trolley. A cleaver, a bush craft knife and a Balisong.

'Bloody hell. You don't think Jez—?' The connection was dawning.

He looked closer, straining to make out the constituents of the scene against the pixelating effect of poor exposure. Then he spied something that made his blood run cold. It lay amongst the tools; the grain of the image obscured the finer details but its general form was quite distinctive. A large-faced, opulent metallic watch.

He dropped the photo into the desk and buried his wrists between his knees, rocking backwards and forwards gently in an effort to calm his racing pulse. He clamped his right hand around his watch face, reassuring himself that it was where it should be.

'How do you know it's her?' he managed through clenched teeth.

Woods held out his open palm before Wilmington. The Constable reached down to the side of her chair and retrieved a large manila envelope. With his eyes not straying from Scott, Woods took the envelope, unwound the string from around the washer-seal and tipped out a driving licence, wrapped in an evidence bag. It bore Finn's digital likeness. The monochrome image was blotted with two dark beetroot fingerprints.

'Her licence. Her photo. Her blood type. I dare say her fingerprints too, but until we find her fingers we can't be sure. We need to know where she is Scott. Her *mother* needs to know where she is.' The unrest in Scott's demeanour had surely not escaped Woods's attention.

Scott braced himself to revisit the photograph. Could be a warehouse. Not a large enough space for a warehouse. A workshop of some kind. Then he noticed the walls featured dark, vertical floor-to-ceiling panels. But they weren't panels, the walls were corrugated. It was a shipping container.

'Notice what's missing?' He held more prints in his hand.

Scott's eyes frantically scanned the photo. He made out the tip of a meat hook protruding obscenely from her crotch.

Bloodied stumps flanked it either side.

'Her le—'

'Her legs.' The policeman slapped down his trump card. A pile of neatly butchered thighs, shanks and shins. Her feet, hacked off at the ankle, stood together next to the severed limbs like a pair of neatly stowed shoes. Painted toes; red gloss; the very same polish she was sporting the night he had bedded her.

'Oh… fu—'

He felt the g-force of a white-knuckle ride careering in reverse through a three-sixty loop, back to the moment he'd received Finn's cryptic missive the night he was out with Kulbir.

You said you wouldn't speak to any other girls while I still had legs.

Finn hadn't sent that message. She was already dead. Which meant that the similarly perplexing texts he'd assumed were from Kulbir and Cheri…

'Oh God. Water, please.' He cupped his mouth and baulked.

'Fetch the man some water please Dawn.'

The foreground of this picture was illuminated by strip lights. The doors at the back of the container had been unbolted and one side was propped open. It was taken on an overcast day or at dusk. The background was barely distinguishable, but to the educated eye, belonging to one who had on many occasions offloaded goods into containers at the Quays, Scott could make out the briefest glimpse of studded, criss-cross metalwork. The Transporter Bridge. Over the River Mersey. By the side of the River Mersey. *Riverside.*

He wondered if it was possible for the police officers to see his blood pounding through the veins in his neck.

'Pretty girl.' Woods hadn't finished yet, another likeness appeared - a radiantly beautiful Asian girl wearing a short sleeved, dark blue tunic with the word 'Doctor' embroidered across the breast pocket.

'Christ, not—' He realised the pointlessness, and self-incrimination, of completing the sentence, even as nausea was threatening to gag him.

'She ain't pretty no more.' Woods made as if to flip another picture.

'Please… don't.' Scott raised his hand. Wilmington placed

a plastic cup of water in it. He gulped its cooling contents, as if trying to keep his throat from closing. 'I don't understand. How?'

'We were hoping you'd be able to help us with that Scott. We have *her* ID too. Same MO. Bloodied fingerprints. Her photo. Her blood type. Her father and brother are distraught.'

'And a third girl' he continued, 'she had a very distinctive tattoo across her shoulder and back. I can show you the picture if you like.' He turned up the edge of a face down photograph, taunting Scott, who simply raised his palm and looked away.

'The sick bastard has carved the tattoo clean off in one sheet of flesh. Displayed it on the table in front of her.' He held the picture in question up to his own eye level, surveying it mockingly. The light that shone through it showed Scott the gruesome scene in reverse. 'Takes a very specialised knife and a skilled hand to do that kind of work, wouldn't you agree Scott?'

Scott's brow creased. His jaw slackened. 'No comm—' He spluttered as phlegm snagged in his throat.

'We've studied these images closely. They have a number of things in common, aside from all being in a similar location; aside from showing the girl skinned and dismembered. They have one more thing in common.' Woods drew Scott's attention back to the professed image of Finn's legless, hanging corpse. 'Who is this at the back?'

Scott strained to make out a dark, ill-defined form in the shadows.

'Perhaps this will help.' He dealt another image.

The lower right section of the photograph had been enlarged and enhanced. Blocky though the image was, in the corner of the shot it was now just possible to make out a sinister figure, crouching in the darkness. One knee was bent, propping up an arm; the other knee planted on the floor. One hand served as a supporting buttress; in the other a slim blade shone with a needle of light. A balaclava covered the face. The long rubberised apron draped over the chest and legs gave way to a para style boot on the visible foot. It was a hunter posing with pride next to their latest trophy.

'Who is this? Jez? Who shot the video?' Woods held it centimetres from Scott's nose.

'Video?' The word was barely audible.

'The stills are from a video Scott. Very likely one that has been streamed online on some sick dark web channel for a clamouring audience.' Wilmington interjected.

'How do you know?' He tugged at his collar.

'Because the video file was emailed to us.' Woods answered.

'Who from? Can't you speak to them?'

'If we knew who it was from, we wouldn't be asking you. It was from a very cleverly encrypted source.'

Scott looked at him blankly.

'How does it work Scott – you lure them and he kidnaps them? He kills them and you take the trophy shots?'

'You don't think *I*—' Dread hit him in full the face like a bucket of ice-cold water.

'Think you *what*, Scott?' Detective Inspector Woods crossed his arms and nestled into a pitiless glare.

'What evidence do you have to link my client to these alleged crimes?' Mitton paused his note-taking to butt in. 'Do you have any bodies? Any witnesses?'

Woods eyed Mitton wearily then turned his attention

back to his suspect. 'Let me tell you what we *do* know. We *do* know that each of these girls...' He put the smiling prints of Finn and Kulbir side by side as his colleague placed down next to them the seductive selfie that Cheri had used for her profile.

'… was active on the *Date with Fate* website.'

He paused to read Scott's expression.

'We *do* know that each of these girls were in contact with a member known as Best-Bet-7. We *do* know that BestBet7 sent messages from an IP address registered to the *Move it with McCabe* Haulage Company.'

'No comment' Scott blurted out.

'We *do* know, Scott, that each of these girls is missing.' He placed his splayed fingers across their faces and pushed the three photographs across the table towards Scott.

'If I may.' Mark Mitton interjected again.

'Mr Mitton.' Woods conceded with an irritated sigh.

'If I may ask my client a question.'

'Go ahead.' He lay the floor open with a wave of his arm.

'Scott, if Detective Inspector Woods can confirm that messages were sent to these girls from your business computer – am I correct in assuming that is what you're suggesting Detective Inspector?'

'You are.' He looked unamused.

'*If* that proves to be correct', he paused as Woods waved his hand dismissively, 'If that proves to be correct, is it possible that Jeremy Steele had access to that computer?'

'Yeah.' Scott nodded with visible relief. 'It's possible.'

'It wasn't password protected?' Woods interrupted.

Scott looked at his solicitor. Mark nodded.

'Yeah, it was password protected but I'm fu— friggin useless at rememberin passwords so I have 'em written in a folder.'

'In a folder.' There was derision in his tone.

'The folder is on me desk.' Scott tapped the table with his fingertips.

'Could anyone else have had access to the office computer?' Mark said.

'My cousin Iain, he runs the farm businesses. *Technically* he's me boss.' Scott sneered. 'All the drivers were in and out. You know, lots of people… I suppose.'

'Lots of people. Very well. We can obtain a warrant to seize it. Determine the patterns of communication.' Woods watched Scott carefully as he added. 'And your home computer. I presume you have a home computer Scott?'

Scott swallowed.

'And your phone.' He micro-glanced at the handset edging out of Scott's lapel pocket.

'Be my guest.' Scott reached for his phone and tossed it onto the table. His new phone. His pay-as-you-go. The one that he'd never used for *Date with Fate*. Or the onion.

Mitton picked up the device and handed it back to Scott.

'Get your warrant Detective. In the meantime do you have any further questions for my client?' Mark symbolically snapped his laptop shut.

Woods turned to Wilmington. 'Tell them what you've been doing, Constable.'

'Mr McCabe, as I speak we have two officers scouring CCTV footage of the areas in and around where each of these girls lived and worked.' She pushed her glasses onto her forehead. 'They are looking through hours of video, frame by frame, tracking their movements around the dates that they were last seen.'

'Very good, thank you Dawn.' Woods flashed a satisfied smile. 'Do you have any information that might assist us in determining where and with whom they might have been before they disappeared?'

'No comment.' Scott gulped.

'Imagine how it will look, Scott, if we identify you in the company of any of these young women.' He adopted a solemn tone. 'Imagine how it will look to the Crown Prosecution Service that, when given the opportunity, Scott, you declined to give that information to us?'

'No comment.' His eyes stung from trying not to blink.

'I notice that you've had a haircut and shave. Why the sudden change of image?'

'No comment.' He mopped his top lip with his sleeve.

'Very well. Mr Mitton, we will require Mr McCabe to surrender a DNA sample and fingerprints in order to eliminate him from our enquiries.'

'Sure.' Mitton turned to his client. 'Scott that's routine. Just a swab of your tongue and an electronic scan of your fingertips.'

'Due to the potentially serious nature of the offenses under investigation we will also reserve our right to detain Mr McCabe until we have run a side-by-side analysis of his fingerprints and the prints found on the ID of these women. It'll take a few hours.' Woods jutted his chin forwards triumphantly. 'During which time we will apply for our warrant.'

'Then I'll anticipate you releasing my client within twenty-four hours or else bringing a charge?' The solicitor's question was a rhetorical affirmation of his client's rights.

'*Twenty four hours?* I've got to collect my son from after school club. I need to get back.' Adrenaline dizzied his head and churned his insides. He needed to get on to Kirk before the warrant was issued.

'We'll ensure you can make arrangements for your son until our analysis is completed. Who would you like us to contact?'

Scott slouched in his seat, shook his head and said with resignation, 'Angela Capote. Jae's grandmother.' Then after a pause he said 'Hold on a minute, don't I have the right to make the call myself?'

'Technically no.' Woods exchanged glances with the solicitor, 'but in view of your circumstances, I've no problem.'

Scott lifted his phone from his breast pocket, tapping the sequence that was Angie's number from muscle memory. It rang out. 'No reply.' He looked at Woods, who nodded.

His finger hovered over the keypad. He could call Roy, he had the landline for the farmhouse branded into his skull. Then he thought better of it, and wracked his brain for Charley's number. Why hadn't he transferred his contacts? 'Come on…' Scott, said to himself, drumming his fingers on the desk.

'Anyone else you can try?' Woods tapped his biro on the back of Scott's hand to silence his drumming. Scott sighed, kneading his forehead. Emma and Kirk would both be caught in the rush-hour frenzy. With a reluctance he couldn't quite place, he dialled Roy's number.

'Aye Scotty lad.' Roy answered within a beat.

'Aye Uncle Roy. Can you do us a favour?' The question

was still rolling reluctantly off his tongue when Angela's return call pealed through it. He wasted no time in switching lines.

'Angie? Thanks for calling back. I'm sorry to ask this again but please can you pick Jae up for me? Got stuck somewhere and might be a few hours.' Scott shuffled in his seat, mumbled a few instructions, then hung up.

'Very well. If that's all gentlemen, Dawn, I'll call the interview terminated at seventeen-twenty-seven. The desk Sergeant will book you in.' Woods said with a hint of victory.

As Wilmington hit the stop button on the heavy duty recording deck the *thunk* rang in Scott's ears as if it were a hangman's trigger for the trap doors.

***

The stench of ammonia from the disinfectant tablet in the urinal stripped the lining of his nostrils like smelling salts. Stale piss would have been easier to stomach. Perhaps it was designed to give the short-term holding cell patron a splitting headache; to keep them alert as a form of torture. Sleep deprivation is, after all, a military technique for loosening a prisoner's tongue, he mused.

Scott sat on the edge of the bench and pressed down the blue plastic-covered mattress with the heel of his hand; designed no more for comfort than it was to be pleasing to the eye. Nevertheless he felt emotionally exhausted. He lay back and, in lieu of a pillow, crossed his palms behind his head, staring vacantly at his reflection in the convex ceiling-dome mirror that enabled the Custody Officer to see his every move through the letter box slat in the solid steel door. That's when he wasn't monitoring Scott via the CCTV camera that was trained on him from the corner of the six foot by eight foot cell.

The white glare of the cornice strip lighting burned his eyes but every time he closed them Finn's skinned, dripping corpse swung overhead. He could smell the grease on the chain; could taste the cold, metallic blood on his tongue.

He couldn't rest. He sat upright and swung his legs over the side of the bed base. He had to get hold of Kirk. Had to get his computers and phone permanently sanitised. It was only a matter of time before Woods got his warrant.

Only a matter of time before a search of his office and cottage gave up every bit of hardware he owned.

Only a matter of time before forensics scrolled through an inventory of every email, every text, every call he'd made to Finn, Kulbir and Cheri. Every website he'd perused.

Only a matter of time before Wilmington caught a blurred, monochrome glimpse of him walking hand-in-hand with one of them through the dark, damp streets of Sale, or Manchester, or Warrington.

How much evidence do the CPS need to bring a charge?

Fucking hell he needed to get out. He instinctively tugged at this breast pocket for his phone. Only it was in a locked box behind the custody desk along with his wallet, belt, trainers and his watch. His watch. A watch that bore a striking resemblance to the timepiece in the photos.

Was it his?

How could it be his?

How long had he been sitting there asking himself questions he had no answers for? He had no way of knowing, and no way of knowing how much longer. He looked down at his socks. He must have stood on some motherfucking bad luck drain.

'Toast' he said to himself as moisture stung his eyes. He

stood and paced up and down. If these girls really had been kidnapped, was he the last person to see them alive?

Had they been taken hostage on the same night?

After they had been with *him*?

Had they been followed?

If they had then the abductor would *surely* be on the CCTV too. He tried to pacify himself with that thought and sat down again.

Yes, *if* the girls were abducted on those very date-nights the killer – because let's assume that's what he is; she is; they are - the killer would *surely* be seen close behind him as he left?

DNA. D-N-fuckin-A. Jesus, Jesus, think. What did he do?

He used a condom with Finn. With Kulbir… he didn't go inside Kulbir, at least he didn't remember going inside her. He remembered cleaning her, after… He flushed the tissues and wipes. Cheri – Christ knows what happened with Cheri, he was utterly fucked. Still, if the state of Finn's body was typical of the others – he shuddered at the image burned onto his retinas like a sun-glare negative – if it was, then it's unlikely that any of his DNA would be found on the bodies. If they ever *find* the bodies. Their flats, though; their houses. Hair, skin… Chrissake the pigs would have a flamin field day. How long does it take for DNA results to come back? Would it prove anything? That he had been there? No, they could have picked up his hairs and particles of his skin from being somewhere else with him. He'd seen that on cop shows. His DNA could have been transferred to their homes by *them*. Would that hold in court? Would it be cause for reasonable doubt?

Circumstantial. That's what they call it. Circumstantial.

Drinks.

Wine glasses.

Saliva.

Fingerprints.

He was on his feet. 'Oh fuck oh fuck oh fuck.' He struggled for breath. Then a thought struck him in the side of the head like a slaughterhouse bolt.

Kat.

Why hadn't Kat returned his calls or messages?

Why wasn't she at home when Lee called by to take her to the Clover?

He hadn't met Kat through *Date with Fate*.

Does that make her safe?

Or was his every move being shadowed?

He resumed the pacing, searching the ceiling for answers. He caught his hall-of-mirrors alter ego in the reflective dome. He looked scared. Terror-stricken like Munch's *Scream*. He needed to calm down. They would be watching him. What would make him look more guilty, being calm or being restless? Christ, if only he could smoke.

Scott walked up to the door and pressed his ear against it to listen for the segs of a copper's boots clipping the floor tiles. All quiet that is apart from another captive, no doubt sodden with booze, wailing *You'll never walk alone*. The irony didn't escape Scott who felt very, very alone. Between the erratic bouts of the drunkard's stanzas, a melodic verse hovered towards him on a thermal somewhere above his reeling thoughts. A familiar tune rendered in an unfamiliar way. A haunting, solitary voice. Did he know the voice as well as he knew Dave Grohl's lyrics? Singing of crimes. Of doing time. *A Matter of Time.*

He found himself accompanying the soloist in a feeble whimper. Where was it coming from? Next door? The corridor?

'Who's there?' Nothing.

'Are you screwing with me?' He slapped his palms and forehead against the cold steel and, feeling helpless and desolate, he started to cry. Who will look after Jae? What will they tell him? Will he see him again?

'Oh God, get me out of here. Get me out.' He desperately needed to speak to Kirk. Anything to buy himself some time to figure out what to do.

Was he being set up?

MrMacabre? Mr No caller ID? Fucked up messages from all three girls?

Who did that?

Was that the killer?

What if they wanted him put away?

Who would want him put away?

'OK, OK, OK, calm down Scotty boy. You're bein a paranoid eejit. A dopey dick. Come on now. Sit yerself down and calm down' he whispered as he pushed the tears from his cheeks, slowly turned and made his way back to the bench. He lay down, placed his right hand over his thumping heart and closed his eyes.

'Lay down Sally. Rest you in my arms. Don't you think I want someone to talk to?' Saline leaked out of the corners of his eyes and into his ears.

'Lay down, Sally, no need to leave so soon…' He could taste the salt in his throat as he swallowed.

The cornice strip lighting dipped out for a moment. He lay there wide-eyed in the darkness, frozen.

'Breathe… Breathe Sally.' He tried to slowly breathe in through his nose and out through his mouth. 'Breathe Sal…'

It flickered back into life, stuttering and flaring as it snagged on the starter.

'In… Out…'

Pressure on his chest.

'In… Out…'

Lightning flashes.

Like a storm moving in.

'In Sal…'

'You in Sal?'

Flashes of light. Darkness.

'Sal?'

Flashes of light. Stuttering.

'Sal… You in?'

Lightning flashes. Freeze frames. The hall. The stairs. The bedroom door.

A beam of light. Sweeping. Left. Right.

Swinging shadows. Breaking the beam. Left. Right.

Legs swinging. Woman's legs. Woman's legs. Girl's legs. Girl's red legs.

'Watch this.'

Beam sweeps round. Jez's face under lit with red fire. Jez's face like a demon.

'Watch this.'

He raises a blade. Sharp blade. Slicing. Slicing through slimy, glistening tissue.

Slicing his tongue in two.

'Wath thisssss…' he hisses.

Not a blade. A watch. A big, opulent gold watch.

'Wath thisssss…'

Swinging left, then right. Left. Right. Catching the light.

Jez's face. Darkness. Jez's face. Darkness. Jez's face. Roy's face. Jez's face. Roy's face.

Roy's eyes. Roy's twitch. Roy's voice.

'Shut your little fuckin mouth or I'll rip your little fuckin tongue out'

Upright. Reaching for air. Heart pounding. Strip light blanching the cell with hot, white light.

'Brenna.'

Tuesday: 05:48

The clanking of the lock, rapid firing through its seven-levers, bounced off the harsh brick walls like a pinball hitting play-hardened rubbers; like a rollercoaster carriage ratcheting up to the sightless pinnacle of a steeply climbing track.

Scott grasped the edge of the mattress and braced himself for going over the edge.

'Let's go.'

Whilst the stolid expression on the Custody Officer's

face hardly shouted 'scream if you want to go faster' Scott could yet feel the giddying g-force of plunging at full tilt. He was done with this ride. He wanted to get off.

'Go?' Go where? Back to the interview room to be charged? Back to Woods for more interrogation?

'You're to be released.' The copper signalled for Scott to check out from his overnight stay with a jerk of his head. Scott didn't stop to ask exactly what *released* meant. Released on bail? With conditions?

He shuffled in line behind the Officer whose heels, torturously slowly, ticked out the seconds as they hit the concrete. He didn't dare look ahead, instead he looked at his socks slapping against the cold, glossed, uniformly grey flooring. Blue steel doors flanked them on either side. *Tick. Tick. Tick. Tick.*

They passed through a solid, heavy door and turned into another corridor. Same floor but different doors moving through his peripheral vision. Wooden doors. Scott chanced raising his eyes to his left as the Officer seemed to be slowing.

INTERVIEW ROOM 4: DO NOT ENTER WHEN
THE RED LIGHT IS ON

His chest sank.

'Alright Dave?' Another Officer jovially greeted Scott's chaperone, who responded with a laid-back salute. They picked up pace again. They passed room three and room two. Scott pre-empted the halt outside room one. The Officer walked on and pushed open a beech-veneer, semi-glazed door.

'This way.' He was nodding towards the front desk. 'Well d'you want to be released or not?' There was a faint flicker of a smile on the policeman's face. It smacked more of derision than warmth.

Scott was escorted to the desk and left standing at the glass window in front of the Custody Sergeant.

'Mr McCabe.' He looked up and waited for an affirmative. 'Mr Scott Thomas McCabe of number two Tied Cottages, Oak Grove Farm?'

'Ye-ah' his voice cracked. 'Yes.'

'OK Scott.' You're to be released without immediate charge.'

'Immediate charge? What does tha—?'

'It means the fingerprint analysis came back clean.' He licked his finger tip and leafed through some forms, picking the top two up and placing them on the desk in front of him. 'The prints found on the young ladies' belongings did not match yours. At this time there is insufficient evidence to bring a charge.'

'What time did the results come back?' Scott's eyes flitted around the room, trying to gauge how long he'd been there.

'Depends on how busy the technician was. Can take a couple of hours. Can take longer.' He clasped his hands in front of him, looking like he was in no hurry to process his detainee. 'You've got your solicitor to thank. He's been quite persistent.'

'So that's it? I'm free to go?' He tried, unsuccessfully, to temper his surprise.

'For now, Sir. Pending the review of further evidence. And searches.' He paused to eye Scott impassively. 'This is your notice in writing to that effect. I am obliged to bring your attention to the part of the notice that states a prosecution may be brought if further evidence or information comes to light.' He slid the notice under the window.

The Sergeant pushed back his chair and sauntered over to a half-height wall of small, black-fronted boxes. He turned the key in one of them and brought it back over to the desk. He studied the contents and compared them to his inventory list.

'Wallet.' He pushed it under the window. Scott open it, flicked through the contents and nodded. The Sergeant placed a tick against the item on his list.

'Phone.' He glanced up at Scott as he passed it to him. There was something about the expression that shadowed the copper's eyes that made Scott shiver. He fired up the handset and nodded.

'Tobacco; Lighter. Those things'll kill you.' He eyed Scott smugly as he ticked them off.

'Drink's too wet without one.' Scott snatched them up and defiantly started to roll a compact, white trumpet.

'Watch.' He plucked the gilt eyesore from the box and laid it across his own palm. 'Expensive watch.' He scrutinised the piece like a collector might, then looked up at Scott. 'Very distinctive.'

Scott pinched the tab between his lips and held out his hand impatiently. The copper wasn't very subtle and frankly he didn't need to do anything to make Scott feel any more shit-scared than he already did.

'Last, but not least, your trainers.' He flipped them over to examine the tread before unclipping the lock on the kiosk window and sliding it up a little. He shoved Scott's stained, well-worn Vans through the aperture. Scott seized them and retreated to the seating area to put them on, suddenly realising that his chilblained toes were stinging.

He pocketed the other items, bar the Clipper, and turned towards the exit.

'Detective Inspector Woods may need to interview you again.' The Sergeant was on his feet. 'Don't think about leaving the area without informing us of your whereabouts.'

'Yeah, yeah, bloody yeah.' Scott dismissed the comment with the back of his hand and lit his cigarette, hoping this show of casual disdain for authority would attest his blamelessness.

He pushed his shoulder to the door and upturned his collar against the pasty rose of dawn.

06:15

'Six fuckin fiftain.' Too early to call Kirk. Too late to call Brenna. Scott sheathed his watch and leant against the sandstone stanchion between the arches at the main entrance of Arpley Street police station. He'd belligerently placed himself underneath the *No Smoking* sign to drain what was left of his smoke. He tossed the stub, pushed his hands into the groin pockets of his jeans and surveyed the street. Sod all in spitting distance; a typical northern street lined with a motley array of 1930s two-up, two-downs in various states of neglect and reclamation, for all he knew a flimsy façade propped up by a timber frame. The Rovers and the Kabin would have looked at home. Lord knows he felt like he was living a farfetched soap opera storyline, the type that writers resort to when viewing figures are on the wane. And for all his grip on what is real and what is imagined; what is recollection and what is fabrication, he may as well have been a player in a Westworld set.

To his left was the corner of Museum Street and on it a three foot tall red brick enclosure boasting the skeletal remains of council-planted shrubs. He strolled over and sat on the wall to contemplate his next move. He wanted to get out of ear shot of the cop shop, plus the smell of bacon was making him feel sick. He sat down, pulled out his baccy and papers and rolled himself another Rich Tea. He peeked at his watch again; six eighteen. Still too early to call Kirk. Still too late—

'Fuck it. What time is it in Ottawa? Five hours back…' His finger traced the time difference back through the hours around his watch face. 'Twenny past one. *Sod* it.'

He rose to his feet, lit his cigarette and continued down Arpley Street away from the station. Flashbacks appeared before him like holograms. Brenna as a young girl. Brenna in her school uniform. Brenna posing pigeon-toed in red tights. Brenna's red legs kicking out. Brenna's red tights ripping. The visions split his skull and took his legs. He doubled at the knees, careening towards the tarmac, grazing the fleshy underbelly of his hand as he broke his fall. The stinging barely registered; his pain receptors were already engulfed. Why hadn't he seen it before? Why hadn't he recognised the voice behind the venomous hissing or the smell of his stale-coffee steeped breath? He shuffled over to the kerb and started to sob. He sobbed until his diaphragm ached.

He dried his face with his sleeves and took out his phone.

'It's not too early. It's too fuckin *late*.' He brought up his short list of contacts, thumbed his sister's name and hit dial.

The international dialling tone sounded like the line was engaged, he knew it well though and hung on. And on.

'Pick up Sis, pick up.' He cuddled himself and rocked back and forth. He was about to give up when the line clicked.

'Scott?' Brenna whispered. 'Do you know what time it is here?' He could hear her shuffling. 'Hold on, Nate's asleep.' More shuffling then silence for a few moments.

'What's wrong Scotty?' She spoke in a timorous voice. 'Something must be wrong if you're—'

'I'm gonna kill him Bren' he spat. 'I'm gonna slice his slimy little fuckin throat from ear to ear. *Slowly.*'

'Who? Waddaya talk—?' Her brother's laboured breathing coursed through the ear piece.

'For what he did to you. I'm gonna cut his little shrivelled balls off. Him and who else? Who else Bren? I know he brought others. I can *feel* them.'

'Oh God, it's come ba—'

'I'm gonna fuckin scalp him. Killin him's too good for him. I'm gonna string the fucker up and skin the dirty cunt alive.'

'*Please* don't mention anything to Mu—'

'Dirty fuckin dirty pervert. I'm gonna cut him Bren, so help me fuckin God.'

'He's Mum's brother, Scott, please don't.'

'Why didn't you tell me Bren?'

'It would kill her…'

'*Why?*'

Brenna listened helplessly to the anguished cries of her brother's awakening, knowing that any attempt to comfort him would be futile, but perhaps some measure of explanation would palliate his pain.

'I needed you to remember Scotty. That's why I sent you the book. My therapist said the memories needed to come from you. That it's the only way to heal.'

'Heal? *Heal?* Bren this is off the fuckin scale!'

'You'd never have believed me…'

'I *would've* believed you Bren. I would've. I'd never doubt you Sis. But Why? Why did you let that pervert take Jae in when I lost the plot? Why would you do that?'

'I didn't know Scotty. They didn't tell me. By the time I found out you'd got your shit together and he was back with you. I just prayed… *prayed* that he'd never touched Jae because he's never touched you. It was always me. Only me. You were just made to watch—'

'Just? *Just?*'

'Jesus Scotty, I wish I was with you now. You can't deal with this alone. You can't.'

'I've got to get out of here Bren. Got to get Jae out. Can't stand another fuckin minute—'

'Get a flight Scott. Just do it. *Please*. You could be here within 24 hours.'

'I can't.' His voice failed him. 'I can't Sis. It's outta me hands. It's fucked up.'

'What is bro? What's out of your hands?'

'My life. Jae. The whole fuckin lot.' He paused to re-light his dead rollie and inhaled.

'It's just a matter of time.'

***

06:53

Kirk stood at his front door rubbing his eyes; his face still scared by the folds of his pillow. 'Christ mate, what a bloody mess. Unbelievable.' As he watched the cab driver pull away, he self-consciously pulled his tight fitting T-shirt over his paunch. It bounced back up over the waistline of his flannelette striped pyjama slacks. 'What flamin time is it anyway?' he asked rhetorically.

'You gonna let me in or what? I need a strong coffee.' Scott darted a barely smoked rollie into the mound of soil that was Kirk's neatly turned over flower bed. He paced up and down whilst his friend came to.

'You've gotta help me mate. Before the pigs seize me computers. What was it, that hack you mentioned? A booby trap?' Scott looked over his shoulder then pushed past Kirk. He pressed his back flush against the wall of the hallway as if trying to blend into it.

'I dunno mate.' Kirk scratched his head. 'If I go searching for stuff like that—'

'*Please* Jim. I need this. What are the chances that any other bloke was messaging those three women on that site? All three? What if the pigs see those emails? Find out that I met up with every single fuckin one of 'em? I'm dead meat mate. Dead meat.'

'Not trying to be funny Scott but hearing you say it, it does look a bit bloody dodgy.' He made his way towards the back kitchen and put the kettle on.

'Exactly.' Scott followed him at close quarters, then it dawned on him what his oldest friend meant. 'Jesus Christ Kirk, you're my best mate. You've known me for thirty bloody years. What chance have I got in front of a jury if *you* don't believe me?'

Kirk swallowed and silently observed his friend. Scott looked gaunt and grey, he had dark shadows weighing heavy under his eyes, which were quivering with mania.

'I think I'm being set up. I don't know why. I don't know who.' Scott took out his tobacco and started to roll another cigarette. His hands were shaking so badly he could barely manage it. His eyes darted between Kirk and the back window.

'It's a bit farfetched ain't it mate? You been smokin that wacky baccy again? It's frying your brain Scott, making you paranoid.' Kirk finished brewing up and passed a mug of steaming coffee to Scott. It wobbled in his grip, spilling the piping hot liquid over his hand. Scott barely perceived the burn, but hastily deposited the mug on the table and lit his fag.

'There's nothing flamin paranoid about the pigs giving me the third degree and holding me in a cell.' He took a deep drag. 'You should've seen those pictures. Twisted…' He turned, holding the smoke in his lungs, and scampered over to the French windows. Unlatching them he slid the door open a smidge and blew the stream of vapour into the dusk, anxiously checking the back garden for snoopers.

Kirk picked up Scott's coffee and took it over to him. 'Areet. Give me a minute to throw some threads on. I'll see what I can do.'

Scott scoped his friend's eyes, flitting to the left and to the right. He couldn't work out whether the reluctance in Kirk's tone was a good mate trying to manage his expectations or a turncoat thinking about squealing.

'Thanks mate, I owe you big time.' He had no choice but to place his faith in him.

'Can't promise anything Scott.'

***

07:26

Kirk took his place at the office desk and hit the standby button on the tower.

'Right, so all me passwords and shit are in here.' Scott

yanked open the desk drawer, tugged out a folder and slapped it down. Kirk lingered on the open drawer. Sally's portrait smiled up at him.

'Poor Sal.' He moved as if to touch the edge of the silver frame. 'She was…'

'Kirk, mate. Please can we get this done?' Scott hovered over him, skipping from one foot to the other. He pushed the drawer shut. As Kirk looked up at him an uncharacteristic coldness swept across his eyes. 'She was a troubled soul' he finished.

'Sorry to hassle ya mate, *please*.' Scott tapped the side of the keyboard.

Kirk flipped open the folder and started typing. Scott made his way round the desk and unlocked the large drawer on the other side.

'Drink?' He pulled out the whiskey and two glasses.

'You're kiddin aren't you?' Kirk said. 'Too early for me mate.' He turned his attention to the screen and tapped an entry into the browser.

'Just need to slow me head down.' He poured a good double and strolled over to the window. His phone tickled his thigh. He pulled it out as Emma's name was fading from its screen.

You OK matey? Kirk texted to say the shit has hit the fan. Wanna come over?

He necked the drink in one and glanced at his watch. Seven-forty-five.

'Gotta go get the little man, Kirk.' He took out a bunch of keys and worked one of the rings free, tossing it onto the desk.

'Them's the spare cottage keys, mate. Let yerself in when

you're done here.' He moved quickly to the door.

'Like I says Scott, can't promise.'

'Just try. If it doesn't work I'll fuckin torch the lot. I'd rather go down for butchering evidence than butchering women.'

CHAPTER 23: MY SALLY

08:18

The Land Rover's breaks squealed as he pulled up, announcing his arrival. He'd blue-toothed Emma en route and left a sprawling, barely sensical voicemail giving her a synopsis of the last twenty four hours. Even the most lucid recanting of the tale would have sounded deranged.

He didn't have time to press the doorbell before Emma stood before him. 'Christ, you look like shit.'

Scott rubbed the bristles on his chin. He couldn't remember when he last had a shower and shave. His jeans were shiny with ingrained grime. His jacket was stained, like it had been sprayed with dirty engine oil. He smoothed down the front of his crumpled shirt. 'I need your help Em. I don't know where else to turn.' He pursed his lips around an unlit cigarette and patted himself down for his Clipper.

'Try your solicitor?' She watched his trembling hands cupped around his lighter, trying vainly to flick the flint into life and realised that her customary cynicism was misplaced. 'Scotty, babe, I'll do anything I can for you, but you need professional help.' And not just from a barrister, she left unsaid.

'I know. I know.' It eventually sparked into life and kindled the tip. 'Just need to get me head round this. Need to work it out.' As he inhaled his legs buckled. Scott threw himself against the frame of the door.

'Jesus, matey. Come in. Take the weight off. I'll stick the kettle on.' She slipped her arm around his waist, flung his arm across her shoulders and heaved him over the front door step. They wobbled serpentine-style into her living room.

After a few moments she emerged with two mugs of coffee. Scott hadn't moved. He sat staring at the carpet. Emma sat down next to him and rested her hand on his knee.

'How can I help you matey?'

'I don't know, Em. I don't know anymore. I forget things. I do things and I don't remember.' He twisted his knuckles into his eye sockets. 'I wake up from a daydream and don't know where I've been. Or how I got there. I find notes to myself. I don't know who I am any more Em.'

'I don't understand, Scotty. What are saying?' She reached around his back and cradled him.

'What if I *did*?' He implored her with his eyes, wide, wet and red. 'What if I did those things and I can't remember? I had sex with Josie and I don't know how I got there. What else have I done to women without knowing?' Tears leaked down his cheeks.

'Oh matey. Come on this is insane. I *know* you. Look how you are with Jae. You couldn't—'

'Jae.' He collapsed into his hands. 'I can't lose him Em. My little man. I can't. They'll give him to someone else. I can't bear it—'

'Now you listen Scott. That is *not* going to happen. I won't let it.' Emma leant over, grabbed a tissue from a box on the coffee table and handed it to him.

'That's why I came to you Em.' He dabbed his cheeks. 'I don't know who else I can trust. If I didn't do these things then why is it all pointing to me?'

'You think you're being framed?' Her perplexity offered little comfort. 'But why? Who? Who would want to set you up?' She picked up her coffee and warmed her hands around it.

'Get in line. Frank fuckin hates me - thinks I as good as killed his sister. Trev? Could he know about Josie? Roy and Iain? Believe me they've got every reason to want me out of the way. Jez? Does he think I've grassed him up? He *might* be the friggin psycho for all I know. Kat's jealous ex? He's a violent drunk... Take yer pick.' Running through the roll call seemed to imbue Scott with fresh hope, he stood up, energised by his hypothesis.

'That's why I need you Em. You said you wrote about this hacking stuff. What if I'm being hacked?'

'It's possible, I guess...' Emma looked ponderous. She rose to her feet and made her way over to her desk.

'Emma, what can you tell me about it? Kirk's working on my computer now but if he can't clean it up I need another angle. Before the pigs get their warrant.'

'Could someone else pretend to be you? Is that what you mean?'

'Could they?'

She waggled her mouse to rouse her dozing laptop then started typing.

'This site.' She tilted the screen back to reveal a trashy looking gaudy webpage with a bright purple, mottled backdrop and an array of clashing fonts. 'It's something some geeky kid has built from his bedroom just because he can.'

Scott looked at her blankly.

'Basically you can type a text message and send it to someone but make it look like it came from a certain number.'

'So it could look like I sent it when I didn't?'

'Yep. Something else too.' She returned to the search engine, tapping away.

'This site gives hackers a guide about how to hack someone's social media profiles. Steal their identity. Given the inclination even *I* could probably figure out how to do it.'

'Jesus—'

'I told you matey, if your passwords are weak, they could crack into your dating account in no time. Any of your accounts for that matter. I managed to.'

'Yeah, but you know me.'

'Doesn't matter, these people are well crafty. Take a look at this.' She typed another search term, scrolled down the list of results and clicked a link. 'Someone with the know-how could be monitoring your activities, like, everything you do on your PC gets copied into another IP address. Spyware. Technically, someone *could* be watching your every move and intercepting it. The police sometimes use these tactics. And the secret service.'

'So if the police can, then somebody else could?'

'In theory, if they know the hacks.'

'How can I prove it's not me?'

'Dunno. There's probably an audit trail if you know how to find it. But I just write about this stuff mate – I don't really know how it's done. Kirk's your man for that.'

'Kirk built my computers Em. My work one and my personal one…' He looked at her. 'He built them from the ground up. Could've fuckin put any trap doors in there.'

'*Kirk*? Are you insane? Why the hell would Kirk want to set you up?'

'I dunno, I'm clutchin at straws. But he's always making

me out to be an asshole for looking at women, like I should feel guilty. Like I'm letting Sal down.' He paced up and down tugging on his cigarette, then turned to push the stub into a ceramic bowl on Emma's desk. 'Christ, he was *in love* with Sal for all I know.'

He searched Emma's eyes for clues. Her cheeks flushed.

'What? He *was*? You know something?'

'I— I don't know anything matey' she stammered and cleared her throat. 'Apart from the fact that you're being ridiculous.'

Scott resumed his pacing, nodding his head as if having an epiphany. 'I've left him messin with my computer Em. What if he's covering his tracks as we speak?'

'Bloody hell Scott. Settle down and get your head straight. This is nuts. Why would Kirk go to all this trouble to frame you? Do you realise what you're saying? If he did then that means he's got something to do with the girls disappearing? It's so completely ridiculous it's actually making me feel angry.'

Scott sighed and clamped his temples between his palms.

'Sit down. You *may* have something with this theory but get a grip. It's not Kirk. If anybody would know about this stuff it's Frank. He was in cybercrime wasn't he? You said it yourself he's a certifiable nutter.'

Emma straightened up and started to browse her bookshelves, walking her fingertips across the spines of the multi-coloured hardbacks. 'One that was trained to be a killing machine' she added.

Scott resigned himself to the sofa and buried his face in his hands. 'I don't know any more Em. I dunno who I can trust.'

'Hold on a minute.' She precariously eased herself up onto the swivel chair to peruse the titles of the higher-stacked volumes. 'I've got a book somewhere that explains all this stuff, take it to your lawyer. Now where…?'

She continued to leaf through the titles on the upper levels, pushing herself up on tip-toe. The chair pivoted sharply forcing her to grab one of the shelves, dislodging a box. It fell to the floor spilling its contents like a magician spreading out a pack of cards. 'Oh shit, that was close. Can you grab that for me matey?' she threw the comment over her shoulder as she steadied herself to pursue the search.

Scott slipped to his knees and started to scrape together the fan of postcards, photos and envelopes. Amongst the array he spotted a floral motif on the corner of a notelet. The botanic design and sickly-sweet perfume were familiar; both had faded with time but the memories they conjured blazed in his chest like heart burn. Swallowing, he teased the letter out from its place in the pack, unfolded it and started to read.

My beloved Emma,

I've let you down. I promised you that I wouldn't fall in love. Yet love you I do.

But they're last year's words already. I imagine next year's words will be spoken by another. Or others.

I read your message to Scott. Tread carefully my love, he will let you down. He let me down. And so have you. Not again. Enough.

Do you remember that I said when it hurts too much, when I can't stand it anymore, to let me go?

So let me go.

I can't look at my precious boy anymore knowing that I want to be somewhere else. Anywhere else. With someone else.

Emma, I thought you were my beginning, but all I can see is the end.

I have to go now, while I still can.

I love you. I love too much.

Your Sally xxx

'I love you...'

'What's that matey? You getting sentimental on me again?' Emma quipped in blissful ignorance, still searching the shelves of her bookcase.

'I love *you*.'

'What?' She glanced down from her perilous perch.

He looked up. '*You* Emma?'

'Scott I—' Blood drained from her jaw-dropped face.

'*Your* Sally? Sal loved you?' He rose to his feet. 'What the fucking fuck were you doing with my wife? She was *my* Sally.' He could barely see through the film of tears.

'Scott, please— I can explain, if you let me. Sal thought you'd had an affair and—'

'An affair? It was a shag. A stupid, idiotic, *literally* senseless shag. I didn't love Josie. Christ I didn't even like her. Did you love Sal?'

'I was—'

'Did you?'

'...getting there' she finished, easing herself down to his level.

'Getting there? What the hell do you mean by that? Did you love her or not?'

'Yes' she resigned, slumping onto the chair. 'Yes, Scott, I did love her, but she wouldn't have known it. I was trying to play it down, trying to do the right thing and let it go. You're my mate Scotty, you were then. I was trying to let Sally go—'

Scott stared at her incredulously, his tear ducts brimming with fresh grief. 'Let her go? *'Let her go?* Emma?'

His words hung in the air between them.

'You always said be careful what you wish for' he spat through gritted teeth.

'Don't... please... do you think I haven't—' She reached for him.

'And me, Em?' He batted her hands away. 'Do you think I haven't too? Every day. Every fucking, insanity-inducing day?' He grabbed her shoulders and shook her. 'Do you think I fucking haven't thought it was all my fucking fault? *Every fucking day?*'

Scott eyes blanched with fury, it blazed in his chest. He threw her back into the chair, stuffed the letter into his pocket and careened towards the door. He stopped and turned.

'And all this time I thought she hadn't left a note. *All this fucking time.*'

The door slammed so hard the walls shook.

***

09:27

He pulled off Dingle Lane just shy of the blind corner and nestled the Land Rover into the discrete clearing next to Dingle Brook Bridge. Angela should be here any minute. Scott climbed down from the driver's seat and strolled over to the gate, resting his elbows on the top of the stile that marked the start of the footpath. The narrow strip of tarmacked walkway twisted away into the distance, flanked on one side by a ghostly sparse Dingle Woods and a balding green on the other. The brook trickled under the bridge to his left. He was so exhausted he almost felt peaceful.

He pulled out his papers and tobacco. Just a few dried and dusty remnants in the crease of the pouch but enough to roll one or two, if he was frugal. As he rolled he left the stile and wandered along the perilously narrow pavement that lead to the moss and lichen carpeted wall of the stone bridge. He lit his tab and sat on the wall gazing vacantly at the water ambling over brush and pebbles.

Ping.

The text alert delivered a shock from his breast pocket, defibrillating his repose. He stalled. He hands tremored with apprehension. Could be Emma begging forgiveness. He couldn't bear that. Could be Woods with his warrant, or worse. He ignored it and sucked out what life was left of his paltry cigarette, seeming to drain his own reserves in the process.

Ping.

He had to know. If Woods was on his way over to the farm he needed to alert Kirk. He wiggled the phone free then closed his eyes and breathed in. He squinted at the screen.

Kat.

His lids sprung open.

Kat: Had to go underground. Sorry.

He hastily swiped the message banner from the screen. His mind reeled, spinning through a vortex of thoughts. Kat is dead. He's being taunted. He swept the area for movement; any rustling in the bushes; any silhouettes crouching and shifting. All quiet but the babbling brook.

The throaty purr of a twin air turbo motor emerged from behind him. He spun around. Angela's Fiat 500 slowed and swept into the layby. Jae's grinning face just visible above the dash, he waved excitedly at the sight of his Dad. Scott ran over, tugging the door open.

'Hey big fella. You've grown since yesterday.' He crouched down and released the seatbelt as Angela surfaced from the other side. Scott sank to his knees, scooping Jae up in his arms. He held him, swaying gently, planting kisses in the curve of his little lad's neck. 'God it's good to see you Jae.' He pulled back and took in his son's face. 'I've missed you so much Monkey.' He cupped Jae's jawline and stroked his cheekbone with his thumb.

'I saw you yesterday Daddy' he said, giggling.

'I know lovely. It's just been a very long day.' His kissed him on the cheek and rose to greet Angie.

'Oh good lord Scott, you look dreadful' she said softly, ushering Scott out of earshot from Jae. Jae obliviously skipped over to the bridge and looked over the wall.

'We could play Poohsticks Daddy.'

'In a moment fella. You find some sticks while I have a chat with Nonnina.'

'What's going on Scott? Why did the police keep you in?'

Scott glanced over each shoulder before responding.

'They could be here Angie. Could be following me right now. Had to meet somewhere quiet. No CCTV.'

'Why Scott? What do they want?'

Scott couldn't answer. His beseeching eyes moistened as they moved from Angie to Jae then back to Angie again.

'I can't stand it Ange. I don't know how to stop it.'

'What can I do?' She touched his cheek. 'Tell me.'

He clasped his hand over hers and closed his eyes flushing tears down his face.

'I can't lose him, Angie. What am I going to do?'

Angela hooked her hand through his elbow and steered Scott towards the gate.

'When you have a child they think you're always going be there. It's like a silent promise you make the day you bring them into the world – I'll always be here for you. They don't know it's a lie.'

'The first of many.' Scott let himself take Angela in. Time and wealth had been kind to her. Wealth, at least.

'They can't imagine the world without you. The day it dawns on them that their parents can't live forever is the most terrifying day of their lives. Scott I can live with the fact that you break that promise if you've made your best efforts to keep it. But to *wantonly* break it, it's like you're saying to Jae "I don't love you enough". You owe your wellbeing to him. You *have* to be there.'

'I don't know how Angie.' Her eyes were Sally's, sweet and warming like cocoa. He longed to hold her.

'You have to forgive yourself, show Jae how to love himself. So he can live in the world without you. Sally's already broken her promise to Jae; to God.' She drifted inwards. 'We've been purchased, and at a price…I searched Corinthians for answers, it brought me little comfort. Believe me Scott.' Angela took his face in her hands. 'You don't want to live to see the day that Jae believes this world is a better place without him.'

A cold, empty shadow swept over his heart, like Sally was passing through him.

'She loved Jae too much to stay with us.' He dissolved into Angela's embrace. An embrace across time. With Sally again. 'She loved too much.' He pulled her close. 'I love too much.'

***

10:14

He reversed into the garage and pressed the green button on his key fob. The door slid from its resting place and lowered itself slowly to the ground, cloaking Scott and Jae in darkness. His head flopped back onto the head rest. He closed his eyes.

'Are you sleeping Daddy?'

He jolted. 'Sorry sweetie. Just tired. Come on.' They slipped out of the four-by-four and through the door adjoining the cottage. The last thing Scott needed was Iain seeing the four wheel drive in the yard and calling the pigs. He and Jae seem to have slipped in unnoticed.

He handed Jae his backpack. 'Pop upstairs and pack a few of your favourite toys in here sweetie.'

'Why?'

'We're gonna go on a little trip Monkey. A secret trip.'

'Why is it secret?'

'It just is. Hop along now.'

He watched as Jae bounced up the stairs and out of view then dashed into the living room. A hand-written note was resting on his keyboard.

Pretty sure I cracked it mate but we won't know for sure til forensics try mining for data. It's a bloody dodgy hack buddy, could land you in more shit but I've done what I can. Bin this note as soon as you've read it. Kirk.

Was Kirk is playing it straight or covering his own paper trail? He pushed the note into his pocket for insurance then uncoupled the hard drive from the monitor, pulled the flex out of the wall and carried the tower into the garage. He pulled the back of the Land Rover open and slid the tower into the trailer. Then slipped back onto the house again.

'Jae?' he hollered up the stairs, 'just popping out for a minute.'

'OK Daddy.'

Scott eased the front door open and scanned the visible terrain. All the wagons were either out on the road or off the road in the workshop. Aside from a couple of cars and customers milling around up near the farm shop at the other end of the yard, all seemed quiet.

He crept out of the door and moved stealthily along the wall to the *Move it with McCabe* frontage. He slipped in, pausing to listen for voices. He tested the office door, it was unlocked. He knew he needed to work fast. Grabbing a toolbox from the shelving unit he threw it open and riffled around for a small screwdriver. The computer tower was asleep. He pulled out the mains plug and set to work unscrewing the casing. He slipped it off and worked on releasing the two hard drive cartridges from their slots. He pulled open the desk drawer and took out Sally's portrait. She would come along for the ride too.

The buzzer on the intercom sounded.

'Dammit.' He scuttled out with his booty and slowly approached the door to the yard. Peeking through the spy hole he saw a delivery driver looming large in the fisheye lens with a parcel in his hand. Scott composed himself and opened the door an inch.

'Yes?'

'Signed-for delivery.' The courier pushed an electronic POD through the gap.

'Right.' Scott scrawled an illegible signature, took the package and shut the door. He stood with his back against the wall and, realising he'd been holding his breath, evacuated his lungs.

He risked another peep outside. Still no sign of Iain. He scurried out from the office and back to his cottage, praying he'd gone unseen.

Back inside the house he shut the door, closed the curtains in the living room and pulled the blinds down in the kitchen. He propped up the portrait of Sally on the kitchen table and sat quietly in the semi-darkness for a few moments. A faint aroma of violets wafted up from inside his jacket. He reached inside. He unfolded Sally's note and smoothed it out on the table next to her image. Then he glanced up at the object d'art pinned to the fridge. Jae's bold artwork leapt out from the bric-a-brac around it. Jae. Daddy. Mummy. Mummy in her cloud.

He rose, poured himself a generous double of single malt into a dirty glass and strode into the living room. At the desk he grabbed a note pad and pen, took a slurp of courage, and wrote "*Dear Angie*".

After a few lines he signed off with "*We'll be a unit again. A family. Love always, Scott and Jae.*" When he was done, he drained his glass, picked up the note and shuffled back to the kitchen table, laying his composition over Sally's, he used the glass as a paperweight. Then he made his way into the hall.

'Jae? You ready?' He stood at the foot of the stairs and waited for his son's curly mop to surface.

'Where are we going Daddy?' Jae lolloped down the stairs dragging his backpack behind him. Norman sauntered over to him and nudged his leg. He threw the rucksack over his shoulder and scooped her up under her front legs. She dangled, half throttled by the drag of her own weight.

'It's a secret Jae.' Scott relieved Jae of his burden, ladling the cat in his arms. He took the bag and shepherded his boy through the door leading to the garage. He opened the rear door of the Landie, forced Norman into her travel cage and slung Jae's bag into the trailer. As he did his eye caught his trapper's knife in its belt sheath. He grabbed it and slid it around his waist, buckling up as he made his way around the side of the wagon.

'Hop in Monkey' he said opening the passenger door. Jae obediently jumped into the seat and waited for his Dad to clip him in. Scott lingered over him, softly kissing his son's forehead.

He walked around the back of the trailer and rattled the rear door. It was shut. Then he appeared next to his son, climbed into the driver's seat, pulled the door to and put the keys in the ignition.

'You ready?' Scott turned and looked at Jae who nodded excitedly.

He turned the engine over.

The CD player erupted through the speakers, shredding sweet Dusty Springfield's poignant pleas for him to stay as she strained to be heard over the spluttering and chugging of the motor. Jae held his hands to his ears.

'Too loud Daddy!'

Scott pressed his foot to the accelerator; the Landie growled and grunted, belching out smoke from its exhaust like a goaded, snorting bull.

He lay his hands by his side. Not on the gear stick. Not on the steering wheel.

The singer begged him not to go away. Had her entreaties made Sally think twice before she leapt?

As the smog billowed past his window he closed his stinging eyes and folded his hand around Jae's. The idling drone of the engine and the gasping of the tailpipe almost drowned out the feeble coughing that drifted through the haze towards him.

Dusty pleaded. He stood firm.

CHAPTER 24: WHERE IS HE?

10:43

Dying for air, Scott heaved into consciousness. He turned to Jae. His seat was empty, the passenger door gaping, smoke swirling through the cab.

'Jae? Where are you?' Panic flooded his chest. 'Oh God, what have I done? What have I done?' Fumbling blindly in the fog, he found his key fob and hit the green button. The garage doors started their ascent. Daylight filtered through the brown fug; fresh, cold air seared his lungs.

'Jae?' he croaked, shouldering his door and scrambling from his seat. Wafting the air, he ran into the smog at the back of the garage. It was bitter and sulphurous and it hitched in his throat, forcing a hacking cough. 'Jae. Where?' he said as he reached the door to the cottage. It was open. He fell through it landing at the foot of the stairs.

'Jae? Jae answer me.' His heart felt like a battering ram against his breastbone.

The front door was wide open.

A movement in Scott's periphery made him turn. Iain was swiftly slithering over the cobbles towards *Store it with McCabe*. Scott's face twitched like a cat with a bird in its sights.

He quickly assessed the situation. The farm was quiet, typical of post-Christmas, pre-pay-day thrift. Still only one or two customer cars in the car park and the owners of those were inside the shop. Feeling the back of his belt for the knife, Scott picked himself up and bolted across the yard. He glared through the reception area window. Iain was in there alone.

'Iain!' He hammered on the pane with his palms. 'Where is he?' His rage was a wave of napalm that wanted to incinerate everything in its path.

Iain turned and darted towards the door in a desperate bid to turn the key. Scott was too fast for him, ripped it wide open and grabbed his cousin by the throat. He pushed Iain backwards over the reception couch and forced him to the floor. Iain tried to raise his palms but Scott tightened his hold. The red blotches on Iain's skin bled together.

'Get off me' he said through a rictus grin.

'Where's Roy? Where's your fuckin pervert of a father? What's he done with Jae?'

'I don't know. I don't know.' Scott pressed Iain's windpipe with his thumbs. 'I swear.'

'Where does he go, your Dad, when he disappears on his business jaunts? Who does he see?'

'I don't know Sthcoth.' His spittle sent cold drops of froth across Scott's face. 'You know Dadth.' He clawed at Scott's hands. 'He wanderths.'

'I know what kind of wandering that pathetic deviant does. You *know*, don't you? You fuckin know. If he's touched Jae—'

'Let me go.' Scott could feel the oil on Iain's skin loosening his hold. The slime of filial fealty oozed from his every pore. 'You lay a hand on me and I'll call the police. I know they're on to you.' Iain's feet peddled in vain against the polished concrete.

'Be my guest you squealing little runt. I'll give that fuckin nonce up. I'll give the law enough on him that they'll hunt him down. Him and his sadistic, twisted cronies. They'll hunt him down and lock him away in a dirty pen like the sick, depraved cur that he is. That's if I don't find him first which he'd better pray I don't.' He pressed his knee against Iain's balls and stared into his reddening eyes as if scanning the retinas for stigmas of a diseased soul.

Iain tried to squirm free but his cousin increased the pressure on his Adams apple, forcing proud the quivering tip of his tongue. Scott pincered it between his thumb and forefinger and squeezed hard.

'Tell me where he is or I'll rip your little, fuckin, snaky tongue out.'

A loud clatter from the back office caught them both off guard.

'He's *here*?' Scott dropped his bleating cousin and stepped over him. He vaulted the reception counter, catching his foot on its edge and sending him slapping to the concrete palms down. Stinging and winded, he pulled himself to his knees. The sounds of a struggle came from the other side of the door, and a feint throttled whine.

'Jae.' He picked himself up and launched his shoulder at the office door. It threw him back, sending a spear of pain through his collar bone. He heard another stifled cry. Desperate, he braced himself and shouldered it again. It burst off its hinges as he tumbled through.

'Dad.' Iain squealed from behind him.

Roy's legs flayed in the air, his feet desperately trying to find the toppled stepstool. His clawing fingers were trapped between a taut cargo lash strap and the bloated flesh of his neck.

'What have you done with Jae?' Scott gritted his teeth,

staring at his uncle twisting and writhing.

'Nothing' he rasped. 'Nothing.' He kicked out trying to gain purchase on anything with his foot. Scott prepared to watch his uncle choke on his final, gutless gasps. But then he felt the sheath for his knife.

'You don't get away that lightly, you cunt. I'm gonna fuckin castrate you. I'm gonna bleed you out.' Scott grabbed the step ladder, climbed it and put the trapper's knife to his uncle's groin. 'I should cut your balls off' he hissed raising the blade to Roy's purple, distended face; scoring the flesh around his bulging eyes. His feeble spluttering and fusty breath made Scott want to slit his throat.

Scott wailed, raising the blade and bringing it down. Roy slopped to the ground like he'd been birthed, gasping and spitting. Scott jumped to the floor, grabbed the ends of the lash and pulled them tight.

'Where is he?' Roy sniggered. 'Where's Scotty? Is he with us now?'

'Shut the fuck up.' Scott twisted the cord around his fist and put the knife to Roy's neck. Roy's face started to fill with colour. Scott's arms shook with the effort of tightening the noose.

'Where's the little boy who liked to watch?' Roy said, grinning.

'You filthy cunt, I should kill you.' He cracked Roy across the face with his knuckles.

'I know ye forget things Scotty.' A bead of blood left his nose and trickled over his top lip. 'I know ye forgot it all. I'll bet ye could kill me right now and forget ye ever did it. It's what makes ye such a good boy.' He gave a chesty cough, 'All I have to do is tell ye to shut your little fuckin mouth—'

Scott's fist slammed into Roy's jaw with a sickening thud.

'Who were the others? There were others, who were they?'

'Like-minded people.' His lips peeled back over bloodied teeth.

'Sick.' He cracked Roy's forehead with the butt of his blade. 'Fucks'.

'Ye Ma never complained' Roy's speech slurred, 'when her B&B rooms were full.'

'Don't you dare bring—'

'Who do ye think made all this money for the farm?' His spittle spray foamed pink. 'Where the cash came from to convert it? That's why my boy runs it. Because I *own* it. It's *my* business.' His head lolled back with laughter.

'No, I don't—'

'Ye work for me Scotty. Your sweet little forgetful brain works for me, and what a perfect, clueless job you've done.'

'You.' He slammed Roy's head into the slabs. 'Piece.' He slammed again. 'Of.' And again. 'Worthless—'

'Scott, no.' A familiar voice called from behind him. 'No Scott. Let us handle it.'

Scott shot a glance behind him. DI Woods and DC Wilmington were at the door, restraining Iain. Woods stepped forward leaving his colleague to pacify Scott's simpering cousin. Roy lay unconscious. The inspector pressed two fingers to his jawline and nodded.

'I should have cut his balls off.' Still clinging to the knife, he slowly shook his head. Woods eased Scott's fingers apart and let the weapon drop to the floor.

'I trusted him with my son. My *son*.' Scott rose to his feet and kicked Roy hard in the ribs. 'Oh Christ, Jae. I couldn't—'

'Don't worry, Jae's with the Family Liaison Officer.

Smart kid. He saw you unconscious and called 999. We found him in his bedroom.' Woods patted Scott on the shoulder. 'And Roy'll get what's coming to him Scott, believe me. There's no justice like prison justice for men like him.'

The two men stood shoulder to shoulder watching the ambulance amble over the stones and out into the lane. Wilmington was guiding Iain into the back of a squad car.

'You think Iain had summat to do with it?' As much as he couldn't stand his pitiful toad of a cousin, even Scott struggled with that concept.

'I doubt he was actively involved. More likely guilty of standing by, but he may have vital information. It's a desperately sad scenario Scott, but often people like Iain are groomed themselves. Never had a chance.' Woods shook his head.

'Neither did Bren. Or me.' Scott pinched the bridge of his nose. 'What lead you to Roy?'

'It may surprise you to know but the alarm was initially raised by the bank.'

'The bank?' Scott pursed his lips around a cigarette and lit up. His hands were still shaking.

'Roy was doing lots of money transfers through multiple personal accounts; making payments in and out of the business accounts – he'd convinced your parents to sign over the farm businesses. Bought them out. Set them up in Spain.'

'The dodgy—' He sharply inhaled.

'Had a deck of debit cards and credit cards. Christ, he was moving cash around faster than a magician in a three-cup-ball trick.'

'And that's an offence?'

'Not strictly speaking, but banks will flag activity like that – money laundering. The more we looked into it the more we became convinced that he was rinsing cryptocurrency.'

'Crypto-what?'

'Heard of Bitcoin? It's a virtual currency – used online to bypass the clearing system. It's anonymous, unregulated and very difficult to trace. That's what makes it so attractive to criminals, to pay for goods and services that fly under the radar. It's used for trading in online black markets. The dark web. So… we set a thief to catch a thief.'

'How so?' Scott swallowed.

'Well, we could see a lot of activity through the banking system but when it comes to tracking where the transactions originate it starts to get very tricky. Merchants on the dark web send communications through a heavily encrypted channel, a specialised browser. It's known as the onion router because it wraps up every internet query in layers of code like an onion. Don't ask me to explain how—'

'Onion?' The penny was starting to drop. 'Jez' he let slip.

'Sorry?'

'Jez – Jez Steele, the driver you interviewed me about—'

'Yes, sorry we went in hard there but we needed to make sure you knew nothing. Lots of leads on our incident board were pointing to you, Scott. It was only when we got our hacker on the case and he started to unravel this mess that we understood why.'

'I don't get it.'

'They were in it together, Scott, your uncle and Mr. Steele. Trading in filth, through mutual connections. Roy was an administrator for a child porn network. He'd been providing perverts with images of abuse for years. He made contact with Jez through ex-jailbird connections. It was Roy who told Jez to apply for your driver's job.'

'Fuck me.' Scott's brain dizzied as it joined up the dots - the contraband and adult content that Jez had tempted him with; the dating site flyer that his uncle had left under his wiper blade. Vulnerable women. Knives. Porn. Christ he'd been played like a fiddle.

'Jez's role was to supply women for another market – one that specialised in sexual torture. The things that turn people on, Scott, it turns my stomach.' Woods rubbed his chin. 'Scott, we had to interview you because they were using you as a conduit. They hacked into your online accounts, assumed your identity, intercepted communications… we could well have been arresting and charging you if our coders hadn't managed to peel the last layer of the onion away in the early hours of this morning. These things… they take a little time.' There was a hint of apology in Wood's world-weary gaze.

'I came close to losing my mind…' Scott wrestled to control his juddering chin.

'We suspect they were trying to do precisely that; to discredit you - make you appear either culpable or insane. In case… in case you found out—'

'Found out what?'

'Oh Lord.' Woods released a deeply uncomfortable sigh. 'Some of the pictures we've uncovered… Some of them were from many years ago Scott. When you were…' He let it hang.

It took a moment for the significance to dawn.

'I should have cut his fuckin balls off.' He strode off across the yard, huffing cigarette smoke into the stiff morning air, pummelling his skull with his fists.

'If it weren't for me being a lawman I wouldn't argue

with you.' Woods said to himself.

'He stole my childhood. He stole Bren's…' His voice broke; he dropped to the cobbles, doubled up and dry-heaved.

Scott stayed on his knees and wept until his ribs were sore. As his breathing steadied he pulled himself to his feet, his legs struggling to support him under the weight of the revelations. The men stood in silence for a few minutes as Scott sucked the life out of his cigarette. Eventually he raised his head and plucked up the courage to ask. 'The girls. The ones… Have you found them?'

'Not yet, I'm very sad to say. We've got enough to nail Roy and put him away for a very, *very* long time. Jez on the other hand is still at large, but we'll find him. And if the girls turn up before he does, you can bet his DNA will be all over the scene.'

Scott's limbs were shaking, he suddenly felt very cold. He bit his lip and hugged himself.

'We'll get him, Scott, but until we do, stay vigilant. Maybe get away for a while – wash this tragic mess out of your hair. What you have left of it.' Woods attempted a smile and extended his hand. 'For what it's worth, I'm very sorry for everything that you and your sister have been through.'

Scott nodded and clasped both of his palms around the policeman's peace offering.

'Speak to the Liaison Officer before she leaves. She can put you in touch with an agency that could help you to… process this.'

'Thank you DI Woods.'

'Michael.'

'Michael, thank you.'

CHAPTER 25: MIRROR MAN

FEBRUARY 2017

Saturday

The blushed, sunset-dusted clouds floated like marshmallows above the horizon line. They hovered above the soothing indigo of fading light, which seemed to roll in towards them on the ripples of the sea as they made their way down Llandudno Pier. The long straight of the boardwalk stretched out before them, lined with wooden benches and delicate lattice work railings that looked as if white lace had been crocheted from wrought iron.

Jae wedged a freshly netted serpent under his arm, the spoils of Scott's not-too-shabby efforts in the firing range, as he licked tomato ketchup and mustard from his fingers.

'Can we go on the fair rides Daddy?'

'We'll see what's what when we get down there Monkey.' If memory served him correctly the oversized rotating tea cups and the swaying cars of Balloon Madness were neither fun nor, for the price they charged, fair. But he did recall that at the head of the promenade, marked with a rather impressive Maharajan-gothic ogee crown, there was an old penny arcade. It was there that they were headed.

To Scott's disguised relief the tea cups and balloon cars were cloaked in canvases. Not only was their visit to the seaside out of season, but the pier was winding down and drawing to its dusky close. Just enough time to push some pennies in the Deck Arcade. They approached the entrance as a mechanical, turban-adorned genie burst into life. He issued a proclamation, the veracity of which was somewhat undermined by his hackneyed Middle Eastern accent and his glazed, vacant stare: 'Zoltar is here to give you the wisdom of the ancients. Do with it what you will. Destiny is not a matter of chance, it is a matter of choice.'

'What d'you reckon Jae – want know what fate has in store?' Jae nodded unconvincingly, eyeing Zoltar with suspicion, as Scott took a coin from his pocket and pushed it into the slot. Shortly after it rattled through the machine a fortune teller card was dispensed. Scott tore along its perforated strip and turned it over.

ZOLTAR SPEAKS

Wonderful things are on the horizon for you. A dear one will return from a long trip and your whole life will be different. You have a patient disposition and your patience is about to be rewarded. Despair not I say for your days of despair will soon be over.

Your Lucky Numbers: *42, 4, 17, 9, 31, 26*

'Looks like it's your lucky day.' A soft, sweet voice purred in his ear. He spun around.

'Oh, beautiful, am I glad to see you.' Scott threw his arms around her the waist, lifted her and planted a kiss on her lips.

She turned to Jae as she landed. 'And you must be Jae. I've heard so many great things about you Jae.'

'Sweetheart, I want you to meet a very special lady. This is Kat.'

'I won a snake.' Jae announced proudly, thrusting his zig-zag stripped fluffy toy in Kat's outstretched hand.

'Ooh, and what a lovely snake it is. What's his name?' she said as she stroked its fur.

'Ssssid the ssssnake' he lisped.

Scott shuddered inwardly, but today was not a day for dwelling on the past. Today was a day for new horizons.

'There's a bar at the back – fancy a snifter?' He smiled, still not quite believing she was real.

'Sounds good. What's your favourite drink Jae?'

Jae stuffed his snake under his arm and took her hand. 'Lemonade' he said as he bolted off, dragging Kat with him.

They settled into a snug corner with their drinks. Scott had come prepared. He unzipped Jae's backpack and handed him a tablet and headphones. As Jae immersed himself in episodes of Spiderman, Scott pulled Kat to him and kissed her gently.

'God have I missed you.' He twisted one of her curls around his finger. Her very presence made him feel clean. 'You have no idea.'

'I'm so sorry, Scott, I just had to get away for a while. Rob was doing my nut in. I was hiding out at Mum and Dad's until the injunction came through.' She stroked his cheek, then cast her eyes down. 'And if I'm honest, I needed space to think.'

'Am I going to like this?' Scott lifted her chin.

'I did a lot of thinking, Scott, and the thing is… I've missed you too. Very much.'

He cupped the back of her head and pulled her towards him. 'I cannot tell you…' they touched lips, '…how happy I am to hear that, beautiful.'

Kat picked up her wine glass and took a sip. 'So what's been going on?'

'You wouldn't believe me if I told you.' He shook his head and slowly ran his finger around the rim of his glass.

'Let's just say that we've both been clearing out our closets. Or at least, in my case, I plan to.'

She looked at him quizzically.

'Kat, there's a lot that you don't know about me. Well to be truthful, there's a lot that I don't know about myself, but I'm gonna try to—'

'What are you saying Scott?'

'While you were away I realised… I realised that you mean the world to me.'

'I know, same for me' she said, beaming.

'But, I don't know if I can…'

Kat pulled away and tensed.

'No, it's not that I don't want to. Believe me Kat I can't remember wanting anything so much.'

'What is it then?' There was a glint of alarm in her eyes.

'I'm pretty fucked up Kat.' Scott started to tremble. Kat placed her hand on his. 'You must've had your fill of nutters…'

'Scott, you are *nothing* like Rob. You're sweet, kind, gentle.' She kissed him. 'You're not a nutter, you're a good man who's been through a tough time. A very tough time.'

'I know I need help, Kat. And I'm gonna get it, I promise, because I *really* want this. I really want us.'

'I want it too. I want to be there for you. And for Jae.'

'The police gave me a number for a therapist, a hypno—'

'The police?'

Scott sighed and took three swallows of beer, it fizzled on his tongue. 'It's a long story. A forty year long story…'

***

'The process of therapy can feel a bit like a rollercoaster Scott. There are peaks and there are troughs.' The therapist paused, clasped her hands together and looked at him earnestly.

'I'm used to those' he said, as he took his seat in the chair opposite her.

'It's important to understand that sometimes it can feel as though things are getting worse before they get better. But when you hit one of the troughs buckle up, stay on the tracks and have faith in the ride. Because if you make it through to the end you'll feel on top of your world.'

'If you're asking me if my heart is in this, it is.' The words came out with conviction but he avoided her gaze.

'Good, but if at any point you feel like getting off the ride you must tell me. OK? So today we're just going to practise using a technique which, over the weeks, should help us to take you back to events that happened in the past. We'll do this gently at first, to give you time to acclimatise. How does that sound?'

Scott, already feeling like a small child in the bloated soft leather of the hypnotherapist's chair, nodded nervously. He fidgeted with his lighter then, glancing at the no smoking sign, slipped it into his breast pocket.

'It's natural to feel a little anxious at first, so let's start with some deep relaxation.'

'Do I need to close my eyes?' His eyes were as wide as saucers.

'Yes, relax your shoulders and neck, close your eyes and concentrate your thoughts on every word that I say.' Her voice was serene and palliative.

Scott rested his elbows on the arms of the chair, folded his hands over his belly and closed his eyes.

'I want you to focus on your breathing... breathing in slowly and deeply then exhaling as far as you can... feel all of the tension leaving your chest as you exhale... feel yourself relaxing into the chair with every breath... allowing the soothing sensations of the most relaxed parts of your body begin to spread down your limbs... and as this warm wonderful feeling of relaxation spreads to other parts of the body... the feeling becomes deeper... and this wonderful feeling now moves beyond the physical reaches of your body... spreading out through your skin to form a bubble around you...'

She paused for a moment. Scott's chest rose and fell rhythmically in signature with the percussive brushes of his breaths.

'Scott, I'd like to start taking you back now... back in time... back to the funfair...'

Scott nodded slowly.

'Imagine that you're walking along a footpath that runs around the perimeter of a park... it's a balmy winter evening... you can see your breath in the air... the park is lined with ornate Victorian railings... inside the railings there's a tall row of trees... too tall for you to see over... but from the other side you can hear the sounds of a funfair...'

He smiled and sniffed the air. It smelt smoky like hot dogs and sweet like toffee apples.

'The sun is setting, casting a golden glow across the sky... and by the time you reach the entrance, the fairground is radiating with colours and sounds... lights are twinkling, and flashing... generators are humming... the music of the merry-go-round is whirling… you stand there surrounded by sights and smells that transport you back through the years… you continue to meander through the crowd and find yourself outside a small tent which bears the sign: 'Fortune Teller'… you duck inside and look around you… in the muted light you can make out a table draped in white cloth… on the table is a large crystal ball cradled by an onyx base fashioned into a pair of cupped hands… the hazy light seems to be coming from deep inside the glowing sphere… and you are transfixed by it as you sit down to wait for the mystic to arrive…'

Scott shifted in his seat.

'In the periphery you become aware of movement inside the crystal ball… you lean forward to see more clearly… the mists that veil the scene evaporate and you find yourself looking at a familiar figure, though at first you can't quite place who it is… then you realise that it's you… it's you in a scene from your childhood… unfolding before your eyes, just as it happened so many years ago…'

Scott hovered over the crystal ball. The scene flickered like it was running through an old Super 8 film projector. It pictured him not as a child, but as he was a few short weeks ago. Scruffy collar-length hair and stubble. As he watched his midriff started to tear, to separate at the waist and his skin peel away. Layer by layer. Like an onion. Each layer he shed revealed new flesh. A new self. A smaller self. One self nested inside the other like a Matryoshka doll. Until he was an infant, watching the scene. Watching helplessly as red legs kicked and flayed.

He started to twitch and twist as if trying to tear himself away. The therapist observed his agitation.

'You decide to get some air… you raise the flap of the tent and make your way out into the fairground once more… people are laughing and smiling… the atmosphere is warm and inviting… as you wander into the heart of the funfair you see the entrance to the hall of mirrors… you can't resist dipping inside and standing in front of them… there are many mirrors lining the walls of the maze… each way you turn you see yourself in another form… one moment you're long and wavy… the next quite squat and round…'

Scott stood in front of a wall featuring five mirrors. The central mirror was the tallest and bore his own reflection. The other mirrors flanking this appeared smaller and two of them, on either side, were only waist height. He studied himself. He looked pale and thin and almost translucent, like he was an apparition. As he stood there trying to bring himself into focus a series of figures peeled away from him, like ghosts. One by one they took their places in front of the mirrors. A little boy in shorts to his far left. A young woman next to him. And to his right a young girl dressed in red. Next to her a man, shrouded in darkness.

'Who can you see in the mirrors Scott? Can you describe what you see?'

'I see other people. There are other people in here with me.' Scott couldn't tell if he was thinking the words or saying them out loud.

'Can you describe the reflections in the mirrors, Scott?'

'I don't know, I don't know who…' he tried to say, forcing his mouth to form the shapes of the words. His throat constricted so that all that came out was a dry whine.

He wasn't sure how to make contact with them. He concentrated hard trying to telecommunicate, first with one figure, then another.

'Who are you?' he managed.

The little boy on his left spoke first.

'I'm Peter. I was born when you were three, but I'm six. When bad things happened I came out so you didn't have to.'

He shifted his gaze to the young woman next to Peter. It was only now as he took her in more fully that he noticed her strong resemblance to Sally.

'I'm Saffron. I was born the night Sally died. You saved me so that I could keep her alive. I look after Peter and Red.'

'Scott, can you tell me who you see in the mirrors? Who is in there?' The therapist's voice was distant and fading, as if she was gently drifting away.

The little girl to his right stepped up.

'I'm Red. I was also born when you were three. I'm nine. You couldn't help your sister so you made me and kept me safe.' Red looked over her shoulder at the man in the shadows. She leaned in towards Scott's ear and whispered. 'We don't like him. He scares us. He's not been in here very long.' Her eyes twinkled with dew.

As if stirred by her double-cross, the man emerged from the darkness. He was older, closer to Scott's age. As he approached, Scott could smell whiskey on his breath and the faint perfume of hashish. His hair was long and unkempt, covering his eyes. He wore a calf-length black leather trench coat and paratrooper boots. As he stepped into the halo of light surrounding Scott, deep shadows formed in the wells of his stubbled cheeks. He looked like a medieval witch hunter.

He slowly raised a gloved finger and pressed it to his lips. 'Sssssh… Don't say a fuckin word.'

Without moving his lips Scott looked at the figure and with his eyes he asked 'Who are you?'

'They call me Mac. And it's *my turn* now.' Mac clasped a gloved hand over Scott's mouth, pulled his head back to meet his lips and said through gritted teeth:

'*Shut your little fuckin mouth or I'll rip your little fuckin tongue out.*'

LATER

CHAPTER 26: MRMACABRE49

BabyBreathless: That's a bit of a strange username you have there.

MrMacabre49: It's a character from my favourite horror film, Mr Macabre – do you watch horror?

BabyBreathless: Not really – bit of a lightweight with scary movies. Too squeamish.

MrMacabre49: Ah, that explains why you didn't recognise it then. Anyway you can talk. Yours sounds saucy. Are you a bit of a bad girl?

BabyBreathless: Oh dear. I worried it would give that impression. I just got it from a random username generator and thought it sounded cool.

MrMacabre49: It sounds very cool. I like the sound of breathless ;-)

BabyBreathless: Is 49 your real age then? You said it was 42 on your profile.

MrMacabre49: No I am 42. 4 and 9 are forbidden numbers in China, they signify death and torture - thought it went well with the horror theme.

BabyBreathless: Ooh, you really are into your horror stuff aren't you? Well, if we go to the cinema you'll have to give me a shoulder to hide behind.

MrMacabre49: I think I could manage that – we going to the cinema then?

BabyBreathless: Are you Chinese? You didn't post any photos…

MrMacabre49: No, learnt about China from someone I used to know. You didn't answer my question.

BabyBreathless: What question?

MrMacabre49: About going to the cinema.

BabyBreathless: Maaaaybe. You'll have to send me a photo first.

MrMacabre49: I can do that now. Here you go.

BabyBreathless: Cute! I see a hint of Cillian Murphy there ;-)

MrMacabre49: Please. Cinema then?

BabyBreathless: OK, so long as it's nothing too scary.

MrMacabre49: I'm sure we can find something suitable.

***

'Oh… *Jesus*.' She arched her back as he traced his tongue down her abdomen.

'Call me Mac. I don't answer to Jesus.' He licked her belly then slipped his tongue between her legs.

'Mac, oh God, that's… '

He stopped, tantalising her for a moment then slid up the bed. He hovered over her, sucking her lips with his. 'Gets you in the mood doesn't it? A dirty movie.' He tightened the belt around her wrists.

'Oh yeah. I've never done any…oh…' He was teasing the bud between her legs with his fingertips.

'Feels good, doesn't it?' He stroked his way up her torso, over her breasts and folded his hand around her neck. He started to give it a gentle squeeze. 'Feels good to be breathless?'

He gagged her with his other hand, purposefully pushing against the tip of her nose. She started to thrutch and twist. Her eyes widened.

He pressed his mouth to her ear. 'How breathless do you wanna get, baby?' He climbed on top of her and forced himself in, applying a little more pressure to her throat with every push of his hips. He moved slowly, being careful with each stroke to graze the rough surface of her g-spot.

Her head rolled to the side. The fear in her closing eyes dissolved into bliss. Muffled moans came faster and louder until, with the last gasp of climax, he released his grip.

Straddling her, he watched the perse hue of her skin blanche as she fought for air.

He kissed her hard and passionate before slinking out into the moonlit street. She clicked the door shut behind him, fell against it and touched her smile with her fingertips. She closed her eyes and caressed her neck, replaying their lovemaking move-by-move on the inner film of her eyelids. The ebbing flame in her loins rekindled. She secretly wished he'd come back.

She straightened her robe and padded across the floorboards into the kitchen. As she filled the kettle her phone purred on the marble counter. It grew louder and more insistent.

She picked it up. Her heart danced. Someone up there was in the mood for granting wishes.

Mac: I think I left my watch. OK to come and get it?

Acknowledgments

I owe a great debt of thanks to my first readers, the very first of these being Andrea, followed by Ben, Sam, Kay, Julie, Steve, Sue, Hiromi, Ed, Simon and Emma. Thank you so much for giving your time to read the fledgling attempt and sharing your kind, candid and helpful feedback. Whilst you may not see all of your observations reflected in these pages, please know that I have learned so much from you as my initial audience and will be forever grateful for your commitment and comments.

Thank you to Kity Walker and all at the Literary Consultancy for assessing the first draft of the book, for your encouraging commentary and your detailed and invaluable critique. It has been an education, as have the fantastic resources and courses provided by the brilliant folks at Jericho Writers, especially Debi Alper.

I'm immensely grateful to my wonderful friend Hiromi, not only for reading an early draft, but also for designing the fabulous cover art.

The biggest thank you of all, however, has to be to my wonderful husband Andy who colluded with me in a pub in Brighton to scribble down the initial idea, tolerated countless evenings of my fanciful plot experimentations and revisions, bolstered me (often with wine!) when my confidence was on the floor and last, but by no means least, read every page with enthusiasm, despite not being 'a reader' (as Bill Hicks would say).

There are many others who have also taken the time to share the benefit of their experience as independently published authors – many thanks, particularly to Carl. Finally, a mention for the Radius JAKKS – you know who you are girls! So appreciate your friendship and support.

And to my future readers – I hope you enjoy the book and if we ever cross paths, the beers are on me.

About the author

K.T. Jayne was born in Cheshire and now lives with her husband and son in Surrey. Having graduated from a degree in Fine Art Film and Video she spent her early years as an experimental filmmaker, touring the indie film festival circuit. She won an ESRC bursary for a postgraduate study in Media at the University of Sussex, followed by a stint of being a lecturer in Film Making and Film Studies at Brighton City College, before moving into her present career as a Learning Consultant in digital technologies. Serial Dater is her first novel.

Printed in Great Britain
by Amazon